WHEN KINGDOMS FALL

CALLIE DAHL

When Kingdoms Fall

CALLIE DAHL

Content Warning: Please note, This book contains explicit content and dark elements that may be triggering to some. It includes mature language, deceased family members, sex and mild nudity, religious extremism, graphic violence and gore, death, physical violence and mutilation, past trauma, drinking and a brief mention of substance abuse. Not intended for anyone under 18 years of age.

For the Ones Who Let Their
Light Die Out.
Wake Up.
It's Time to Light a Match and
Burn, Baby, Burn.

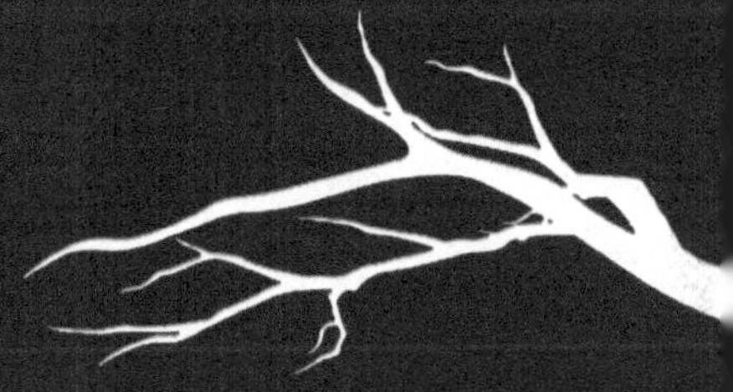

LITHELLE
MENYAMERE MOUNTAINS
DOMNHALL'S RUINS
NIARATH LOCH
THE WYLAN WOODS
THE MINISON OCEAN
TRAIFTON
FANG GULF
KALANDRAE

CHAPTER 1
WILLA

"Bring him back."

Those three words were a broken whisper. Hollow.

Willa finally surrendered to the pain and let go of the waves of emotion barreling through her. The thin, white nightgown she wore was soaked all the way through from the rain. Her feet squelched in the mud as she rocked back and forth, hugging herself while she cried. She hadn't even bothered to put shoes on when she'd left the confines of Traifton.

Brushing away fresh tears, she turned her back to the deity who had turned his back on their realm five hundred years ago. A god who had helped create a curse to taunt and hunt mortals.

She surveyed the sleeping town of Traifton while taking in the fresh scent of wet grass around her. It was against the council's rules to leave the tall walls of the trading town without permission or an escort. And it was dangerous to be out here so close to the Wylan Woods. To be caught outside the walls was cause for punishment by the head of the council, Lord Nalore, and his flock of zealots.

Silver helmets glittered beneath the rain and torchlights as Traifton's sentries paced the fortress built around their homes for protection. Willa's mouth twisted into a defiant smile. They hadn't noticed her slip past the gate. She could have said it was good fortune, but she had done this more times than she could count. It was becoming too easy to do so. Too tempting to find refuge between the walls made by men and the magical wall made by the old gods. She knew she would feel lighter out here amongst the rolling hills and tall grass. And despite the ache in her chest and burning in her throat and eyes, she could finally take a full breath. A breath of clean, natural air. One without the smells of rotting fish, sea salt, and molding rooftops.

A snap of branches sounded behind her. Willa spun back towards the statue of Velithor as four ravens pushed out from the misted wall of magic. Her mouth fell open as they flew out of the tainted woodlands. From where she stood, they looked like ordinary ravens. Untainted, compared to some of the horrors the watchmen had killed and shown to the town as a warning. She followed their flight as they pumped their glistening black wings to pass over her head. They barely spared a glance at her below. Instead, they flew together towards Traifton's walls, calling out to one another in sharp and crass caws as they did. As they passed the guards on the wall, arrows were released, and one by one, they hit the birds. Willa's body stiffened as they all plummeted from the sky.

She shrank back towards the statue of Velithor to hide from the sentries now looking in her direction. They would be hyper-aware of any movement now. She should have grabbed her black cloak. It would have done well to hide her bright auburn hair. It was a beacon of light compared to the muted greens and browns of the surrounding hills.

She stepped behind Velithor's large, scaled leg and watched the walls. Funny that she was finding refuge under the deity she had cursed minutes before.

The guards were shouting to one another now. Her nerves seized as the watchtower's beacon was lit. Signaling movement in the Wylan Woods to the sleepy seaside town.

As flames grew from the watchtower, the hair on the back of her neck stood to attention. A low, warbled call crackled above Willa, numbing her mind and body with icy fear. It was followed by a snapping of what she could only assume to be a beak opening and closing. Chirping echoed around her. Those noises were not like anything she had heard before.

It could only mean one thing: a Wylan Creature.

Willa pushed closer to Velithor's stone leg in muted horror. A soft clicking reverberated over Velithor's scaled belly. Scratching came from above, sending shivers down her spine. Whatever it was, it was walking, maybe even crawling, atop the dragon deity's back. She thought she heard a ruffling of bird feathers as if to shake away the rain. Another raven? No, this was too large; she wouldn't have heard a raven scratching so loudly above her. Whatever it was, her time out here had expired. She needed to return to Traifton if there was this much activity in the Wylan Woods. She needed to get home before she became a meal to a cursed beast.

Her pulse kicked up as the horrible calls continued above her. Her only hope now was the guards, never mind the council's punishment for being out here. If it was a tainted creature, she wouldn't make it back to the town with it sitting unsuspectingly above her now. Her dreams had conjured monstrosities each night who enjoyed tearing her limbs apart, but she had never been this close to the real thing.

A large, black owl swooped down from the top of Velithor's statue and landed in the tall grass before her. She pressed up against the stone, desperate to sink into it like wet sand and become part of the statue itself. But it was too late. She had been spotted.

Its head spun around to get a better look at the dragon's stone paws. Its legs were hidden within the blades of grass, scraping along the mud. Willa tried to swallow her whimper as it stalked closer. A pair of wings sat pinned beneath its frame. But one wing was unnaturally bent and instead of feathers, black smoke rippled from leathered tendons and ivory bone. Half alive, half dead. Her nightmares hadn't come close to the real thing. This was much, much worse. Its beak opened and closed as if tasting the air between them.

But the eyes were the most terrifying of all. Unblinking and bulbous, pupilless and glowing green, they stared into the shadows beneath the statue, searching for her in the dark. Willa tried to hide, but the glow was so bright. So entrancing. She had never seen such a vivid color before, brighter than any blade of fresh grass or cut emerald.

As its head rotated unnaturally, its chest puffed out, moving long feathers and smoke up and down as it did. Another low chirp came from the beak before its head stopped right where Willa stood. Closing its eyes, it took a breath in, and with it, she heard guttural pops and scratches within its throat. When the eyes opened, black pupils floated within the green glow.

A sharp tug jerked Willa's body. The owl made another soft coo, as if encouraging her to succumb to its magical pull.

No, no. No. Move, Willa. Move! Warning bells rattled her insides as her own conscience urged her to run. But she could not.

The beast's eyes glowed brighter, like two freshly lit candle flames. Warmth tickled the top of Willa's head, caressing her hair and shoulders. It slid down her skin like warm honey. As it dripped and pooled all the way towards her bare feet, she wanted to step towards the creature. But why? Why would she do such a careless thing?

"Come out from the shadows, my curious little mortal." A haunting female voice filled her mind as she stared into the bright, glowing eyes.

The owl's beak opened and clicked. A soft tug urged her forward, as though an invisible rope was knotted around her midsection, pulling her gently towards the Wylan Creature.

Willa's legs shuffled forward, away from the safety of Velithor's statue. She dared to watch her slow-moving feet and panicked, realizing she couldn't feel them. How was she walking? But as soon as the panic bubbled up, she was remedied with a gentle humming within. The sound filled her ears, like soft waves tickling her senses.

The woman's voice spoke gently, as if Willa were a skittish alley cat it was trying to coax. "You are so far from your home and so close to mine."

A gentle chortle bounced around her head, but it was warbled and broken. "You are filled with such emotion for someone so young. Tell me, mortal. Why are you sad?"

The tugging around Willa's belly stopped with the question.

Willa swayed side to side gently as her jaw dropped involuntarily. Words belonging to her fell from her lips. But they sounded distant, as if in a dream. "You took my father."

The owl's head twisted in a full circle. Its wings opened in a creaking, unpolished way before its head faced her once more. "Ah yes, Sander was his name. I was there when he entered our home."

It looked to the wall of black, rolling mist, and Willa followed its gaze. She stared at the magical veil without hesitation now. Instead of fear, the warmth around her body seemed to buzz with an odd sort of adrenaline.

The voice in her mind drew her back to the owl's glowing green eyes. "Come, I'll show you the way to him."

"He's alive?" Her tongue was thick and heavy as she asked the haunted question.

Another distorted laugh rang within her as the owl stepped past her, wings still open, towards the veil. The bent and broken wing lifted higher above the ground, popping as it did so, touching the mist. A soft hiss replied to its touch before an opening appeared before them.

Willa's eyes widened as she got a small peek of the Wylan Woods. Rows of dark trees greeted her, followed by a warm honey smell. She inhaled and her lips pulled back into a soft smile.

"We will find him together. Come now, mortal." The voice was playful, eager to show her its home.

An oddly primitive warning sounded in her brain. They were taught about the Wylan Creatures and their magical traps, but for the life of her, Willa couldn't find a single reason to be afraid in this owl's presence. It was being kind to her and she was so warm.

A light appeared within the trees and a deep, familiar call rang out. "Wildfire, is that you?"

"Father?" Willa's eyes widened at the sound of his rich tenor.

She ran towards the opening and paused before it, frantically searching, hoping to hear his call again. Emotion lumped in her throat as a laugh escaped her. Was this happiness? It had been so long. This unfamiliar feeling was euphoric. Addictive.

"Father!" she cried out to the trees.

The owl shifted slightly, pulling the veil back with its wings as it did, to reveal more of the Wylan Woods. Willa eagerly smiled down at the gruesome creature and lifted her foot to step inside.

"Come, friend. Let's greet your father." The voice within her hummed enthusiastically.

CHAPTER 2

WILLA

It had been four years to the day without her father. Willa scanned the Wylan trees with anticipation. Was his rough beard longer now? If it was, it had to be down past his navel at least. Willa's eyes crinkled from the image, and she stepped past the opening of the dark mist.

An intrusive blaze of orange fire sizzled beside her. Willa paused and turned to the owl as a flaming arrow embedded into its neck. At once, its leathery feathers ignited. Willa stumbled away from the forest's opening as the two green eyes watched her within the flames.

The black pupils within the green glow bounced around frantically as the voice within her mind said, "Stop this. Kill them, mortal. Kill them!"

Gone was the female voice. In its place was a sinister male voice, hissing out the violent command. Her body seized at the tone, and she nodded to the burning beast. Willa turned with a vengeful scowl.

"Kill them!"

Willa moved, driven by a force still unknown to her. *Yes. Kill them.* They had interrupted her chance at seeing her father. The owl had done nothing to her. It was her friend. Why would they do such a thing?

In the distance, torch lights were bobbing down the hills. Shuffling forward, Willa's lips curled further into a snarl. The smell of burning flesh hit her nose as the owl screeched in pain behind her.

The owl's panicked cries quickened her pace while the dark voice inside her repeated with fevered intensity, "Kill them!"

Two large hands wrapped around Willa's eyes and mouth. She struggled beneath them, twisting her shoulders, but it was no use. The hands lifted her up and pressed her into a warm body, dragging her away from the screeching, burning bird. Willa scratched at the arms, but it did nothing. She could see nothing. The only sound she heard was her newfound friend dying from the flaming arrow. It was dying, wasn't it? The screams released from the owl were loud and ear-piercing, making her heart twist and crack with each outcry.

Those hands tightened around her as she flailed about. They dragged her backward along the grass and mud for a few more moments, but the creature grew louder the further she and her captor got.

"Willa, stop. Willa stop!" A familiar male voice yelled the command near her ear.

Willa could only listen to the disturbing sounds coming from the dying owl.

"Willa, you're safe. Willa! Willa, it's Ivaan. I've got you. You're safe."

Ivaan. Her closest friend. Her lover. Of course, it was his hands clinging to her now. The sudden realization of who held her had her inhaling his scent. Sea salt and sage. Willa's body went limp within his familiar grasp.

"You can stop screaming. I've got you. You're safe with me."

But she wasn't making any noise. The burning bird was.

Ivaan slowly turned her to face him. Willa's mouth was left open and dry as he dropped his palm from her lips. She closed it and swallowed thickly. As she did, the bird's cries stopped abruptly.

"I was not screaming. It was my friend." It hurt to speak, and Willa practically choked out the words.

Ivaan's brows drew together in an agonized expression. Willa lifted a shaking hand to her neck and rubbed it before turning to look over her shoulder at the owl. But Ivaan's fingers gently stopped her with a soft touch along her jaw. His calloused hand cupped the side of her face and pulled her back to focus on him. Why did he look so frightened? His blue eyes searched her meticulously from head to toe. His mouth was pulled into a tight grimace and his sandy blond hair was ruffled as if he had recently awoken.

"You're trembling. Gods, Willa how long were you out here for?" Ivaan's hands roamed her shoulders and arms as he continued his attempt to warm her before pulling her into his chest for a hug with a resigned sigh. Willa smothered her face against his velvet cloak, staring unblinking towards the bobbing torch lights coming closer to them.

"I heard him." It still hurt to speak. And she was suddenly cold. And...empty.

She had been so warm before. Filled with euphoria and awe. Delirious with the joy of seeing her father again. No. Delirious with magic.

The terrifying realization washed over Willa.

"I was the one screaming?" Willa asked, her dry throat rasping.

Ivaan pulled away to study her. He gave her another squeeze and nodded grimly before looking towards the torches and men.

The voices were calling out to them now. Willa looked at them and frowned.

She thought of the owl burning and shifted uncomfortably in Ivaan's arms. She had been yelling out in pain from the Wylan Creature's death, because of how easily its magic had manipulated her mind, while the bird burned silently. Willing her to stay ensnared. Willing her to kill the ones who had harmed it.

Ivaan's voice was thick and unsteady as he whispered, "Willa, I'm so sorry. I'm so sorry."

Why was he sorry? He had saved her.

She searched him anxiously for the meaning behind the words and remembered what had happened before she broke the council's rules. They had fought earlier in the evening near Traifton's docks. The argument had escalated enough for her to run from him, leaving him to sort through his temper and thoughts alone. If he was apologizing for their argument, she no longer cared. She was too tired to care.

"Don't be sorry," her voice cracked as she spoke. It sounded as though she were on the verge of crying like she had been during their fight.

Ivaan pulled her back into his chest. "Please don't cry."

But she wasn't going to cry. He held an empty shell with no emotion. No sadness, no anger, no confusion. Nothing.

Ivaan whispered a few more apologies above her and then explained, "I didn't know where you went when you left me at the docks. I went to your home, but your brother refused to let me in. He said he hadn't seen you."

Tybalt had lied. She had confided in her twin as soon as she'd arrived at the house. He'd been waiting for her by the hearth when she had run in, tears streaming down her face. Call it twin intuition, something their mother had always sworn by, but he had told her he knew she wasn't okay, and it was why he had stayed awake. Tybalt always knew what to do and say. A trait Willa envied often. He knew she wouldn't want company, especially Ivaan's, for the rest of the night after she went to her room. And, as always, Tybalt was right. She needed time to think. Alone.

She wanted to smile at the lie Tybalt had told Ivaan. But her body wouldn't even allow such a simple gesture. Instead, she only watched as the men talking to one another closed in on them in a tight, torchlit circle. Willa took in their features, separating the guards from the heavily robed council members as their conversation died out to study her and Ivaan.

Ivaan's voice was rushed now as Lord Nalore, the head of Traifton's council, pushed past his men to walk towards them. "You said you were going to find your father and ran off. What was I supposed to do with that? And when you weren't at home, I feared the worst. You're always sneaking out." His tone changed as if he was lecturing a small child. "Head full of ideas, but I didn't think you would actually do it. He's gone, Willa. He's gone. We should have packed and left tonight before you could do this to yourself. I can control the ship myself now, you know, we could have done it."

Color ebbed into her cheeks from his berating words.

She hadn't planned on being entranced by dark magic...She hadn't planned on going into the cursed Wylan Woods with a possessed, half-dead owl.

Willa lifted her hands and pushed away from his chest, ending their close embrace. "It's not like I asked for the Wylan Creature to come to me. I...I don't know what happened. I had been sleeping. I had a nightmare. Gods, I just needed some fresh air for once besides the smell of rotting fish and wet cobblestones. I needed some time to think. You asked me to leave, Ivaan. Without my family? Without him?" Tears blurred her vision as she spoke. "Did you ever think maybe it's still too soon, or did you just assume I'm fine now that it's been another year?"

Ivaan was crying too, she realized, but the tears falling from her face were emotionless. Empty just like her, as if the owl had taken her soul before dying.

Lord Nalore was speaking directly behind her, his nasally voice grating the back of her neck as he spoke of the creature's charred remains. The dancing flames of torchlights illuminated Ivaan's tense expression and wet lashes. He wiped the tears from his face, and as he did, Willa caught something new in his gaze. Guilt.

Unnerved by the sudden change in him, strange and disquieting thoughts began to race through her mind. If not for their earlier argument, what was Ivaan apologizing so adamantly for before the council and guards arrived? Willa's eyes narrowed in on Ivaan's, but he was no longer looking at her. Instead, he straightened his stance and nodded to Lord Nalore, who was still speaking behind her.

She masked her inner turmoil with the familiar, empty calmness and prepared herself to explain the night's events. She turned away from Ivaan to face Lord Nalore and was abruptly caught by both elbows. Two sentries stood on either side of her, gripping her rain-slicked skin tightly. The pressure of their grip made it impossible for her to pull away.

Confused, she looked back over her shoulder. "Ivaan? What's going on?"

Ivaan refused to look at her, ignoring her question. The guards pulled her further from him so she had no choice but to look at Traifton's leader.

But again she tried, "Ivaan? What—"

"Silence, child," Lord Nalore cut her off. His voice was harsh and clipped. His beady eyes glittered in the torchlight, taking in her wet nightgown with a tight-lipped scowl. Rain pelted softly over his dark brown garb of heavy robes, and the light from the dancing flames carved deep shadows into his sunken, weathered features.

He looked to where Ivaan stood and asked, "Did she touch the creature? Did she touch the Wylan's veil?"

Willa tried to turn but the guard's grip on her arms tightened, halting her movement. She could only watch as Lord Nalore's scowl deepened, followed by a curt nod. His dark gaze turned vicious when his eyes returned to hers. Before Willa could explain, one of the guards holding her spoke.

"I saw it myself. The creature almost had her inside the Wylan when we got word from Ivaan of someone breaking your rules."

Willa gave the guard a sidelong glance of disbelief. The guard ignored her shocked expression as he spoke eagerly to Lord Nalore.

A cold knot formed in her stomach as Lord Nalore replied to the guard gripping her too tightly. "Thank you for your work, Branlon. Ivaan, please come here."

He waved a bony hand to Ivaan while Willa repeated the guard's words in her head.

She took in a quick, sharp breath as Ivaan stood beside Lord Nalore. When their eyes met, a jolting shock ran through her. No. He couldn't have turned her in. Wouldn't. Even if he was concerned, he would never do that to her.

The guard beside her seemed to beam from Lord Nalore's praise.

Branlon puffed out his chest and continued, "Lord Nalore...I also heard her screams, and they were..." He paused. Shifting slightly in his grip around her arm before finishing. "Unnatural."

Willa's mind raced louder than her erratic pulse. Her heart refused to believe what her mind told her: Ivaan had turned her in. She glared at him with the burning, silent question. A glazed look of despair spread over Ivaan's face, tears falling from his blue eyes.

She had rejected his offer of running away with him, and this is what he did to her?

Even knowing the punishment, the bastard turned her in.

A jarring tension stretched between them. Startled hurt turned to white-hot anger. Her fury and shock bubbled up with violent fury, making her lean over and retch onto the dirt. The guards stepped away but still held onto her with disgusted grumbles.

Lord Nalore murmured hastily, "It could be the magic making her sick. Ivaan, how was she when you found her?"

Willa blinked at the vomit on the ground with rattled gasps. Strands of her auburn hair swayed before her as burning bile and hatred coated her mouth.

Ivaan spoke at last. And the word he said next was Willa's undoing. "Wild."

Wild.

Willa thrashed and kicked as the guards lifted her up and dragged her back towards Traifton. Lord Nalore pulled Ivaan to walk alongside him.

Amidst her attempt to break free, she sputtered out, "Lord Nalore, please! Please! I'm fine. He got me before anything could happen. It was a night terror. I sleepwalk. I swear to you, Lord Na—"

"Silence." The head of the council's voice echoed around the valley with cold finality. His angered face swung back to hers.

Red hair blurred her vision as she breathed heavily, with wide, terrified eyes. He looked her over with disdain, seeing her only for what Ivaan had called her. Wild.

"I will not hear your voice until I am absolutely sure it is you, Willa Thesalor. And not a poisoned creature grasping your soul within your mortal frame. Take her to the square. She will answer to Forsetyr now."

CHAPTER 3

SOREAN

Sorean held his fingers above the flame. He held them there until the smell of burning flesh had him alert once more. A prince born from the Queen of White Flame shouldn't have felt the small, stinging burn. A prince's skin would not shrivel so easily beneath a simple candle's burning wick. He had seen it with his other siblings. They had the ability to put their hand within the hearth and hold it over the dancing flames for minutes without pain or blemishes. And yet here he was, examining his charred fingertip with a dissatisfied curl of his lips.

He had magic, like all faeries did, but he was different. His magic was foul and devoid of flame, unlike the rest of the royal family. His mother and her court advisors overlooked his questions. They said his changing magic was a rare gift. Magic to be proud of. Magic the realm could benefit from. Magic that would alter the course of history when he became king.

Sorean sighed and pinched his burnt fingertip over the calloused pad of his thumb. The library was deserted at this time of night. The surrounding candles had been his only companion for the past two hours. But even they were tired. Their wax had spilled to run and harden over the stacks of scribbled notes surrounding him. Notes he had read enough times to recite each and every sentence.

At first, like every young faerie discovering their gifts, he had been filled with wonder and awe of his abilities. Faeries controlled the elements, each one appointed to the ground beneath them, the air above them, or the water and fire running and hissing beside them. And like most of the royal bloodline, he controlled all of them. Fire and air were the strongest in the House of Valkian. Only as a child, had Sorean held the ability to call the white flame. He could manipulate air to camouflage objects, including himself. But as quickly as he learned to hone his magic, it just as quickly changed. Like an apple rotting inside of him, his normal powers withered away to something else entirely. Those white flames died within—snuffed out by something made of malice. While other's magic grew with the changing seasons, his magic shriveled in the light of the surrounding flame. Only stirring awake in the quiet evenings when all was at rest and dark.

Sorean had dedicated the last four, almost five, centuries to reading all of the books within this tomb of a library to find magic like his. And yet he'd found nothing. How could he rule Lithelle when he didn't even understand what was inside of him? And to rule a hidden realm, invisible for nearly five hundred years...

What if he made a mistake? What if he lost control of his magic? It could risk them all.

A female voice brought life into the quiet library. "You look like shit."

Sorean blinked in surprise and looked up from his hand. His second in command sat across from him with a wry smile. Iara was too well dressed for the late hour. Gone were her regular training leathers, and in their place was a navy silk gown, clinging to her rich brown skin.

Sorean whistled and leaned back in his chair. "And you look—"

Iara cut him off, "Don't. It wasn't my idea." She held up a hand in surrender before lifting two empty drinking glasses in her other.

Firm hands clapped his shoulders, making him jump. Only one person touched him so casually.

"You're coming out with us, Prince." Harland hit his palms on Sorean's shoulders once more before setting a bottle onto the table in front of him.

He stepped away from Sorean's chair and pushed the bottle to Iara. It nearly toppled over as it slid over the notes and books sprawled about before she quickly swiped it. She smiled to herself, pouring the bottle of dark liquid into the two cups and lifting one to Harland. He gave a mocking bow, his dark brown curls falling over his shoulders as he did, before grabbing the glass and handing it to Sorean, who lifted the glass and sniffed the liquid with hesitation.

"And what is the occasion?" He raised his brows to the two faeries and took a small, careful sip. Wine. Fermented berries kissed his tongue and coated his throat instantly.

Harland only laughed in reply and took the bottle back from Iara, pulling straight from the amber stem. He never was one for formalities, despite being a royal faerie himself, and a highly regarded archer of the queen's guard.

When he was done, Harland wiped at his black beard and explained with a grunt, "You have two weeks left of freedom. I'll be damned if you waste those nights in here."

Sorean finished his drink in one smooth motion. He didn't need the reminder. He set his glass down delicately beside his quill and ink with a pointed look to Harland. As if to show him what real manners looked like. Harland's eyes glittered in the dim candlelight and he pulled from the bottle, letting the wine's juices run down his beard and silver tunic. Sorean shook his head. These faeries were insufferable.

He ignored them both, instead looking over the messy table with a frown. He wouldn't find anything else tonight. Sleep was what he really needed, not a night of drinking. Something squirmed deep within his stomach as he imagined his bed. No, he never got a good night's sleep with his magic. Any distraction would be better than his night terrors.

Sorean pushed his hair back, tucking the chestnut curls behind his ears as he did. He shoved the restless stir of his magic down deeper, ignoring its soft call, and looked to Iara and Harland. "I'll only go to Lady Talarin's Tavern."

Harland took another pull and gave Iara a sideways glance as he did so. Iara simply nodded and finished her own glass of wine.

Pushing her chair back, she stood and straightened the two thin straps on her shoulders. "A room is already arranged for you."

An intrusive breeze had him sitting back to watch Iara's casual magic. A wave of her hand was all it took to conjure and bend the stale air to her will. With another flick of her wrist, all of Sorean's notes and papers were floating off the table before falling into a neat little stack of organized chaos.

"This dismal room will be here if you decide to sneak away from us." Iara pushed back the rows of small braids from her shoulder. "Let's go."

Iara's braids swung low over her bare back as she stepped between the aisles of books and shadows, with Harland trailing quickly behind her. Before he went after the two, Sorean lifted a hand to the few candles left burning beside the now neat stacks of parchment. A soft manipulation of air was all it took for all of them to die out, casting them all into the dark.

When they were out of the castle, Sorean tugged the bottle from Harland's hand and took a drink. He wiped at his mouth and sighed, looking back at the twinkling lights of his home. The queen's chambers were dark. Late was the hour at hand if she was already asleep. Harland walked casually beside him, following Iara's lead through the dimly lit back-alleys of Lithelle.

"Nothing will change when I am crowned, you know. We will still have time for trouble." He took another drink and smiled from the immediate buzz washing over him. "My mother will still control anything she can. I am nothing but a puppet on a string."

Harland huffed out a breath and retorted, "The crown is heavy, no matter the task. Especially for you." Sorean's shoulders straightened from the comment. Harland continued, unfazed, "You are a mystery to the people. Dark and broody, much like your magic."

"And do the people like this or fear this, Harland?" Sorean flinched mid question. Did he really want to know? His hours in the castle told him one thing, while his late nights around the lower quarter of Lithelle had him questioning the high bloodline's constant stream of compliments.

"Well, the girls of the court certainly love it." The brute faerie only laughed as he reached out to steal the wine back from him.

But Sorean quickly dodged his hand, holding it up with a smile. "*But?*" He raised a brow at his friend and long-time confidant.

Harland jumped for the wine, and again Sorean dodged him with a throaty chuckle. Harland shook his long hair in resignation. He gave a comical, longing look to the bottle before giving Sorean an answer. "*But* there are some who are hesitant of your claim. Your magic has been compared to King Ammanar's brief display."

"King Ammanar was a mortal fool who stole magic from the elves." Sorean practically growled the words mortal and elves. His deep tone echoed around the stone walls they walked between. "I am no elf. And I am no mortal."

His father had said such things before he drew his last breath. Kindness had never been in his father's tone when he spoke to Sorean. It was no surprise, being chastised for his differences even before death's release.

"Obviously, *Prince*." Harland took advantage of Sorean's dampened mood and yanked the bottle from his hand. "They don't fear you or what you have. Those who voice these concerns survived the breaking of the scales five centuries ago. They saw what the gods did. Because of it, they only fear change. They fear different. So much, it blinds them."

The Prince of Lithelle pinched his lips and examined the dark alleyway. He had been born into this hidden realm. He hadn't witnessed the day of desecration in the Kingdom of Domnhall. But he had heard of the horrors many times. The people of Lithelle—his people— had good reason for concern. But he was no mortal king. And he was not elvish. Even if his magic was different, it would never be what the elves had.

Iara turned ahead of them, waiting impatiently. Harland noticed, walking with faster steps. At least his second in command scared Harland enough to hurry along. Sorean was tired of this conversation; he wanted to forget about it all now as the wine numbed his limbs.

But Harland spoke as they passed a restaurant's open door reeking of garlic and spilt ale. "Perhaps different magic is what this realm needs, Sorean. Too long have we been hiding. The gods' curse has taken on a life of its own outside our veil. Balance is perpetually skewed. And yet we sit here night after night, surrounded by mirrors to showcase our own magnificence. We are wasting potential."

Sorean scanned their surroundings, assuring the three of them were still alone without the shadowed alleys' privacy. Sparing a glance to his friend, he whispered sternly, "If the queen heard you speak so openly, you would be dead by her flame."

Harland was drunk already. This conversation needed to end before they reached Lady Talarin's back door.

Lithelle was hidden to keep their magic alive. To keep the faerie race alive. When the gods cursed the mortals for what King Ammanar had done, they abandoned their two magical creations: Elves and Faeries. Queen Morielle had hidden their realm out of protection. And hidden they had stayed for hundreds of years. Never to be found and never to be killed by the wrath of what the gods had left for the mortals.

This was the way of the fae now: Hidden and safe. What could he do differently without risking his people?

It wasn't until Iara opened the back door to the tavern that Harland turned to him and said, "I only ask that you use the weight of the crown to make this long life a little more exciting for me, Prince." He winked and ducked his head into the crowded room.

Sorean's head was pounding. And his mouth...Gods, something must have died within it. It took him a few moments to get the red velvet tapestries above him to stop spinning. He blinked furiously at them, rubbing his eyes a few times until he could see clearly.

A slender hand tightened around his waist. Turning his head, he found a sleeping female faerie with tousled blonde hair covering half of her face. The rest of her half-braided hair lay in long strands atop the black silk sheets. Sorean took in her bare shoulders and then the arm trailing beneath the sheets. He sighed through his nose. He didn't recognize her.

The night was a blur after walking into Lady Talarin's discreet rooms. Rooms filled with all of the intoxications a troubled prince could hope for: Faerie women, faerie men, faerie wine, and faerie substances to snort through the nose and smoke through filtered pipes.

The queen's spies never entered Lady Talarin's tavern. They rarely ventured this deep into Lithelle. And even if they did, Lady Talarin was paid handsomely for her discretion of what the prince and his friends did there night after night. But one could never be too sure. Sorean watched the sleeping fae and tried to recall her name. He vaguely remembered the two of them dancing atop of the bar, but the rest was fuzzy. Much like the ringing headache growing between his ears.

Sorean sensed his mysterious bedside companion waking up by the sound of her heavy breaths subsiding. He smirked, his dimple creasing as he did. Her hand tightened on him, the stinging pinch of her nails digging into his skin nearly making him moan with arousal. He could now recall every hazy second of what had transpired here only hours before.

"Good morning, Prince." Her voice was rough and tired.

Sorean cleared his throat, searching for her eyes within those straw-colored strands of messy hair. "Good morning."

He turned on his side and reached out to push the hair away from her face.

She was stunning, as most faeries were. Amber eyes ate him up as he studied the small freckles brimming her tanned nose. He had always loved freckles. "Forgive me, but I seem to have forgotten your name."

A light, flirtatious giggle fell from her swollen lips. Lips he had clearly kissed before and was now thinking about kissing again. Her hand left his waist slowly, making him raise a single brow.

She trailed those sharp, long nails up and down his outer thigh in a teasing manner and answered, "Dasyra, Your Grace."

"Dasyra. Of course." He smiled and pushed up from the pillows, reaching for her face in one smooth motion. Running a hand through her hair, he whispered near her ear, "Allow me to make detailed amends for whatever happened previously in this bed."

Dasyra let out a soft, breathy moan and whispered, "Of course, Your Grace."

Sorean smiled while planting soft kisses down her jaw. "I shall never forget your name again. But after we are done, you will need to forget mine."

"Again," Iara insisted with returning impatience.

"I'm trying." Sorean retorted through clenched teeth. Beads of sweat dripped off his nose and onto his outstretched palms.

"If you'd put half as much effort into this as you did with the random tavern faeries, perhaps we'd be seeing more progress in the young heir apparent."

Sorean dropped his hands and wiped them off on the thighs of his leather pants. The corner of his mouth twisted with exasperation, and Iara's narrowed eyes drilled into him with disapproval.

"And what about you?" Sorean shook the curls away from his brow. "Or are you still pining over the one you cannot have?"

His second in command managed to keep her face masked with cold annoyance, but Sorean caught the small twitch of her lips before she let out a resigned sigh. Iara rolled her eyes, as if knowing Sorean was straying from the topic at hand. A pitiful attempt to ignore what was going on. His unruly magic would not listen to him. Whatever was inside of him was petty and temperamental. There was no other way to put it. And Sorean had ignored it for days now, not bothering to use it or pay attention to its constant stir within his belly. Sleeping tonics mixed with faerie wine had aided in a week's worth of good rest, which also meant his magic couldn't reach him in his dreams. Now he was being punished for it.

For hours, Iara had barked commands at him while he strained to lift the small collection of rocks in the modest training arena they stood in. He had only managed to conjure a small breeze, enough to stir the dirt and make them both sneeze.

Sorean straightened and rolled his shoulders back. "I should be working on veiling. That, I know I can do." He could hide the whole arena easily with the little air magic he still had control of. A simple matter of shifting the air around him, enough to make pockets of darkness to hide in plain sight. It was how Lithelle had stayed hidden for so long, thanks to his mother's veiling.

"Which is why we don't work on veiling anymore. Because you can do it. Pining and plotting are two entirely different things, Prince. For example, you are pining for a different reaction from your magic when you choose the wrong actions to call upon it. Your essence is smart—smarter than you—and you know it. So act like it. Make a plan, bargain with it even. Get it to come out." Iara shoved away from the wall she had been leaning on and strolled past him towards the water table. "As for me, I am biding my time with whom you speak of. And dying slowly watching you try to be something you are not. She will see me for my worth one day. I am patient, although it is hanging on by a thread today because of you, Sorean."

"This doesn't look like much training." A female's voice crooned behind Sorean, playfully.

Sorean flared his nostrils to hide his breathy laugh. This morning was turning around for the better. He gave a smug, knowing smile to Iara, who practically choked on her water from the faerie's voice.

Running his damp hands through his mess of curls, he turned around, looking his betrothed over with a widening smirk. "Haven't seen you around for a few days, Farren. How is our queen?"

"Shouldn't you know?" Farren mirrored his snarky look before turning to grab a glass of water.

No. Sorean had been avoiding his mother as often as he could manage.

He watched Farren with amusement as she pointedly ignored Iara standing beside her, taking a slow drink from the glass before setting it down on the table.

There were no feelings involved with Farren when it came down to their contracted betrothal. The contract had been set and signed in ink before either of them were born. An alliance of strong faerie lines for magic and nothing more. A means to an end to keep Lithelle safe and sound within their bubble of protection.

The two had tried it once, after more than a few drinks at Lady Talarin's tavern. No spark came of it, in fact it was quite rigid and awkward for the both of them. In the morning, Farren confessed her taste being of the same sex as hers. Sorean had suspicions, after hearing rumors at the tavern, but he himself enjoyed tasting both male and female faeries and had assumed she was the same after hearing the gossip. Neither of them wanted to be married for different reasons. His for the chains of the crown and hers for the chains binding her to produce heirs.

It was then, under the banners of a brothel, the two had made an agreement to keep the titles and do what they wanted—who they wanted—in the whispers of shadows. And when he was king, he would find a way to end their marriage without scandal, before they were pressured to produce heirs and pass down his uncontrollable magic.

"I'm actually here on behalf of you, Prince."

Farren stepped away from the table and straightened the ties of the dress hanging from her midsection. Her dark brown curls bobbed along her pale shoulders as she fumbled with the satin ropes. Sorean waited patiently, knowing she would continue when she was ready. Farren was not one to be rushed, like most royals.

When she'd finished fixing the satin strings, she jutted her chin to bring Iara closer, and whispered, "It's Noi. He's back and will only speak to you."

"The deserter?" Iara hissed. "Where has he been hiding all these months to only come back now and ask for the prince?"

"The Wylan Woods."

en feared monsters. Yet fear made men do monstrous things.

Willa sighed through her nose as she flexed her hands, watching the red scars on her palms pull and twist with the clenching and unclenching of her fingers. Shadows from the surrounding torchlights and candles dramatized the markings, deepening her scowl.

It had been a year since her punishment, yet the large star in her right hand and sunburst in her left looked as fresh as the day they had been burned into her. Designs forever embedded in her skin from the abhorrent Ritual of Vitality: A branding upon the palms of a mortal to assure their blood was not tainted with the Wylan Wood's cursed magic. To assure they still harbored the grace and good balance to be favored by the old god, Forsetyr.

Balance. Willa nearly snorted at the mere thought of the word. The Ritual of Vitality was not a test of balance. It had nothing to do with the divine gods and every bit to do with the power Lord Nalore and his council held over this fearful town. If Forsetyr was still alive and out there somewhere, he would have felt the pull of balance being abused by Traifton's leader. The God of Balance would have seen what fear had done to man in his absence. But then again, the horned bear god himself had helped create the curse upon Kalandrae, tainting its once beautiful creatures. He had helped instill fear in men because of a mortal king's mistakes.

King Ammanar's purpose was to be the mortal beacon of balance between two magical species: Elves and Faeries. But greed outweighed rationality when Ammanar found a way to kill the newly crowned elf king and steal his magic while doing so. Blind with raw power, the mortal king destroyed everything in his path until the gods intervened and struck him down. The death and betrayal of King Ammanar ended the treaty of peace and harmony between the three races. It had been five hundred years and still, mortals suffered for King Ammanar's foolishness.

"By the laws of the scales, the fire, the water, and by the grace of the old Kingdom. Together we will be in the grace of Forsetyr's balance once more." Lord Nalore's prayer cut through Willa's thoughts like a dull, rusted blade. Dropping her hands back to her sides, she peered through the smoke-filled room with pursed lips.

He was watching her. His dark and beady eyes looked her over from the terrace where the rest of the robed council sat. The Lord of Traifton clasped his hands together and waited for the crowded room to repeat the words—waited for Willa to repeat the words. But Willa said nothing. Instead, she rested her back on the statue nearest to her and crossed her arms defiantly. She smiled at the lord and tilted her head to the side, her dark red curls bobbing near her face with the movement. He ignored her silent brazenness and looked to those approvingly who repeated the prayer.

"You're pushing your luck this morning," Tybalt whispered to her.

Willa turned her head and smiled at her twin brother, who leaned on the God of Chance beside her. She waved away the stream of incense smoke between them, the burnt smell of orange and pine trailing after the dissipating smoke. She scrunched her nose and fought off the tickling sensation of a sneeze. Her clothes would reek of it all day, but at least it was a pleasant smell. There could be worse punishments than having to endure morning prayers.

As Lord Nalore moved on to a droning chant of an old song, she whispered dryly, "Do you figure Nathayus can get us out of here early?"

Tybalt gave her a tight lipped smile. He still believed in the gods, unlike her. But he joined her in ignoring the off-key chanting and looked to the statue they both rested on.

A sea serpent's neck hovered above them, twisting and winding all the way towards the Hall of the Divine's glass ceiling. Nathayus had always been Ty's favorite of the three gods. Her twin studied the stone deity with a sort of longing, hopeful look. A small twang of jealousy nipped at her chest. She sometimes longed for the blind faith he still held. It would be nice to believe in something again.

Out of the three gods, Nathayus answered to the waters and the waters only. And Traifton's history was unclear regarding his disappearance on the day of the Kingdom of Domnhall's destruction. He had only arrived after King Ammanar was killed. He had taken the mortal king, holding the betrayer with his pointed fangs, and dragged him below the black waves of the Minison; a display of an unholy burial. But he never came back to help the other two gods curse the mortal lands. Some prayed to only him, hoping he would hear their call before Forsetyr and Velithor. Hoping if he hadn't appeared to help them make the curse, then perhaps he disagreed with what they had done. Willa noticed the sea serpent sigil swaying slightly from her brother's neck. Though her twin never said it, Willa knew Tybalt was one of those who prayed to him most.

Tybalt's short, curly red hair, matching hers in stubbornness and vibrant color, fell away from his forehead as he trailed the serpent's long neck and detailed scales. Even in the dim light, she could make out the freckles dotting his narrow nose and pale cheeks. The similarities between the two of them ended with his dark brown stubble covering the rest of his face and chin. The older they got, the more he looked like their father. Willa took in his tall and slender form and then looked down at her own. Her breasts pillowed out beneath her unbrushed hair, hiding the rest of her curved frame. She was tall like Tybalt, but it didn't take away the curves, making any pair of pants she wore a bit too tight. If she laid off the morning bread she stole every day from the market, perhaps they would loosen.

But bread made her happy. Pants did not.

The thought of fresh bread made her stomach gurgle and she nudged Tybalt with her tucked elbow. "Pray harder. I'm hungry."

Her brother snapped his head from the statue and gave her a threatening look. Willa uncrossed her arms and covered her mouth to suppress her brimming giggle. He opened his mouth to reply, but closed it abruptly as a robed councilman appeared before them.

Willa dropped her palms and straightened, squinting into the robe's hood. Her smile soured and fell away as Branlon pulled back the thick black velvet to give Willa and Tybalt a tight-lipped grin.

Branlon had once been a sentry but was now a guard and active member of the council. It seemed his ass-kissing had worked in his best interest. His job had changed shortly after he'd helped pull her from the Wylan behind Ivaan and Lord Nalore.

He was the one who had tied her to the statue of Forsetyr so she could be mutilated and publicly humiliated before all of Traifton. And he had smiled while doing it.

But it seemed his servility to the Lord of Traifton only went so far, since he was always appointed to trail after Willa and keep close watch on her. And what a terribly boring job it was for him. Because of her punishment the previous fall, she didn't have much trouble to get into. What they were hoping to catch her doing was unknown to her.

Each day was the same. She was here each morning, as instructed. Forced to attend prayer in the Hall of the Divine—a foolish hope of ingraining faith into her once more. Then she worked at the market, selling her mother's salves and ointments. She was usually fruitless in sales, since she was a walking symbol of what not to do. So why would anyone trust what she had to sell? The only sales she did make were older regulars: temporarily abandoning status by conversing with Willa to get what medicine they needed from her mother's gracious and hardworking hands. And when the market closed for the evening, she returned home and never left. Even if she wanted to, the sentries stayed posted outside her bedroom window and the home's front door. On occasion, she would even be sent to the council's homes to polish their floors, clean their chamber sheets and pots, and wash their heavy robes.

During the Rituality of Vitality, one would have thought bleeding red, not black, would have been enough humility. But no. Just because she wasn't tainted didn't mean she was trusted. She was the town rebel. Unpredictable. Scarred. *Wild.* Those who were her friends before now walked in the other direction if they saw her. Whispered about her. Laughed behind her back.

Branlon spoke in a sniveling tone, "May the balance of Forsetyr ring true through you both on Murock Day."

He reached into his pockets and pulled out two white candles, pushing them towards her. She rolled her eyes, making no attempt to grab them. Instead, she crossed her arms and mirrored his pretentious smile. Tybalt pushed away from the statue and plucked them from Branlon's hands, distracting him from Willa. Taller than the guard by at least a foot, Tybalt looked down his nose at Branlon with a scowl but said nothing. Keeping his patience in check, her brother quietly bent to light the wicks from ones already burning on the stone ground near Nathayus' curled tail.

Branlon didn't care about their attitudes. He was too arrogant in his new position, considering himself untouchable. "Be careful tonight. With so many activities going on, one might assume it would be easy to slip away in the night."

His smile curled, turning sinister, and he gave a pointed nod to Willa, "I don't have to remind you what the cost is for upsetting the balance. Thought you would have learned after what happened to your father."

Tybalt stiffened, and Willa snatched the candle from her brother's hand. She pushed off the stone serpent's belly and stalked towards the guard with clenched teeth.

A few of the townspeople nearest to them, still chanting their prayers, turned their heads. But when they saw Willa, they all returned to what they were doing with rapid speed.

Branlon stepped back, raising his chin. "Have you got something to say, Willa?"

Willa's temper flared hotter than the candle's flame dancing in her hand. He and the rest of the town could say what they wanted about her. But her father had been brave and selfless. No one spoke ill of his memory.

Branlon had crossed an invisible line.

CHAPTER 6

WILLA

Willa spoke on emotion alone when she hissed between her teeth, "You know, Branlon, some days I wish they would have found cursed magic in me."

An older woman, kneeling directly behind him, overheard and choked with surprise, fumbling the words of her prayer.

Branlon only snickered in reply. "And why is that?"

"Because with a snap of my fingers, you would fall before me." Willa tried to keep her shaking voice quiet, but a few more were turning to gawk at her now.

"Empty threats are all you have, Willa. I'm not scared of you." Branlon looked at the few still daring to listen in and drawled, "My only hope is to pray for you now. Pray the gods sort out the skewed scales within you."

Willa heard Tybalt hissing out a warning for her to stop, but she lunged forward, shoving Branlon back into the praying townspeople of Traifton. Her lit candle touched the arms of his robes as she shoved him, and she gasped as the flames eagerly latched onto the cloth.

Branlon stumbled back into the crowd from the shove, slapping at the flames dancing on the heavy material. His footing faltered as he staggered backwards, and before Willa could blink, he was on the ground, dragging an innocent townsman down with him. The poor man's lit candle hit the ground as he fell, and within seconds, the man's flame was crawling over the stone floor, eagerly eating the oils and dried flowers on the cobblestones.

Lord Nalore had stopped his chant now. In fact, the entire hall had grown silent. Branlon shimmied out of the arms of his flaming robes as quickly as he could. But the fire was faster. It eagerly licked and crawled up his shoulders and down the sides of his black velvet draping. Most of the townspeople backed away from the scene, while a few others ran past, calling for water.

Willa thought to run while she still had the chance, but the outburst had unleashed something within her. She took slow, deliberate steps towards the guard struggling to free himself from the hungry fire. Branlon was too focused on getting out of his robe to notice. He didn't spot her until it was too late. Until she raised her leather boot and kicked his chest with her heel. Branlon fell back, landing on the burning robe he had managed to get out of with a startled yelp. He hissed and tried to sit up, the flames nipping at his short black hair. Willa used all her weight to hold him down.

It felt good to look down at him. To see fear in his eyes, if only for a moment.

She leaned forward, pressing his chest further into the flames. They were eating at her other boot now, crawling up towards her thin pants. But she didn't care, she would be punished soon, anyway. And it would be far worse than a few burns on her leg and holes in her boot. Time was running out. Better make it count.

"If the Wylan's veil ever falls, I hope the creatures enjoy manipulating your soft mind until you become their meal. I hope you feel pain like I have."

The smell of burning flesh brought her back to the night she was branded. Her body trembled with the memory, but it only fueled her rage.

She continued with a smug smile, "But maybe you are feeling it. I would ask if it hurts, but I know better than anyone."

"Fuck you," Branlon replied in reckless anger, finally managing to grab hold of her ankle. Squeezing tightly, he shoved her leg off him. He was stronger than her and did so easily.

Willa laughed and stepped back before he could touch her. She continued to back away as he jumped up, slapping frantically at his burning backside.

She knelt and patted away the small flames, still clinging to her. "That's not very divine of you, *councilman*. Perhaps it is you we should be praying for."

Cold water fell over Willa's head, soaking her instantly. She lifted her hands and pushed away the dark red curls from her eyes with surprised gulps. Branlon was coughing up water as well, two council members quickly covering him and the ground in thick linens to snuff out the small fire she had caused.

"What's the meaning of this?" Lord Nalore bellowed.

Willa covered her chest and shivered. She looked over at the lord, who held an empty bucket. His eyes were narrowed on hers as he waited for an explanation.

"I was provoked!" Willa threw a hand out to Branlon, who was being stripped from the top down to assess whether he was injured. He had hardly been touched aside from the singed hair on the back of his head, making for an unattractive, blistering bald spot. She arched an eyebrow with smug satisfaction, but Lord Nalore stepped in front of Branlon, hiding him from her view.

Lord Nalore was breathing heavily as he looked at her, his face bright red. He had been waiting for her to act out again. He had been testing her patience for a year, practically drooling over the chance to punish her once more.

"What was I supposed to do, my lord? He poked fun at my father's death. A member of *your* council once upon a time, if memory still serves you properly."

Lord Nalore's face deepened into a dark crimson.

"Four lashes to be served." His yell echoed around the large hall, and Willa's mouth fell open. "Here and now!"

She was to be beaten for this outburst? And in the Hall of Divine, of all places?

Tybalt yelled her name, but Willa didn't dare look his way. She wouldn't get her twin involved in her careless mistake.

Two guards grasped her arms and pulled her onto the podium before she could argue further. Within minutes, the early morning prayer had become a show hall for her punishment.

Lord Nalore explained the reason for her sanction while a table of incense and parchment was wiped away and cleared for her to lay atop of. "One lash for provoking a council member! One lash for attacking a council member! One lash for the attempt to desecrate our sacred hall of worship! And one lash for the lack of participation in prayer!"

Willa winced in frustration. The first three were somewhat warranted. The last, however, was not. That was simply because of how she had spoken to Lore Nalore. For embarrassing him. *Not* because of her lack of participation. For if that were the case, she would have one lash for every day she stepped into this hall for morning prayer.

She barely had time to cover her breasts as her wet tunic was cut down the back. A council member shoved her face down onto the empty table and she hit the wood with a startled cry. She braced her hands on either side of her face while her back lay open and vulnerable to all, her pale, freckled flesh like a blank canvas to those who stood behind her.

Shuffling and whispers moved below her. Willa's composure was a fragile shell around her as she waited for what would come next. She had never been lashed before, though she had seen it. A quick reprimand often used by guards if they caught a thief at the market or near the docks. It couldn't be worse than branding, could it? On the bright side, maybe she wouldn't be allowed to attend the Murock Day's dance as another form of punishment.

As if reading her mind, Lord Nalore spoke with finality to those watching. "Willa Thesalor is a reminder of why we purge our shadows this week for the crimson moon. Let her remind you of what this red moon stands for tonight at the dance when you see her face. Unleash your desires tonight, so tomorrow and the rest of the week, you may be cast in the moon's shedding light and Forestyr's good graces once more. Pray for Willa as we help her purge now, before the gods."

So she would be forced to attend tonight. To dance and drink around those who whispered about her below in the hall. To wear a dress to rub on her back and remind her with every breath what happened when she broke the rules.

Two hands rested on either side of Willa's face upon the table, pinning her to the wood, and Branlon's voice spoke low in her ear. "I will enjoy this."

CHAPTER 7

SOREAN

Noi shifted in his seat uncomfortably before speaking. "Something has happened."

"Clearly. Speak plainly, fox." Iara's tone was harsh and clipped.

Tilting his head to one side, Sorean stole a slanted look at Iara, but remained passive, waiting for Noi to continue.

The shifter grasped the stem of his glass tightly before glancing out of the booth they sat in, his pointed ears twitching through his matted red hair as he scanned the faeries. "We couldn't have gone anywhere else?"

It was telling how long the faerie shifter had been in his animal form. He looked half wild and unkempt. His shirt hung from his torso in a wrinkled state. It took everything in Sorean not to scrunch his nose at the smell coming from his skin.

Faerie shifters were becoming more and more uncommon with the state of magic keeping Lithelle hidden. Fae shifters used the natural elements of the ground and soil to shift into their animal forms. Simply because animals were of the purest form of nature. Predatory, innocent, and bred of their own volition. But now, after centuries of being veiled and hidden, there was nothing natural about Lithelle. It was all magical tricks to give the look and feel of a natural realm and kingdom. But the air was different—magically tainted—as was the water, soil, and food growing from it.

Because new fae were being born into a realm of false nature, the only faerie shifters left were those who were alive before the gods' curse. Almost all of them were used by Queen Morielle to act and serve as spies—to be the eyes and ears outside Lithelle. To keep tabs on the other realms. Noi was one of her spies. But the fox had been gone for months now, making Queen Morielle announce him dead or a deserter. And to be a deserter was punishable by death. It was law.

Noi studied the bustling crowd around them with narrowed, untrusting eyes. The rims of his golden irises were nearly all black and dilated.

Sorean rested his elbows on the table and cleared his throat to get his attention. "It would be too obvious to speak within the castle. You know our queen has eyes and ears everywhere." Noi's golden eyes flicked back to Sorean's with hesitancy, but the prince continued, "Lady Talarin is the only tavern owner I trust. What happens here is no one's business. Especially the crown's."

He looked at Iara and Farren, who sat on either side of him. They both nodded in agreement.

Harland was keeping most of the tables preoccupied with his magical parlor tricks. Water droplets fell around the tables but never soaked a hair on one faerie's head. The tavern's regulars loved his performances and charm. And Sorean loved the drowning sound of water coming from his acts to hide conversations which required more privacy.

"The Wylan is much worse than I feared, Your Majesty."

"Sorean is fine, Noi. You've known me since I was a boy." Sorean attempted to give a comforting smile, but he was growing impatient. His mother would be expecting him soon for the evening festivities at court.

Noi bowed his head and set his now empty glass down. Pushing it away, he said, "The cursed magic has taken on a life of its own. Even the water tastes different now. What animals were in there are no longer of the same mind."

Noi swallowed thickly, as if he'd known some of them personally before. Perhaps he had with how often he traveled through the Wylan Woods to keep tabs for the queen.

The shifter continued, "They are tainted. Warped of skin and flesh. I even saw creatures made of magic itself. They are horrific."

"We already know this to be a fact, Noi." Farren drawled, her tone bored as though she were at court beside the queen. She tilted her head. "Unless there are new species we need to add to our records?"

"There are new ones I will describe to you later, but it is not what concerns me. What concerns me is how these new creatures act. Their trail patterns were odd, as was their communication."

"Communication?" Farren asked. "You mean to say they have their own dialect now? Before we were told they would destroy one another if crossing paths. We know them to be practically dead, lifelessly walking around without purpose."

"At first, I thought it to be my own paranoia. But I had been trailing one for three, maybe four nights. Night after night, it called out into the woods. It howled and whined as if it were hurt. I heard the same noises echoing its call before a different creature appeared. I watched and waited for a fight to break out when they eventually met within the trees, but they did not." Noi's eyes brightened as he spoke of what he witnessed. "Instead, I watched them speak to one another through these low, distorted noises.

They traveled together as if they were part of a family. Two entirely different beings hunting together, sleeping near one another, looking out for each other. Curious, is it not?"

"Curious, little fox," Iara mumbled. Despite her distrust in him, she was leaning closer on her chair, clearly invested in what Noi had encountered.

With the queen's death sentence above him, Sorean didn't blame Iara's lack of trust in the fae shifter and this gathering, but this was news indeed.

Noi ignored Iara and continued, "I followed them for weeks until I realized they were going to the old kingdom." Iara and Farren stiffened beside him. "It was there I discovered something worse than what I could imagine. The Kingdom of Domnhall is gone. Where there was an empty, crumbled castle, is a massive hole in the ground, the size of Lithelle."

Sorean had only seen drawings depicting the grandeur of the old Kingdom of Domnhall. The gods and mortal kings had put a lot of pride into it. Its size was colossal, like Lithelle's. For there to be a pit the size of it was almost unimaginable.

He shifted in his seat and asked, "What's created this pit, Noi? Or has the cursed magic begun to eat away the continent itself?"

Maybe it was a metaphor from the gods. Another symbol to show what once was could never be.

"I'm afraid nothing inside the Wylan Woods is simple, Sorean. I do not know how the pit was created, but I did see what came out of it."

Iara cursed and took a long drink before announcing she was bringing back a bottle for them all.

Noi's eyes were distant now, glassy, as if he were seeing the horrors for the first time. "The gods' cursed magic has become its own entity now. It's producing its own species in this pit. Poisoned magic, now breeding life made of leathered skin and shadows. Worse than what we've recorded thus far. Ten times the size." Noi visibly shivered before continuing, "What's worse is they wield magic. As if they have faerie magic or elvish essence."

Farren stood from her chair. "Queen Morielle needs to hear of this at once, I will go—"

"No!" Noi barked out. He stood abruptly, leaving his chair to fall to the ground as he did.

Those nearest to the table paused to look over at the sudden disruption. Sorean gave a pointed look to Harland, who instantly brought their attention back to him with a new trick. He pulled wine from a faerie's goblet and constructed it into the shape of a dragon. The floating red wine hovered over the faeries like a dream conjured of the fire breathing creatures of old. Harland made its wine- made-wings flap above everyone in the tavern, spinning it in circles higher and higher towards the ceiling.

Sorean tried to imagine what Noi had witnessed in the old kingdom. He was grateful the dragons had left with the dragon God of Justice, Velithor. If they had resided in the Wylan Woods when it became tainted, the realms would have been reduced to ash by contaminated dragons centuries ago.

"Noi, you know whatever you've seen in the Wylan Woods has to be reported to my mother."

But Noi wasn't listening to Sorean. The shifter was panting up at the wine-made-dragon with all black eyes. His lips were curled into a snarl, as if he were offended by the dragon creation. A small whine came from the back of his throat, and he shifted back on his heels nervously. Not offended, Sorean realized, but scared. He needed to control this situation before Noi shifted and caused a scene.

"Noi," Sorean said in a commanding tone.

He needed to know what had caused such alarm when Farren had mentioned the queen. He needed to know why Noi was so afraid of a simple faerie parlor trick.

Sorean spoke louder this time, "Noi!"

Noi snapped his head towards him with curled lips, showing off his elongated canines.

"Please," Sorean spoke calmly and pointed to Iara's empty chair, "If there is something you wish for us to keep from the queen explicitly, you need to be clear."

Farren was still standing, ready to go to Queen Morielle with this information, but Sorean pointed to her chair as well. She pursed her lips, but heeded his silent command.

Sorean offered Noi a comforting smile. "May we continue?"

Once seated again, Farren crossed her legs and tilted her head to Iara's still empty chair, then back to Noi. The shifter studied Farren and Sorean with wide, dilated eyes and shook his head. He dipped his chin, as if to remember the company he kept were to rule this kingdom soon, and sat back down.

Straightening his wrinkled shirt, he cleared his throat. "There is more. I ran after seeing what crawled out of the old kingdom. I ran until I reached a lake that whispered sweet nothings to me. The fog above the water calmed me instantly. It helped me forget. So I stayed there, hidden in the reeds, for days."

There was only one place within the Wylan Woods with the power to do such things.

"Niarath Loch," Sorean stated. A historical lake where mortals and magical beings alike had ventured to find prophetic answers in the murky water before the curse.

Noi nodded and continued, "It seems to be the only thing still untouched by the cursed magic. It was there I heard what is happening outside the gods' cursed veil."

Iara appeared, silently filling all their glasses before lifting Noi's fallen chair up and sitting on it.

Noi gave her a sidelong glance while speaking. "The water speaks in riddles, and riddles only. But from what I could gather, the elves have re-appeared. And they are searching for something."

CHAPTER 8
SOREAN

Iara set down her wine and looked to Sorean with a concerned frown, while Farren shifted uncomfortably beside him. Sorean ignored them both, desperate to keep Noi focused. "What could the elves be looking for, Noi?"

The elves, much like the faeries, had left after the gods' cursed Kalandrae and turned their back on all their creations. No one had seen or heard from them in centuries.

Noi drank from his cup deeply before answering. "The water has many guesses. But the whispers confirmed there are some elven families who stayed in this realm, keeping to the shadows. Hiding in plain sight. But because they stayed behind, they are now feeling the effects. Their magic is weakening without us and the gods' old construct of balance."

"But?" Sorean prodded. There had to be more. He needed something more concrete to bring back to his mother.

Noi leaned forward and grabbed onto Sorean's wrist.

Iara gripped the shifter's arm and squeezed until Noi winced, releasing him. "Careful, shifter."

Sorean waved her away with furrowed brows.

"One whisper in the lapping waves of the lake set my hair on edge. The water whispers concerns of a new era of gods. One where elves control the mortals for what was done centuries ago." His voice dropped to a whisper. "They are back for revenge."

Sorean smiled while taking a drink of his faerie wine.

It was time to go. It was news to bring the queen, but nothing new by her predictions. His mother assumed, if the elves still lived within this realm, this would happen eventually. She knew the elves would want to hurt the mortals for what their late king had done. Anger harbored for so long could easily fester into vengeance.

"We owe the mortals nothing." Sorean shrugged and set his cup down.

The mortals had put them in this mess. Why would they stop the elves from seeking vengeance if they were making themselves known again?

Sorean gave Noi another reassuring smile. "Thank you for the report, Noi. The queen will be pleased. With your detailed recollection, I'll be sure to have the bounty on your neck taken away."

"I'm not done, Prince. The water's whispers had more to say. They spoke of an item ancient and forgotten now by almost everyone in the realm."

Sorean dropped his polite smile and clenched his jaw. He drummed his fingers along the tabletop, waiting for the shifter to spit it out.

"A piece of an artifact has been found. The Key of Sanctity."

Sorean paused his thrumming fingers. "I thought it was destroyed along with King Ammanar."

Noi nodded eagerly and pressed on. "So did I, Prince. So did I. But the waters sensed its awakening in the southern isles a few months back. The elvish piece has resurfaced."

Farren set her cup down and raised a finger. "I'm sorry, what is the Key of Sanctity? And what does this have to do with the elves?"

The Key of Sanctity was practically lore to the fae now. A story passed down from the elders after too many drinks. In moments like these, Sorean forgot the princess was younger than him and Iara by two hundred years.

Noi poured from the bottle Iara had brought and Sorean answered while the shifter drank.

"The Key of Sanctity is what held Forsetyr's Law of Balance in place. The mortal kings were bred to hold a singular token of power, having none for themselves."

"It was a symbol of peace to show mortals were important," Noi added, still clutching his glass.

Sorean refrained from laughing and continued, "One piece was forged from elven essence, and the other half was made from ours."

"And the mortals?" Farren asked. "What part had they in this key?"

"A mortal king held both pieces as a pillar between the gods' magical races." Noi said, his attention seemingly drifting to Harland and his dragons once more. Thankfully, he didn't react, but his gaze wouldn't land on anything for longer than a breath.

"If I remember correctly," Sorean said, scratching his chin. "The gods sensed faeries and elves growing restless with their power after the mortals appeared. Mortals are weak. They are beneath us. But some went too far with the knowledge and killed mortals for sport."

Iara nodded with a sigh. "They even used some as slaves or playthings before the fae or elves tired of them."

Silence filled the table, and Farren's brows knitted. "And what of the elves and us? Did we play well together, sharing the human slaves?"

Sorean took a drink from his cup before answering. "No. Faeries and elves were beginning to feud over differences in magic. The gods grew tired of the wars and mindless killings. We were created to be extensions of the gods, yet we soiled their name with our actions. So the mortals became a tool and a reminder that they were necessary for the maps to thrive and grow. They wanted us to learn from them, help them, become idols to them, so one day we might do what the gods did."

Farren spoke confidently, "Even if a piece has resurfaced, the Law of Balance is gone. The gods are gone. There are no mortal kings left to wield the symbol and, even if there were, it's not like the key actually does something important, right? You said it was a symbol, nothing more."

He hummed in agreement. "It is interesting to hear it has appeared after centuries, but it seems irrelevant to the elves' return and the magic in the Wylan."

Noi's dilated pupils glittered beneath the candlelight. "You forget an important part of the history, young prince. The gods didn't just put our essence into those pieces, but our entire life force. We knew this at one point. Which is why it was such a huge symbol for the mortals to hold onto. A dangling piece, hanging above both elves and faeries to behave or..." Noi clapped his hands loudly and rubbed them together. "Poof. We'd be gone. If the artifacts had been destroyed when King Ammanar died, the elves and fae would have died with him. Even now. If it were to be resurrected, and somehow destroyed, we'd be gone."

There was a lengthy pause before Noi asked, "If your magic was weakening, Prince, would you do something to fix it?"

Sorean retracted from Noi's question and pursed his lips. If his essence was normal, the answer would easily be yes.

The shifter took his silent brooding as a sign to rephrase and asked instead, "What if every faerie in Lithelle was weakening? Would you try to fix it then?"

"Obviously," Sorean snapped.

Noi gave a grim smile. "As I said, the water whispered of the elves' essence beginning to grow weak because of the broken scales. Their race is dying. They are desperate. But if there is enough essence within the artifacts, they could be cured."

"But again, Noi, they would need our piece to even wield the key." Sorean wearily finished his glass, rubbing at his neck.

"If the elves are desperate for revenge—desperate for stronger magic—desperate for living in this realm, they will do anything to make it happen." Noi frowned. "If they were to find both pieces, and wield it with a mortal in the middle, they would be able to take the faerie essence from our piece and use it for their own."

"Killing us all," Iara whispered in horror.

Noi continued, "And why would they care when we have been missing for five centuries? To them, we are already gone."

"But to mix magic is forbidden," Sorean muttered. "Its law is greater than the Law of Balance."

It was curious to imagine what mixed magic could be like for an immortal and how powerful they could be. A combined creation would almost be considered a demi-god in the eyes of the old deities. Perhaps the gods had also thought of this, and set the law to assure their own creations couldn't come close to their own, omniscient strength.

Sorean asked, "You think the elves, even suspecting we are dead and gone, would stoop so low after rivaling us throughout history? Would they not consider it an abomination to share their magic with our own?"

Noi cocked his head and looked at him, his face growing somber as he studied the white markings running up and down Sorean's neck. "Your Majesty, if I may speak plainly, I did not bring this to the queen for a reason. Here we are safe, and she would say those words exactly. She would laugh and let the elves try this fool's mission, but you and I both know the strain of keeping this realm hidden. No one wants to admit it, but our magic is also waning. We are doing all we can to hide it, but balance has been unkempt for too long. If our artifact is out there somewhere, and the elves find it and act out this plan—"

"It could destroy the veil and us along with it," Sorean finished, pushing to his feet.

Noi nodded gravely. "For too long, we have sat back and done nothing. Queen Morielle was wise to hide us, but there is too much going on outside of our world. And it will find a way to harm us in the end. I ask you now, Prince Sorean, what will you do with the crown?"

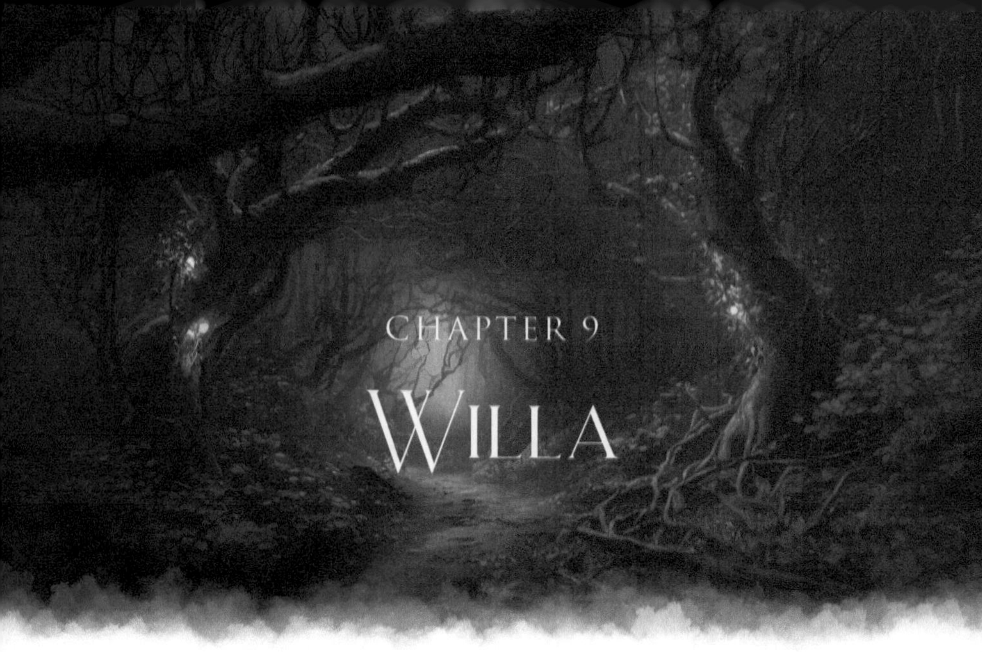

CHAPTER 9
WILLA

Willa stared into the water of the metal basin, quietly holding her knees towards her chest, as her mother tended to her welts with a damp cloth. Tears fell from her eyelashes with each delicate pat placed upon her skin.

"You're lucky these didn't open or you wouldn't be able to walk, or work, for at least a week. But you will be sore and uncomfortable. And I'll bet every copper you get nasty bruises too in the coming days. Best get ahead of it with my peppermint salve." Corvina clucked her tongue with disapproval. She dropped the cloth into the water behind Willa and stood. "I suppose they want it to happen. For you to be uncomfortable."

Willa wiped at her swollen eyes while her mother circled around the washroom, checking the numerous shelves for oils and balms. Twenty-four years of age and her mother was looking after her like a small child. Corvina stepped back to the iron basin and poured sweet-smelling liquids into the water. Lemon, sage, and lavender quickly enveloped the room and Willa lowered her lashes, inhaling greedily.

"For what it's worth, I am sorry." Willa dipped a finger in the water and swirled it around, watching the oils sink below as she did. "I would have kept quiet if it weren't for the comment about Father."

"Your father would have been upset at how you acted. As am I, Willa Thesalor."

Her mother sighed and kneeled so she could speak to her at eye level.

Corvina tucked a few wet curls behind Willa's ear and continued in a more delicate tone, "Sander also taught you and your brother how to speak up when something wasn't right. We taught you to stand up for what you believe in, despite what others may do or say. It doesn't mean I condone lighting a council member on fire, because they did not act how you would act if the positions were reversed."

Shallow sobs tore through Willa's hunched back as her mother brushed through her hair with her fingers.

"But your father would have laughed so hard you'd worry his sides were about to split if he knew what you did. He never did like Lord Nalore or how the rest of the members groveled at his feet. I am sorry you did not have more time with Sander. He may have called you Wildfire, but I swear the man was born from embers." Corvina stood and walked towards the door. "He would know how to help you and your temper. You are more like him than you think."

Before giving Willa some time alone, Corvina spoke again, "Don't ever forget him or his memory, Willa. But remember, he also was on the council. He had his own opinions in this home, but walked with grace among the town. Follow his steps tonight and the rest of the nights forward. I'll be back to help you dress."

The door to the washroom opened and shut, leaving Willa in a cocoon of steam and her own thoughts. She closed her eyes, feeling utterly miserable.

Her mother was wrong. She was nothing like her father. No matter how hard she tried, grace was not a word associated with her sailor's mouth and hasty actions. She was a woman, acting no better than a bratty child. She wasn't brave or selfless like him. She wouldn't have rushed into the Wylan Woods to save a small child as he had. No one else would be so brave. They wouldn't have returned from those woods, like him, if they had.

Willa soaked for a few more minutes, imagining her father's face and memory. When there were no more tears left to fall, she pushed herself out of the bath. She grabbed a towel and patted herself dry, flinching at the stinging throbs from her back as she did.

She needed to stop acting on her temper when the townspeople or council provoked her. She needed to be better for her family and her father's memory. They were the only ones standing behind her now, and Willa knew what that meant for them.

Tybalt was having a hard time keeping a job. He was an excellent worker, but he was having to find a new place to work anytime she opened her mouth. She hoped this morning's act wouldn't hurt his new job down at the docks.

Out of all of them, her best friend, Claire, had been doing her best to separate herself from Willa in public. With her newfound position as captain of her family's trading ship, Willa understood. It was easy to be separated, with Claire having been away on a sailing route for three months. Would she be back for the week-long festival? Gods, Willa hoped so. Although, with her outburst this morning, Claire might not even speak to her now for fear of tainting her new title.

Willa padded to the tall mirror resting on the wall in the corner of the room, turning to look at the red, puffy marks below her shoulders. The pain hadn't been worse than the Ritual of Vitality. She had managed to keep her mouth covered as Branlon let the whip snap in the air. His anger lined those lashes. The fourth one had nearly turned her silent sobs into a plea for mercy. But she hadn't wanted to give him any more sick satisfaction. And when he was done, she'd stood with her trembling chin held high, and walked off the terrace and through the silent crowd, ignoring their stares and whispers. She'd walked home much the same—swallowing the remaining sobs in her throat with desperate determination, holding onto her cut up shirt as a sentry trailed behind her.

A soft knock on the door had Willa looking into the glass to find her mother stepping in with a wrapped bundle. "This was left for you at the front door."

Corvina walked to the racks of neatly dried herbs and set it down.

"Who is it from?" She looked at the package with curiosity. It was wrapped in a fine silk cloth and tied together with what looked to be twine used for fishing nets.

Her mother was watching her intently with furrowed brows. "I'm not sure. There was no note."

Puzzled, Willa pulled at the knot on the string. Removing the silk folds, her eyebrows rose to touch the wet messy curls atop her forehead. It was a gown.

Willa lifted the heavy velvet and let it drop from the wrappings. The navy-blue dress splayed out in layers of light, shimmering chiffon atop the blue velvet underskirt. The sleeves were long and form-fitting. The top of the dress was simply designed. Lines from the corset beneath fell into the chiffon bustle of skirting. It had a high cut to clasp around her neck. Willa smiled at the thumb holes at the bottom of the sleeves. They would cover her scarred palms nicely. It was like this dress had been made specifically for her. Willa turned the dress in her hands, her smile faltering when she saw the wide open back.

Corvina took the dress, muttering the names of fabric workers who could have made it, and shuffled towards the mirror. Willa followed and dropped her towel to step into the folds of the mysterious gown.

"This doesn't seem like a Traifton made gown, Mother." She sighed. "But I can admit it's gorgeous. I only wish the back weren't wide open." Who had brought this to her?

Corvina shimmied the dress up past Willa's hips and mumbled, "Let all of Traifton see what the council did to you. If Lord Nalore wants to use you as a display of his cruelty, be one of beauty and grace." Corvina pulled the rest of the gown towards her chest and let Willa slide her arms into the sleeves.

As her mother worked on the ties in the mirror, Willa noted her cheeks were more hollow than usual. Her eyes were sunken in and besides the puffiness from crying, they were shadowed and purple above her freckled nose. She hadn't been sleeping well, with the usual night terrors of the Wylan and its creatures. But despite her tired face, this gown did well to make her feel beautiful. Her red hair seemed to glow above the navy color, and even her tired eyes seemed brighter in their mossy green color.

Corvina pulled Willa's wet hair to the side to tie the shoulder pieces together near the nape of her neck. A surprising, sharp poke pricked her skin while the corset pulled tighter over her chest.

Willa hissed and raised a hand. "Wait, a moment. Something is piercing me."

She stared at her mother in the reflection while reaching her hand in between her breasts to grasp at whatever had poked her skin. Paper touched her fingers, along with something sharp and slender. Willa pinched at both and pulled them out of the dress.

A crumpled piece of parchment and a small hair clip sat between her fingers. She took the hair clip first with her other hand and held it up in front of the mirror. The metal clip opened and closed easily with her movement. But the metal design atop of the clip had her pinching her brows together in confusion.

Its design seemed to be half of a star. Slender lines formed sharp points of the star's design, but it looked to be torn in two. The edge where the missing half should be was jagged and slightly rusted.

"It looks like the Star of the Scales," Corvina mused.

Willa pulled her right thumb out of the velvet sleeve and rolled up the material. Spreading her fingers, she held her branded palm out towards her mother, who put the clip near the scarred design of the large northern star on her palm. The two of them nodded in unison at the similarities of the elongated points of the star. But why was it broken? Willa remembered the paper and eagerly unfolded it.

She immediately recognized Claire's messy handwriting.

Willa read the words aloud with a wide smile, "I heard about this morning. Had to make a scene on Murock Day, really? And a fire in the Hall of the Divine, of all places. You really know how to cause a scene. What happened this morning is the reason I couldn't deliver this to you in person. I hope you understand. The journey has been long, and I need my men to listen to me more now than ever. I hope to explain it all to you later, but for now, enjoy the gown. I can't wait to see the look on the daft lord's face when you arrive in it."

Of course, her best friend had found this gown for her. She wished she could see Claire now and forget the festival all together. She wanted to hear all about her travels. Who she'd seen, where she'd been, and what she meant by her crew needing to listen to her.

"She didn't say anything about the hair piece, did she?" her mother pressed.

Willa squinted at the crumpled paper, reading it again before flipping it over. There was something else hastily written upon the backside of the parchment. It was still Claire's handwriting, but it looked to be rushed.

"...Essence apart. Whispers true..."

Confused, Willa read the four words aloud. Claire loved her history and had endless journals of research. Maybe she had used the piece of paper from her journal to write her the note and simply forgot what was already on it.

Her mother said nothing to the odd words on the back of the paper. Instead, she tugged at Willa's damp curls until two braids were falling behind her shoulders. Corvina's face was pulled tightly in concentration while she set the broken hair clip in her mouth and twisted the two braids together. She twisted and lifted them from Willa's shoulders, so they rested around the back of her head like large, twisting red vines. Holding the hair up with one hand, she pulled the clip from her mouth with the other and shoved it in between the twisted hair. Willa fussed as it scraped her scalp, but her mother continued, despite her prickly demeanor.

Corvina stepped away and clapped her hands, announcing she was finished. Willa folded the note back up and pushed it into the dress where she had found it. The clip wasn't visible within the thick twists of locks, but the points pinched and rubbed her scalp as they held the braids perfectly. Yet another piece of Claire's gift made specifically for her.

Her mother took in her work from the mirror's reflection and nodded to Willa, who gently poked at her hair. "Those sharp edges will hold it up nicely if you dance. If I didn't know any better, I'd wager this was a dress fit for the elves."

If Claire had run into the elves and managed to buy clothing from them, she truly did have a story to tell.

Corvina continued with a smile, "You look lovely, Wildfire. It really is the perfect color to bring out those eyes."

Willa returned the smile, despite the aching wave of grief, trying to drown her heart from hearing her father's nickname. Turning, she pulled her mother into a soft hug.

Corvina was careful not to touch her back as she rested her head on Willa's shoulder and whispered, "Remember what I said, Willa. Go with grace tonight. And—"

"Keep your wits about you." Willa said the words with her mother in unison.

The two of them broke apart and laughed at their joint reciting of her father's words before leaving the room together, hand in hand.

Tybalt was waiting for them near the hearth, with two cloaks resting over his crossed forearms. He whistled and looked Willa up and down. "I thought you were going to blend in tonight, not come looking like an old Domnhall royal."

Pulling her cloak from his arm, as her mother laughed behind her, she rolled her eyes at him. "You can thank Claire for this one. And did you even bathe?"

Willa leaned in towards his neck and sniffed. Scrunching her nose, she pulled back and made a fake gagging sound. Tybalt suddenly looked nervous. He took to inspecting his black tunic and velvet pants. Was it the mention of Claire being home or her joke on his smell?

She swallowed her mocking giggle and patted at his chest. "I'm only teasing. You look fine."

"You look like him." Corvina's somber, matter-of-fact tone had them both looking over to her. She had taken a seat in their father's old reading chair.

Corvina gave them both a pained smile with glassy eyes and nodded.

Tybalt stepped to their mother and bent down to place a kiss on her cheek. When he turned, Willa caught him wiping at his eyes before shouldering past her towards the door.

They walked silently in the rain, and the sentry followed a few feet behind them. The rain was coming down harder than usual, the wind from the Minison's waves threatening to whip off the hood of her cloak with each corner they took. The alleys were empty, save for the scattered stacks of crates and barrels. The only sound was an alley cat hissing at them as they dodged puddles and holes in the cobblestones.

Willa knew Tybalt was chewing on their mother's words. Talk of Father always put a heavy rain cloud, made specifically for the Thesalor family, above their heads. Where Willa was often foolishly outspoken, Tybalt was reserved. Observant. Though they had both grieved together, he had handled their father's death differently than she had.

Willa had to speak loudly through the pelting rain bouncing around them, "I want to apologize for this morning."

Together, they rounded their last corner and stepped into the main square. Tarp-covered market stalls and the large statue and fountain of Forsetyr greeted them. Forsetyr stood on his hind legs. A giant brown bear nearly eight feet tall. His mouth was open, a silent stone roar calling into the sky. Antlers rolled from the crown of his head, casting ominous shadows on the surrounding ground from the torchlight. His two front paws were extended out before him. The bear's left paw was open, claws pushed out, stretching towards the open night. The other was turned down, and claws fisted towards the pool of water surrounding him.

As they passed the God of Balance, Tybalt answered. "You have nothing to apologize for. I should have stopped you. I should have said something to Branlon."

"No." Willa raised her hand to cut him off and continued, "I am not your responsibility. What I did was worth four lashes. Maybe even more."

"What they have done to you is barbaric." Tybalt's voice dripped with resentment, making Willa pause with concern.

Hatred was how she had handled their father's death. It was unlike Tybalt to sound so angry.

Willa sighed and did her best to lift his spirits as she tugged his hand and led him towards the temple. "Forget the council. This week is about having fun. Acting our age for once. I will behave tonight, so you need to get into some trouble for the both of us." Smiling she mused, "Maybe even ask Claire for a dance."

Tybalt practically tripped over his feet, and Willa managed a choking laugh of surprise. This explained why he had acted so nervously inside earlier. He had always tried to join in on their meetups, trailing after her best friend like a love-struck puppy while he did. But did Claire feel the same towards her brother? It was hard to tell with her sometimes, and despite being her closest confidant, Claire was good at keeping her thoughts and matters private.

Two sentries stood in the rain near the rows of torchlights leading to the Temple of Domnhall. A hall filled with more statues, but instead of gods, it displayed the old mortal kings from the mortal's old kingdom. Willa gave a wide, mocking grin to the poor bastards having to stand in the cold night while the rest of the town danced and drank.

Traifton's autumn festival brought many walks of life from across the Minison ocean. Though it was clear most came for the veil hovering over the Wylan Woods. They'd stay and partake in the town's events and dances for the week, to go home and spread the word on what the curse looked like. Security would be heavier this week, to make sure no one left the walls. To ensure no deaths happened from the Wylan's wrath under Traifton's watch.

The smell of fresh bread and savory meat greeted Willa's nostrils the closer they got to the Temple's open doors. Merry music rolled towards the twins as they stopped in the doorway to shake off their cloaks. She remembered her mother's words when the humid air kissed her exposed back. She had half a thought to put her cloak back on before anyone could see the welts. But her mother was right, if she had to attend, Willa would let them stare and whisper. At least she would look damn good while they did.

Willa threw her cloak onto the pile of others and observed the temple. The pulse of the band's drums rolled through her boots and tickled her legs. Clusters of Traifton's people, and those from across the Minison, mingled and laughed before her, causing her lips to spread into a thin smile.

Her mouth watered from the feast laid out along one side of the large banquet room. Golden-flaked pastries, stacks of dried meat and cheeses, bright-colored fruits, and vegetables had Willa's stomach rumbling louder than the drums around her. Steaming meat pies filled with fish and fowl were already being picked apart.

"Come on. Let's get food before all the good pies are gone." She wrapped her arm around Tybalt's and steered him eagerly towards the tables.

Her brother didn't argue as she pulled him along. But he wasn't eyeing the table with doe eyes like Willa, instead, he was searching the crowd with a determined look. Willa's nose crinkled in amusement and she grabbed two plates, giving him more time to search for their friend. She filled both of their dishes until she could hardly carry them. She groaned with regret when they reached the dessert table.

Fresh rolls glistened beneath the candle lights, teasing her. As did the various bowls, filled with different sized brown squares that were sweet, melt in your mouth, rich in taste, and slightly milky. But the sugar-crusted pies were what had her half considering dumping her vegetables and cheeses for a clear plate. She groaned and looked longingly at her favorite treat: apple pie. Apples were hard to find in Traifton, as most of the orchards had once come from the groves within the Wylan Woods. But each year for this festival, ships brought back enough crates to make fall ciders and desserts like her favorite, sugar filled pie. And with the morning she'd had, she wanted nothing more than to take a whole apple pie for herself and leave the dance so she could revel in the saccharine taste in silence.

A puzzling, deep male voice pulled Willa out of her sugar-induced vision. "I've never seen someone look at dessert with such longing." The accent was strange and rich in baritone, yet sweet sounding, like the treats she was currently drooling over.

She pulled her gaze from the dessert trays to study the cloaked male standing across the table from her. There were enough candles and torches around them to show half of the stranger's face, though most of it was still framed in shadow from the hood. She could only make out a strong, chiseled jawline and plush, pouting lips. Gods, he was tall. Taller than those who waited impatiently behind him with their filled plates.

Willa gave the mysterious person a sour look before turning to hand Tybalt his plate, but he was nowhere to be found. Had he been out of the line for quite some time? She looked back down the line to search for him, only to find a row of men and women glaring at her to move faster. She scowled back at them before moving forward.

"You mock me," she said to the hooded stranger.

"No, I envy the desserts. I've never been looked at in such a way."

Willa scoffed. *Men.* "Perhaps it is because no one can see your face."

He had to be from the south. The accent was not of her town, and clearly he didn't know who she was, or he wouldn't be speaking to her. Willa contemplated throwing her plate of food at him from across the table. She'd most certainly have it cleared and ready for apple pie in doing so. But as she moved past another plate of sugared rolls, the shoulder of her dress rubbed on her back enough to remind her of what would happen if she were to step out of line tonight. She pushed back her shoulders, allowing her welts a moment of reprieve.

This week would be filled with more strangers like this. Some even wore masks on the eve's festivities to hide their stature back in their homelands. For this festival was one of reveling in sin. To unleash your shadows was to be embraced in the divine's lasting light of good balance and fortune. There was no telling what would happen with the travelers and Traifton's members this week, with enough drink and delicacies in their bodies to make them warm and courageous against the biting wind and cold outside.

An older woman with a plate ready for desserts and a face pinched with impatience coughed loudly beside the stranger. The hooded man turned to her and gave a half bow. As he did, he stepped away from the table, allowing the line to continue. The stranger turned into the crowd and walked away without another word. Willa shrugged off the oddness of the encounter and turned away from the table herself.

Beyond the dance floor and band was a long table, seating the council. Willa noted Branlon's new robes and lifted her chin victoriously. Unlike the rest of the members, his hood was up to hide his bald spot from this morning. She would take the little triumph and cherish it forever. But Willa's lips thinned with anger when she moved from Branlon to Lord Nalore. Traifton's leader sat at the center of the table, looking out to the crowd with a half-smile, while pulling from a large silver goblet. She eyed him and the rest of the table warily before returning to search for her brother's red curls.

It took her nearly three minutes to get to the other side of the crowd without spilling the plates of food, and she blew out a sigh of relief when she found her twin behind the table she had been headed for. He was leaning on a statue of a mortal king Willa hadn't bothered to remember the name of. Mortal kings went too far back for her to memorize all of their names. Besides, King Ammanar was the only one worth noting now.

Tybalt greeted her with a lazy smile. He traded her a plate for a glass full of red wine. Willa nodded her thanks before copying his stance.

Eyeing the crowd, she asked, "Did you find her?"

The three of them usually did this, forgoing small talk with strangers sitting at the tables, to people-watch in the shadows of old kings instead. After Claire's note and Willa's morning, she feared if her friend were here she wouldn't be caught dead near them tonight.

Tybalt took a long sip and pointed his head towards the council's table. Willa followed his gesture. Claire was there now, standing among other sailors, shaking the hands of the council. Though she could only make out her mess of tightly coiled curls, the dress she wore was stunning. It was vibrant gold, like the sun before setting, and it lay atop her radiant brown skin like melted copper.

Willa watched the exchange between Lord Nalore and Claire curiously. Lord Nalore was laughing at something she'd leaned forward to say. Willa bristled as his eyes trailed past Claire's neck towards the deep cut in her gown. Though both hers and Claire's dresses were clearly tailored by the same skilled hand, the neckline was certainly different from her own high collared dress.

Tybalt caught the look, too, and leaned forward to set his plate of food on the table. "I'm getting another drink."

Before Willa could say anything, he was gone. He shouldered his way through a crowd of giggling women dressed in brightly colored silk and satin. As if alarmed by his rudeness, they all stepped away from him before pressing closer once more to whisper. Eventually, they caught Willa's stare and turned towards her with their chins pointed up in disgust. Willa lifted her drink towards them with a sneer and took a long swig, ignoring their giggled whispers.

Setting her cup down on the table, she grabbed her plate of food. Without Tybalt, she could have sat down at the half filled table before her, but nostalgia had her resumming her standing position to better watch the crowds. She chewed lazily and gazed over the crowd with boredom. The ritualistic Murock Day dance would begin soon. And although she and every person in this room knew the steps and motions by heart, she didn't dare push her luck by joining in tonight. It's not like she would find a partner who wanted to dance with her anyway, unless it was a stranger from a different town.

The thought of travelers had her absentmindedly searching for the tall, cloaked male from earlier. One would assume with how tall he was, and an obvious hood over his face, she would be able to spot him easily. But on the third round of searching the large room, she gave up to finish her food.

Setting her plate next to Tybalt's, she groaned at the warmth in her belly and tightness of the corset against her ribs as she reached for her wine. But a smacking on her wrist had the cup tilting and wine spilling down the front of her dress.

"Whoops. Clumsy me."

Willa held her hand in the air above the fallen glass in shock. A woman dressed in a tight red satin dress stared at her with glazed eyes. Blonde hair sat high on her head, sticking out in different angles, making her look like an exotic bird with ruffled feathers.

"Penelope," Willa said through clenched teeth. "Too much wine already?"

Penelope only laughed and stepped over the fallen drink as she continued walking. "Interesting dress, I love the back of it especially."

Wretched hag.

Willa seethed at Penelope's back while she walked through the crowd. She needed to behave, but the gods were truly testing her willpower. She looked down at the ruined velvet and cursed. She practically stomped to the drink table, envisioning what she would do to Penelope one day, if given the chance.

Tybalt was still there, leaning over the bar top, flirting with one of the barkeeps. Willa had seen the girl before, working in many of the taverns nearest to Traifton's docks. She ignored their banter and grabbed the girl's wet towel. Bending over, she wiped at her satin shoes and the parts of the soaked skirt.

"Willa?" Tybalt's voice was low and concerned.

"I didn't do anything, for once in my bloody life, Ty. Just leave it," Willa snapped. She regretted it immediately, not meaning for her anger to be directed towards him.

"No. Willa—"

"What?" An unwelcome blush crept along her cheeks, her voice hoarse with frustration.

Tybalt gave an apologetic nod to the woman on the other side of the bar. She stepped away, giving them some privacy, and Willa threw the damp rag on the table, crossing her arms to hide the stains.

Her twin didn't question what had happened, but said, "Nora says Claire's ship isn't the only one anchored for today's festival."

Willa blinked at him slowly, trying and failing to hide the irritation in her gaze. Why should she care what ships came and went?

Tybalt searched her face before downing his glass of dark ale. She gave him an annoyed look, willing him to spit out whatever it was he was trying to say. She wanted to go and cry over a plate of apple pie.

But before he could explain, the main doors to the temple burst open.

"What is the meaning of this?" Lord Nalore pushed his chair back with a screeching echo of wood across stone.

A sentry ran in, sweat beading his forehead as he yelled. "Lord Nalore, m-my lord!" stammering between heavy panting he rasped, "An uncharted ship has dropped anchor on our soil."

SOREAN

Sorean slowed his horse's gait and dropped the reins, wiping the sweat from his brow and rubbing the back of his neck with a soft groan. The invisible noose tightened with every mile they took on horseback.

To leave Lithelle without reason was cause for death by order of his mother. But Noi was right, he was going to be king soon. It was his duty to protect his realm, and he could no longer deny it was possible from the safety of a hidden throne.

The lie had been simple. In a week's time, he would be crowned. Shortly after, he and Farren would marry. He had asked Queen Morielle for a few days of reprieve from the court and its duties immediately after speaking with Noi in Lady Talarin's tavern. He and his closest companions would go to the veiled cabins in the Menyamere Mountains to rest before the court's crowning festivals began. To enhance the lie, Sorean had explained it would be safer to train his unruly magic in the mountain range without fear of hurting anyone or anything in its path. He was surprised when Queen Morielle agreed to this idea, saying she had been much like him in the weeks leading up to her coronation.

The path from Lithelle to the cabins in the mountains was unveiled for only a few miles before their party would be hidden once more. Although they all had magic and were prepared to use it, the queen had insisted he bring some of her guards.

Sorean looked at Iara, who rode beside him with a tense posture. He dug his right heel into the side of his horse, who instantly jumped and side stepped with alarm. Grabbing the reins, he made a loud fuss over how nervous Lithelle's horses were before having the horse stop amidst their lineup.

"When's the last time you rode, Prince?" Harland joked as he and his horse strolled past.

Sorean ignored Harland, which only made the fae bounce on his saddle with laughter as he continued ahead of him. Two sentries leading the back of the line with supplies and food slowed their pace, but he waved them ahead, sliding off his saddle and pretending to inspect it.

Iara slid off her horse to stand beside him. "What's your plan?" She tightened the straps of her saddle packs before turning to Sorean's horse to help him.

He lifted a pouch to show Iara what he had brought.

She patted his steed's neck and eyed the bottle. "So you mean to poison your mother's sentries?"

"It's not strong enough to actually hurt them, but it will knock them out long enough for us to get away. I was warned it gives hallucinations as well, so they are in for quite the experience." He shoved the bottle back into the pouch and rolled his shoulders.

Iara ran her gloved fingers through the horse's coarse hair. "And when they wake up?"

"It will keep them asleep for a few days if given enough. It gives us plenty of time to get to Niarath Loch and confirm what Noi said. They wouldn't dare return to Lithelle without me. And if they do awaken before our return, we can say we were out training." He adjusted the high collar of his jacket and said, "It honestly doesn't matter what we say, you know they won't question me, regardless."

Iara gave a slight tilt of her head and hummed.

Sorean tensed. "If you have a better plan, speak it."

He looked at his second in command as she turned to him with folded arms. Her thin rows of braids were pulled back in a low ponytail, hanging low over her shoulder. Her fur-lined jacket fell well below her knees, covering her training leathers beneath. The air was much colder outside of their hidden realm, and the mountains would be worse. But they weren't going to be staying in the mountains, with any luck.

Iara rubbed at her arms with her gloves before giving a pointed nod toward his hands. "There is another way. Save us all the time, Sorean."

Sorean shook his head immediately, reaching for the horn of his leather saddle and sliding his boot into the stirrup. "No. I won't risk it."

"Won't risk it?" Iara huffed a sarcastic laugh, a puff of white air following her breath as she grabbed his horse's reins. "The concoction you carry is traceable once in a faerie's system. If they get sick or have lingering effects, the queen will have them checked. It will get back to whoever made it based on your orders. *That* will lead to questions, Sorean."

Sorean ignored her and pulled himself onto the horse. Swinging his leg over, he tugged at the reins, but she pulled them closer to her. His horse whinnied with irritation.

"Save us all time and use what's within you. They will be unaware of what happened, not having witnessed what it does for themselves. It will give us more time and give you the much-needed practice." She let go of the reins and turned.

Sorean scowled at her back as she got onto her own horse.

As if feeling Sorean's glare upon her, Iara glanced over her shoulder, her voice smug. "Besides, the queen believes we're out here to train anyway, so now is your chance."

She clicked her tongue against her teeth and rode off.

Sorean let her go on ahead to give himself time alone. Frustration had him cursing into the cold breeze, his hot puff of air lingering before revealing the snowcapped mountains before him. Raising both hands, he pulled off his fur-lined gloves, marveling at how his fingers trembled. He looked down at his tawny skin and flexed his fingers into fists before releasing them. Could he even do it? His training had been barren the last few weeks.

You know why that is, Prince. Too long have you ignored us. We are eager to please you. Let us out so we can play.

Sorean dropped his hands into his lap as the voice of his essence whispered to him. His magic stirred beneath his skin as it crawled and clawed its way through his body. His horse shifted beneath him, as if knowing what was inside him.

Sorean fumbled while reaching for his gloves. He shoved one on quickly but paused as the glove pushed back the sleeve of his thick jacket to show the marks around his wrist and forearm. They were glowing a pulsing white as his essence purred and stretched inside him. His eyes widened as the color darkened to a deep blue, nearly black, before he pulled the sleeved down and donned his other glove.

It was already late into the evening when they reached the cabin. Glittering stars winked and twinkled above them, a stark contrast to the blood moon discoloring the snowy terrain. To the non-faerie eye, there was nothing but snow covered rocks and thick pine trees. But to them, four large log homes sat nestled at the base of the mountains, with glowing lanterns surrounding the little pathways, smoke barreling from small chimneys, and a barn sitting a few yards away, open and ready for their horses.

When they reached the property, the air shifted, making Sorean's ears pop as he stepped into the veiled magic with his horse. Once inside the veil, his senses settled down, but his horse did not. It seemed eager to be rid of Sorean as he led it to the stables. Harland had already gathered and tied the rest of the group's horses.

Harland's usual cocky smile fell away when he looked at the prince. Sorean grimaced as Harland openly stared at the few markings on his neck, still visible above his high collar.

"So we're going with Iara's plan?" the faerie asked in a surprisingly serious tone.

Sorean said nothing as he followed Harland through the stables, watching as he tied his horse beside his own.

He pulled a bottle of wine from his saddle pack and threw it to Sorean. "For the nerves."

Sorean caught it and pulled at the cork with his teeth before taking a long, hearty drink. When he was done, Harland grabbed the bottle and took a long pull himself.

Wiping at his black beard, he asked, "Do you want me to hold your hand when you do it, Prince?"

Sorean threw his head back, surprising himself with a laugh, before reaching over to grab the bottle from Harland and shoving him in the shoulder. Harland gave a throaty chuckle in reply.

He took another long pull and gave the bottle back to Harland, but he waved him off. "We have a long night ahead of us."

Sorean looked at the bottle and nodded, his stomach twisting at the thought of where they were going. "Get all the sentries in the cabin for dinner. And be changed by the time I get back." Sorean put the wine back in Harland's pack and turned. "Make sure to watch the horses, too. They won't like this next part."

CHAPTER 12

SOREAN

Sorean tripped over his own feet in the dark. He cursed himself as he stood and pushed into a run. A gut wrenching scream came from the cabin behind him as he ran through the trees.

Swirls of shadows danced around his vision as he fumbled past the tree trunks. Another sentry cried for help, putting ice in his veins at the sound. But his essence ate away the chill within him, purring and warming his belly before whispering, *More.*

"No," Sorean bit out through clenched teeth.

The shadows darkened in front of him, dimming his vision. When he made it to the back of the stable, he slid to a halt, snow kicking out around him.

Panting, he looked to Iara and Harland waiting on their horses. The beasts pawed at the snow and huffed nervously at Sorean, watching him with wide assessing eyes and twitching ears while he doubled over to catch his breath. Sorean's horse reared up and kicked into the air when the guards within the cabin shrieked and wailed in unison. Harland pulled at his reins to settle him down.

"Sorean, your nose," Iara said while calming her own horse down.

Sorean lifted a shaking hand and wiped at the moisture on his face. Blood glistened on his fingers when he pulled them away. He cursed and wiped again while turning to look at the cabin. Though he hated it, his body thrummed with energy with every sharp inhale, whistling through his nose.

A pulsing knot within him demanded more, but Sorean ignored it, biting out the command. "That's enough."

His essence recoiled at his tugging command, and he turned his back to Iara and Harland before lifting his shaking hands. He frowned at his palms, covered in dark, snake-like tendrils of mist, and called his magic back.

It protested, but with each sharp inhale, it begrudgingly dissipated and sank back into the glowing marks on his skin. His shoulders dropped as the last of the shadows dancing around his vision disappeared.

Anxiety still gripped at his throat. Memories of what his magic had done before threatened to rise to the surface, urging him to run back to the cabin to assure the queen's guards were alive. But there was no time to check. They would be back within a few days, and the sentries wouldn't even know they had left. He wiped at his nose and turned from the now silent lodge.

Harland and Iara said nothing as he jogged to his horse and stripped out of his warm clothes. He glossed over the dark blue marks along his torso and arms while the cold air bit at his bare skin. He pulled on his riding pants and thin white tunic before donning his bow and satchel of arrows.

His horse stepped nervously beside Sorean as he tightened the saddle before mounting. He knew why. It had heard the sentries' cries for help. It sensed what he'd done. It feared what was inside of him.

When he was ready to ride, Iara handed him a cloth. He took it without meeting her eyes and kicked his horse into a walk. He wiped at his nose only to find blood still running from his nostrils.

"They will be fine," Iara called over the horse's quick steps. "For what it's worth, you did better at drawing it back in this time. Since you've used it again, it won't fight you as much the next time you call."

Sorean cursed into the cloth held to his face. She was always training him. Pushing him.

"I hope I don't have to use it for a very long time, Iara."

She smiled and kicked her horse into a canter.

"Where we're going, you might need to." She galloped away, winding through the trees to pass Harland.

A startling realization washed over Sorean. She'd wanted him to stir his essence so it would be ready for aid if they needed him. Needed *it*.

Lost in his own reveries, Sorean flinched in his saddle as his essence whispered, *We're ready for more when you are, Prince.*

CHAPTER 13

WILLA

Willa and Tybalt both turned in unison, along with the band who had stopped their song mid-chorus, towards the open door and rainy night beyond it. Willa rocked back on her heels, anxious to witness who would be entering the temple now, so late in the evening on a rogue, undocumented ship.

She thought of Claire and did a quick scan over the crowd. She found her sneaking towards the small back exit of the temple with members of her crew trailing behind her. Claire and her crew threw on their cloaks within the shadows of a statued king before slipping through the door.

She wanted to follow her, to ask her what was going on, but Tybalt's hand grabbed her forearm. Willa frowned down at his hand before looking back to the open doors.

Hooded sailors sprinted inside the temple. The men dropped their cloaks, revealing Ivaan Jepsen, among other members of his crew.

Willa's breath hitched as she watched the man she'd once loved cross the dance floor, pushing toward Lord Nalore. The man who had turned her into the council because she'd refused his grand, selfish gesture of running away together. Her fingers clenched near her sides and she dug her nails into the material covering her palms, counting from ten to steady her breaths and racing temper. Tybalt gave her arm another knowing squeeze.

Ivaan looked different. Older. His sandy blond hair, once tightly cropped, now touched his shoulders in soft rippling waves, like the water he had come in on, and his cheeks were tanned from the hard sun. He had been gone at sea much longer than Claire had. His father's ship was the biggest of all the trading boats to come from Traifton, and because of that, their routes were long and dangerous.

"Gods, Willa, your hand."

She barely heard Tybalt through the panicked breaths, whistling through her nostrils. His voice was distant, bouncing down a long tunnel. Had he said something about her hand? Willa slowly looked down at her clenched fist. Tiny droplets of blood splattered onto the stone floor near her wine-stained skirts. Her fingernails had managed to curl under the velvet and pinch into her scars.

Red blood. Not black. Not tainted. Breathe.

She relaxed her fingers, shifting uncomfortably from the immediate sting. But it had been enough to ground her. Enough for her to climb back into her body, even though she wanted nothing more than to run. Was it Ivaan and his crew that had made Claire leave? The two had always competed with one another for trading, but Claire was not one to run from challengers.

Tybalt whispered her name, turning her away from Ivaan and the council so she could better focus on the still open doors of the temple.

A ripple of awe ran through the crowd, raising the hairs on her exposed back, stinging her welts as she tensed and looked through the temple doors. Like the calm before a large storm, an electric hum tickled Willa's ears and hovered over the crowd. Anticipation clawed at her turning stomach, quickening her already racing heart.

Her eyes widened as two hooded figures entered the temple. They were tall—taller than everyone in the room—and covered by long velvet cloaks that flowed behind them like black Minison waves hitting Kalandrae's shoreline. Another two appeared, then another pair, and another. They stepped through the doors so swiftly, Willa feared if she blinked she would miss another pair entering. Three more pairs of cloaked figures entered the room before Lord Nalore ordered the doors shut. Shuffling her feet, she gave a nervous glance at her twin, who looked as confused as she felt.

Lord Nalore leaned forward from behind the table, resting his palms on the wood. "Please, show yourself, guests of Traifton."

Willa looked between the hooded figures and Ivaan, who stood beside Lord Nalore with a hand on the hilt of the small dagger sheathed at his side.

The closest figure stepped forward in answer, a gloved hand pushing back their hood in one smooth motion. Willa gasped. A long-pointed ear stuck out from beneath a curtain of silky, silver hair. The gloved hand unclasped the velvet hood and they turned, nodding to the others, who stood eerily still in rows of two. At the silent command, the other hoods fell back.

Willa counted the delicately tipped ears, sticking out from black and silver hair with an open mouth before looking back at the one who stood nearest to Lord Nalore and Ivaan. Long ashy strands of hair framed a face seeming to be cut from the same stone as the surrounding statues. His skin's complexion was pale, much like the hair on his head, but his eyebrows were black and his eyes a deep cinnamon brown. Willa examined his perfectly cut form in wonder. Despite his large, defined body, he looked almost mortal. But when she looked at his pointed ears, studying the way they narrowed at the tip, a shiver crawled down her welted back. The way they moved, like an animal's, twitching from every soft sound, was not natural in the slightest.

The visitor was magnificent and fearsome. She had seen drawings in books, but nothing compared to what stood before her and all of Traifton now, practically glowing beneath the candles and torchlight.

He was ethereal.

He was an elf.

Kauis looked out at the crowd of mortals like a hawk searching for its prey. It took everything in him not to curl his lip in disgust at the pathetic creatures gawking at him and his men.

The smell of fear and anxiety rolled over his shoulders like thick, humid air. He had just escaped the southern islands and their suffocating humidity, yet this was almost worse. The scent of the town's salted food and the sweat clinging to the mortal's fragile skin stung his eyes.

Was this what the mortals of Kalandrae had been doing all these years? Praying to the gods who cast them out and cursed their land? If they were smarter, they would have been training to fight the creatures made from the curse within those woods. They would have found a way to better defend themselves from the gods' punishment. Not groveling and praying at the feet of these statues. Prayers did nothing to gods who didn't listen.

And the curse beside this lowly trader's town was growing restless. Hungry. If he had to guess, the veil surrounding the

Wylan Woods would find a way to break. Like a dam, it would fall and devour the rest of the continents in this realm. He felt it now, here within the town. He recognized the pulse of the cursed magic the gods had put into the ground. It called to his elven essence, like a whisper between silken sheets, tempting him with every sharp inhale he took.

For centuries, they had avoided this wasteland. Their magic was waning without the old law of balance. And it would be so easy to take from the gods' cursed creation—to take magic for their own so they could stay strong. But Kauis wouldn't taint his body, or his men's. No desire was that desperate.

"Announce yourself at once."

Kauis bristled at the pudgy mortal's tone. But he bowed to the man with a curled smile, noting the sailor boy with sandy blond hair beside him. Kauis recognized him. They had followed his trading boat in from the storm. The boy, not realizing they were elves, had helped guide their ship to shore, presuming they needed help navigating the Minison's tepid waters. He should have killed him and his crew when he had the chance, landing outside of the gulf quietly like they had planned.

Kauis took a delicate step forward, his smile widening as Traifton's guards moved closer. He counted the half-sheathed weapons and struggled to contain his smugness. They knew what he was by now, and weapons were no match for him.

Mortals were foolish, spineless beings. Though he would have reveled in witnessing each and every guard wet themselves at the snap of his fingers, now was not a time to instill fear. Regrettably, it was a time to be amiable. They could work with this change in plan. They would have to be patient—to hide in plain sight while they searched for what had brought them back to Kalandrae after so many years. For what had brought him back home.

Kauis ignored the slowly gathering guards and spoke loudly for all to hear. "I am Commander Enrel." He put a hand on his armored chest plate. "I come from the line of Sylpetor Elves. As do my men."

Whispers broke out, tickling and twitching his ears. The pudgy man's jaw fell open, practically hitting the table beneath him. The sailor boy dropped his hand from his knife, and the guards inching closer paused.

Kauis released his hand from his chest and waved it back to his comrades, who watched him stoically. "We have come for aid, in exchange for yours."

The man stood and returned a swift bow. The rest of his robed figures, gawking from the table, were quick to follow. Kauis hadn't been to court for quite some time, but it was obvious who ruled this seaside town.

"I am Lord Nalore, the leader of Traifton and a distant descendent of our late King Ammanar. I believe I speak for all in this room when I say we are shocked and honored to be sharing space with elves once more." The Lord of Traifton stood tall, wetting his lips and glancing at his council before continuing. "It seems our prayers for redemption towards your race have been answered. But why now? After all this time?"

Kauis' jaw ticked at the man's words. There was no such thing as redemption between mortals and elves.

His mask slipped only slightly as he retorted, "It is because of your last king and relative that we are here now."

The Lord of Traifton swallowed thickly. Kauis watched his wrinkled neck bob with the movement. He'd forgotten how quickly mortals aged. This distant royal before him was younger than seventy years, yet looked like he might roll over and croak tomorrow. Kauis had not a single wrinkle even after six long centuries.

He took a steadying breath to regain control. When he was able to swallow the quick lash of his temper, he continued. "For five centuries, we have lived with a broken scale of balance. King

Ammanar destroyed an unbreakable oath. He killed our king and made an entire magical race disappear, along with most of ours."

His eyes landed on a statue of the ancient mortal king he spoke of. He gave the statue a slow look over, curling his lip. He could easily destroy the statue with his magic without even lifting a finger. He could destroy all of the mortals and statues in this hall without ruffling a hair on his head. All for what their king had done to his kind. "We had a choice, after the gods took control of Ammanar's short-lived massacre."

Kauis looked back to Traifton's leader., "The faeries disappeared and the gods were leaving to another land, fresh with possibilities. We were offered a place in their new realm. Most of our kind took the offer, while we and a few other elven families stayed behind. Those who stayed behind were given a task. We were instructed to watch the mortals. To study how they interacted with one another and how they maintained their short life spans without the gods' watchful eyes."

Kauis studied the crowd and smiled. These mortals were eating the lie right out of the palm of his hands. They had been given no such task. Those who stayed were given a warning. After the gods cursed the mortals and their land, they had warned the elves that if they chose to stay and dwell among the traitorous race, their elven essence would wane. And without their magic, they would eventually die like mortals.

But revenge was stronger than life at the time of their king's sudden death. They needed to know how a mortal, with no magic, had killed their immortal leader. They needed to know how a mortal had stolen their essence and taken it for his own.

The gods had wiped their hands of this realm, eager to start fresh without malice and greed between races. But Kauis could not wash the blood of the past from his hands. Not with so many unanswered questions. Even if it meant shortening their lifespan because of it.

But centuries had passed and Kauis could feel his magic waning now. It was too soon. He needed more time to find answers. Answers he would take to the gods and the kin who had left him and his family to search on their own for centuries. And if they wouldn't listen to him, Kauis would find a way to strengthen their essence and provide certain immortality. Even if it meant sharing their time with putrid souls like the ones surrounding him now.

Kauis turned away from the mortal council and clapped his hands together. A small ripple of his essence immediately rose to the surface. Like a blustery breeze, it snuffed out the candles and torchlights, drenching the hall in darkness. Gasps tore out around him, and he allowed himself to smile fully at the smell of fear rising within the embrace of familiar shadows.

Another clap of his hands brought forth the familiar bright purple light from within his being. The warm glow fell from his fingertips like a cascading pool of smoke and water, drifting down towards his legs and slowly crawling over the marble ground.

He allowed the mortals to whisper and stare at the magic they had never seen before. It was too easy to play with their emotions. They were desperate for hope. They reeked of it. And his magic was the bearer of such things for them.

Moving his fingers, he called the purple light back towards him, lifting it high into the air. It pulsed above him and the rest of his comrades like a large puffy cloud, and like moving pictures on a drawing book, he shaped a glowing replica of their ship. He pushed the ship's sails on a breeze of his own doing, to float above the crowd as if they were the waters to hold it up.

"We are here to decide whether or not the mortals are worthy of forgiveness. This is also a test for our kin; for what Ammanar did to our king was unforgivable. But mercy is our task. An ultimate test of balance, by Forsetyr himself, to bring the elves and mortal men together once more. If the two of us can work together again, the gods will return and strike up the old oaths."

Kauis formed the magically made ship above him to shift into a familiar sea serpent. "On our travels across the Minison, Nathayus came to us with a message. The repairing of the scales is to start on Kalandrae. It is to start with you all."

He smirked as the pale serpent crawled around the heads of mortals in the temple. Some had fallen to their knees in prayer at the sight of the God of Chance.

He raised his voice, silencing the hushed prayers and whispers. "And we agreed. We have been watching Traifton for some time. We have heard stories of your unwavering faith. We have seen the penance you have paid. With our magic, and your might—if we can end the curse beyond your walls and work together—the gods will return to our favor."

Kauis had never met this serpent deity. Nathayus was gone like the other two gods. The scene above him played out a narrative of false hope. Of bringing peace back to Kalandrae and the mortals residing on it. All lies.

They just needed time to search.

His eyes narrowed to scan the faces surrounding him and his men. Where was she? With her boat at the docks, she had to be close. Within a town of high walls, she couldn't go far.

"The God of Chance is alive!" The Lord of Traifton called out and clapped, cheers and cries of joy bouncing around the stone floor and statues as he did. "If we work together—if we bring down the gods' curse and restore balance once more..." The man paused and ran a trembling hand through his greasy, slicked back silver hair. "Does this mean there will be a chosen king of mortals once more, Commander Enrel?"

Kauis frowned. The man was sweating, his body odor making Kauis nauseous.

Of course, the mortals only thought of that. Greedy creatures through and through.

Kauis pushed his shoulders back and forced a nod before lying through clenched teeth. "If one is worthy enough, the gods may find the need for mortal kings again."

Another round of clapping and cheers rang out from the mortals.

Something tugged deep within his body. *Greer.*

His companion had taken to the cliffs around the town to keep watch for them while they planted false seeds and searched for what they had truly come for.

Kauis clapped his hands together. At once, the torches and flames lit among the crowd. His purple light dropped immediately, falling back into his body, warming him from the inside out. He planted his feet and braced himself for the wave of exhaustion to follow his small use of magic. But no one noticed, they were all too eager to celebrate the lies he had spoon fed them moments before.

He excused himself from Lord Nalore and the council. His men didn't move as he walked by them, staying in the middle of the hall as he strode through the crowd, the mortals parting quickly at his fluid gait. Two sentries scrambled forward and opened the large oak doors for him with a bow.

When Kauis stepped outside, he loosened his shoulders and inhaled the scent of rain and mud. His second in command followed him out, waiting for the doors to close behind them before letting out a groan.

"They reek of desperation." Visha's graveled voice held an arrogant tone to it as she inspected the empty square and dilapidated market stalls.

Greer tugged at their connection again with more urgency, and closing his eyes, Kauis called at the bond with an inhale.

His body was tired from the little stunt he had performed, but to shift into Greer's sight was something of a different nature. He kept his eyes closed and waited for the familiar hum of the ancient griffin's energy to click with his. When he opened his eyes, he was looking out over the Minison's rolling waves instead of Traifton's pathetic market square.

"I'll never get used to that." Visha's voice was distant now, the faint whisper barely reaching his delicate hearing.

Kauis ignored her comment. He knew what he looked like when he shifted. The shift left a mark on his soul when he left his body to enter another. Even if it was his bonded companion. His body would bear the mark for hours after. Hair stained black and pupils blown out as though he'd had no color or depths within them to begin with.

"No one leaves the hall without an escort." Kauis' voice was strained as he gave the command to his second.

"And then what, Commander Enrel?" Visha asked. "How long must we stay here and pretend to like these condemned traitors?"

"As long as it takes. We are close. It has to be here." Greer was turning his head towards the docks. Ships of all sizes bobbed up and down, tugging at the ropes and anchors holding them down. A light appeared on one of the smaller trading ships. Kauis recognized it at once.

"No mistakes this time, Visha." Kauis closed his eyes and severed the connection with Greer. When he re-entered his own body, he opened his eyes and blinked away the droplets of rain trying to nest upon his eyelashes.

Visha's cold eyes darted nervously back and forth before settling on him with a stubborn scowl. The sky blue markings along her tawny neck and face emitted a soft glow around them. With the blue glow, the design on her skin looked like a bolt of lightning, complimenting her fierce nature. She was pushing out her magic, trying to feel for what they had been hunting. Her silver hair seemed to glow when surrounded by the blue pulsing light, making her a beacon of rare and rigid beauty beside the bleak gray and brown undertones of Traifton.

"How do we know we are close? We don't even know what it looks like. It's been dormant for hundreds of years and my essence..." She pulled away from his unblinking gaze and looked down at her hands, wiggling her fingers and shaking her head with irritation. "What if our magic is too weak to feel it?"

Kauis had no answers for her. He had wondered the same thing for years now. What they searched for was a myth at this point. A riddle. A hunch and a few prophetic words were all he had to go off.

He stepped further into the rain and lifted the hood of his cloak. "Keep an eye on Merellian."

Visha shifted as if to follow him. "You task me with a fool's mission. Merellian does what he wants when he wants. He barely even listens to you."

"As my second, you are my voice when I am gone," Kauis said sternly over his shoulder.

"Something you remind him of constantly. He loathes me for it." Visha spat near her feet with anger. Her pale blue eyes met his stained and depthless gaze with unmasked bitterness.

"Keep him reined in, Visha. If he has a problem with it, he will answer to me later." He answered her disapproving frown with a coy smile. "Indulge. Mingle. We are gods to them for a night. Enjoy it."

WILLA

Earlier that morning, Willa would have laughed in someone's face if they'd proclaimed elves still existed and a god had returned. But now she was surrounded by weepy, drunk mortals who chanted the sea serpent's name as magical immortal beings regarded them stoically.

Willa picked at her apple pie, studying Traifton's new visitors scattered about the temple, the hair on her arms still standing from the crackling energy of Commander Enrel's display. She may no longer worship the gods but now the elves were here in the flesh before her, how could she deny the bitter bite of hope hovering around their cloaks and shining armor?

As she ate, she noted none of them bore weapons. Their armor, although beautifully intricate, was freshly polished, as if they donned it for decoration only. With magic in their veins, she doubted their need for mortal weaponry like swords and arrows. How could Traifton help the elves take down the curse the gods had put on Kalandrae? The guards and sentries had weapons, but everyone was terrified of the creatures in the Wylan. This change would not happen overnight, although everyone around her certainly celebrated like it would. Though the elves had magic, there were no more than twelve around her. The Wylan Woods covered most of Kalandrae before stopping at the base of the Menyamere Mountain range in the north. There was no telling what was within the veil now and whether twelve elves and a few hundred mortals could take them down.

If Nathayus had appeared to Commander Enrel and the rest of his company, he had to know where the other gods were. Which meant they really were still alive. Were they truly listening and observing the mortals through these elves?

Willa shoved another mouthful of apple pie into her mouth to suppress the guilt of how she had cursed the gods for a whole year now. She cringed while chewing, recalling all of the curses she'd spat at them when passing their statues. Her stomach twisted with the memories. But even if they were out there, it didn't fix her anger or grief.

Willa swallowed her last bite of the sweet and sour delicacy with a sigh, her eyes wandering to Lord Nalore. Her favorite treat spoiled in her stomach while he laughed and drank with two of the elves. Of course, he had asked about mortal kings. If Forsetyr and Velithor were still out there and listening, Willa hoped they would see how terrible of a man Lord Nalore was. She nearly vomited at the thought of him ruling over all mortals in the realm. Surely more men would come from the southern isles to claim their place as the rightful king if the old scales of balance were brought together again. There had to be someone greater than that sweaty sack of shit.

It surprised her how quickly these immortals blended in with their festival and customs. Aside from their height and swift, graceful steps, they seemed normal. Some seemed to laugh and smile like mortals. But when they resumed their stoic stances, Willa had to remember her manners and not openly gawk. It was almost like they didn't have to breathe like she did. They were so still, so alert.

Predators.

The hair on Willa's neck stood. Yes, they were powerful and otherworldly. She tried to shake away the goosebumps pimpling her bare back while watching them drink with those from her town. She wanted to observe more of their magic. She wanted to learn everything about them.

Willa reached for her goblet and washed away the taste of pie. Tybalt was on the dancefloor with the barkeep, laughing and spinning her in clumsy circles. She smiled, washing away the jealousy that came with being a spectator during such a huge night of celebration with another drink of wine.

A plate was set beside her, followed by a cup.

Willa pushed back her chair to stand, practically knocking the chair to the ground with her hasty movements.

Ivaan lifted his hands while she backed away from him. "Willa, can we talk?"

His voice was like another glass of wine being spilt on her. Sickly, sour, and humiliating. Willa pointedly ignored him, straightening her skirts and making to step around him instead of answering. She would keep her composure for Tybalt, but she didn't have to endure this conversation. She had attended the dance as instructed. Lord Nalore wouldn't notice her absence between the elves keeping him entertained and the ale in his belly.

Ivaan half turned to stop her and Willa hissed, "I said you were dead to me the last time we spoke and I meant those words."

Ivaan blanched, taking a step away from her. Willa didn't so much as spare him another glance as she walked around him.

She had only made it two steps when he said, "You can't leave without an escort. I overheard the elves talking earlier when their commander left."

Willa furrowed her brows towards the closed oak doors in frustration. Two sentries leaned on the wood as well as a female elf with blue markings along her face and neck. The female elf bore a hardened expression as she observed the mortals with icy blue eyes standing out from her bronze complexion. She roamed over each mortal with careful precision before landing on Willa. Willa shriveled from the cold, unyielding gaze of the elf. She turned away, noting the elf's markings pulse, moving along her skin.

Her words were bitter as she looked back at Ivaan. "Because of you I always have an escort. Day and night I am followed in this town. I have no doubt I will have one the moment I reach for my cloak."

"I was hoping I could be your escort. Give me the chance to apologize, Willa, and I swear I will make amends to you for the rest of my life." His voice was too soft. Too kind for the raw emotions bubbling inside of her now, mixing terribly with the wine and pie.

Did she want forgiveness? The anger she carried was exhausting, but speaking to him now was much more draining. She rigidly held her tears in check and clenched her fingers into fists. As she did, she remembered her scars. She chose anger. Forgiveness could hurt her more in the end.

Willa lifted her chin. "You are a ghost to me now. I do not consort with the dead and the dead cannot help me."

Ivaan's eyes narrowed. The long, deep look they exchanged clawed at her mind, eating away at her nerves and fragile control. His cheeks darkened with the heat flaring to his tanned skin. Within seconds, his apologetic mask had slipped and true anger lingered in his gaze.

Adrenaline pumped through Willa's body as she remembered every fight and argument they'd had before he turned her in. A kind, innocent sailor to the town, but a temperamental boy who lashed out when he didn't get what he wanted. Before, his kind, apologetic words would have coaxed her skittish heart back to him. But she remembered now. She knew what lay beneath his false mask of magnanimity. A mask she no longer saw with their broken trust and her broken heart. It was a kindness to him that she didn't announce to the whole temple what he had really been like behind closed doors.

She gave him a smile, one full of teeth and malice. How could she have ever chosen forgiveness? He deserved nothing of the sort. She turned and walked away.

"I see you haven't changed, Willa," he called after her.

His chiding tone fueled her anger. She stopped and pushed her shoulder blades back. He probably thought she would lash out—turn and yell at him or throw him more insults. But instead, she remembered Father's words. *"Keep your wits about you."*

Ivaan's anger bore into her in rippling waves of tension, making her straighten. She winced at the pain in her back as she tensed, but still smiled, despite the stinging throbs. She stood there, silently, allowing him to study the markings Branlon gave her.

She needed him to understand that because of his actions, she was forever condemned within the walls of Lord Nalore's watchful eyes.

You haven't changed. Her smile widened. As if that were an insult.

It was true, she hadn't changed like he had hoped. If this morning was any indication, she had grown more feral. To him and the council she was still wild, and for the first time in a year, she was grateful for it.

CHAPTER 16

KAUIS

Kauis kicked his feet onto the table. The girl tied up across from him said nothing. Even if she'd wanted to, she couldn't with the cloth tied around her mouth. "Your crewmembers are loyal to you, I'll give them that much."

Her honey-colored eyes narrowed on him. He gave her a teasing sort of grin and looked around her cabin. It was simple. Plain. Maps were littered beneath his boots, along with candle wax and dried quills. The shelves behind the desk were empty aside from a few field journals. No trinkets or keepsakes. Even her trunk was empty. But judging from the state of the deck above them, they had embarked on a long journey. This room should have been more lived in from the long months on a route.

"I'm going to ask you what I asked them." Kauis dropped his crossed ankles and sat forward on his chair. "What were traders from Traifton doing in the Chasm?"

He leaned forward and pulled at the cloth on her face. The loose knot behind her neck gave and it fell away to drop along her slender, dark brown neck, glistening with sweat.

"Why do you care, elf?"

The lack of fear in the girl's voice had him raising a brow in curiosity. He liked her feisty nature. It reminded him of Visha, even Merellian, when the two weren't irritating him. It was a shame he'd have to kill her for her lies.

He shrugged. "I wasn't aware members of the highly theocratic Traifton worked with sea robbers, is all."

The Chasm Isles were filled with troubling company. None that this girl, in a sophisticated, albeit sinfully low-cut gown, should have been involved with.

The girl licked her lips and shifted in her seat. Kauis smiled as the invisible bindings of his magic held her thighs to the seat of the chair with little effort.

"I've heard there are groups down in those islands who found a way to create their own magic," he continued. Her breath hitched slightly, and his smile widened. "Sorcerers is what they used to be called. I'm not sure what mortals call them now. From what I know, there are some who still make spells out of the elements with mere rune marks on parchment. And deals with sleuthing shadows in the caverns at low tide for unnatural gifts. Gifts only elves and faeries should have by nature."

He waved a hand in the air between them as if to call on the wind itself, much like the fae used to do before they disappeared. The girl ignored his waving hand and lifted her chin to glare at him. The veins in her neck bobbed with her racing pulse, a thin line of sweat beginning to bead down a narrow trail from her coiled curls to her black, furrowed brows.

"I don't know what you are talking about."

The lie came from her lips easily, but Kauis saw the tick in her tensed jaw.

He traced his fingers along the maps on the table. Leaning further across the paper, he pointed to a red line on the map between them. "This was your route, though? You stopped at

Nudrith's port for trading." Sliding his pointer finger past the drawing of Nudrith's harbor, he stopped and tapped it over a small speckle of islands further south. "That is only a day's ride on horseback, and another by boat, to reach the gambling and drinking dens of the Chasm's pits."

"Is that where your lot has been hiding this whole time? Sounds like you can tell me more about it than I could ever hope to."

"Let's cut to the chase, sweetheart. We saw you and your crew dealing with a sorceress. Gambling with her, even. We'd been pursuing her for weeks when we saw you two dealing cards in plain sight."

It had called to him when walking into the gambling den. A low thrum of elvish essence had tickled the back of his neck. A gentle nudge he had chased all the way to Kalandrae. Five centuries they had searched for the Key of Sanctity. A piece of home. A way to find certain immortality. The artifacts were dormant when separated from one another. The only explanation could have been sorcery. The false magic could have been enough to arouse it from its deep slumber for a minute or two before growing dormant once more. Enough for Kauis to hear its whisper, and taste desire for the first time in centuries.

"Tell me, what makes a captain so desperate she has to make a deal with an unbalanced? And what did the captain get in return, I wonder?" His hair fell from his shoulder and grazed the table and he noted her chest rise and fall, faster than before. Her stubborn facade was beginning to slip.

"I have an addiction to gambling. It started a few years back when we were stuck down south from the Minison's early winter storms. I lost everything. Clothes. Jewelry. Heirlooms. I went to her to try and get it back. All I got back were a few dresses like the one I wear now."

Kauis took in her evening gown and nodded. It wasn't from Traifton, that was clear. She was telling some truth at least.

He opened his mouth to ask about the artifact when a bonded tug from Greer alerted him.

Leaning back in his chair, he smirked as the girl studied his sudden shift in demeanor with confusion. More sweat fell from her brow, and her nostrils flared. If he couldn't get her to talk with conversation, what he would do next would scare her enough.

When he opened his eyes, he was looking through his companion's bond and seeing the foggy land through Greer's watchful eyes.

The town of Traifton was a speck below the large black wings pumping on either side of him. The black feathers glistened from the earlier rain as he dipped through a cloud to get lower.

Kauis searched the ground through the large black griffin's sight. As if Greer's body were his own, he pushed the beast to go lower so he could see what was so urgent. A small pang of irritation came with Kauis taking over the griffin's movement, but Greer allowed it. He always did.

Past the northern wall of Traifton lay a small valley of rolling hills and rock. They weren't focused on the valley or the mortal town, but instead the looming curse beyond it. Greer neared the wall of black mist that covered the Wylan Woods. Tree tops were moving violently beneath the mist, enough for Kauis to slow Greer's speed before getting too close. Something was beyond the wall of the veil, and pacing on the other side.

Greer dipped lower on his own accord and Kauis scanned the pulsing mist. They dove low enough to be even with the stone statue of the dragon deity, Velithor, standing as an old entrance to the ancient woodlands. Greer was almost the same size as the large stone statue, his wing brushing against the dragon scales as Kauis pushed him to fly beside the magical wall.

A sudden breeze pushed at Greer's wing, too quick for either of them to catch. Before Greer could veer away from the mist, the veil opened beside them and a mangled, four-legged beast was jumping towards Greer's side.

"Up! Up!" Kauis urged.

Greer didn't need his internal push. He was an ancient beast, much older than Kauis. When it came to survival, Greer would know what to do. It was how he'd survived thousands of years before even meeting him. Kauis often wondered if he resented him for the fated bond placed on the two of them. He was no longer free to roam and constantly put in danger because of it.

The griffin let out a screech and pawed at the lunging beast with his back feline haunches and claws. The creature fell from Greer's swift kick and rolled in the grass with a low growl. They didn't look back down to study it. Instead, Greer pumped his wings wildly up into the night sky, pushing every emotion of shock and anxiety into Kauis as he did so, matching Kauis' own surprise.

So, that was a Wylan Creature. It was as he suspected, they were feral and rabid mutations from the gods' poisoned magic.

Kauis needed to get back to the girl and let Visha know what had left the woodlands. If they could kill this beast now on the loose, it would be a perfect opportunity to gain further trust from the mortals. Kauis had Greer turn back towards the docks and promised to find him a few mountain goats or sheep from the cliffs before parting from the connection once more.

Soul shifting was never easy. It always took Kauis a few minutes to collect himself when he came back. More and more his soul protested falling back into the confined cages of his two-legged primordial body, and it took a fair amount of coaxing to command his essence back into his skin. And even when it did return, it seemed to sit, irritated, right below the surface of his limbs, itching to be let out once more.

Kauis pushed away from the agitated feeling of his settling essence while he grounded himself, quietly taking in the familiar surroundings while getting used to his body again. He let his ears twitch and move, waiting for the girl's nervous breaths across from him to tickle his senses and pride. But he heard nothing. All was still and calm. Something was amiss.

Ever so slowly, Kauis pried open his eyes to find the chair across from him empty. Before he could stand to look for the girl, a heavy object hit the back of his neck, darkening his vision.

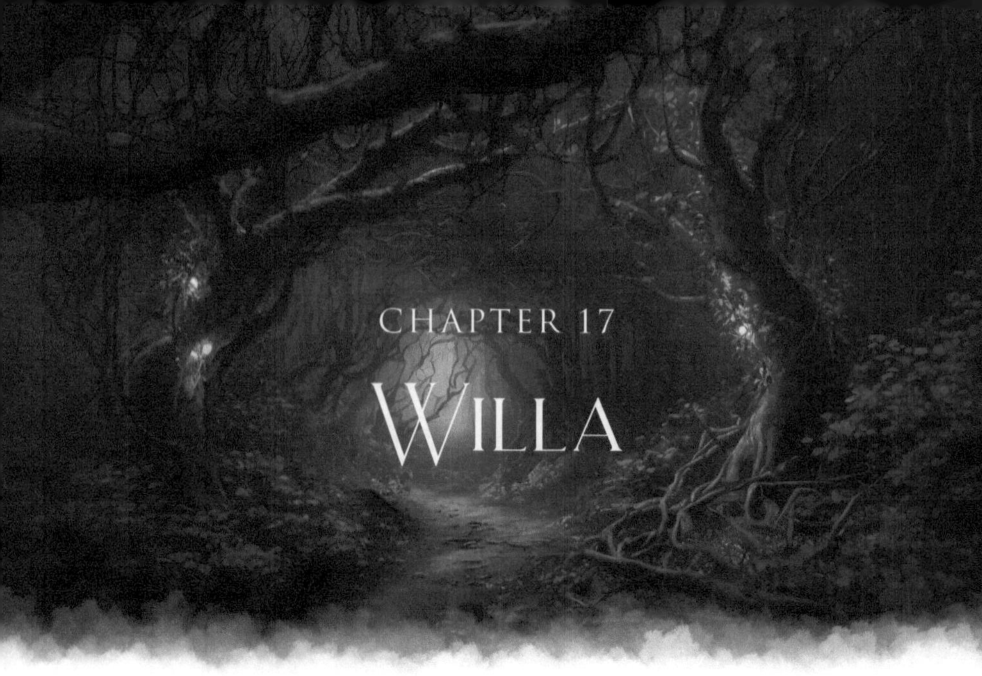

A sentry followed Willa out of the temple doors. She hadn't bothered to worry Tybalt with her leaving; she wanted him to enjoy the night. As for her, she was ready for sleep and maybe even another bath to ease the pain on her back.

She adjusted the hood of her cloak and stepped into the rain, the sound of her and the guard's footsteps all she heard, until a male's voice called out, "I'll escort her from here, mortal."

Willa recognized his voice straight away and raised her brows beneath her hood. Through the torchlights, she saw nothing, but a shuffling of feet had her turning to find the guard backing away from a tall, hooded figure.

The hood fell back to expose an elf with long black hair and radiant features. Pale, plump lips were pulled into a smug smile, settling above a strong jawline. The guard looked at both of them for a moment, as if unsure of what to do. But when the elf cut him a stern look, the guard bowed and immediately turned back to the temple.

Willa gave a low whistle as she watched the guard shuffle away. "I would give anything to scare them so easily."

The elf replied to her bitter words with a graveled chuckle. The sound was rich and hearty, warming Willa from the inside out and reddening her cheeks. "I knew you were an interesting little mortal."

Words failed her while she attempted to calm her racing breaths. He pulled his hood back up, casting his face in shadows once more. His profile spoke of power and ageless strength as the two walked beside one another.

Willa cleared her throat. "So, you're the mysterious male who mocked me at the dessert table."

"I was not mocking you. I was simply curious." There was a trace of laughter in the elf's silky voice, pulling Willa's lips into a nervous smile.

She hummed thoughtfully. She had also been curious, but she would rather go back into the temple with Ivaan than admit she had been searching for this rogue stranger after the two had parted from the dessert table.

Willa noted the way he walked and balked at how simple steps seemed effortlessly commanding when he did it. She couldn't tell if it was her own frayed nerves sending ripples of energy all around her, or if it was his own powerful presence pimpling her skin.

"Why the mystery before the grand entrance?" she blurted, scarcely aware of her own voice.

"I get restless if left alone for too long. I was bored and decided to explore."

Willa caught his smile and, disarmed, she smiled back, mentally cursing the flush warming her cheeks and neck as she did.

The elf continued, unfazed. "Commander Enrel wanted an entrance. Dramatic effect and all. I took it upon myself to look around while he fretted with the petty details."

"You two must be close for you to talk so casually about your leader," Willa mused as she led them through the empty square and into an alleyway.

The reply was swift and surprisingly cold. "We grew up together."

Willa slowed her steps. "So you're friends?"

She noted his broad shoulders straighten, the small smile he had held earlier gone. In its place was a clenched jaw and tight lipped scowl. The two clearly had history. It had her pondering how old the elf was beside her and how old his commander was.

She looked down at her bustling skirts to consider a simpler question. "What is your name?"

"So many questions..." Back was the teasing, warm tone, lifting her spirits. It was nice to speak to someone who didn't judge her. After a few quiet steps, he spoke again. "If I give you my name, will you give me yours?"

Willa rolled her bottom lip between her teeth and hummed playfully. She led them out of the alley and into another, darker one. "Is it wise to speak so casually to an elf?"

He let out a surprised bark of a laugh, his chin lifting enough for the hood of his cloak to slide away. Rain pelted his pale skin, streaming into the black silken strands of his hair. The red moonlight pooled over his handsome face, enhancing the elegant ridge of his cheekbones.

He looked down at her from the bridge of his nose and teased, "It depends on who you ask, mortal."

He smiled, showing off white, blade-sharp canines. Willa inspected his teeth nervously, her gaze moving past his ethereal face to study his ears.

"Is it wise to wish poor mortal boys dead?" the elf asked with mock severity.

Willa's gaze snapped back to his as if she had been slapped across the face. "You were eavesdropping on my conversation?"

"I wouldn't call it eavesdropping when it was easy enough to overhear." The elf's warm brown eyes twinkled humorously.

He remained rooted in his stance while Willa walked ahead, letting her nerves riot within her. She thought of his pointed ears and wondered how well they could hear and what limits they could test with their agile, immortal bodies.

The elf drawled behind her, "For someone who likes sugary desserts so much, I am surprised at the bitter bite from your mouth. Tell me, is he the reason for the markings on your back?"

Willa spun back towards him, the hood of her cloak falling back as she did. Red curls had fallen from her braids, and they clung to her neck and cheeks instantly in the rain.

She crossed her arms, glancing around the dark alley before answering. "The short reply is, yes. He is the reason for it."

She caught herself curling her fingers towards her scars, but stopped herself. Willa instead rolled her shoulders back and straightened, as if to roll away all remaining thoughts and feelings of Ivaan.

The elf assessed her with a half-cocked head and raised brow. He towered over the crates beside her, casting a dark shadow over her whole frame. "I can take the pain away if you let me. Or, I can kill the boy. Say the word, mortal, and it is done."

Willa's mouth parted in surprise, letting out a surprised choke of a laugh.

"What? With your magic?" She wiped rain away from her cheeks and lashes, her laugh hanging in the air between them as he stalked closer, bridging the gap between their bodies.

"I could. It would be easy, too. I could even make it look like an accident if need be." He took another step closer.

Willa could not move as his eyes drank her up. She flushed, but remained silent. He seemed amused by her reaction with his raised brow and devastating smirk.

When he was close enough, he brushed her arm with his wrist. The simple touch had heat flaring from the tips of her fire red hair all the way to her toes. The electric hum of magic from the temple returned, stilling her core as she lifted her face towards his.

The elf ran a gloved finger up her wrist and forearm slowly before stating boldly, "I could also do it with my hands. We are much stronger than you." He halted his lingering touch and raised his brow in a silent question.

Willa eyed the muscles beneath his wet shirt, clinging to his outstretched arm. He could kill Ivaan. Rid her of him once and for all. But no, she wouldn't have him killed, tempting as it sounded in the moment. She was no monster.

"I do not need you to kill Ivaan. Though your offer is appreciated." She smiled despite how wicked she sounded, and the elf chuckled. Willa looked back down at the hand hovering above her elbow. "You can really heal my back?"

"Not without knowing your name first." His voice deepened, making her feel bashful at how close the two were standing in a dark and deserted alleyway.

She pondered, staring at his slender, gloved fingers. If he was offering to use magic and show her more on what elves could do, she wasn't going to pass up the opportunity.

She turned so her back was facing him and lifted her hands to the clasp of her cloak. But gentle fingers stopped her. The elf reached over her shoulders and around her neck to unclasp it himself. Willa shivered as the cold air kissed her exposed, stinging skin.

"Willa," she whispered. A ripple of excitement had her pulse racing.

"Willa."

He was much closer than before. Close enough for the sound of her own name, which she had heard for twenty-four years, to send a flare of warmth down her spine before pooling restlessly in the pit of her stomach.

"My name is Merellian. With your permission, Willa, I am going to touch you now."

She nodded at the wall and sucked in a breath.

"Your word, Willa."

"Yes," she said with a slight wheeze.

A soft whisper tickled her ear, followed by warm breath as the elf spoke into her hair. "What you mortals call magic, we call essence. It is its own entity within us." He paused, as if trying to figure out how to explain it in a way she might understand. "It's as if we share our body with another soul. It doesn't need food like you or us, or water, or light. But it does feed off our desires, emotions, and actions."

Willa didn't dare move with his face bent so close to hers now. Instead, she gave a meek nod towards the brick wall of the alley and asked, "Desires?"

She jumped as a cold hand touched the small of her back. In an instant, the static buzzing feeling of his magic zapped her skin. It was as if she had been struck by lightning.

She was suddenly lit up from the inside out, a new kind of roaring inferno inside her touched and tickled every bone and crevice within. The Wylan owl's magic from last autumn paled in comparison to what this elf's magic was doing to her with a simple touch. She had never been so alive, or awake, with the brush of his magical essence.

Dizzy with the euphoric feeling, she stumbled forward, reaching out to the wall as she did. Merellian's other hand quickly slid around her waist to hold her upright. He let out a low chuckle, caressing her tingling skin.

He dipped his head to speak in her ear and continued his earlier explanation, as if she could hear anything besides the buzzing swarm of friction between her skin and his. "Whatever urge you desire, the essence feels strongest when acting upon it. Each essence has a will of its own, as do elves. As do mortals. No matter the race, we all have different personalities and traits. For example, your desire for sugar and pie would stir your essence to life at the salivating thought of it. Essence has its own needs as well. Needs that become temperamental when ignored for too long. Eventually, you become bonded with your essence and feed into each other's needs and wants to stay strong and skilled."

Merellian shifted slightly, moving his hand up her waist to adjust the pressure on her back. "What you are feeling now is my essence, running through you. I am quickening your natural healing process with a simple touch. Because you have never experienced this, your body is opening glands that have never been awakened. You are feeling what I have lived and breathed for centuries. This gift is not passed lightly, Willa."

Willa's eyes closed involuntarily as his words washed over her like a soft lullaby. His hand roamed her back slowly, igniting the other pulse he spoke of. Her blood coursed through her veins like an awakened river as his hand slowly moved along the welts on her back. But they didn't hurt as he touched them. Nothing hurt. All that remained was an insatiable hunger deep within her belly.

He hummed behind her and asked, "How do you feel?"

"Weightless." She sighed and leaned into his hold. When she opened her eyes, they were hazy and heavy, blurring her vision as she tried to focus on the brick wall before her. "Tell me, elf, what do you and your essence desire the most for me to feel this way?"

Merellian made a low, strangled noise before she was spun around, her bare back pressed against the cold brick wall, but there was no pain to follow. He had healed her.

The elf dipped his head, running his nose along the small of her neck, as he whispered roughly above her pricked skin.

"Power." He brought his lips below her chin, whispering another word. "Control. It craves undivided attention."

He had it. Every ounce of her being was focused on him alone.

Her mind was obsessed and her body was taut with the anticipation of what he might do or say next. He inched his face lower so he could look directly in her eyes, his gaze dark and sultry. Willa bit her lip to soften the small tremble of her chin.

He smiled, his eyes flicking down to the motion as he voiced another word, "Lust."

Merellian's lips crashed into hers. The two collided in a heavy fever of breathy sounds while they frantically tasted each other. The kiss sent new spirals of ecstasy through Willa. His soft lips pushed over hers with such a force, she opened her mouth to gasp. Merellian took the opportunity and nipped at her lower lip, stinging her sensations.

She should have stopped him, should have pushed him away and walked home. But the ache within her was too strong, too overpowering, as his tongue slipped into her mouth to taste her fully. She moaned against him and the noise had him pushing her harder into the wall.

Something scratched at her head as he roamed his hands down her sides.

She pulled away and rasped, "Wait."

Merellian stepped away in one fluid motion, eyeing her with concern. She touched the back of her head and remembered the jagged hair clip holding her braids. She wanted to undo it so they could continue, but as he stepped away, the rush of warmth and weightlessness was gone.

Reality pressed down upon her shoulders. Sheepishly, she adjusted the skirts of her dress and brought a shaking hand to her swollen lips.

"I am sorry," he said, his voice suddenly cold.

He cleared his throat and bent down to retrieve her cloak, and she grabbed it from him before he could straighten.

Merellian let her and continued, "I forget what it can do to mortals. And I am sometimes weak to my essence and its longings."

A sting of embarrassment hit her with his apology. What had transpired wasn't a natural feeling. They knew nothing about each other. She was a mortal, seeing magic for the first time. *Feeling* magic for the first time. How naive she must have looked to him. He had explained it to her as he healed her back. The elf had only wanted to help her and she'd practically shed her clothes at the sight of him while he did it.

Mercifully, the red moonlight hid the extent of her flushed humiliation, but she still pulled her hood up over her hair, wincing at the scratching pain from the hair clip. Shame guided her clipped steps through the alleyway.

Merellian caught up easily. "Lust between two beings is perfectly normal, Willa. But the rush of desire you had was entirely my own. My essence likes control, and I had you puddled beneath my grasp."

Willa froze. He had said control. He had also said power. *Predator.*

"You do not need to fear me, Willa." Merellian reached for her. Grabbing her wrist, he gently pulled her towards him. "I am glad we stopped when we did."

"And if we hadn't stopped? What would you have done?" Willa searched the brown tones of his eyes as he pursed his lips in contemplation.

"I would have claimed you as mine forever. And I do not share well."

Willa was too startled by his words to say anything further. She wanted to explain she was not one to be wanted or desired after. She wanted to ask more about his essence and what other elves desired. She wanted to know more about how he'd healed her back with a simple touch. And if he could heal the welts on her back, could he take away the scars on her palms as well? Instead, they walked together in a tense silence.

When they reached her front door, she turned and pulled back her hood. "Thank you."

Merellian gave her a half smile, though it didn't seem to reach his eyes. His black hair was slightly ruffled, as was his cloak, from what had happened in the alley.

Willa continued with tears lining her vision, "Tonight you have shown me kindness. And that is something I haven't received from a stranger in a long time."

Tomorrow, he would learn more about their town and traditions when Lord Nalore was sober. He would see how she was treated and hear about her and her wild nature. Tomorrow, he wouldn't look at her like he did now.

"I will not forget you and how you made me feel weightless. If only for a few moments."

Willa leaned on the front door of her home, and as it clicked shut, she pulled her thumbs out of the gown's sleeves. She studied her branded palms in awe, processing how easily Merellian's magic had healed the welts on her back. Could his elvish essence take away these scars? She traced the marks with narrowed eyes, her face contorting into a bitter scowl as she did. The welts were surface level but the scars went deeper than what she saw. Even if he could erase them, it wouldn't take away the humiliation from the night of her punishment. Nothing would erase how the town saw her. But it would help to not hold a reminder so openly on her skin.

She took her cloak off and patted her exposed back as best as she could. Smooth. No pain or blemishes. Her morning discipline had vanished beneath the hands of the ethereal elf. She swore under her breath and shook her head in wonder. She would give anything to have magic like his.

Her mother was fast asleep in her father's chair, and Willa smiled to herself as she adjusted the blanket around her shoulders. All was still in their humble home, aside from the crackling fire behind her.

A thud from down the hall pierced the silence.

Willa stilled and waited for another noise. It was an old home, with leaks in the roof from the constant precipitation, so creaks and pops were not surprising. But when a jolting crash echoed down the hall, Willa stepped around her sleeping mother and grabbed the nearest item she could find.

With a heavy, wooden rolling pin gripped tightly between her hands, she tiptoed past the washroom and Tybalt's empty room. Her door at the end of the hall was slightly ajar, and she could see nothing aside from her bed, illuminated by the light coming through her window. Another noise from within sounded, and Willa kicked the door open.

Running blindly into the dark room, she lifted the rolling pin and found Claire standing by her open nightstand.

Claire whipped around with wild eyes and ran at Willa. She stepped back and raised her hands in alarm, dropping the rolling pin.

"Claire? What in the gods' names are you doing in here?"

Claire's face was drenched in sweat, with dried blood caked beneath both of her nostrils.

"What is wrong?" She reached up to wipe the caked blood from her friend's face, but Claire waved her away.

Her friend turned and ran to shut Willa's bedroom window, explaining how she'd got in. Her room was a disaster. Clothes hung from her nightstand and were scattered over her floor and bed. Her notes and books were torn, littering the floor. Baskets and boxes, once holding small trinkets and keepsakes, were thrown about.

Claire sat on the edge of her bed and leaned forward, running her hands through her curls. "Willa, I am sorry for this, truly I am. But I need to know if you have it." Claire looked to Willa, wiping her eyes and nose.

Willa's eyebrows knit together with concern. "Are you alright? What happened to you?"

She joined her friend and sat beside her on the bed. Claire covered her face with her hands and let out a frustrated grumble. How badly was she hurt? She had only seen the blood beneath her nose, but was she hurt elsewhere?

Willa wrapped her arm around Claire's shoulders and pulled her into a tight embrace. "What are you looking for? How can I help?" She thought of the note still inside of her gown and asked, "I read your note after receiving your gifts. Is it your crew? What am I missing here?"

Claire dropped her hands and Willa released her. She looked towards Willa's scattered belongings, blinking away fresh tears. Her mouth hung open for a moment before she turned to Willa. "You said gifts...but I only gave you the dress." Her amber eyes narrowed on Willa's with a fevered intensity.

Confused, Willa reached for her hair and pulled at the hair clip Claire had given her. "I assumed the clip was a part of the gift. It was in the corset of my dress with your note. Here, take it. I'm sorry, I didn't know."

Claire lunged towards Willa as she pulled at the coiled braids around the sharp edges of the metal star. She'd tugged one braid out when Claire clasped her wrists tightly. "Stop. Willa, leave it. Listen to me. I need your help."

Willa left the pin within her hair and eyed her friend warily. Claire was the one person besides her family she'd do anything for, knowing Claire would easily do the same for her. Whatever she needed, Willa would help.

Leaning over to grab a black tunic on the ground, Willa pulled at the bottom seams until a strip of fabric ripped away. She stood and hustled to the wash bowl atop her nightstand to dampen the material. Claire was standing when Willa turned back to face her.

Claire flinched when Willa gently patted it below her nose, her eyes distant and glassy.

To better understand, and to get Claire to come out of the frenzied shock she was in, she started from the beginning. "What happened on your route, Claire?"

Claire met Willa's assessing look and released a shaky breath. "I made a mistake. I am the reason they are here."

Willa tensed. "Who?"

She thought of the elves and pursed her lips. No, it couldn't be them.

As if to read her mind, her friend answered, "The elves are not what they seem, Willa. They chased my ship to Kalandrae. I brought them here. I have brought a sickness worse than what is inside those woods."

Willa thought of Merellian and Commander Enrel's speech. Claire hadn't been there; Willa needed to explain why they had come.

But her friend paced in front of her with crossed arms and a determined scowl. "They will do anything to get what they want. They will say anything, even if it means lying through their pretty little teeth. They are dangerous. Their magic is dangerous."

She couldn't be talking about the elves Willa and the rest of Traifton had just met. She couldn't be talking about the elf, Merellian, who had healed her ailments with a selfless touch.

Willa retorted, careful to hide her exasperation. "The elves are here to help bring balance to Kalandrae. They are here to help bring back the gods and the old oaths. They are here for us."

"They don't give a damn about mortals." Claire scoffed and shook her head. "You sound like the lovestruck girl you were when we were younger. I was the same when I first met them.

One of them in particular was fond of me. Merellian was his name."

Willa's mouth parted in shock as she looked at Claire with wide eyes.

Claire paused and let out a surprised, brazen laugh before leaning over to cough. "Oh, that is rich. He is charming, but I saw him for who he really was before getting to my ship in the southern isles, Willa. We had help escaping from friends down in the pits, but with a raised fist, Merellian dropped them all, killing them instantly. Five of my friends dead because of him. And he laughed while doing it. They're wicked, immoral beings." She straightened and wiped her nose, now dripping with fresh blood.

Claire had been to the Chasm's gambling pits? Speechless, Willa handed her the wet cloth but her friend waved her away again.

"I'm okay, really. It's only the cost."

Willa scrunched her nose. The cost? The cost of what? She opened her mouth to ask but Claire continued.

"We need to leave Traifton."

CHAPTER 19
KAUIS

Kauis awoke on the deck of Traifton's port, wrapped in a thick rope with heavy knots around his wrists and ankles. A note, nailed to the board in front of him, swayed in the sea's breeze. Lines and circles dotted the parchment, creating a design of a rune mark.

Sorcery.

Kauis cursed at the paper and called out to his essence.

Nothing stirred.

The hair falling over his face was still black from soul shifting with Greer. Was he truly so weak? Again, he called for his essence, but instead of its shifting reply, there was a gnawing emptiness.

Fucking sorcerers.

Kauis swore and pulled at the ropes. They should have given easily with his strength, but they seemed to grow tighter the more urgently he pulled. Not only had the captain been consorting with a sorceress, she was one herself.

A loud call from the sky had him sighing with relief.

Greer circled the pier twice before landing on the docks. The boards creaked and bowed beneath the large beast's weight as he stepped towards Kauis. He looked at the ropes and then at Greer's leathered talons. The griffin swiped at the ropes with ease, and they sizzled away like ash. Sorcery did not work on creatures like Greer or the old dragon lines from Velithor.

Kauis laughed and pushed himself up. His essence greeted him immediately when he called this time.

He smiled at his old friend. "I've never asked, do you fancy the taste of mortal?"

"I wouldn't ask for your help if I didn't believe you could do it. In fact, you might be the only person on this cursed land brave enough to pull it off."

Willa stood after lacing her brown boots and nodded at her friend. Claire handed Willa her cloak with a serious look and nodded back. She clasped the cloak around her neck, and winced at the anticipation of such a heavy material irritating the fresh marks on her back, but remembered what Merellian had done. Claire's recollection of the roguish elf had her stomach revolting at the thought of their fevered kiss, only an hour earlier.

Looking down at her brown pants and tucked in tunic, she shook off the memory of Merellian. It wasn't the warmest outfit for what she planned to do, but if she needed to swim, at least she wouldn't drown with this matcrial. Lifting the hood over her hair, she gently reached for the metal hair clip once more, making sure it was secure.

A light, cold object was dropped into her open palm. Willa looked at the small fishing knife and raised a brow. This knife had helped them escape a wandering fisher's net when the pair had snuck out for a midnight swim near Fang Gulf's coves. Claire saved their lives that night with this knife, though she swore Nathayus was there beside them, helping their chances of survival while she cut and hacked away the ropes to free them.

Willa looked at her friend, the one who'd taught her and Ty how to swim, the one who'd stolen wine with her on trading ships only to puke it up later while giggling and stumbling to their homes. She'd gotten Willa out of trouble as much as she'd gotten her into it, and was the one person she could share her true feelings with. Claire had helped put Willa back together after Ivaan betrayed her. And Willa had helped her gain the confidence she needed to run her own trading ship. Though Willa didn't need to do much, aside from a few strong-worded pep talks, Claire had blossomed into a fearsome and courageous captain in such a short amount of time on her own. A captain with still so many stories to tell. A captain with secrets that, when she was ready, would be divulged to Willa so she could understand what had happened to her on her travels.

Claire's bloodied nose, and her wild eyes were enough to secure Willa's loyalty, if their years of friendship—sisterhood—hadn't.

"You'll get my family out of this if this goes south?" Willa asked.

Claire smiled and walked to the window. Shoving it open, she teased, "Don't let it go wrong, and we won't have to worry about that."

Willa looked towards her bedroom door, picturing her mother sleeping in the chair. Corvina wouldn't survive if anything happened to her or Tybalt. Not after Father. And what if she were caught again? The council would destroy this family for her actions.

"Your word, Claire, or I'm not doing this. Promise me you will make sure they're safe and out. Even if this goes right and the elves are what you say they are, I don't want any of us on Kalandrae when they enter those woods."

"I promise to do my best to get them out when the time comes. But your brother and mother are tougher than you think, Willa. You are Thesalors. You are made of fire. If I can't get here fast enough, I know your brother will watch over Corvina. Right now, you are the priority."

"What hides in my hair, you mean?" Willa gave Claire a knowing look.

Her friend didn't sugar coat Willa's halfhearted question. "Right."

A knowing silence stretched between them.

Willa still didn't know what the hair clip was or why the elves were searching for it. Claire was too paranoid to speak of it in Traifton. She only knew these immortals would do *anything* in their power to find it. Even if it meant destroying all of Traifton. All of Kalandrae.

But if Willa could sneak it off Kalandrae while the elves searched for Claire, Traifton—*her family*—might survive these immortals. Forget the town and council; let them fall for the elf's pretty lies and false narratives of hope.

Branlon had poked at Willa's rebellious nature earlier in the temple, but he had no idea what she planned to do now.

She rocked on the balls of her feet and let out a nervous, breathy laugh. If she did this, she hoped for a gods-damned thank you from Lord Nalore himself when the elves left this continent to search for the clip elsewhere.

"I'll have a member of my crew waiting on the coast for you past the gulf."

Willa cast one last nervous glance to her father's old maps spread out on her bed. The maps were littered with hand drawn trail lines crawling all over Fang Gulf's bluffs. Traifton's watch towers were blind to the high rocks and anything on the far side of them. And most sailors wouldn't dare anchor their ships near those rocky walls of teeth. Most sailors weren't Claire. A bit of distraction is all it would take to get her boat out of the trading port and on the way to Willa.

"We will leave as fast as Nathayus will push us. Afterwards, I will explain everything. *Everything,* Willa. I have so much to tell you." Claire smiled, tears brimming her eyes as she did.

Willa pulled her into a hug and wiped at her own eyes. "You're sure you can distract them and get to the ship in time?"

Claire laughed into her shoulder. "I have learned a few tricks at sea. The God of Chance would be proud."

Willa swallowed thickly, desperately trying to shove away her nerves and lingering doubts. They could do this. She would do this for Claire, despite not knowing everything, her friend was in trouble. Her family could be in danger.

"What comes after storms, Claire?" she whispered before ending their close embrace.

"Clear skies, Willa." Claire pulled away and winked. Her eyes twinkled mischievously as she followed the old, superstitious sailor's motto with, "The gods have never met us and they should be grateful. They wouldn't know what to do with the both of us in death's dark realm. Let's keep it that way."

Willa winced, but Claire clasped her shoulders, shaking her gently. "We can do this. We must."

Willa adjusted the velvet hood of her cloak, pulling it forward, making absolutely sure it covered her whole face while waiting for Claire's signal. She counted down from ten in her head, tapping at her foot while watching the east wall.

She hadn't even made it to five when a burst of flame lit up within the eastern watchtower. Claire had gotten there faster than she thought. As predicted, the guards above her shouted orders to one another. Willa dipped into the shadows as far as she could to watch them all run towards the east tower.

"Fools," she whispered, before slipping between the bars of the gate.

She headed west, clinging to the side of Traifton's high walls as she ran. The landscape was ominous under the red moon's glow. Long flowing grass in the rolling valley crawled up and down the hills like waves of blood. Mud and rocks squelched loudly beneath her boots as she ran towards the end of the wall, the soft rain pelting her rippling cloak.

More guards were running above, shouting about the eastern beacon being lit. She relished in the brief victory of their plan before readying herself for the next part. This was the trickiest step to maneuver. A few yards of running in the open, where anyone or anything could easily spot you, before reaching the rocky, tree-lined path that led to the highland cliffs of Fang Gulf. No one was looking her way now with the distraction, but Willa hesitated to catch her breath and still her nerves.

She had sworn to never leave the walls after the Ritual of Vitality. Yet here she was again, about to run down the same path. And she didn't dare look over her shoulder at the Wylan Woods beyond the valley. Not when her nerves were already so close to crumbling.

Get over the bluffs and climb down to the coast. Claire will be there waiting for you. Willa stretched her fingers and wiggled them while rocking back and forth on her heels, exhaling and narrowing her eyes at the path beyond the patch of barren dirt and black, rocky sand.

If she got caught this time, the council would most likely kill her.

She couldn't get caught.

She sprinted out of the shadows and away from the dreadful thoughts of what could go wrong. She ran as fast as she could, pumping her arms wildly while her boots kicked up wet sand below her. A few more paces and she would hit the tree line, giving her the privacy to slow down.

When the row of thick pine trees was close enough to touch, sand turned back to grass and mud, giving her the leverage to go faster as she neared the entrance to the rocky path. A loud yowl sounded above her and a massive black shadow crawled across the sky. She gasped and dropped to the ground, sliding through the mud and grass towards the rocky terrain. She looked out from the tall grass, waiting to spot the shadow before she moved.

Another loud, screeching yowl sounded. It echoed on the cold sea breeze before Willa saw it pass beneath the red tinted stars.

Wylan Creature.

Willa jumped up and sprinted to the trees, faster than she had ever run before. She didn't stop when she hit the rocky, winding path. Even as it inclined, she pulled herself over the large rocks as quickly as she could. She would not be caught by a beast of the Wylan again. That was a fate worse than being caught by Lord Nalore.

Her lungs burned, her throat aching from the cold air. Her arms and legs were struggling to keep up as she neared the top of the path. The trees hugging either side of her and the rocks she scrambled over were beginning to thin out. A frigid gust of wind pushed away the hood of her cloak as she rounded the last boulder and bent over to catch her breath. She wheezed, puffing air between her pursed lips to lift the fallen strands of hair dancing before her eyes. Although her body wanted to drop to the ground and rest, she stood tall, ignoring her burning lungs.

Fog was thicker here, nearly close enough for her to reach up and touch. The blood moon tinted the clouds red as she waited for her galloping heart to slow. Carefully, she stepped one foot in front of the other.

Cold gusts of wind slapped her cheeks, blowing her hair around wildly as she crept over the flat rocks. She pulled her hood up to protect her face from the cold wind, but it was torn away the moment it rested atop her forehead. Narrowing her eyes, she studied the black rock in front of her to make sure it didn't stop or decline.

Her steps slowed when the rock before her disappeared into a thick red cloud. Crouching, she traced the rock with her fingers and followed it until it abruptly cut off, leaving her hand to dangle out into the frigid air. The sounds of crashing waves hitting the jagged cliffside below greeted her senses while she recoiled her hand. She squinted through the condensation with growing tension. She needed to wait for Claire's next signal or she would risk the descent for nothing.

"Come on," she croaked. "Come on, Claire."

Her friend had said she had tricks up her sleeve to get to her ship swiftly, but dark thoughts crept into Willa's mind as she shifted side to side in her crouched position.

What if a guard caught her? Or worse—an elf?

A small yellow light cut through the shifting clouds and endless dark below. Willa nearly cried out in relief at the sudden burst of light. Claire's ship was out there in the mass of midnight waves, and the yellow light was the rowboat heading towards shore.

Relief calmed her trepidation. Her friend had made it. Claire truly did have the luck of Nathayus to get away from the distraction in town to her ship so rapidly.

Willa just had to make the climb and they would be safe. She wiped her sweaty palms on her pants and looked at the marks upon them. She should have grabbed gloves. The climb could tear fresh wounds into her skin. She'd have to go slow and steady, for the cliff was wet and sharp. Footholds would be hard to find, especially with no light. But she had done it before when she was younger. Several times, in fact. But that was a lifetime ago. Before she'd met the wrath of monsters from the Wylan and the true monsters in Traifton.

Willing herself to move, she leaned forward in her crouch to stick her head out over the ledge. The wind beat at her senses as she tried to find a good place to begin. But despite the howling gusts of air, an eerie yowl of a Wylan Creature sounded. She stood slowly, careful not to slip or let the wind push her forward, and looked up, but all she saw was red, rolling fog.

A jarring, thunderous boom had her spinning back to where Claire had signaled.

Terror grabbed her by the throat and held her in a vicious chokehold as the ship out in the black water went up in flames.

She stood paralyzed as the flames licked up the black sails, turning from a bright orange to white. *Claire!* To Willa's horror, the flames changed color, licking and spitting into a bright royal purple with white and blue ends.

Magic. Magic like she had seen in the temple from the elf—Commander Enrel.

Another haunting call came from above, pushing Willa into action. She turned from the burning scene below, catching the mass of black feathers cutting through the red fog towards her. Willa dropped into a crouch as the feathers passed over her. A long black tail followed the massive beast, whipping over her head as it went. She watched the tail disappear over the side of the cliff and dip down towards the flames.

The large black, feathered creature—big enough to be a dragon—flew across the water. She stared, open-mouthed at the silver-haired rider atop the beast. The elf who had stood before Traifton and promised to help the mortals, was controlling it, and they were headed right towards Claire's burning ship.

"The elves will do anything to get what they want." Claire's voice pounded in her chest as Willa let out an anguished cry of alarm into her fists. She sobbed while the large beast dove into the flames.

Commander Enrel had destroyed Claire's ship, all for whatever *she* carried.

And if Claire truly had made it onto the ship...No. She couldn't consider that now. She had to get down there, she had to do something. She needed to make sure her friend was alive.

Willa searched for a starting point with panicked hiccups, but another call from the large beast had her looking back to the ship. A long, black feathered wing dipped above the burning sails and turned back towards the cliff, right towards her.

"Whatever happens. You are the priority. This cannot get in the hands of elves." Claire's words had her turning from the floating inferno. Those words had her running for her life.

She would break her neck if she ran back down the rocky trail, so she veered to the left and sprinted over the slick, black rock as fast as her body would allow. The western bluffs crawled back into the valley like tiny mountain ranges before reaching the veil of the Wylan Woods. If she could reach the tree line when coastal rocks turned to patchy groves, maybe she could hide within them. Surely the beast was too large to get through the patches of trees.

A grating, echoing shriek sounded from the sky behind her. It was too close to her, and its loud piercing call hurt her ears, making her grit her teeth as she ran blindly in the dark.

She almost made it to what looked to be a small grove of wind whipped pine trees when large talons bigger than her face snatched her shoulders on either side. The ground beneath her fell away and Willa was lifted into the air faster than she could blink.

Gusts of wind tunneled above her as black wings pumped up and down beside her face. Willa grasped at the talons with her nails, clawing and digging into them with all the strength she could muster, but it was no use. Below her dangling feet was nothing but red fog. The wind swallowed her cries as she helplessly watched the clouds shift and move while the foul winged beast lifted them higher.

She looked back up to focus on what carried her, only to find the elf leaning over to watch her. But something was terribly wrong with him. His eyes were black, like two empty sockets, and the silver hair whipping around his face was changing—growing darker by the second as the creature called out towards the crimson moon. She had been afraid before, assuming this creature was from the Wylan, but now true terror laced every panicked breath.

The elf's lips curled into a sinister smile and the beast cried out, tucking its wings close to the talons holding her. Willa's stomach lifted into her throat, as they plummeted through the fog and back towards the ground. She gasped and closed her eyes as they neared the valley, waiting for impact, but the beast leveled out, flying right above the rolling hills. Low enough for grass to hit her shins and boots as her legs flailed uselessly behind her.

An abrupt, sharp pain tore through her right ankle. Willa howled, looking back to find two green bulging eyes. Long claws clung to her boot as a Wylan-made monstrosity gripped onto her eagerly. The winged beast screeched and lurched to the side, its talons shifting, releasing Willa.

She landed in the dirt beside a moaning mass of shadow and gnarled, leathered bone. Red flames hit the grass around her as she coughed and tried to regain feeling in her body after the jarring fall. Sentries were shooting at the creature, she realized. Had they seen her yet? Would they hit her too, for once again breaking the rules?

Commander Enrel had his beast kicking off from the ground to ascend into the red clouds above, leaving her alone with the leathered monster beside her. As if he thought it easier to have the Wylan beast kill her for him.

The Wylan Creature growled at the flaming arrows landing around them and Willa sat up with another desperate gasp for air. As the beast stood and shook the mud from its sides, she stared in horror at the four gangly legs protruding from a hunched and bony spine. It was massive compared to the owl she had seen before. She didn't know which poor animal it had once been. It looked to be a construction of the gods' cursed magic. A new creation entirely.

The walking nightmare loosened another distorted snarl, stepping forward, but stumbled back as another arrow pierced the ground before its large, sniffing snout. Willa backed away with a helpless whimper, gulping for air like a fish out of water. She needed to move. She looked at her boot, shredded by the creature's claws. It throbbed, but there was no blood. She could walk, but not run.

She could do this. Another arrow whizzed past her face, and the beast let out an irritated bark.

Willa pushed up and turned away from the distracted creature. She limped through the grass, hissing at the pain shooting through her leg with each step. She scanned the sky for the elf's winged beast with a grimace.

A pained howl had her turning back to the Wylan Creature falling to its side.

Before it stood Merellian.

Hand outstretched, he clenched his fingers into a fist. Willa covered her ears to muffle the Wylan beast's high pitched sound. Merellian's eyes snapped to hers as if he'd caught her movement. His dark eyebrows shot up in surprise before returning his focus on the creature still writhing in pain below him.

Power. Control.

Those were the words he had used to describe his essence. The essence which effortlessly tortured the cursed creation now. Claire's warning rattled inside her like a booming thunder cloud.

The flames from the arrows caught fire in the patches of grass and Merellian dropped his fist. The Wylan Creature's cries died out instantly, its head falling into the dirt with a loud thump.

For the first time in years, Willa sent out a prayer to the old gods.

She whispered towards the flames and prayed for the shadowed monstrosity to rise back up and attack Merellian. She waited for it to lunge up from the ring of fire and rid Kalandrae of the true predator before her, but it didn't move again.

<h1>CHAPTER 22</h1>

WILLA

The shouting of sentries pushed Willa further through the valley. She had nowhere else to run but towards the very thing that terrified her the most. She dragged her limp ankle through the grass, crying out in frustration as she stumbled up the hill. Pain pulsated up her leg as she focused on the black mist of the Wylan Woods.

Something knocked her to the ground and she rolled onto her back. Merellian hovered above her, pinning her beneath his legs.

The elf's raven hair was wild around his face, his breathing erratic. "What's a pretty thing like you doing out of bed?"

Willa shifted her hips to loosen his grip, but he was a dead weight above her. The commander and his winged beast were back, calling out from the clouds above. They circled high above them, casting ominous shadows over them. Merellian bared his teeth at the red tinted sky.

His chest heaved and he snarled at his commander before looking back at her with dark and dangerous eyes. "And what did you do to ruffle the *magpie's* feathers?"

Willa shook her head and pleaded, "Let me go!"

To her surprise, Merellian peeled away from her to glare up at his commander. He seemed focused only on the beast in the sky, circling closer and closer.

Torch lights were bobbing towards them. Silver helmets as well as silver hair meant elves and sentries were headed their way. She tried to stand, but crumpled back into the wet grass. Strong, slender hands lifted her and set her upright.

"Let go of me, elf!" Willa pulled from his grasp and stumbled back.

Merellian tilted his head back to let out a bark of a laugh. His shoulders trembled in a chuckle as he inspected the elves and guards nearing them. Reaching up, he unclasped his cloak and lifted his fingers behind his neck. The silver breastplate covering his front torso dropped to the ground with a loud thunk, his black tunic rippling in the breeze.

He rolled the sleeves of the tunic up with a smirk. "You did something, didn't you? You've made Commander Enrel mad. He wants you now."

Willa made a careful step back and Merellian laughed.

"But I don't do well with sharing, Willa. I've tasted your desires. Our wants are more alike than you could ever imagine."

He was wrong. She was nothing like the elf assessing her with cold, calculating eyes. Adrenaline thrummed through her like the hot wave of pleasure he had given her hours earlier. The thought turned her stomach sour as she thought of Claire's ship burning— of what his commander had done to her friend.

Willa took another timid step back, her boot slipping in the mud as she did, but she caught herself before falling. She tried to mask her pained hiss from the stinging in her ankle, but failed. Merellian's ear twitched, his smile widening along his face. The red moonlight carved into his perfectly cut cheekbones and long neck, amplifying his vicious smile. Willa trembled at his stillness.

"Willa!" Ivaan's voice surprised her as he called from the group rushing towards them.

Before she could say anything to him, Merellian pushed against her side, whispering in her ear. "I'm going to give you a head start, girl. Run as fast as you can and let me enjoy the chase."

A zap of energy hit her, adrenaline coursing through her louder now, taking the pain away in her leg.

Merellian backed away from her, his mouth forming one word before curling into a snarl. "Run."

Willa turned on her freshly healed ankle from Merellian's magic and sprinted up the hill. Arrows flew past her as she pumped her arms in the direction of the Wylan.

"Run, Willa. Run!" Merellian called out behind her.

Willa glanced over her shoulder. He was still walking through the grass, letting her get away.

Predator.

An arrow landed right before her, making her jump to the left. Merellian laughed.

A blood curdling scream had Willa flinching as she ran. She looked back, not daring to slow her pace, as the creature she thought Merellian had killed attacked Traifton's sentries.

Willa slid to a stop and helplessly watched the beast latch onto one of the guards and shake him within its shadowed maw. Merellian hunched over with a bubbling laugh and Willa's jaw dropped in terror at the crazed sound.

Ivaan had managed to get away from the frantic sentries, focused only on her and Merellian. But the beast's green eyes narrowed on Ivaan's back as he pulled away from the group. It dropped whatever poor soul it had in its mouth to chase him.

Willa rushed forward, yelling out a warning, but it was too late.

The beast tackled Ivaan and dragged his body back and forth above the ground with a bone crunching finality. Ivaan's cry of alarm was clipped as the beast stepped over him to rush towards the next powerless mortal. Willa gaped, horrified at his lifeless body on the ground.

A screech cut through the Wylan Creature's sickening sounds as Commander Enrel's winged beast barreled towards the massacre. The commander's beast picked up the Wylan Creature effortlessly and carried it away, causing Merellian's crazed laughter to halt.

If there was ever a moment to keep her wits in check, like her father had always said, it was now. A calm wave of resolve washed over her as she turned. Time slowed as she focused on the black mist and ran from the nightmares behind her.

Run, Run, Run.

As she ran as quickly as her body would allow, she thought of the horror in Claire's eyes as she'd warned her about the elves. They would stop at nothing to get what Willa had hidden in her hair, and now Claire was dead because of it. Ivaan was dead. Willa knew she would also die in these woods before the night was over.

She didn't stop running until her scarred palms touched the veil of cursed magic. Sucking in a breath, she closed her eyes and ran into her chosen coffin.

CHAPTER 23
WILLA

"Willaaa!" A cold, teasing yell sounded out behind her. She kept her eyes closed and pumped her legs and arms through the thick, moving veil. It didn't slow her down or try to stop her as she pushed through it blindly. She ran until the heavy mist dissipated and humid air touched her neck and tear stained cheeks. Falling forward, she clenched the dirt around her and opened her eyes.

Gnarled tree roots twisted and rolled in front of her on the forest floor. Wet leaves kissed her face as she pressed her body into the dirt. She needed to stay hidden atop the floor of the cursed forest. Merellian wouldn't dare enter these woods alone, would he?

The thought of Ivaan's lifeless body had her trembling. She had run from a cursed beast who had killed Ivaan so effortlessly, only to enter its home. She had wished Ivaan dead and now he was. Though she didn't want to believe it, if Claire was on her ship, she was as good as dead, too.

Claire had been right. The elves were worse than the sickness around her.

Air whistled through her nose and out of her lips, moving the damp leaves around her. Red moonlight trickled between the branches above, making the shadows from the trees sinister.

"Willaaaa!" Merellian's voice came from beyond the mist near her feet. "Willllaaaa! Come now, girl!"

His chuckle reverberated through her skin, his teasing dark tone chilling her to the bone. She couldn't move. Not with him so close. Would his elf hearing catch her movement beyond the mist? Of course it would. She was a clumsy mortal and her adrenaline was fading.

Willa attempted to hold her breath, fearful of him catching her frantic panting, and counted down from five to calm herself. She had reached three when slender fingers wrapped around her ankle and dragged her back. Willa kicked her other leg and heard a soft grunt.

Merellian's fingers loosened around her ankle, enough for her to kick away. Clawing at the dirt, she rose, attempting to sprint forward, but he tackled her into the dirt.

The two rolled over one another until she was flat on her back, his muscled legs pinning her to the ground as he straddled her stomach. His arms caged her face, forcing her to look at him, and tendrils of hair fell in dark curtains towards her trembling chin. His nose bled into his teeth, staining them completely red as he smiled at her. Willa lifted her hands and clawed at his neck and cheeks. He snarled and snatched both of her wrists, pinning them by her ears, causing her to yelp.

"You are full of surprises, little mortal. Why does Commander Enrel hunt you from above?" His voice was dark and grumbling through his clenched teeth, and she squirmed beneath his grasp. "The coward won't come down and handle this himself, so I will. Like I always do."

"He killed my friend," Willa stammered. "Even Ivaan is dead!"

He squeezed his fingers around her wrists and snarled. She gasped in pain as he pushed his hips over her stomach to keep her down. His blown out pupils roamed her neck and chest before looking to where their bodies met. She stiffened as he gazed at her slowly, like a meal he was about to feast upon.

"You wanted him dead. I tasted your anger before." The elf bent forward, growling in her ear. "I practically drowned in your waves of resentment. Your hatred was stronger than anything I've ever tasted. It was divine."

He inhaled the scent of her hair before letting go of her wrist to trail a single finger down her neck. Willa whimpered and squirmed beneath him, but it was no use. He was too strong.

Commander Enrel's beast called out from outside the trees, snapping Merellian's focus away from her. He sneered up at the branches and murmured, "Run along, Magpie! She is mine."

Willa took his moment of distraction to reach within the pocket of her pants. The hilt of Claire's fishing knife greeted her fingers and she yanked it out. Merellian looked down right as she thrust the dull blade up towards him.

A sick, squelching sound followed the small blade sinking into his throat, and Merellian hissed, slapping away her hand.

He stood in one fluid motion, grasping the hilt with both hands. Pulling it out swiftly, he laughed as a small stream of blood squirted from the wound. Throwing the knife into the trees beside them, he thumbed the small cut and smirked.

His fingers were covered in blood as he lifted them to his lips and licked them clean. "Like I said, your anger is positively ravishing, girl."

Willa had no time to move as Merellian lunged for her. He straddled her and put both hands over her neck with a vile laugh. She kicked beneath him, but he tightened his fingers around her esophagus with little effort, making her cough and sputter.

Reaching her hands up, she clawed at his wrists, which only seemed to excite him more.

Leaning forward, his nose touched hers, blood falling from his neck and dripping onto her chin. His dilated eyes held the same bone chilling hunger. Squeezing her neck again, her hips bucked and her shoulders lifted from the ground. Willa slapped at his cheeks and pulled his hair, but he only squeezed tighter. Black spots danced between them as the air left her lungs. Her hands went limp from the drain of life within her and fell to the ground.

Merellian looked at her fallen arms before leaning back and sitting on his heels, releasing his grip entirely. Willa gasped for air, sucking in greedy gulps, as the elf's hand moved to his bleeding neck as though surprised. But his brief astonishment twisted into something darker, as his lips curled back into a corrupt grin.

As she drifted in and out of consciousness, he took her hand in his. "I want you to feel my body repair itself, mortal. I want you to know that I cannot die."

Willa gagged and coughed for air, looking anywhere but the wound she had given him. He lifted her other hand, pressing both palms into the warm blood now trickling down his neck.

Suddenly, the skin beneath her palms burned hotter than the brands that had scarred her. She choked out a cry of alarm between her gasping breaths and Merellian's brows knitted together, as if he could feel the sudden rush of heat between them and his wound.

The blood from his veins crawled between her fingers. She could have sworn it sizzled as it touched her skin. This was not the same as when he'd healed her. Was it his dark essence coming out to touch her while it healed the wound she'd placed upon its master? The elf's blood trailed along the scarred designs on her palms, making her stomach turn. And it burned, oh gods, it burned. Hotter than any fire. Worse than any branding.

"I don't want to feel this. Just kill me." She gasped.

Merellian continued to frown. Wrapping his fingers around her wrists, he tried to pull them away from the wound, but the burning sensation flared back with a vengeance as he tugged at her hands.

"Let go," he commanded darkly.

Willa tried to pull away, but she couldn't. An invisible force kept her stuck to his open, bleeding wound.

"I can't," she wheezed.

It was as if her palms had been dipped in the hearth of a fire itself as blood squelched from beneath her fingers. Merellian coughed, blood flying out from his teeth and spraying her face as he did.

"Let go!" He gripped at her wrists so tightly she thought they might break. Blood fell from his neck, mouth, and even nose, as he clung to her wildly. "Let go!"

She couldn't. Couldn't move or fight him off as he pushed and pulled at her hands with rising panic.

His vice-like grip dropped from her wrists as his eyelids drooped shut and he coughed out the same two words, "Let. Go."

Another burst of hot, lacing agony crawled beneath her skin as more blood rushed from Merellian's small wound. His eyes opened and he cried out in alarm. Before, Merellian's eyes had held only raw, viciousness—a vast hunger, desperate to swallow Willa whole. But now, as the two stared at one another, she saw a glimmer of terror matching his panicked pleas and heaving shoulders.

He coughed out more blood and dropped to the side. Willa, unable to release her grip on his bloody neck, rolled with him. The two screamed in agony together as the pain and heat increased between their fused touch before everything faded to black.

CHAPTER 24

WILLA

Everything burned.

Willa's skin itched and crawled beneath the clothes she wore. She tried to lift her head, but it was too heavy. Too painful.

A gurgling sound bubbled beneath whatever she rested upon. Willa opened her eyes and winced at the aching in her temples. Warm liquid trailed down her arms as she shifted her body to rise.

An elf stared up at her with wide eyes, blood pouring from his nostrils and mouth. And the blood didn't stop there. Willa shoved away from him to find she had been resting on his chest and neck. His pale skin was covered in dark red blood, and as it fell from the wounds on his neck and rolled down his chest, it seemed to run eagerly towards her hands. When it touched her fingers, she gasped as fiery pain tore through her.

The world went dark once more.

Willa awoke with a large, gulping breath. Remembering where she was this time, she pushed away from Merellian's chest and fell back onto the ground.

The elf's body was lifeless, red moonlight illuminating his bloodied form. His eyes were still open, blood no longer pouring from his throat, nose, and mouth.

Dead.

But how? How was he dead? He was immortal...

She reached for his hand and grasped it. It was ice cold.

Willa's shirt and pants were soaked in his blood and she lifted her hands, trembling at how it had caked around her scars. They no longer burned. In fact, nothing hurt like it had before. Nothing at all. She wiggled her hands and watched the scars dance in front of her. A rotten iron smell hit her senses. Leaning forward, she vomited away the shock in her system. Heaving atop the leaves, she puked again, wiping at her lips before pushing herself up into a stand.

Shaking fingers reached up to touch her neck, tender where Merellian had squeezed her windpipe. She tried to speak, but winced in pain. *She* should be dead. Not him.

The knife. She needed the knife.

Kicking at the leaves, she wheezed a pained note of relief as the blade appeared a few feet in front of her. Bending over, she lifted it up and stared at the dark blood crusted around the blade before bringing it to her pants to wipe it clean.

Willa huffed a dry laugh. It was pointless. She was covered in so much blood. And why was she laughing? She had killed an elf.

Shock.

Willa jumped at the startling male voice and spun around, clinging to the blade in her hand.

You're in shock.

The voice was barely audible and distant, as if it came from within her, not around her. She looked at her shaking hand holding the knife and frowned.

Shock. Right. It was the shock.

Shaking off the oddness of the voice, Willa studied the wall of mist and took a careful step forward. Listening to the silent rustling of trees around her, she cursed. What would she do now?

A muffled voice sounded on the other side of the veil and she stepped forward, pressing her cheek up to the mist to listen.

"Bring them all to the temple for questions. The girl Merellian chased into the Wylan was trying to escape on the very ship we chased here," Commander Enrel's voice said.

Willa covered her mouth to silence her breathing.

A female answered sourly, "And what of Merellian? You saw how he acted. He did nothing when the creature attacked their men."

"I will handle him, Visha."

Willa clenched her hand tighter over her mouth to stop from vomiting again at the thought of Ivaan—of Claire—dead, because of this commander.

The female elf asked, "And the girl?"

His voice hardened ruthlessly. "She's mine. With any luck, she'll be dead by dawn."

Willa choked back a cry and fell away from the veil. She stepped quietly past Merellian's body, trembling with every timid step, until she was further amongst the trees. A loud call from the Commander's winged beast sounded out from the other side of the veil, giving her the push she needed.

Branches snapped at her cheeks as she zigzagged between the thick, gnarled trunks. Little trickles of red moonlight were her only guide as she fumbled forward in the cursed woodlands.

The air was different here. Thicker and stale. Ancient. It clung to her skin like a second layer of sweat as she ducked under twisting vines covered in black moss.

After a few minutes, she slowed and rested against a tree to get a better look at her surroundings. Her lips were cracked and her throat ached. She needed water badly. But she could only see endless rows of trees and bushes.

Aside from the fallen, molded leaves, a thin layer of mist crawled along the barren forest floor. The mist was lighter than the black wall encasing the forest, with a certain tint of color to it. The thin clouds crawled near her feet until she could perceive what color it was. She whooshed out a breath as she picked out the green tint and shivered. Green like the eyes of the creatures within these woods. Cursed magic from the gods. She looked back up at the tree tops and red light streaming through their openings.

Leaning her head back on the trunk, she tried to come up with some sort of plan to at least prolong her death.

No birds called from the trees. No branches broke. No sounds were made except for her rattled breathing. She closed her eyes and thought of her school studies on the Wylan before the curse. If she could get to the river, she could drink, and maybe even follow it out. All water had to lead somewhere, right? But she didn't know where she was now. It was hopeless. Rubbing at her sore neck in frustration, she opened her eyes to try to see past the few trees around her in the dark and dingy red light and was met with a pair of green, glowing eyes.

Willa forced her eyes shut before she could be entrapped with magic. She waited for the creature to move closer as she reached for the knife in her pocket, but nothing made a sound. She waited a while longer before opening her eyes only to be met by the dark shadows of trees.

A branch snapped behind her, breaking the eerie silence surrounding her. She pushed away from the tree and ran forward, looking everywhere for those green eyes. A startled yelp whooshed out of her as she found herself falling from a sudden ledge, readying herself to hit the ground. But before she could, a black mass of shadow latched onto her with brute force.

Kauis was a boy the first time he had soul shifted. He had fallen asleep for his nap and woke to find himself flying over the old castle of Domnhall. He thought it was the best dream he'd ever had as he flew above the castle with sudden, intoxicating freedom. Kauis had loved it as the air pushed the black and white wings of a magpie on either side of him. He'd circled his tower and called out from the beak he could see between his eyes. But suddenly, pain had laced through him and his wings gave out. He'd plummeted past the windows of the castle tower and landed on the ground with a bone breaking thud. He'd wanted to wake up but realized he was stuck. Stuck inside a dying body.

Footsteps had walked towards him, and suddenly he was being plucked up from the ground. He'd opened his beak to scream at the pain of being lifted by his wing, but only a crass caw came out. His closest friend, Merellian, had looked at him with a feral smile, laughing before shaking him by his wing. Then Merellian had pointed a finger at Kauis' head. Pain had swept him into a world of darkness.

When he'd opened his eyes again, he'd found himself holding a dead magpie between slender, pale fingers. An indescribable feeling of depravity overwhelmed his senses, like a heavy rainfall beating upon his nature, souring his breath. Kauis looked down, realizing it was not his own body but his friend's.

Merellian's hands had flown up to clench his temples, the bird dropping to the ground.

"Get out!" Merellian had screamed.

The scream had bounced around Kauis like white lashes of a whip, swallowing him in a painful darkness once more. When he awoke, he was finally in his own body, drenched in sweat.

Kauis never spoke of the violation that had passed between the two of them. In fact, he didn't speak on any of it until the shifts became more and more frequent. It wasn't until he accidentally shifted while awake that it was brought to others' attention. It was a rare gift of elven essence to be able to shift in such a way. From there, he was separated from his group and trained privately.

Merellian never said it, but Kauis suspected he was jealous of the attention that came with the rare gift. When Kauis rejoined the elves his age, he'd heard Merellian whisper the name 'magpie'. Kauis had practically fumbled over his own feet before looking at his friend with a silent question. The look on Merellian's face told Kauis he knew what had happened when they were children. It was his nickname from then on, a silent omission consistently held over Kauis' head. And the feeling of entering Merellian's mind festered, nagging the back of his consciousness, when Kauis witnessed his friend's short temper and use of his essence. Compared to their peers, Merellian's magic was disruptive and vile. Dark and dangerous. Kauis kept him close for that exact reason, for above all, Merellian was loyal.

And it was better to have his sort of unruly magic behind him and not against him.

When Merellian had chased the girl into the woods, Kauis' soul had stretched and pulled within him. Despite his weak state from using so much magic, his body had lurched and convulsed atop Greer while they landed near the horrified mortals below.

One moment he was holding onto Greer, seeing through his eyes, and the next he was looking down at a mortal girl with blood splattered over her face. Raw fear had rattled his insides. Within another breath, he was back in his own body, sliding off Greer and into the mud.

Now, Kauis stepped through the misty veil of the Wylan Woods with a scowl. He flicked the tendrils of mist off his shoulders as it rolled around his arms, but it desperately crawled back to him, like it was trying to greet an old friend. Greer flew above the treetops, calling out to him as he stepped further into the veil.

Sniffing the air, Kauis groaned at the feeling of such powerful magic rotting the air around him. The gods had done this to curse mortals, but did they realize how badly it teased the magical races? Unlimited power hovered here, like a ripe piece of fruit ready for the plucking.

His body tensed as he stepped carefully between two trees and looked around the dark forest, his own essence purring within him. It must have tasted the gods' magic, too, for hunger and jealousy nipped at his stomach. He was weak. The magic he'd cast upon the girl's ship was enough to drain him for weeks. He would have stopped Merellian sooner if he'd had anything left to use.

You could use what's around you, his essence whispered, deep within his mind.

Kauis shook the thought away as he stalked through the foliage. Tempting as it was, the creature from the valley was telling enough of what this magic did to those who were around it for too long. A few birds rustled above, high enough to make his ears twitch. Aside from that, the forest was silent. Odd for the reputation this place had. He narrowed his eyes, searching the forest floor before him. Rounding a tree, he froze.

Merellian's body lay still on the forest floor. Eyes wide open, his friend stared with an open mouth towards the red moonlight trickling in from the empty branches.

What sort of joke was he playing? It wasn't funny. There wasn't time for things like this. He had always had a sick and twisted sense of humor.

"Get up," Kauis sounded the command with no emotion as he stepped towards him.

He didn't move. Kauis stilled. Something wasn't right.

"Get up!" he barked.

Kauis quickened his steps, dropping to his knees as he reached his body. Blood was everywhere. Merellian's tunic was drenched in it. Kauis realized he was shaking as he carefully bent forward to touch the wound at Merellian's neck. He hissed and fell back as a sudden, searing pain nipped at his fingers, now caked in his friend's blood. How could this happen? Elves couldn't be killed by small wounds, and yet his blood was all over the forest floor.

Lifting him by the tunic, Kauis shook Merellian violently as though he might wake him from whatever stupor he was lost in. The elf's head lolled to the side and Kauis yelled, "Get up!"

But his body lay limp in his grasp. Dead. He was dead.

Kauis' essence roiled beneath his skin as he closed Merellian's eyes and gripped his cold hand. Emptiness clung to him, a single tear rolling down his face, which he quickly wiped away.

His men often teased him for his lack of emotion. They joked he was as soulless as his black eyes. He was a temperamental leader and stern toward those he cared for. He had to be with the fate of his lineage hanging by a fragile thread.

Lowering Merellian's body to the ground, he sat beside him in tense silence. He stared at the hole in his neck and fought the memories of his father's own death when they had both been so young. Too young to understand that their lives were going to change for the worse. Too young to realize he was an orphan of the crown, harbored with the elder elves who chose to stay and avenge their fallen king. And through it all, despite their tense friendship, Merellian had stayed by his side.

The memory of his father's death had Kauis opening his eyes. He thought of the soul shifting with Merellian and remembered the mortal girl's face covered in blood. An elf's blood. His *friend's* blood.

Kauis pushed into a kneel, raising both hands above Merellian's head, and whispered, "Forgive me for this."

His essence rolled eagerly within him and latched onto Merellian's skin. Kauis' eyes closed as his soul left his primordial frame.

Fire burned within every cell of his being as Kauis stared down at a frightened girl. He coughed as his blood speckled her face.

"Let go," he croaked.

The girl tried, but the tugging of her hands had his lungs squeezing like a snake, tightening around his throat. His essenced drained away, along with the blood leaking from him. His neck seared like it was being torn in two as he tried to rip away the girl's palms.

When he awoke again, the girl hovered over him, covered in blood. She reached forward, checking if he was alive. He was, but barely. His vision darkened and his bones ached. Every pain his body had ever been through now echoed through his centuries old frame. Was this his immortality leaving him? Suddenly, the girl's fingers touched his chest. A bloody palm with a strange mark upon it was moving along his shirt. The blood from his neck trickled down to her, eagerly greeting her flesh. Hot pain hit him in the chest like a blast of lightning. And then nothing.

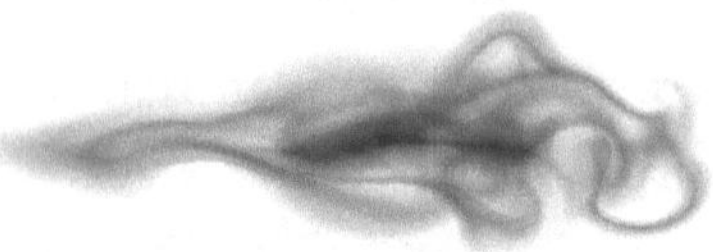

Darkness filtered all around him. Kauis found himself standing in an endless field of black within his own elven body. But this wasn't his body, was it? This was somewhere in between. He spun around and shouted, his voice swallowed instantly by the thick black clouds surrounding him.

Now he was looking out into the forest, running towards a valley within the Wylan Woods. Two bloody palms reached out in front of him. They bore the marks of the old kingdom.

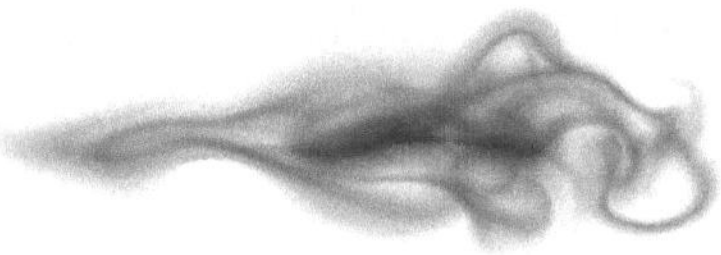

Kauis fell back into his own body and vomited. He trembled with the phantom pains of what Merellian had gone through. What that mortal girl had done to him. Was it her he had shifted into in the end?

A nagging tug beat at his chest. Greer called out from above. Concern rolled through their taut bond and Kauis fell back onto the cold leaves near Merellian's body.

"Find her," was all he could shove down their bond before sleep overtook him.

Willa yelped as a large, slimy creature clung to her. Together, they rolled down the hill, hitting rocks and bushes as they went. Willa shoved at whatever held onto her with slick limbs, but it was too large, and they were falling too fast for her to get away from it.

A massive fallen tree stopped their momentum. The creature clinging to Willa took the brunt of the hit and, as it did, Willa pushed away from it. She somersaulted a few yards further until she, too, was physically forced to stop by tumbling into the base of a tree trunk. The sudden stop knocked the air from her lungs.

Crawling forward, Willa sucked in air as she looked back to where the creature lay. It twitched atop the fallen log before stilling on its side.

Enough red moonlight trickled in for her to get a quick grasp of her new surroundings. She had landed at the base of a valley. Water rushed behind her, loud enough for her to turn and look for it before returning her gaze upwards to the opening in the trees that spread out above her in the valley as far as her eyes could see. The crevice she sat in was surrounded by long, gnarled roots sticking out from the tops of the hills. Vines hung on either side of the valley, swaying gently in a deep green color, with black moss dripping from them.

Willa looked back at the water. It was a river by all accounts, fast moving and large enough to fit a boat. She followed it towards an opening of the hills, where green mist hovered.

She turned from the river when a clicking sound came from where the fallen creature had landed. The Wylan Creature slowly pushed into a stand, revealing its full horrific height. Two glowing eyes monitored the surroundings before focusing on her from the fallen log it now crawled on top of. Its mouth took Willa's attention as it clicked together two long, pincer-like fangs. A black tongue wiggled several inches from the two elongated fangs, as if smelling the air in front of it. It clicked its teeth at her and hissed, black shadows rippling from its scales.

Time slowed as Willa stood. One word rang in her head, louder than any chime or trumpet. *Run.*

Willa turned and sprinted towards the rushing water. The sound of pincers snapping too closely behind had her crying out in panic as she neared the muddied river bank. She could swim— not well—but well enough to let the rapids push her away from this magic-made monstrosity. She readied herself for the plunge right as a large crash came from the treetops.

A familiar shadow swooped towards her in a mass of black feathers. She ducked her head as Commander Enrel's beast dove towards the Wylan Creature with its massive talons, hoisting it up into the air with little effort. She didn't wait for the elf's beast to turn and reach for her next. Sucking in a breath, she jumped into the wide river while the sound of crunching teeth and talons echoed in the valley around her.

There was a reason Willa had worked at the market instead of taking up a job with her brother and Claire on the docks or ships.

Willa knew how to swim—almost everyone in Traifton learned at an early age, for most ended up with jobs near or on the water—but she had never excelled. Much like everything else she did, she rushed into the act of moving rather than thinking.

Willa was grateful for the rapid, moving waters taking her away from those beasts for a whole thirty seconds until she began to panic at how fast and effortlessly the water was dragging her along. Her fingers grasped at river rocks and mud as the water swept her along, but it was no use. She had barely gotten her head above the crashing waves to suck in a small amount of air before another current yanked at her billowing cloak, shoving her under once more.

Under the water, she could barely see with what little light the red moon provided. The only thing she could make out were sprays of little bubbles fizzing in front of her face. She flailed her arms so she could hold on to anything to get above the surface, but her velvet cloak twisted in the fast currents, spinning her helplessly within the water's rush.

Then she dropped.

For a few brief moments, the waterfall allowed her a breath of air and a second's reprieve from the rushing rapids. But it didn't stop Willa from letting out a terrified squeal as she tumbled towards a dark green body of water. Mist kissed her cheeks before the slap of cold water hit her with an icy force.

The current below the waterfall was nearly worse than the river's as she plummeted below the murky water's surface. She kicked her legs and arms, desperate for air, as her body spun helplessly in the vicious whirlpool. But her body was tired, still aching and, despite her sluggish efforts, she managed to kick free from the waterfall's churning, pushing out towards calmer water.

Little trickles of light danced above as Willa reached her arms up to the surface. She was tired—so tired. Her cloak dragged her down like she was falling. Her lungs burned and bellowed, tightening more and more the further down she went before mounds of sand and water reeds embraced her.

Willa kicked up from the floor and tried to swim, but a force seemed to grab the back of her head and shove her down. Pain ricocheted through her as Claire's metal hair clip slammed into a boulder. Willa tried to move, but she was stuck—the clip was stuck—latched onto the boulder. She frantically reached back and undid the clasp. Her hair lifted around her as she pulled from the stuck piece of metal. Her body started to drift upwards, but it was too late.

The spots dancing in her vision morphed and grew into large, inky blobs, sweeping her into an endless realm of darkness.

"I haven't tasted a mortal in centuries," a woman's voice whispered.

Death had finally come to take her at last.

The voice laughed. The bubbling sound echoed around Willa's mind in joyous, melodic chimes before she stated, *"This is not your death, young one. I see many things through the water. I hear many whispers, but your death is not yet known to me."* The woman paused and hummed thoughtfully before saying, *"The scales, though broken, have seemed to tilt once more."*

Willa waited in the dark for death to release her from the pretty, riddled words. But it did not come. Instead, something poked her skin. A hard pinch had Willa gasping and opening her eyes. Darkness surrounded her.

Her arms floating lifelessly beside her, Willa's lips pursed as she wiggled her fingertips. They moved through the black tendrils weightlessly.

"What is this place?" Willa's voice was muffled and distorted. Her tongue was heavy and hard to lift as she formed the question.

She was met with silence.

Her red hair floated around her, and the sight made her gasp. "The hair piece! I need it!" Something pinched her, this time on the back of her neck.

"The lake takes a gift from the souls who enter our waters. We keep the gifts of those who pass for safekeeping to help you on your way. In fact, we've met another like this. The two will be safe in the belly of our embrace."

"But I need it!"

Panic latched onto her as she thought of Claire and the effort that went into hiding the hair clip. Willa spun to be greeted by a woman's face smiling at her in the dark.

The woman's face was wrinkled and aged, but her brilliant blue eyes had a youthful glow about them, visible between long white tendrils of floating hair.

"Need and want are two very different things."

"Who are you?" Willa whispered.

"I am in the rivers, water, and rain. I hear whispers on the waves, taste desires in tears." The woman's voice was clearer now. Instead of a whisper, it sounded directly in front of her in the dark. "My name will not hold merit to you, girl. But my message will."

A hand came through the tendrils of white hair. Bony and slender, it waved two long fingers around the dark mist until a light appeared. Willa stared, transfixed by its glowing aura. It pulsed and throbbed before her as if breathing. It began to spin, faster and faster, until a shadow spread the matter of the light apart.

"There once was a story of a water serpent. So hungry, yet there were no fish. It searched and searched its cove, but nothing was there." Shadows danced and moved within the glow until a serpentine shape took place as the woman continued. "It waited and waited for unsuspecting prey, hoping the new and pretty traps it made would lure them into its home. But nothing came.

It waited, but never left to search beyond its comfort. Only staying in its cove. It grew so hungry that eventually it found its tail." The serpent shadow began to shrink with every bite it took into its own tail as the woman continued, "So sick and brain muddied from gnawing hunger, it began to eat its tail until eventually it was too late. Was it upset when it realized it was eating its own flesh? No. The serpent had grown so fond of its own company that he thought he tasted better than anything else he had tried before."

The serpent within the light disappeared and Willa blinked. She looked at the woman, confused. "I don't understand."

The woman smiled and again the light appeared. This time, a kingdom sat within the light. Tall shadows of a pointed castle grew as light stretched high above her.

The woman said quietly, "I have seen many kingdoms rise and fall. An endless cycle, beginning and ending with an unsuspecting serpent. An endless wheel engaging in the Law of Balance time and time again."

"But balance is broken. There are no kingdoms left to fall," Willa whispered as shadows crawled along the walls and the white light turned a dark red crimson.

Fire rolled over the castle until the shadows crumbled away into the darkness surrounding Willa and the mysterious woman. Willa looked at the woman with a perplexed gaze.

The woman laughed. Jagged teeth, each tipped in a sharp point, glistened in the dark as the woman bubbled a rumbling, happy giggle. Willa crossed her arms, silently willing the woman to stop her mocking laugh.

When she did, her smile dropped before speaking. "Balance is never broken, young one. The scales are merely scattered across the maps. Some eclipsing out in deep waters. Some left to rot within malice. Though the essence has grown far apart, the whispers remain true."

Willa had heard those few final words. But where? She closed her eyes for a moment and saw Claire's note and the hasty words written on the back of the page. When Willa opened her eyes, the woman was gone. A whisper crawled along her neck and Willa blanched. The woman rolled past her right shoulder as if she were swimming lazily on the planks of her long white hair.

"There are many kingdoms, Willa. Ones not yet made and ones not yet broken." The woman's face bobbed before her before disappearing.

Willa spun around to find only darkness as her company.

"Just remember, girl. When kingdoms fall, a new dawn rises. I fear you will go down many hard paths, young mortal. Yet there is something more to you I cannot quite place." She hummed, the sound caressed Willa's skin, sending shivers along her spine. "What comes after storms, Willa?"

Without thought or question, Willa answered immediately, "Clear skies."

That was an old sailors' saying, one she had heard and said many times in Traifton. A motto her and Claire had said to one another before parting. Emotion lumped in her throat, realizing those were the last words she had said to her best friend. She shook away the thought, knowing if she settled into the grief it would drag her to the bottom of this lake and hold her there indefinitely.

None of what this woman had said made sense. Willa opened her mouth to voice her questions, but the woman cut her off.

"Very good. Very good. Dawn is approaching, Willa Thesalor. Will you be the fire to cast the new sun down or the rain before it?"

Those piercing blue eyes and sharp teeth appeared again before Willa. She blinked at the woman, unsure of how to answer. Unsure of what to make of any of this.

The woman's smile only widened before her face snapped upwards. "Interesting."

"What's interesting?" Willa whispered.

"Three into one created by slaughter." She sighed. "I hope we meet again, mortal, so I may learn more of your time before coming to me."

Water flowed into her lungs and rushed around her as sharp, black talons gripped her shirt, pulling her up and out of the lake she had fallen into.

The air was thick and suffocating. It *tasted* strange. Sorean's senses had been overwhelmed from the moment he left the safety of Lithelle, his pointed ears twitching constantly from any movement around him. His companions sensed it, too. They were all on high alert and abnormally tense.

A tainted deer stepped timidly through the trees. Sorean nocked an arrow. Endless hours of research in Lithelle's tombs had done little to prepare him, and the hundreds of drawings within the spies' bestiaries paled in comparison to the actual creature before him now. Bones could be seen clearly along its ribs and legs through black, matted fur. It was as if the cursed magic were picking it away slowly. Antlers grew from its head normally at first, before twisting and winding into one another like entwined tree branches after a storm, the ends of them as black as its fur. Moss swung from the twisted horns as the deer looked around before continuing past another tree.

What frightened Sorean the most was its eyes. The Wylan Woods was dark, the moon shining a dim red color around the forest floor, making for an eerie scene. But the deer's eyes glowed a bright emerald green color, emanating through the dark, endless expanse of forest oaks as they searched mindlessly.

Sorean followed the creature with the tip of his arrow. It would be a kindness to kill this deer. Better to kill it than for it to attack them. He had heard stories of the cursed creatures using magic to entrap those who stared upon them for too long. Even as faeries, Sorean knew this cursed magic was powerful.

His essence rolled restlessly as he stalked the unsuspecting deer from where he perched on a branch. It was hungry for more time out of his body. As though it could feel the power around him as the cursed magic sank into his skin like a humid layer of precipitation.

Sorean's arrow released and hit the deer right above the heart. The deer screamed and dropped. Deer shouldn't scream. The sound grated against his sensitive ears, loud enough for him to bare his teeth in irritation. Despite the chilling noise, Sorean knew the deer would not get back up. Their arrows were coated in fae magic—a poison that would kill anything within minutes. Sorean could only grind his teeth and watch the deer struggle to stand before its green eyes rolled back into its head with a distorted groan. Dead.

A whistle sounded to his left, and Sorean peered through the tree branches to find Iara hunkered down on a branch. Her legs swung back and forth silently before she dropped down. She hopped from branch to branch, as if she had done this a hundred times over, before landing softly on the forest floor. This is why they trained in Lithelle, to be ready if the veil ever fell, or if they ever left its safe and cushioned bubble.

Sorean scanned the forest while Iara ran to the deer and knelt before it. They were at least a day's ride away from Niarath Loch and Sorean was eager to get to the water and ask questions. He needed to confirm what Noi had said with his own ears before taking it to the queen. When he was crowned, he would take action, whether she liked it or not. This was only a small step for change. But admittedly, he was ready to return to Lithelle. It would be nice to not constantly hunt or feel like he was the one being hunted with each passing mile. And although Iara and Harland assured him several times, Sorean also couldn't stop worrying about the sentries at the cabin. What his magic had done for them to get away. The noises from the cabin would be added to the list of things to haunt him in sleepless nights to come.

Sorean pulled the bow over his head and let it rest on his back with the string around his chest before grabbing his fletching of arrows. He stood on the branch, looking around one more time, before crouching to begin his climb down.

A jarring, startling screech above him had him standing defensively. He reached for his bow and readied an arrow within it, looking up through the green mist and barren branches to find pockets of the night sky.

Another shriek peeled out before a massive black shadow enveloped him in darkness. Without hesitation, Sorean released his arrow before nocking a second one and firing through the branches again. The shadow replied with a piercing cry, so loud it shook the branch he balanced on.

He had hit his target—whatever it was. Better to kill than be killed here, especially if it was one of the flying creatures from their scout's bestiaries. Sorean backed up to the tree's trunk and searched above him frantically. He listened and waited for another call or shadow to fly above him, but all was hauntingly quiet now. He counted down the minutes and listened with calm breaths. Another two minutes and the poison would kill the intended target. Whatever it was, it was not coming back now. Sorean climbed down from the gnarled tree as quickly as he could.

Iara and Harland were beside him instantly, the latter scanning above them as he whispered, "What was that?"

"Something much bigger than a deer." Sorean tilted his head to the deer's carcass, walking over and kneeling beside it.

He had to fight his gag reflex at the putrid smell of rot and decay, and he pulled the arrow out with one swift jerk and stood.

He wiped the arrow's tip over his thick riding pants and turned back to Harland and Iara. "Let's get back to camp and pack up. If we travel tonight we can get to Niarath Loch by morning."

Harland nodded. "The sooner we get out of this poisoned place the better."

Sorean waited for Iara's confirmation, but her brows were furrowed slightly and her lips were pursed.

"Speak plainly," Sorean said. If Iara was hesitant about the plan, he wanted to know why.

Iara pulled her low ponytail over her shoulder as she continued to scan the treetops above them. "Two days in these woods and we've only spotted and killed a handful of Wylan beasts. Noi's report had me anxious for more bloodshed upon entering the Wylan. Don't you find it strange?"

Sorean watched her carefully. "Noi was also closer to Domnhall than we are now. He ran this way, towards Niarath Loch, to get away from the beasts in the pit he spoke of."

A shiver crawled along his spine at the thought. It had him scanning the trees with paranoia as he awaited her reply.

When she didn't answer, Sorean sighed and stepped closer to her. "Why are you so adamant on proving the fox shifter wrong?"

Iara glanced at him and spoke with a casual shrug of her shoulder. "Why wouldn't he run back to Lithelle after witnessing such monstrosity in the old kingdom? Why run clear to the other side of the woodlands?" She sighed and moved her braids back to fall behind her neck and turned to face Sorean fully. "It just seems too easy. And no matter what the waters say to you, we broke the law all on the word of a deserter. I only want to make sure we did this for the right reasons and not for—"

"For what, Iara?" Sorean cut her off. Shifting his weight, he crossed his arms and looked her up and down slowly.

"Are you sure this isn't you running from the crown?"

Sorean scoffed and took a step away. Unbelievable.

Iara was quick to follow with raised hands. "I will follow you anywhere, Sorean. You know this. But I need to know right now if this is an act of rebellion. If I am to die by the queen's white fire, I need to know this is worth it for you."

Sorean clenched his jaw. "I am doing this *for* the crown. I need answers before I can accept this burden."

Iara laughed and dropped her hands. "Burden? Half the realm would kill to have your position."

"And what position is that? Court matters, day in and day out? Grand parties?" Sorean paced in front of her while anger nipped at his clipped steps. "We hide in a bubble of fake light, fake air, fake water, fake food, for fuck's sake! All while this is happening right on our doorstep. I will not become a fat and lazy lord while the rest of those on this map suffer in silence!" Sorean hadn't realized he was yelling until he closed his mouth and wet his dry lips.

He turned from Iara, walking away. "I will accept the crown, but not until I know what it is exactly my mother has been hiding from all of these years." When he heard her footsteps following him, he turned and raised a hand. "Go back to camp and help Harland. I'll walk until you catch up."

Iara opened her mouth to argue, but closed it promptly and nodded. He watched as she turned on her heel and ran back to their veiled camp.

Sorean walked through the trees, attempting to fight off his lingering irritation. Iara was right to question him. He had never wanted the title of king before. He had made it clear several times when around her. But to assume he would desert the realm entirely was absurd. He was no coward. His essence purred beneath him with his angered gait. It seemed to like it when he was angry. He clenched his teeth and ignored its silent pull, continuing in silence.

A bird chirped through the trees ahead of him and Sorean slowed his walk, listening. Another bird echoed the first, ringing out from the east, and he peered up into the branches, stepping towards the sound.

As he walked, he readied his bow with an arrow and held it near his hip. Another bird replied in the trees before him. Sorean's dimple popped in his cheek as he smiled to himself. He had always reveled in the hunt. The chase excited him. Especially now that the hunts were real and not simulated by faerie magic in the training rings. He crept along for minutes on careful steps as he followed the bird's calls.

Use us instead, save your arrows. Sorean physically shook his head to get rid of the whispers of his essence.

He ignored the plea and stopped behind a large bush filled with thorns and thick vines. Squinting through the shrubbery, he watched the tree branches, preparing to find green eyes. But nothing appeared. He crouched further and listened, waiting for another bird's squawk but the forest was silent.

The skin on Sorean's neck pimpled at the stillness of the air around him, and he stood, slowly scanning the trees, unable to shake the feeling of being watched as he looked out through the dim red light.

A wail tore through the forest. Not a beast's, but a normal scream—much like the sounds of the sentries back at the cabin. He spun towards the sound, waiting to hear it again. When it did, it echoed through the vast expanse of trees like a siren's call in the Minison's waters. It was a woman's voice.

Let us out, Prince! Sorean shook his head and ran forward towards the call, ignoring his hungry essence as he ran.

One minute, Willa was being pulled up through the trees by the elf's large beast, and the next, she was crashing through the branches by herself. Something had hit the Commander's beast as it carried her above the green mist of the Wylan. The creature had been so startled it dropped her. She had tried to stop her fall and silence her screams as she crashed through the branches back toward the Wylan Woods, but she'd fallen too fast to grab ahold of anything.

It was foolish to admit relief had flooded her when the beast dropped her back into the poisoned woods. But anything was better than being with the elves again. The air was knocked from her lungs as she hit the ground, pain ricocheting through her body in little currents, making her vision spin wildly as she gulped for air. One would figure after so many falls and brash collisions, her lungs would be used to such a forceful hit to her breathing.

Willa pinched her eyes shut as a bird chirped, another answering seconds later. Willa had heard these noises before from the owl that had tricked her. The chirps were not normal—they were distorted and broken. After a few agonizing gulps, she coughed into the dirt and wheezed before falling onto her back to look up.

Hundreds of small, glowing green eyes surveyed her from the treetops.

Unblinking, they pulsed their green light, casting an eerie glow around her body and the forest floor she lay on. Ever so slowly, Willa pushed herself up. She was surrounded. No matter which way she turned, multiple pairs of eyes floated within the dark branches of all the trees surrounding her.

A female's voice crooned in her head, *"An elf in our midst? He will be pleased with our findings."*

A harmony of whispers bounced around between Willa's ears. *"Ye-es. Yes! Yessss."*

The pull of the Wylan's magic greeted her like an old friend.

Standing, she wiped at her still damp clothes and answered through thick, honey flavored air, "I am no elf."

Her voice sounded strange and she realized she was warm, and free of pain and anxiety. The sensation caused her stomach to flip, but she ignored it and smiled up at the familiar, friendly green glow.

The same voice entered her mind, *"You cannot lie to me, she-elf. I can taste it on your breath."*

Another warbled voice asked, *"What does elf taste like?"*

The first voice replied darkly, *"I do not know. I've never met one until now."*

Willa smiled, but her lips were numb, leaving a tingling sensation on her face as she asked, "How could you possibly know I am an elf if you have never met one?"

Again, her stomach rolled and flopped, sending a bundle of nerves up and down her body. But once more, she ignored it and gave into the warm glow of the green eyes coaxing her with cursed magic. Willa moved her hand from her lips and looked at her palm. The scar of the sunburst seemed to glow beneath the green light, and she giggled.

When she looked back up, a pair of green eyes was growing larger than the others. A flat nose sat beneath them, and under the nose was a wide, underbite of a smile. Rows of teeth jutted out above the creature's thin upper lip, but it was the ears and wings that took her attention. Huge floppy ears, stuck out on either side of the leathery skin. The wings were leathery as well. Willa could practically see little lines of veins through the material as it flew towards her. The closer it got, the wider its mouth opened, showcasing more and more rows of tiny, jagged teeth.

Willa curled her lips and smiled with all her teeth, as if to copy her new friend flying towards her. She giggled, but stopped when all of the green eyes shifted and moved in unison. Branches and leaves fell towards her, and she spun around, listening to the sound of snapping wings growing closer.

With a whoosh, the beast landed, standing taller than her by a foot at least. It reminded Willa of cave bats near the shores of Traifton, but this one was much larger and more curious. More of the creatures began to land behind the one watching her now with its wide-open maw. Their wings and ears took up most of their frame as they pushed each other to make their way to her. She was surrounded.

Despite the warm glow from their eyes, something itched in the back of Willa's mind. Her stomach rolled and twisted before she blinked away the haze.

You need to run. The deep, timbre of a male's voice spoke through thick water. The sudden thought was so quiet, she barely heard it.

"See-ee-e. I heard it now. You are an elf!"

Willa frowned at the largest, bat-like creature, shaking her head. What was this beast talking about? She wasn't an elf; she was running from one. Her hands started to tingle, and Willa hissed. Both of her palms were glowing white around the markings of her scars.

Run. The voice inside her was much clearer now—its urgent command seeming to eat away at the cursed magic entrancing her.

Willa spun from the large bat and jumped as another, smaller one suddenly lunged for her. She backed up, gasping as something sharp grabbed hold of her back legs. Willa kicked blindly, but a beast from the trees swooped down, grabbing onto her cloak.

Another came from above, grabbing more of her cloak, and then she was in the air, fighting the flapping wings. These creatures were nothing compared to the winged bird who had carried her so effortlessly in its talons. But for any wiggle and flail she made, the more clipped and irritated the ones below became. And for every movement, another latched onto her legs or clothing with their tiny clawed toes to lift her higher. There had to be five or six of the smaller ones carrying her into the air, and as Willa fought desperately to release herself from their grasp, fear rippled through her when she saw where they were taking her.

They had been flying together in unison, lifting her back towards the largest and original one that had lured her. She was as high up in the trees as it had once been, but now it stood on the forest floor, looking up at her with a wide smile. Its mouth widened, bigger and bigger. Willa could have sworn she heard its jaw tick and break with each moment it opened wider and wider, until all she could see was a hole filled with teeth, and two black, leathered wings on either side.

Willa thrashed her shoulders and elbows. But so many held onto her wrists, ankles, knees, clothing and hair, making it impossible to move. She could hear nothing aside from the rushing wings beating furiously around her to hold her steady and in the air. She was helpless as the one below made a gurgled noise with its open maw. The bat-like monstrosities all chirped and chortled to one another in unison and, before her next breath, she was falling into the wide mouth of jagged teeth and slimed leather.

Her rasps echoed in the slimy cavern, the leathery walls tightening and expanding around her, pushing her further and further within the creature's body. Enveloped in darkness, she blindly pressed her hands into slime coated walls. Willa hissed from the immediate sting that came from her palms and pulled back. In the dark, the scars on her hands were still glowing a faint white color. The burning sensation tingled beneath the marks, making her bare her teeth.

Lifting her tingling hands, she slapped them on the leathered wall and yelled, "Let me out!"

A gurgle shook around her, loud enough to silence her demand.

She clenched her hands into fists and pounded on the slimy wall. "Let me out!"

The tingling in her hands roared, becoming so hot, she moaned from the pain. It was happening again, much like with Merellian. This was no hallucination, this was unimaginable pain within her veins, roaring like an unforgivable inferno. But the leather walls were closing in on her so tightly she couldn't move.

She was being suffocated within the beast. Swallowed whole and eaten alive.

Willa's hands pushed against her chest while the leather on either side of her squeezed her.

"No!" She wheezed and unclenched her hands, pushing at the slimy insides of the bat beast before another burst of pain rolled through her body.

Lifting her hands, she frantically clawed at the beast's innards as it tried to swallow her further and further within its being.

Ask me what you need and I shall give it. Back was the male's voice, echoing deep within her panicked mind.

What in the gods' name did that even mean? How could a voice within her own mind help her now? This had to be the effects of shock or the aftermath of once again being entranced by the Wylan's magic. Another squeeze of the beast around her had her gasping for dear life.

"Let—" She wheezed and the walls around her tightened with her intake of breath. "Me out."

Her mind grew fuzzy as the fire beneath her hands flared up.

What will you do when you are out? Willa closed her eyes, focusing only on the voice as it lectured her with soft clarity, *They will only chase you. Hunt you down until they can trap you again. You are weak. Helpless to this world.*

She was unable to take a full breath now. Her palms were up near her face, pushing and clawing at the leathered slime shifting around her body. Willa wished for magic in that moment. She envisioned Merellian stopping the Wylan creature with a simple lift of his hand. She envisioned Commander Enrel burning Claire's ship without even touching it. Willa would give anything to have that now and stop this slow, agonizing death.

The voice chuckled. *I knew you had some spark within you. I believe we'll have some fun together, mortal.*

Willa opened her eyes and screamed as a sudden burst of burning agony rushed from her neck all the way down to her outstretched palms. A white burst of light appeared between her fingers and the belly of the beast before the pain pulled her under.

CHAPTER 29

KAUIS

Kauis awoke on the forest floor of the Wylan Woods, clasping his chest. He rolled over with a startled gasp at the pain lacing every fiber of his body. Clutching the dirt, he panted as black and white hair fell past his face. He had done too much by shifting into Merellian's faded soul and now his body was paying for it.

When he tried to stand, another wave of pain hit him so violently, he fell face first into the dirt with an agonized groan. A pleading tug within him sent another surge of misery through his body, but this pain was something else entirely. This wasn't his own.

Greer was hurt.

Kauis hissed through his teeth, pushing himself up from the dirt and stumbling forward, blinded by the pain beating at his soul with sharp, poisoned claws. He had read many tales of those who were magically tethered to animal companions, but unfortunately, each case was too unique for him to gain any sort of clarity. There were only a handful of facts that seemed to stay the same within all stories of these bonds.

The first being that the animal and the being with the tethered cord didn't choose such things. Fate, if such a word existed, is what linked the two together when crossing paths. The second was ways of communication. Each story of those bonded stated they could connect to one another through one magically long cord. This cord of connection had no limit to distance between the two, though was stronger the closer and more often the pair would use it. Through the bond, the pair could send each other their emotions and talk to one another. But it seemed only Kauis could go so far as to jump into Greer's own mind with his unique soul shifting abilities.

Kauis stumbled through the trees before falling into a trunk, leaning forward and vomiting bile. He waited for the cramping in his stomach to subside so he could catch his breath. Wiping at his mouth, he scanned the dimly lit woodlands and groaned. He couldn't shift again, not like this, but he needed to find Greer and understand what had happened.

His emotions and memories were still accessible through the bond, so Kauis could at least do that. Sliding down the tree's bark, he closed his eyes and tugged on their connection.

A vision of crashing through the canopy of the Wylan's trees came instantly, followed by surges of pain. Another vision came after. Blurry details of tall grass and bushes. A long black wing was sprawled out, and in between the feathers was a wooden arrow. Dark liquid crawled towards the hazy blinking of the griffin's sight. Greer looked back at his wing before closing his eyes.

Kauis stood and ran, weaving his way through the scattered old oaks as fast as his immortal body would allow. His ears twitched furiously, checking for predators as he focused on the only thing that mattered now: reaching his bond.

A griffin such as Greer would live an abnormally long life alongside Kauis and his elven magic. However, if one were to die, the other wouldn't last long in a world without their companion. If Greer was dying, so was he.

Kauis had seen arrows like the one in his vision before, but it had been centuries. Faerie made arrows, tipped in fae poison, killing any creature, magical or not, in minutes. Greer was large and stronger than most, but Kauis could feel it as he ran deeper into the Wylan. The ancient griffin was dying.

With each breath passing through Greer's beak, the poison crawled further and further into his bloodstream. Guilt overwhelmed Kauis. What might the griffin have been doing instead of being bonded to such a selfish immortal like him? Greer had followed him for centuries without question when he could have had a peaceful life of his own. But because of Kauis, the two were back in the dreadful land where they had first met and formed their living, breathing connection. A connection that was beginning to dim.

Kauis couldn't die. Not when he was finally getting answers. The arrow confirmed the faeries were still alive, and closer to him than he could have ever imagined. They had searched Kalandrae first, after the gods left them to fend for themselves. But they had found nothing aside from the newly cursed forest and remnants of the old Kingdom of Domnhall. Had they truly been here this whole time, hidden in plain sight?

Kauis reached a large rolling river, deep within a natural made valley, and he grabbed his sides, surveying the rushing waters through clenched teeth. Waves of pain and adrenaline continued to battle with one another in his head, and he took a few steps back before blowing out a rattled breath. With quick pumps of his arms and legs, he ran towards the water and pushed off, landing on the other side and pushing back into a sprint.

Greer was getting worse. Kauis rubbed at his temples and eyes to force away the slow forming shadows dimming his vision.

He pushed a message to Greer through the waning bond as he searched the trees and hills before him. *"I am with you. Hold on."*

A feeling of anguish rumbled back to him—the only answer he would get from Greer now. But something else came with it, one that had Kauis pushing past his own pain to begin his run again. *Fear.* Greer was scared. An emotion he had never once received from the ancient beast.

A vision flashed before Kauis, and he skidded to a stop in the dirt. Glowing green eyes, blurry through Greer's hazy vision, watched as two bare feet crunched through the brush towards him.

A foreign, accented voice whispered, "We meet again, old friend."

Kauis blinked and panted as the vision dissipated. Wiping the sweat off his brow, he tugged at the connection. He had heard this voice once before, but it had been so long now, it was like a distant dream. Another burst of pain rumbled through his body, starting from the top of his head and rolling all the way down to his shoes like crackling lightning.

Growling at the aching in his limbs and muscles, Kauis pressed forward. He was so blinded by his own pain and Greer's, he didn't notice the creature swooping from the trees above him until it was too late.

Kauis moaned, his fingers grazing over the soil and wet leaves, failing to listen to his frantic mind and grasping at anything he could. A low warbled bark sounded above his head. Kauis lifted his chin, wincing in pain. A black mass of shadow had been dragging him through the trees for minutes now. Or maybe hours. His body was so weak and weary.

When the ground stopped moving, Kauis opened his eyes. He stared up at the trees and blinked until they stopped spinning wildly in his vision. Someone was speaking beside him, but Kauis couldn't hear anything over the pounding of his heart. His pulse was moving too slowly.

Greer was dying. He was dying.

A sudden burst of pain had Kauis sitting up. He yelled and clutched at his chest before rolling over to vomit in the dirt. Greer was lying on his side, only a few feet away. Kauis tried to stand, but only made it halfway before falling back onto the soil. The sudden fall had pushed away the roaring sound of his pulse, only to open his ears to the sound of frantic cries from Greer.

A voice was chanting around them, its lilted accent and rolling r's danced around Kauis as he lifted his head up enough to vomit again.

Something, or someone, reached for his arms and pulled him up into a kneeling position. Kauis' head rolled to rest on his shoulder.

Cold fingers grasped his chin and yanked his head upward. "We meet again, Prince."

Kauis was no prince. Not anymore. But he opened his eyes and looked at the person who held him upright. Gray, long hair covered a bony, wild face. Darting black eyes, set high within time-worn sockets, assessed Kauis hungrily.

"I can help you, but I will need to hear the words from your own tongue to do so," the man crooned in his rich accent.

Kauis' eyes wandered to the scarred patch of skin beneath the man's pointed chin at the center of his neck. The Mark of the Damned bobbed up and down as the man swallowed—a long curled line crawling down his neck like a twisting vine. At the end of the curled line were three branches. Three lines for the three gods, rolling downwards along his neck and not up, for a symbol of eternal damnation.

Greer let out an agonized yowl and Kauis winced, his eyes falling shut as he embraced the warm darkness behind his lids. "Help us."

A cold sting struck his cheek and Kauis opened his eyes, looking up at the man with a curled lip.

The man smiled and closed his beady black eyes. "I want you to see what real power can do, Kauis. So when the time comes, you know what to do with it."

The man's eyes opened again to reveal glowing green irises, and when he spoke, his voice was different. Darker and slightly distorted. "You love this creature."

It wasn't a question, but an observation.

The man caught Kauis by the shoulders and led him towards Greer, dropping him beside his dying companion. Kauis reached out a hand and Greer's beak brushed his fingertips. The smell of iron stung Kauis' nose as he took a deep inhale at the same time Greer did.

Kauis heard the man shuffle around them before sighing loudly. "Love is a hindrance, much like this bond you two share. If I cannot save you both, I will save only you, Prince Enrel. You are too valuable to me."

Kauis gathered enough strength to rasp, "I will leave my body if you do not save him first."

If he let his soul shift now, it would not come back to his dying body. Nor to Greer's. It would float until it could attach to a new creature, or maybe it wouldn't. His soul might be too weak for that now.

The man chortled behind him. "A shifter elf bonded to an ancient creature from the old, forgotten realms. If I didn't know better, I would call this a gift from the gods themselves."

There was a lengthy pause, then he began to speak in a language Kauis did not recognize. Kauis ignored the banished man's chants and stared at his friend.

"I am with you," he pushed through the bond, before closing his eyes with the griffin's.

Kauis awoke to cold droplets of water on his forehead, rolling down his nose. He groaned and opened his heavy eyelids. Even with his elven vision, the darkness surrounding him was too thick to make out where he was. Kauis opened his mouth and swallowed thickly. His tongue was heavy and his lips were dry and cracked. He sniffed the air and scrunched his nose at the stale, putrid air. It was cold, his neck and face tight from the frigid atmosphere. But his backside was warm. Kauis pressed further into the warm wall he had been resting on to take away his chill.

A puff of hot air blew out over him before an irritated grumble shook the ground beneath him. Kauis turned and ran his hands over Greer's side, feathers and fur tickling his fingers.

"You're alive," Kauis whispered. He scratched behind Greer's long, catlike ears and smiled as the griffin turned his head to further lean into his fingers. "How are we still here?"

Kauis reached for the bond to feel for Greer's emotions, frowning when nothing happened. Dropping his hand he closed his eyes and tried again. The same, unfamiliar feeling of fear hit him with such force that he gasped and clutched his chest, opening his eyes to find Greer eyeing him with narrowed glowing green eyes, like the tainted beasts of the Wylan Woods.

Kauis reached a hand out to his companion and tried to feel for their bond, only to be hit with another wave of dread. "Who did this to you?"

"I saved him."

Kauis spun around to find a glowing lantern illuminating what looked to be a cave surrounding them. The light bobbed as it neared, brightening the surroundings the closer it got. Kauis took a step back towards Greer protectively and bared his teeth.

A deep laugh echoed and bounced around him. The man he had met in the forest stepped into the light. Without the cloud of death hovering over his mind, Kauis recognized him instantly.

Ulrond, the Disowned Deity of Chaos, smiled at him. "Do not worry, prince of old. I am not here to hurt you. I am here to help you."

CHAPTER 31

WILLA

An irritating buzzing sound had Willa slapping the air near her ears. Sitting up with a startled rasp, every bone argued with her sudden, rattled movement. Her neck and throat ached, along with the rest of her body, and she tried to stand, only to slip and fall back onto a steaming pile of warm liquid.

Pieces of skin and leather were scattered about, black blood steaming near her boots, which were covered in a thin iridescent slime. She lifted her shaking hands to find her palms still glowing beneath a layer of sticky, brown liquid. Noises from above cut through the dull ringing in her ears and she found multiple green eyes watching her, like before.

She ran without a second thought of what had happened and how she could still possibly be alive. Something whizzed past her face, narrowly avoiding her cheek, and Willa gasped, ducking before hearing a thumping sound behind her. She looked back to find an arrow sticking out of a fallen beast on the ground. Its eyes blinked at her before closing and drawing a rattled breath.

Willa turned and pushed back into a run, searching the dark rows of trees for whoever or whatever had shot at the beast, but found nothing.

Something grabbed at her from behind a tree and she yelped as strong hands pulled her back. Despite her attempt to shake them off, warm fingers covered her mouth and nose, an arm wrapping tightly around her chest and pulling her closer to the tree's trunk.

She let out a muffled shout against the hand clasping onto her, which only had their fingers tighten around her with more force. Whatever held her shifted, and the sensation of warm air prickled around her nose. She had witnessed it in the Temple of Domnhall. She had been ensnared from it at Merellian's touch. *Magic.*

Willa inhaled sharply and wiggled. The energy was so sudden she nearly sneezed, but the hand covered her nostrils as if it could feel her about to do so.

"Do not move," a deep, male voice commanded lowly in her ear.

A lilting accent, much like the elf Merellian, had her quaking in his grasp. The voice was aged and dark, demanding respect with those three clipped words. She had been found.

Her eyes widened over the hand clinging to her as she thought of the metal hair clip. But red, sticky curls waved in front of her vision. She didn't have it. The lake did. She wanted to laugh at the irony of it all. The hair piece had sunk to a forgotten lake, much like Claire had in the Minison. Her friend's secrets of whatever the broken star was and whatever it meant to the elves would die with the both of them now. Hidden in deep waters.

A tear ran down Willa's face as she accepted her fate. She even thought of Ivaan as her heart twisted in pain. So much loss in such a short amount of time. And she was in the middle of its storm.

A loud warble of a cry cut through her drowning thoughts. The sound was answered by several wings snapping and pushing through the trees around her and Willa shifted, looking around wildly. The bat-like beasts flew on either side of the tree and sturdy body she was pinned to. They passed without a second glance, winding their way through the forest in front of her, calling out to one another as they did.

The sweltering layer of magic seemed to thicken as the creatures flew past them, unaware of her and her mysterious captor. Like a dry, summers' day with little breeze, or a tight woolen blanket, it covered the top of her head, all the way down to her soaked toes.

Willa tried to turn her head to watch the creatures but the arm around her chest tightened to hold her still. Again, the deep voice whispered above her ear. "I said, don't move."

A vivid memory flashed before her eyes as the steeled edge of her captor's voice reminded her of Merellian once more. The thought of him pinning her to the ground with strong hands squeezing her neck, filled her with blind panic. Her throat seized with the recollection, as if the elf's ghostly hands were crushing her now. Fear had Willa kicking at her captor. Surprised, he loosened his grip enough for her to fall forward.

A beast flying over her shoulder turned. She had been spotted. It flew towards her with green glowing eyes, chirping loudly as it did. She gasped and shielded herself with her arms before she was pulled back into the buzzing blanket of magic. A hand lifted out in front of her face towards the beast still nearing them with snapping teeth. A sudden burst of shadows, darker than the pockets of night between the distant trees, snapped from the outstretched palm. The flying beast screeched and reared back with a quick flap of his wings, but the shadows continued to flow from her captor's hand.

She watched helplessly as another hand closed around her mouth, pulling her closer. Warm breath tickled her neck as she watched the shadows crawl like tiny beasts from her nightmares through the trees. Up and up the shadows grew until she could see nothing but black mist before her. Loud screeches of pain echoed through the mist, followed by breaking, popping, and snapping sounds of guttural cries and warbles.

Willa stared at the hand stretched out in front of her with wide, terrified eyes, watching markings along the tanned wrist glow a deep blue color, like Minison water lines running in his veins. Willa shifted behind the hand holding her firmly and whimpered.

"Stop it." The voice was strained and angry. Very angry.

A creature's cry rang out before a sickening crunch silenced it. His magic was doing this. Killing those beasts with a simple, raised hand.

This was a worse fate than by the vile hands of Merellian. Fear bit at her insides, making her squirm, and she jabbed her elbow into the body behind her. His hand loosened on her face, allowing her to lean forward. If he was busy killing these beasts, she could try and run from the true killer latching onto her now. She had somehow managed to survive the flying creatures before. Maybe Claire's fishing knife was truly blessed by Nathayus himself. Maybe luck would help her one more time.

She kicked at him again, harder this time, and was dropped instantly. But she fell into the dark shadows coming from her captor's hand. The trees looked darker within the black shadowed mass, enveloping her in rolling waves of ink. Willa took a hesitant lunge forward before a large shadow figure lurched towards her. It stopped before touching her and dissipated.

A voice crooned in the moving, inky mist, "Willa!"

Willa spun around and whimpered. It was her father's voice.

She started to run, but another shadowed figure stepped in front of her.

"Wild, wild Willa, come to play at last!"

Willa grabbed her ears and crumpled at the voice of Ivaan Jepsen.

Strong arms laced around her waist, hoisting her up through the dark, teasing shadows. Willa kicked at the captor, but went limp in his arms when his angry voice yelled, "Don't fucking move or I will kill you."

She closed her eyes to hide from the shadows still whispering and teasing her with the voices of her past. Then she was falling, dropped to the ground like a sack of flour. Willa rolled onto her back and groaned. Opening her eyes, she looked at her captor.

An elf stared down at her with enchanting, forest green eyes, haloed in a shimmering silver color, beneath knitted brows and a deep scowl. Dark brown curls covered most of his forehead, but what captured her gaze was the glowing, white and blue lines crawling across the olive skin of his neck in swirls and patterns of leaves and curling ferns, towards his strong cut jaw. They were breathtaking. *He* was breathtaking.

His strong, ageless features twisted when his eyes finally met hers. A lethal calm sat in his narrowed gaze before icy contempt washed over him. With one dark and impaling stare, Willa knew, with calm finality, this elf would be the one to take her life.

The elf mumbled something, in a language much like she had heard Merellian use, but she barely had time to take a breath to speak before the scent of hot and heavy magic overwhelmed her, pulling her into a deep slumber.

Sorean studied the girl near his feet with caution. Bile bubbled in his throat from the stench clinging to her torn clothing. She was covered in remnants of Vokreat. Nasty creatures who haunted the forest in the night, mimicking the sounds of birds. Practically blind without the glowing green magic pulling their line of sight, they hunted on scent and noise alone. He should have known better.

Reaching out a finger, he pulled a tangled clump of vibrant red hair away from her cheek to find her ear. The tainted beast's stomach lining coated her damp mess of curls, held together in tangles of braids and knots. Tucking the hair back, his scowl deepened from her round, simple ear. Not pointed like an elf or faerie.

A mortal this far into the Wylan Woods? Impossible.

He recoiled, as if she were the poison coating the arrows hanging from his back. Her cloak was barely hanging on to her, covered in thick, black blood. His lips curled in disgust as he roamed his way back up to her pale, plain face. Light brown freckles covered her narrow nose and cheeks. A few even lined her chapped lips.

None of the bestiaries could have prepared him for a mortal. There were no drawings of them within all the notes and books lining the catacombs at home. None, save for the few drawings of the old mortal kings. Her pale skin lacked the immortal glow the two races seemed to emit. Her hair was dull and her features were less sharp and clear cut. She was so ordinary, aside from her mass of vivid hair and freckles. Her body was shorter than any faerie he had ever encountered, and although her frame held natural curves to them, she looked so...fragile. So weak. It somehow made her look innocent, even covered in Vokreat guts.

Remembering the stories of King Ammanar, Sorean stood, his skin crawling as he put distance between them. Mortals were far from innocent. What lay before him was the reason these woods were tainted. She was the reason for his hidden realm.

A deep hatred coated his vision as he watched her chest rise and fall. His air magic sat like a veiled bubble around her and every few seconds, he tightened the pocket of air to pull her further and further into a deep sleep. In a few minutes, the lack of oxygen would ruin her mind and not allow her to wake again. He leaned on the trunk of a tree as her breath quickened.

He would enjoy watching this. No mortal deserved an easy death.

His essence hadn't stopped moving, despite him calling it back. Iara was right. It had listened to him this time without question. But never had it stirred like this, directly beneath his skin. It insisted on staying there, too, no matter how hard he fought to push it down and lock it away. Sorean looked at his hands and rolled up his sleeves, eyeing the glowing plants and leaves amidst his prominent veins.

We like her. Her fears tastes sweet, Prince.

Sorean rolled his sleeves back down, his jaw ticking. Ignoring the whisper of his essence, he went back to watching the girl's death. Her breaths were slowing now. Any minute and she would be gone.

Her fingers twitched in the dirt, pulling his brooding glare away from her face, as something on her hand caught his eye. He didn't want to touch her, but his curiosity was too strong. Begrudgingly, he bent over, and reached for her wrist, turning it to look at her palm. That was certainly interesting. The Dawn of Harmony had been burned there—a large sunburst splayed out in light pink against her skin.

He dropped her wrist and scowled. The girl made a soft whimpering sound and twitched before letting out a breathy wheeze. Sorean reached for her other hand. A large northern star was sprawled across the palm. The Star of The Scales. Two symbols when put together, helped to create what the waters had whispered to Noi—the Key of Sanctity. Why would these symbols be branded onto a mortal girl?

The sound of hooves had Sorean pulling away from her freckled face. Iara and Harland were weaving their way towards him, his horse trailing behind theirs.

"What is that thing?" Iara called before sliding off her horse, mid trot. She jogged towards Sorean and the girl, freezing a few feet before them. "Is that a mortal?"

"She was being chased by a swarm of Vokreats. She somehow survived them." The girl was convulsing now. A satisfied smile crawled along Sorean's face as he watched her body jerk and twist on the forest floor. "Maybe they don't like the taste of mortal."

He thought of her marks and dropped his sneer. They had come to the Wylan for answers, and maybe she could help. Sorean sighed and lifted the magic blanketing her. He would kill her after finding out why she had the marks, and why she was so deep into the tainted woodlands.

"You stopped it? Kill her!" Iara spat at the ground and covered her nose. "She is no use to us."

Don't kill her, she's ours to play with. We've never met someone like her.

Sorean swallowed thickly, in an attempt to push his essence's curious whispers away.

"She smells terrible," Harland grumbled, covering his nose as well. "Her scent alone will lead any hungry creature to us."

Sorean looked at both faeries while he nudged the girl's hand towards them in the leaves. Harland crouched and cursed in their faerie language. Iara bent down to the girl's other side. She touched the girl with hesitation, as if the mortal would jump up and attack her like a crazed beast.

Iara frowned at the mark. "Mortals are more barbaric than I thought to mutilate their own bodies like this."

Harland grunted in agreement. "Do you mean to question her, or are we killing her in a different manner? Maybe having her for bait is not such a bad thing."

Sorean ignored Harland and Iara, staring at his still glowing marks while he wiped dirt from his pants.

"You used your essence again?" Iara asked quietly.

Sorean nodded as he wiped slime off from his shirt. Holding the girl had proven to be quite revolting, and now he was covered in blood and guts from her clothing. "She surprised me by fighting back. She fell out of the veil I had put around us. A Vokreat caught it instantly and came for us."

Harland laughed. "She managed to surprise you? A mortal girl?" He grabbed his thighs and leaned forward to let out a bark of a laugh.

Sorean snapped, "I took care of it."

Iara stood and backed away from the girl. Wiping her hands, she ignored Harland's taunts. "I had wondered if it was you or something else. There are guts littering the trees and forest floor back there. Whatever Vokreats were chasing her, they are no longer."

Iara gave him an apologetic look, but Sorean kept his face neutral. He gave a hard nod and pushed away the thought of the sentries back at the cabin.

She spoke again, "We don't know what mortals have been doing while hiding from the shadows of the gods' wrath. I wouldn't trust a word from her mouth." Sorean clenched his jaw and listened while she turned to the horses. "She's better off dead, especially after being touched by the tainted creatures. We don't know what this magic can do to mortals, Sorean. This is a huge and unnecessary risk."

Iara was right. She usually was. There was a reason she was his second, no matter how much she irritated him with her harsh critique. But he had made up his mind.

"We will take her to Niarath Loch. The waters will not lie to us." Grabbing her waist, he lifted her up easily and hoisted her over his shoulders.

They rode all night in tense silence. Sorean had tied the girl's wrists together on the horn of his saddle to keep her upright while they traveled. Thankfully, nothing had latched onto her scent or theirs as they hurried to Niarath Loch.

They didn't reach the mythical waters until small trickles of dawn painted speckled dots along the forest floor. Stopping below a waterfall crashing into a dark lagoon, Sorean pulled the girl off and held her up with one arm beneath her legs and the other behind her shoulders. Her head lolled onto his chest and Sorean scrunched his nose at the still rotten smell of Vokreat guts upon her. She would sleep for some time, judging by how close she was to death by his magic. Her breaths had been deep and steady throughout the night. Dreamless. A small part of him envied sleep like that, for it was something he hadn't had in years.

His essence rolled beneath him as his gaze roamed the girl's freckled cheeks.

Let us play with her, Prince.

Sorean shuddered, ignoring the whispers. His horse eagerly trotted back towards Iara and Harland, who lingered in the trees behind him with watchful gazes.

"Send a signal if you see or hear anything."

The two fae nodded before scanning the trees surrounding them and the roaring waters.

Sorean adjusted the girl in his arms while stepping through the tall reeds circling the murky lake. Mud squelched beneath his boots and he slowed his steps, focusing on the rippling water. Mist hovered above the lake from the rushing waterfall, and humid air had sweat rolling down his neck. The air tasted sweet here, like freshly plucked flowers. But the sweet scent was dampened by the stench from the girl. He flared his nostrils and set her on the bank behind him, the half-smile resting on her face making him scowl.

When he turned back to the water, he was startled to find a tall man with long, silver hair standing in the middle of the lake. His head was cocked to the side, his expression one of faint amusement as he studied Sorean with brown, glittering eyes.

"Essence apart. Whispers true." The man's voice carried a unique force. It was timeworn and gentle, yet held a tone of command that only came with age.

The waters lapped eagerly towards the toes of Sorean's boots, as if desperate to taste or touch him, and he dipped his head slightly in respect. "I am here to confirm what the fox heard. I am here to inquire about the elves."

An easy smile played at the corner of the man's sharply lined face and he moved his head to look past Sorean. His hair shifted, showcasing a delicately pointed ear, much like his own. This man's ear was longer, sharper, even. For he was an elf. Shock jarred Sorean's senses with the realization. His hair stood on edge and his body tightened with rolling adrenaline. Sorean took a slow, defensive step away from the water.

The elf only raised both hands and let out a sharp, boisterous laugh. "I am only what you wish to see. The lake is a mirror of your deepest wants and desires."

He had no desire to speak to an elf. Only to know whether they truly were back.

"If I am seeing you, does that mean what the fox heard is true?" he asked hesitantly. "The elves are back?"

The elf studied the grass behind Sorean for a moment before focusing on him. He nodded with the same, odd smile, but said nothing.

Sorean frowned, crossing his arms. "And why have they returned?"

The elf watched him with a curious intensity before mimicking his stance. "You have had the answers within arm's reach all along, Sorean. You will not find them with me."

His eyes hardened, shadowing with infinite depth, as he looked Sorean up and down. Taking in a breath, the elf looked at the water before waving his hand towards Sorean. "Come. Step into the water. There are more pressing questions I sense in you now."

Sorean lifted his chin, ignoring the elf's evasion. Entering these waters meant giving a piece of yourself to the lake. According to legend, Niarath Loch was particular when choosing its endowments, depending on the answers one individual might seek. Some had brought family heirlooms, paintings, or jewelry to the waters for answers. Others were more drastic, giving up a piece of their magic or memory. Sorean wouldn't go into the waters. He had nothing to give.

He watched the rippling, murky water kiss the toes of his boots and bit out, "You say answers are within arm's reach, but I know nothing of the elves and their wants."

"What does your queen think of the elves?"

Sorean narrowed his eyes and cocked his head. The elf copied his mannerisms, his playful smiling widening into a mocking grin.

"Wouldn't you rather learn more about the marks upon your skin? And what sits hungry right beneath it?" The elf's eyes seemed to glow now as they danced along Sorean's arms before looking back up at him with a curious, raised brow.

A flicker of apprehension ran through Sorean. Could the lake truly give him the answers he had tried to find for centuries? And now that he had the chance to understand, did he really want to know what made him different from the rest of his family? Sorean looked at his hands in deep contemplation, his essence eagerly whispering about the mirage above the water.

As if hearing his essence's call, the elf laughed. The rich and throaty chuckle was loud enough to send ripples of water towards Sorean's feet.

He took a slow and careful step forward, allowing his boot to sink below the water's surface. The cold water sent a shiver through him as it touched his shins, sinking into his riding pants with little effort.

The mortal girl stirred behind him, stopping his hesitant walk. He furrowed his brows and grimaced. His questions were not important now. Maybe one day he would come back to the lake. Right now, he needed to know more about the elves and the mortal.

The elf sighed, as if understanding Sorean would not commit to entering the deep waters.

"So soon the girl returns to us and yet she has changed so quickly. Her paths are altered by the course of a new fate. But we have been enjoying the whispered stories from her token in her absence, while it rejoins the other gifts within our belly."

"She has been here already?"

The elf hummed in reply.

Sorean looked over his shoulder to where the girl lay. Watching her chest rise and fall, he pondered on what a mortal with nothing but tattered clothes could have given the lake to satiate its omniscient hunger. The elf had said 'rejoined', as if her token was a returning gift. But that would be impossible: to take and give the same item to these waters. Sorean turned his head from the girl and surveyed the lake's surroundings as the elf spoke.

"The fox speaks the truth. The elves are desperate because of mortals much like the one behind you."

"But why is she in the Wylan?" Sorean fixed his eyes upon the elf's glittering gaze once more. "No mortal should be here. And why would the elves be so desperate?" He recalled all the whispers Noi had heard, and hoped the elf before him would answer with clarity.

"Those two questions wield the same answer, Prince."

Sorean rephrased his question, trying and failing to hide his irritation as he asked, "Why is she here?"

"The elves are hunting her."

Finally, an actual answer. Sorean narrowed his eyes. "Why?"

"You'll find your answers with her in Lithelle, not the lake."

He tilted his head and let out a bitter laugh. "My mother will kill her on the spot."

The elf seemed to glide towards him with the same blade sharp tone. "Ask yourself why that is, Sorean Valkian. Why is she so quick to kill anything straying from her warm embrace? Or anything that enters her den?"

Fear made his mother paranoid. Fear and nothing else.

The elf continued coldly, "Fear is all consuming. You know this more than anyone. You battle with it every day. Yet you do not ignore it like your mother. Instead, you wish to learn more about it. You're eager to rid yourself of the unknown. Your road ahead may test you, Sorean."

Sorean nodded at the rippling water. "Like being crowned."

An agreeing hum from the elf had the water rolling towards him in soft waves. "A king bred to harbor balance tilts his scale to purge fate's pain."

Sorean half listened to the riddled words, leaning forward to better see his reflection. In the water, a crown sat upon his head, but something was off. He bent closer and studied the design upon his brow. Something dark glistened against its usually golden glow. He was close enough for his nose to touch the water when he realized it was blood that coated the crown. The red liquid dripped over his face as his reflection smiled wryly. Sorean failed to choke down his alarm and stumbled backwards through the water like a newborn fawn.

The elf's deep laugh crawled its way into Sorean's soul, nestling within his bones to shake him from the inside out. "Run along to Lithelle. Unless you are ready to ask what you really want to know."

The lake's mirage was sinking into the water now, the elf's legs disappearing like mist above the water until only his chest and neck stuck out from the middle of the lake. The silver hair floated around him like a blanket of white snow as he awaited Sorean's reply.

Sorean looked back to his reflection. Reaching a shaking hand to his forehead, he nearly sighed with relief to feel nothing was actually there. The elf's laugh nipped at Sorean's soaked heels as he turned his back on the riddles and tricks of Niarath Loch.

"Do not ignore those whispers for too long, Prince of the Scales," the elf crooned as Sorean picked up the mortal girl. His essence rolled beneath him in reply to the elf's warning and he left the lake with more questions than answers.

Willa was dreaming. The taste and feel of the vision around her was a familiar nightmare she had carried with her since her father's disappearance into the Wylan Woods.

Walking along an empty road, howls and moans harmonized throughout the trees. Something was tugging her along, as if a rope were tied loosely around her waist, pulling every few seconds to assure she kept moving. So she did. One foot in front of the other, she walked absentmindedly, not worrying over the haunting noises growing closer to her with every step.

She didn't stop her slow and casual walk until she reached the top of a hill. There was a valley below, filled with more trees and a rolling river. This was different from her dreams before. This was the actual Wylan Woods. It was a memory of where she had met the Wylan beast before falling into the river. But her clothing was fresh and clean. No guts or blood covered her. Perhaps she had died within the lake, and the rest had been a vision within the confines of death, and this was her tormented limbo—infinite visions of her demise.

Willa frowned, surveying the woodlands, when something new caught her eye at the bottom of the hill. There was a mound right before the rolling waters. The small hill was covered in grass and twigs, looking like a nest of some sort, for there was a gaping hole at the foot of it.

The tug along her waist pulled, and she listened. Step by step, she walked down the hill until she reached the curious mound. Crawling onto all fours, she peeked her head into the darkness of the small opening. The tug again came and soon she was falling through dark shadows. Whispering wails echoed around her as she plummeted through dark mist.

She landed with a loud *oomf* onto a bed of leaves. An empty, vast darkness surrounded her. Willa lifted her hands to her face, but she saw nothing as she did. The darkness was too thick and suffocating.

"Who is here?" A deep male voice called out in the dark.

It sounded so far away as it echoed to her in the black blanket pushing around her, that Willa said nothing, for it was only a dream. She got up from the bed of leaves and stepped forward into the murky tendrils. Spinning around, she squinted into the thick darkness, but was unable to adjust her eyes to the endless depths around her. Panic squeezed her lungs, forcing her breaths out in quick and heavy pants.

A clapping noise made her jump, but a blue light appeared, floating above her head. The curious ball of light, no bigger than a bug, flitted around until it exploded. The light broke off into multiple, tiny fragments, looking like stars twinkling in the sky. She watched them with quiet trepidation, calming her building panic.

Adjusting to the sudden light, Willa blinked and spun around slowly. She seemed to be in a dark cavern of sorts; condensation along the stone walls rolling in slow drips.

The sound of rustling fabric had Willa turning towards a large dais. On it was a stone throne, and on the throne was a man wrapped in shadows. The shadows were moving around him so rapidly she could hardly make out any features.

"Who are you?" The man's stern voice came from the center of this shadowed storm, twisting and breathing upon the stone.

Willa countered curiously, "Who are you? This is my dream, after all."

The man grunted as if annoyed. "I could say the same to you. Everything was going quite peacefully until you landed here, stumbling around so loudly, my head nearly exploded from your stomping and dramatic panting."

Willa blanched. "So, what? You were sitting in the dark before this? On a throne, no less?" She crossed her arms and studied the little balls of twinkling light. "If my trying to figure out where I ended up in my own night terror was...dramatic, you sitting in a dark hole in the ground with no noise and light is the most dramatic form of brooding I have ever witnessed."

The shadows around the man on the stone throne seemed to twitch a bit at her words, slowing down enough for her to make out a tight lipped frown. But the shadows covered the rest of the face too quickly for her to get any sort of clarity on who he was or what he looked like.

"You may leave whenever you wish to my... brooding, if that's what you call it."

Willa lifted her chin towards the man hiding in the shadows. "I think *you* should leave."

"If I leave, so does the light," He countered quickly. "And you'll be stuck in the dark again."

"Oh, *great* lightbringer, please don't go." Willa raised her hands to the lights, spinning around before laughing dryly. "Please. I've been through worse things than the dark."

The man clapped and the blue, twinkling lights were gone.

Whispers came suddenly. Familiar ones, much like from night terrors in the past.

"Willaaaaa. Ah, hello old friend." The owl's voice crooned inside of her mind. *"Come to find your father?"*

Willa tried to stay calm, but the voices grew and grew until she eventually dropped to her knees with her hands over her ears. She knelt there for an eternity as the whispers fed her fear.

The shadowed man's presence hovered in front of her, as if to revel in her cowardly display so soon after she had mocked him. He eventually sat beside her and sighed before clapping to let the blue light hover and expand above them once more.

"Even I couldn't have made up those horrific voices," he mused quietly.

Willa dropped her hands, blinking up at the light, and gathered herself.

The man nudged her side, still ensconced in shadow, and asked, "So, you're not my own imagination?"

Willa shook her head. Tears were falling from her face, she realized. Embarrassment flooded her. After all, she had asked for this. Said she could deal with the darkness and now look at her. She focused on the twinkling lights, feeling the man's clouded eyes observe her as she did.

She heard his breath hitch before the shadowed figure pushed into a stand and backed away from her with fluid steps.

"Oh, I recognize you." His voice was chilling as he let out a dry laugh. "This is my own making, then. I'm being haunted in my sleep, is that it?"

"What do you mean?" Willa stood and followed the shadows returning to the stone seat.

"You are the very mistake which has altered my course for the worse."

Willa halted and frowned. How could she be a mistake to a person she had never met?

The shadowed form plopped onto the stone throne dramatically.

"Back to brooding?" she scoffed.

"If you are of my own making, I shall simply ignore you until I awake."

Willa tilted her head to the side, raising a hand to push back a few curls hovering over her cheeks. "Is this how you handle all affairs?"

"How did you get those marks?"

Willa paused and looked at her lifted hand. The brands glowed softly beneath the blue lights. She tucked her hand into her other arm and crossed them in front of her chest. "I believe fear sometimes makes monsters. I brought out both in a man who holds too much power."

She thought of Lord Nalore and her family, hoping her mother and twin were still alive. She would give anything to see their faces again.

The man hummed. The noise was graveled and muffled by the moving shadows around him. "Power can also reveal who is a monster."

Her mind went to the elf Merellian and she shuddered. "Yes."

"Look at me," the male's voice commanded with a deep, unnerving vibrato.

Willa obliged and was met with the swirling shadows only inches away from her face. She took a hesitant step back and whispered, "I cannot see your face or form. You are covered in darkness."

Though she could not see his eyes, his hidden gaze had the hair on the back of her neck standing at attention. "You are the reason I am wrapped in darkness now."

Through the mist, Willa watched with wide eyes as a large, pale hand appeared. She moved her head away, but the hand paused right in front of her. Slowly it lifted, as if to touch her cheek. She twitched as the fingers grazed her skin before pushing back a strand of her red curled hair.

"I can hardly see you with all of this hair in front of your face." Two fingers ran through the curl Willa hadn't noticed laying lazily over the bridge of her nose. The pale hand pulled it behind her ear before sinking back into the shadows. "Your hair is like blood."

Willa bristled. "That is the worst compliment you could ever give a woman."

"It wasn't meant to be one." His answer was all too serious before he asked, "Where are you now, freckles?"

Willa rolled her eyes. "I have a nickname now, too?"

Despite herself, her lips twitched in amusement. She didn't have many nicknames, and none that were kind.

"What other nickname would you have me say? Outcast, perhaps?"

Willa's budding smile faltered. Her brows rose and she opened her mouth to speak, but the shadows lunged for her.

"Or maybe Murderer? It's a fitting title, is it not?"

"I don't know what you're talking about," she choked out as she clumsily backed away from the shadows moving faster now before her.

The blue twinkling lights were beginning to dim, one by one, slowly drenching the two of them in the thick darkness once more.

The voice laughed darkly. Bitterly. "Tell me where you are and I will make your death swift when we meet again."

Willa bit out her reply with a shake of her head. "I am stuck in a cave with a brooding man made of darkness."

The voice laughed darkly before the shadows raced for her, and Willa screamed as they enveloped her whole.

Willa had always enjoyed the feeling of sailing, despite her fear of swimming within the waters below the boat. The way the waves rolled and the wind pushing you forward... It was an easy rhythm for her body to fall into. The rhythm was relaxing and the open water was freeing, if only for a few minutes or hours. She had never traveled far across the Minison, only a handful of fishing excursions across the rocky bays with Claire and her crew.

Sighing as the boat swayed beneath her, Willa leaned back against the wooden mast, allowing nature to run its course and lead her wherever it wanted to go. The wooden pole was so firm and so warm. It kept her steady while the rolling water tugged beneath her. Willa's core hummed as she leaned back and nuzzled into it. She sighed and turned her face towards the water to feel the warm, humid breeze tickle her skin.

A dry cough came from behind her and the pole she was desperately trying to snuggle up against shifted, jolting her awake.

Willa lurched forward, sliding from what she'd thought to be a boat. A pull at her wrists held her up as a mane of thick hair bobbed before her, whinnying as it trotted through the thick trees. She gagged as something dry sat across her tongue, stopping her from making any noise.

Letting out a muffled yell through the cloth, she spun her shoulders back, only to find herself sliding to the other side too quickly. A hand grabbed her hip and pulled her back into an upright position. Willa froze and stared at the moving creature below her legs. She had heard of horses before, but had never seen or rode one. Traifton had no use for them. Her stomach lurched. They were so far from the ground—she hadn't realized they were so large. And her clothes were different. A thin blue tunic with a high collar and loose sleeves fell well past her waist. Black, thick pants made of wool clung to her thighs. Her boots were her own, but they had been cleaned.

Her brows pinched together as she studied herself. One moment she was in the beast, suffocating, and the next she was running. Covered in its guts. An elf had found her. Willa let out a muffled gasp and shifted forward with a lurch. The hand still gripping her hip tightened.

"Must you always wiggle?" the same, deep voice that had found her in the woodlands asked with irritation.

Willa turned her head to look over her shoulder. An arm wrapped around her waist as she did to keep her from sliding on the leather, continuously shifting beneath her.

She did her best to glare at her captor before taking in his features. Unruly brown curls bobbed atop of his forehead. His sharp and high cheekbones glistened with humid condensation, his nose perfectly straight, with skin practically glowing in beautiful olive tones. Yet the silver rimmed eyes watching her were cold. No emotion lay within them as he let her study him.

Willa found herself searching for those patterns on his neck, remembering them from the last time she saw him. The markings were still there, but now they were pale and white, almost like scars. She narrowed her eyes and assessed them further. She didn't remember them looking like that before. Before, they were dark, living, breathing things on his skin. She remembered the dark magic he conjured. Shivering, she followed the markings on his neck up into his curly hair to find a pointed ear. *Elf.*

How long had she been sleeping? It could have been days—weeks even. Her body was well rested despite her foggy mind.Willa shifted forward to gain distance from her elf captor, but his arm only tugged her back towards him. Her back hit his chest and he chuckled.

"Where do you think you could go that I would not find you?" Warm breath tickled her neck as he said quieter over her shoulder, "Even your breaths beneath the cloth in your mouth are loud enough to be heard from miles away. You cannot hide from me."

Willa bared her teeth over the cloth gagging her and twisted her torso to better face him. The elf was smirking at her. A small dimple appeared in his cheek when she deepened her scowl, and before she could figure out a better plan, Willa reared her head back and rammed her forehead against his.

Her mistake. Gods, was he made of stone? Willa bounced off him so hard, she toppled off the side of the horse before he could catch her.

She groaned, or tried to make a noise, but the cloth in her mouth was tight, making her choke upon it as she landed with a loud thump. A laugh echoed above her as she coughed into the cloth and rolled onto her side on the dirt.

A horse trotted past, and on it was another male elf. A roguish grin beamed beneath a large, bushy beard, long brown hair pulled back at the nape of his neck as he laughed down at her without stopping his horse.

Willa tried to sit up, but another horse kicked dust and dirt at her face. A female with long black braids, and dark brown skin to match, watched her through narrow, untrusting eyes. She slowed her horse enough to bare her pointed teeth at Willa before continuing.

Sitting up, Willa shook the dirt away from her hair and forehead. The elf captor slowly turned his horse to walk over to the other two riders. All of them whispered harshly to one another, none more so than the female elf. But her captor only raised a hand to silence their conversation. Willa sat helplessly and watched him slide from his horse in one smooth motion. He said something to his companions quietly before walking towards her with a deep scowl.

The elf made of stone stopped right before her and Willa slowly looked up, wincing at the slight ache from hitting him. The bastard smirked at her from where he stood, bringing his dimple back to life within his tawny cheek. Willa bared her teeth around the gag, but she knew there was nothing she could do. He was right. There was nowhere to hide.

He bent over and grabbed her bound wrists and clenched hands, fitting them easily inside one of his, making her feel even more helpless and vulnerable then she had before. Without any strain, he lifted Willa up.

He let go of her wrists as soon as she was standing upright and lifted his hand towards the material around her mouth. Willa shivered as his fingers trailed along her jaw before reaching for the knot resting on the back of her neck. Would he kill her now and be done with it?

They had to be going back to Traifton and Commander Enrel, but there was no telling where they were now. The trees around them all looked the same to her. She looked back to the other two on the horses and swallowed. She didn't recognize these three from the festival.

Her eyes flicked back to her captor. She would have remembered such a wicked, irritating smirk. The elf's fingers worked on the knot as he studied her throbbing forehead with a smug satisfaction before staring into her eyes. Willa managed to hold eye contact, taking the time to look at the silver circle encasing his green irises. If it weren't for the silver, their eyes would have been similar in color. But even now as he stared at her—into her—her mind panicked at the wild, unearthly look.

The gag loosened slightly, but the elf held onto the knot and lowered his brows before saying, "If you scream, I will tie you up to a tree and leave you for a Wylan beast to feast on your mortal flesh. Do you understand?"

What was worse? The beasts of the woods, or the monsters hiding beneath pretty, unsuspecting faces like this elf, or Merellian? A howl rang through the woods and Willa watched as his eyes shifted from hers to scan the forest before settling on her once more.

Willa gave a slow blink and lowered her chin slowly in submission. The elf's lips twisted into a small bud of a smile.

But his voice was still dark and forewarning as he said, "Good girl."

Those two words made Willa want to hit him again with her forehead. That arrogant dimple was back as he caught her deepening scowl and she fought the urge to tear it from his face. The elf's smile only widened, showing off his perfectly straight teeth, as he let go of the material and retracted his fingers from her neck.

Willa opened and closed her mouth a few times to wet her lips and tongue, now free from the material. The elf's smile settled into an aloof smirk as he grabbed her wrists with one hand, turning and pulling her into a walk.

Willa spit at the dirt beneath her feet and licked her lips. She would do anything for water now to get the taste of fiber out of her dry mouth and throat. "Are you taking me back to Traifton and Commander Enrel, then?"

The elf paused his fluid steps, nearly making Willa collide into his tall and formidable frame. "Commander Enrel?"

He turned his torso towards her, glaring at her from the bridge of his nose as he did.

Willa lifted her chin and drawled, "Yes, *elf*. Your commander. Commander Enrel. Isn't that what awaits me when I get back on your horse? If so, tie me up to a tree like you earlier promised. I will die here."

Merellian's bloodied face hazed her vision. She looked away to hide her trembling chin, as another howl bounced through the trees. It was daylight, for once, and Willa could better see how endless this forest was. It was less daunting in the little daylight they got beneath the forest canopy. But the rocks and roots still looked sinister in the eerie glow of green fog, creeping along the woodland's floor.

A tug at her wrists had Willa stumbling forward. The elf grabbed her by the crook of her elbow and hastily tugged her to the horses.

"I am no elf, mortal."

Willa's mouth dropped. But what else could he be?

He had an air of authority and the ageless appearance of an elf. An elf who demanded respect with his calculated looks and polished steps alone. His ears were pointed. Clearly he had magic. She had witnessed it herself. Even without having witnessed it, there was a dominating presence of power rippling off of his shoulders. It rolled towards her in thick waves of energy, prickling her skin instantly. And that unsettling energy focused on her as he met her wide eyes with an icy glare.

Willa averted her gaze, swallowing her nerves while his gaze bore into her. Even the horse nervously stepped away from him as he reached for the reins. A low warning sound came from his throat when he managed to grab hold of the reins and pull the horse closer to them, despite its protests.

Willa tugged her wrists from him, but his fingers tightened around her. "I can ride by myself."

The female on the horse beside them let out a dry laugh. Willa glared at her and the one smiling beside her. Both their eyes glittered with mischief.

Two hands swiftly threw her up onto the leather seat of the nervous horse and before Willa could grab the reins herself, two arms slid on either side of her and grasped the thin leather pulls. A clicking sound of a tongue was all she heard before the horse took off with a quick gait that had her tipping forward on the saddle from the sudden movement. A hand released the reins to pull her tied wrists over the knob of the seat.

"I think I'll stay on and make sure you don't fall off again, mortal," her captor murmured in her ear.

Willa snapped, irritated by his arrogance. "I have a name, *elf*."

"And I do not care."

Clicking his teeth he lifted the reins, urging the horse beneath them to move faster. Willa grabbed onto the knob to hold steady while the horse quickened his pace. She could hear little else aside from the thunderous hooves close behind them and the tree branches snapping past them as they went. But she did hear another eerie howl call out from the trees. She looked out to the forest, but saw nothing aside from rows and rows of trees and hills.

"Where are you taking me, elf?" she asked, but her words were swallowed by the rush of wind.

A warning snarl rolled along her neck and Willa winced, remembering their ears and keen senses. She shifted forward, trying to distance herself from him, but his hand let go of the reins and reached for her chin. With a swift tug, he turned her cheek so she could see him as he leaned forward.

"Listen to me, *mortal*. I am not a fucking elf. We are the fae." His fingers pinched into her chin hard enough for tears to sting her eyes before he let go.

Willa gasped and turned away from him to hide the shock on her face. His hand moved over her shoulder and side before gripping her hip. A sudden rush of heat crawled along her back as he pulled her closer to him.

"And we are taking you to my queen."

CHAPTER 36
KAUIS

Kauis stood and stretched his rigid limbs while Greer flew into the cavern. The griffin landed with soft steps before tucking his wings into his side, and Kauis snarled at the man sliding from his companion's back. He tried to move towards him, but the chains around his ankles, muting his magic and strength, held firm.

The banished god answered his feral noise with a laugh as he stood beside Greer. "His wing is almost healed. He will be able to fully use it within a week's time."

Ulrond patted Greer's side and, as the griffin clicked his beak and looked down at him with his glowing, green eyes, Kauis fought to hide his revulsion, watching the two speak with one another.

Ulrond nodded and stepped back. "I always wondered what it would be like to have my magic touch a creature like this."

Anger blurred Kauis' vision. His shoulders heaved with the rage reverberating through him. How dare he act like this cursed magic was his own.

Ulrond reached up and swept a hand over Greer's tucked wing. "The griffins could have become deities of their own if they'd held more ambition. I met this one before, you know. Long before you were ever born. He was a rabid creature in those days, one of the fiercest. I also remember *you* being a bit unmanageable when we met in the kingdom." He laughed as he recalled. "Your trainers wanted nothing to do with you and your disorderly temper. But it seems you have settled, and in the process trained this beast to be no better than a common pet. We'll have to change that."

Greer gave an eager chirp in response before looking over at Kauis. The two stared at one another for a long moment and Kauis shifted uncomfortably as those glowing green eyes bore into him. He had tried for nights now to reach out to Greer through their bond, but each time he was met with a wall of fear and anger. The Greer he knew was fading within the confines of the gods' cursed magic. Magic Ulrond had used to save him. To save them both. Their bond was still there, but tainted. Unrecognizable. Much like his companion.

Ulrond followed Greer's gaze and asked Kauis, "Have you thought about my offer?"

Kauis tried not to flinch as Ulrond smiled, his eyes shifting from black to glowing green.

"Never." He spit at the ground near his shackles and crossed his arms, lifting his chin toward the four glowing orbs of emerald light coming from both his companion and the rogue deity. "You desecrate the gods by using their magic. Especially you, who was cast out. What you are doing is abhorrent."

"Yet, it is why you are here now. Your companion lives because of what I've done. And because he lives, so do you. You should be grateful." The deity sighed and stepped away from Greer. "I had hoped a few days alone would help you come to the conclusion that we both want the same thing."

Kauis pressed the back of his head on the cavern wall and scoffed. "Do not act like you know me or any of my wants. We are nothing alike."

"Why did you come back to Kalandrae, Prince?"

Kauis rolled his eyes and looked away.

"Your essence is not what it once was, Kauis. I can feel the change in you. I'm sure it is like this for all the elves now, after so long." Ulrond stopped walking and looked around the cave with a sigh, "You are desperate. I once was, too. I was so desperate that I got myself banned from the gods' council and grace. You were there that night, you saw me leave."

Kauis shifted over the stone and glowered at the god. He had been there. His whole family had. The memory had left a burning imprint on him, for it was the first time Kauis had seen Velithor, the dragon God of Justice.

No one knew why Ulrond was banished. No one asked. Being the God of Chaos, most assumed he had gone too far in his bargaining and balance shifts. Deities like him only existed to keep the balance in check with the gods themselves, but they were temperamental and fickle creations. Never to be trusted. Most had said good riddance to the deranged god. Kauis would never forget Velithor's roar as Ulrond had rolled down the steps of Domnhall's castle.

"You have changed much since I last saw you, Kauis. But the same look remains in your eyes."

Kauis asked sharply, "Which is?"

"A vendetta sits in your gaze. I saw it the night your father was killed." Ulrond tilted his head and stared at Kauis, unblinking, as if he were searching for what he spoke of.

Kauis leaned forward, the memory of his father's death dampening his rising temper, and icing his question with a bitter frigidness. "You were there?"

Ulrond finally blinked and nodded. "You were angry. Rightfully so. But even I paused when I saw the burning hatred upon your face. You want revenge for what was done to your father. I, too, want revenge, Prince."

Yes. He did want revenge, but he needed to make sure he would survive long enough to find out what had really happened to his father. He needed to get power for him and his people first if he wanted to continue to feed the questions burning inside of him.

"If you seek revenge against the gods, you have already won. They are gone and you are free. You even have their magic now to use as your own. What else would you want?" He shifted to rub his ankles where the chains chafed his skin, watching as Ulrond paced the cave before him.

"My father is gone," Kauis continued harshly. Merellian was gone, dead by the hands of a mortal, much like his father. And now Greer, the last bit of family he had left, was changing right before him. "Nothing will bring him back. And I am not a prince. There is nothing to rule. I am merely an elf trying to help my race survive."

"Nothing to rule?" Ulrond repeated. He beamed with a crazed grin, lifting his arms and spinning in a circle as he laughed chaotically. "Look around, Kauis! It is as you said, the gods are gone. Everything is ripe for the taking. You will see soon enough that our wants are the same. That *we* are the same."He turned to walk back to Greer. "A few more days with those chains should help you understand what true desperation feels like."

SOREAN

The girl fell asleep against his chest as they raced through the Wylan Woods. Whatever had been chasing them at the start gave up after an hour of trailing them. Sorean was grateful for that. The girl was enough of a handful when she was awake and would only get in the way of fighting a Wylan beast. Again, he thought of how he'd found her and frowned. If they had more time here, he would have liked to witness what she would do against a creature, so he could understand how she managed to stay alive the last time.

Sorean's curiosity about the girl was nothing compared to his essence's constant stream of wonder. It refused to stop stirring and itching under his skin, the puzzling whispers becoming more and more frequent the further they traveled. Iara had always said his magic was smart, but each time he was near the girl, its whispers surprised him. A simple look towards the mortal, had his essence purring, jealous he could touch her and it could not. It made sense, considering Sorean had never met a mortal, but the constant nagging within him was beginning to weigh heavily on his nerves.

The ground inclined the further they went. Dirt shifted to crumbled rock and roots as they traveled north, back to the Menyamere Mountains. He didn't dare stop until night had fallen, as the terrain was too rocky for the horses to continue in the dim red light of the moon. A night's rest would do them all good before they got back to Lithelle.

The mortal twitched slightly in his arms, murmuring something softly in her sleep. She was dreaming, he realized, as he slid from the horse and pulled her off the saddle. Iara and Harland were already creating a fire and rolling out bedding as Sorean carried the mortal towards them.

Iara's back remained turned to him as she said, "She mistook us for elves."

"An egregious mistake," he replied sarcastically. "There is no mortal alive today who has met a faerie. She is the first in centuries."

Iara grabbed a leather canteen from her pile of belongings and drank from it. "Meaning she has already met the elves to compare us to one. Perhaps she is a spy, sent out into the woods for us to find. Maybe they suspect we already have the Key of Sanctity and are trying to draw us out. The elves are strong enough to control minds with their form of magic. The mortal might not even realize it and that is why she still lives."

Harland snorted before sitting across the fire from them both. "You are too paranoid, Iara. The elves would not use a mortal for a spy. They are not smart enough, and it would be a waste of magic on the elves' part."

"And yet one killed an elf long ago," Iara retorted. "And this one is somehow smart enough to be breathing in a place trying to steal the air from her lungs quicker than you can say faerie wine."

Harland stopped his laughing to roll his eyes, looking up at the trees while he pulled from his bottle.

"She has strange markings on her skin, much like what the elves have been searching for according to Noi." Iara growled in irritation and turned to pull back her blanket. "They *are* smarter than we think. They have had to survive without magic, so intellect is all they can rely on. Don't be so dull. The both of you."

Sorean gave a pointed look to Harland who fought to hide his smile as they listened to her. It was better to let her rant than to cut her off when she got on a roll like this. Iara's wrath was unprecedented sometimes, scaring even Sorean in the years they'd known each other.

Iara continued, "Sorean, the lake said to bring the girl to Lithelle for answers. But do you really believe Queen Morielle will accept a mortal being into the realm? We all know this girl will be dead the second we enter."

Sorean looked at the girl in question. She continued to mumble in her sleep beside his hip, her lips moving with soft breaths. He wondered what she was dreaming of to have such a calm look upon her face.

His essence reared its head within his mind, loud enough to dizzy Sorean.

She's ours, not hers.

Sorean shivered from the sudden cold sweat kissing his brow. A wave of heat rippled inside him, as if his essence was actually angered by Iara's words.

She is not yours, Sorean responded internally. His stomach rolled in rebuttal, but the sudden flash of warmth was gone.

Iara pulled him away from his worrying magic as she continued, "And if she is a spy, she will know where the realm is. They could be seeing through her eyes now! Even if she dies by white fire, the elves will know where we are immediately and could come looking for us next."

"Sorean, she has a point," Harland said across the orange flames.

How quick he was to take Iara's side. Sorean scowled at him. But the lake had asked him similar questions, as to why the queen would want her dead instantly. Out of fear and paranoia, yes. But any ruler would want to know how a mortal had survived so long. They would want to know everything happening outside of their realm to always stay one step ahead. She couldn't kill her. Sorean refused to believe it. So he answered them both with a quiet finality.

"I was told the answers are closer than I anticipated. Revelations my mother may have kept locked away. At the very least, this girl could answer what all three of us have wondered for centuries."

He looked to Iara as he voiced what they had often discussed in Lady Talarin's tavern after one too many drinks. "Are my mother's fears warranted?" He shook a curl away from his head and sighed. "We have seen the monsters now. The lake speaks the truth of what Noi said. We will bring our proof to her in court and the rest of the faeries. This girl is a living piece of what we have hidden from. I want to see what she does when faced with a mortal again. Even if she kills her right away, I want to know why. She will kill her easily with fire, proving our strength. Strength we have wasted on veiling our realm instead of actually doing something. I just want to understand. Even if it means sacrificing this girl to gain clarity."

It was cold to say, but true. A necessary death if it came to it before he would willingly take the title and step in for his mother.

Harland grunted his agreement and Sorean fought to hide his smile as he waited for what Iara would say.

She only laughed. "And after? We will be punished for bringing her to the realm. For sneaking out into the Wylan. Don't presume she won't hesitate to bring you down, even days before your coronation. You have siblings you know. Any one of them will be more eager to rule than you ever were."

"The girl is proof enough that something is going on. Something we cannot ignore." Sorean wrung his hands together and continued, "If the girl was with the elves or even saw them, it should be enough for the queen to listen before killing blindly."

Iara lay back and rolled away from him. "Your love for your mother blinds you from her wrath, Sorean. We will all be dead within a day's time by her flame."

She pulled the blanket over her head, ending their conversation.

Harland whistled and stood. "I think I'll take a piss and cover first watch. Veil us quickly, Sorean."

Sorean nodded as he walked away.

"And feed her," Harland called over his shoulder. "Mortals need to eat more than we do."

Sorean loosened a frustrated groan from his throat and closed his eyes, a quick pop echoing in both of his ears as he covered the camp and horses with his magic. When he was sure the veil was secure, Sorean leaned over to the sleeping girl and flicked her nose with his fingers. The girl's features scrunched at the soft flick, but she didn't wake. Sorean rolled his eyes and grabbed her shoulders. He shook her lightly, enough for her to jolt awake with a gasp.

The girl clutched her chest and looked around wildly before settling on him with sudden awareness. Her lips curled into an amusing, less than intimidating snarl as she looked him up and down. Sorean was in a sour mood from Iara and he didn't want to argue with the mortal now. He needed to sleep and hoped it would be dreamless.

He shoved an open bag of dried nuts and fruit into her tied hands and commanded, "Eat."

The girl looked at the open bag and sniffed its opening before wetting her lips with a dart of her tongue. "Water."

Sorean reached for Iara's leather canteen. Bringing the opening of the pouch to the girl's lips, she tilted her chin up eagerly, opening her mouth as water rushed out, splashing her face. She gulped greedily and sloppily, like a horse drinking from a bucket.

He pulled it away before she could puke it all up and plugged the top with the hanging cork. The girl moaned beside him and licked the moisture from her lips before digging into the bag of food.

"This would be easier if my hands were untied," she mumbled, lifting the open bag to her lips and chewing at whatever made it into her mouth.

"It seems you're doing just fine."

The girl glared at him, and Sorean sneered at the pathetic display as she made another attempt to shake the dried food into her mouth.

Sitting forward, he pulled out the knife he had found in her pocket. "Fine. Only because it pains me to see you act like an animal."

He spun the hilt within his fingers and the girl stared at it with an indecipherable look before leaning over to vomit up the water and food she had inhaled. Sorean's eyes bounced from the girl to the knife with confusion as she continued to dry heave. When she was done, she sat up and refused to look at him.

When was the last time she ate or drank? She had done both too quickly and her body had rejected it. He slowly moved towards her and she flinched, like a rabbit ready to run from a trap.

"Remember your promise?" Sorean threatened before freeing her from the rope.

The girl gave a small nod. Sorean swiped at the rope with her knife and, when he was done, he dropped the blade into the dirt between them.

He wanted to test what she would do. Food or fight first?

The girl didn't make a move for either option. Instead she stared at the fire with a glassy, far away look. She followed the dancing flames and rubbed at the red marks on her wrists before absentmindedly tracing the brands on her palms. A loud grumble came from her stomach. She glanced at him before leaning over and snatching up the bag of food.

Sorean stood and used his own canteen to wash away the girl's vomit in the dirt with pursed lips. Harland's light steps, as he circled their camp to survey the woodlands, had his pointed ears twitching while he cleaned the mess. When he was done, Sorean handed her the leather pouch of water and returned to his bed roll. She took it with a small nod and took three careful sips before wiping her mouth with the back of her hand.

Sighing, the girl wrapped her arms around her shins and rested her chin atop of her knees. "Why now, after all this time?"

Sorean cocked his head to the side and studied her profile. When he said nothing, she inched her chin towards him.

She narrowed her eyes at him and frowned before rephrasing her question, as if he hadn't understood it the first time. "Why have you returned? Or have you been in the Wylan all along and we were unaware of it?"

Sorean fought away his smile and answered like he would in court with the faeries. "We never left."

"That doesn't answer my question," the girl grumbled before looking away from him.

Sorean clucked his tongue against his teeth and leaned back on his palms. "We would be up all night if I answered that question, mortal."

She glanced his way, only to give him a deep scowl. That lifted Sorean's sour mood a bit. Her attempt to scare him was comical.

He looked up to the trees and said, "You and I both need our rest for where we are going tomorrow."

The girl mumbled something into her legs and Sorean raised a brow as he caught the curse words through his fae hearing. Bending forward, he reached for the knife between them, playing with the blade in front of his tucked shins. "How does a mortal defend herself against Vokreats and Wylan beasts with only a dull and rusted blade? What have you used this for, I wonder?" He gave her a sidelong glance. "And since this was all you had on you, I also wonder what you gave the waters of Niarath Loch."

"We would be up all night if I answered those questions, *faerie.*"

Sorean fought his smile, lifting the knife up to study it further. His ear twitched at the sound of her stomach rumbling again.

"I need to relieve myself," she said quietly.

She relaxed her legs and leaned back to stand, but Sorean stood before she could.

The girl frowned. "I won't be running from you. Not in these woods."

"I won't be taking any chances." He extended a hand to her, but she ignored it.

Groaning slightly, she pushed up into a stand by herself and stepped around the fire. Sorean followed as the girl stepped in between two trees.

"I can taste your magic all around me," she said over her shoulder. "What does it mean?"

"We are veiled. The camp is secure from the Wylan's curse."

The girl stopped and turned to him with a raised brow. "Then let me relieve myself in peace. I will not leave and have no need for watchful eyes if your magic covers me."

Sorean gave a frustrated snort but turned. He would hear her anyways with how loud she was. It pained him to listen to the girl's heavy footsteps. Did she realize how effortlessly annoying she was? He never thought something as simple as walking would grate his senses with such irritation. The sound of vomiting had his ears perking up. He planted his feet and listened while the girl puked again after relieving her bladder. He didn't move until she stomped past him with clenched hands. Sorean followed her back to the fire, nodding to Harland within the trees as he sat beside her.

"Are you sick?"

The girl wiped at her cheeks hastily, but Sorean caught a glimpse of the moisture resting along her dark brown lashes.

"Do you care?" Her voice was flat and lifeless.

No. Not in the slightest.

Sorean shifted. "I don't want you heaving on me in the night, or on tomorrow's ride."

She ignored him and continued watching the flames dancing to their own silent rhythm. He would give anything to be on watch like Harland instead of sitting in between Iara and this stubborn girl.

He sighed. "I have something to help you sleep so you don't keep us up all night."

"Just kill me."

"That would be a kindness for you." His lip curled up as he growled, "And I am not kind. You and your people do not deserve a quick death."

"Leave me to the beasts if I am so terrible." The girl turned to look at him and Sorean watched a slow moving tear track down her cheek. Her lower lip trembled slightly as she asked, "Why go through the trouble of feeding me and keeping me alive? Why take me to your queen if you hate me so much? I don't understand what you want. The only thing I know for certain is I have nothing to offer you."

She has much to teach us.

Sorean flinched at the sudden words echoing within.

What could a mortal girl possibly teach his essence? Thin tendrils of shadows edged his vision. Sorean closed his eyes, inhaling slowly to push away his magic, but the whispers persisted.

We've been alone for so long. We like her, Prince.

He was relieved to find no lingering shadows when he looked at the girl this time. But a headache was beginning to grow beneath his furrowed brows from his magic constantly rising and falling inside of him.

"You spoke of elves before—mentioned one's name as if you had known them personally. Our queen will want to know what you know. We keep tabs on the realms to keep our safety impenetrable to others. It is how we have stayed hidden for so long. Information is what we seek." His voice was cold as he said, "However, my company suspects you are a spy for the elves. If this is true, I will kill you now."

"I am not." She shook her head, wiping away the tears from her freckled cheeks. "I have met them, but I do not favor their kind. Please. I have no answers for you."

The fire's orange light danced in her eyes as she glared at him. The look was filled with such animosity, telling him she felt the same way towards his kind as well. The feeling was mutual.

She looked at the knife between them and whispered, "It would be better to kill me now, faerie. I fear what I've done to lead me here has ensured I will have nothing to return to. Killing me is not a kindness. But it is what I deserve. The ones I love are gone. Let me be with them and rest."

Sorean had never heard such pain before. So much sorrow dripped from those words. He watched as more tears fell from her face. He wouldn't kill her. Not now when they were so close to home. If Iara was right, the queen would grant the girl her somber wish before tomorrow's sun would set anyway.

To assure she wouldn't do it herself, Sorean grabbed her dull knife and threw it into the fire. The girl winced as it dropped into the flames, but she didn't reach for it or protest what he had done.

More tears fell and they bounced between her freckles like trail lines on a map. She was a hollow being. It could explain how she had survived; she was practically as numb a creature as the beasts around them.

The girl pinched the marks on her palms with her fingernails, hard enough to draw blood from the scarred lines. Sorean leaned forward, reaching a steady hand towards her clenched fingers. He wanted to ask her about the marks and if all mortals bore the same designs. She said she didn't have answers, but anything would help him when taking her to the queen. The girl caught his movement and flinched before looking down, realizing what she had done. She wiped the self-inflicted cut along her pants.

"You said you were from Traifton?" The girl nodded and he pried further, "And do you all have those marks?"

She spoke quietly, "No. Only I bear these reminders."

"Reminders of what?"

"To never disobey Traifton's council." She sighed through her nose and continued, "To stay away from the Wylan Woods." An empty smile pulled her trembling lips back as she looked out to the trees circling their camp. Her voice seemed to be dipped in the fae poison coating their arrows. "But it seems, even brandings don't work for those who are *wild*."

He looked to his second in command and mumbled, "Iara was right. You mortals are truly barbaric."

At least his mother offered a quick death by the white fire of her essence. To instill deep marks like hers would have guaranteed a slow, painful healing process which had to be worse than the receiving brandings to begin with.

Sorean leaned closer to her, sickened by the thought of mortals and their wickedness.

In one swift motion, before she could scoot away from him, he ripped away the bottom of her tunic. She looked down at the oversized shirt in shock, and as he reached for her bleeding palm, she tried to move away from him. Her breaths quickened, loud enough to make Iara stir beside them. He looked pointedly at her bleeding palm while holding out the piece of fabric but again, when he reached for her, she jumped, leaning further away.

Frustration curled his lips, stirring his restless essence in his stomach. She was terrified of him—rightfully so—but gods, she was stubborn in her fear.

Giving up, he threw the fabric onto the dirt between them and gritted out, "Wrap it yourself, then, mortal. Blood will only attract creatures and you don't want to get infected." Maybe she already was. Iara was right, there was no telling how this cursed magic affected mortals.

Ever so slowly, the girl grabbed for the cloth and wrapped her palm with careful movements. Sorean watched her curiously and noted the detail she put into making the knot upon her hand. It was well enough to pass inspection from the healers in Lithelle, making him wonder what she did for work in her mortal town.

When she returned to watching the fire, ignoring him, he continued to prod. "Is all of your family gone?"

"I'm not sure," she whispered.

Sorean pinched the bridge of his nose with a clenched jaw. He wouldn't get any more information from her; not tonight. He turned to rummage in his bag.

"I want to be very clear, girl," he said as he searched for the tonic to help her sleep. And in turn, to help him sleep without her constant wiggling and whining. "I do not like you."

"You don't know me," she scoffed. "And I have a name."

"I do not care," he replied with a snarl. "And it seems you don't care either with your persistent begging for death."

Sorean turned back to her, shoving the small vial into her hands. "Do not feed me your pitiful sob stories and expect me to pity you. *You* are the reason this forest is cursed. *You* are the reason the gods are gone. Your lost loved ones mean nothing to me when this map is clouded in darkness because of you and your people's mistakes."

The girl's wrapped hand trembled as she stared at the vial. He waited until she looked him in the eye to continue. "But I don't need you running off on your own to take death into your own hands when anything around you could kill you as easily as I could. You say you don't have answers, but anything you tell my queen will help us."

The girl narrowed her eyes, as if unsure where he was taking this when he proposed a small bargain. "If you will speak to my queen, I will send scouts to Traifton. Answers in exchange for answers. I will see if your family is alive, if you explain to my queen why you think they wouldn't have reason to be."

The girl's haunted, blurry eyes searched his with a sudden spark. Sorean let her silently chew on his words.

She pulled the cork from the vial and drank from it with one swift gulp. "I cannot go back home. It will be worse for them if I return. Assure me that my family is still alive." She shivered and said, "Then you will kill me."

CHAPTER 39

WILLA

Sweet smells of honey wafted around Willa as she sat up from the cold, hard dirt. Stretching her arms out, she yawned before letting out a shiver. The fae surrounding her were all sleeping. And the faerie male who had been sitting beside her when the tonic pulled her to sleep was now resting on a tree nearest to her. A small flask glistened in the moonlight atop his chest, his mouth open as he slept with his chin raised towards the night sky. Even in sleep he was striking. Handsome. Yet his natural beauty was tainted by his irritating attitude. The only thing keeping her from stealing his horse and running from camp was his promise to check on her family.

Willa looked up at the trees and noticed the red moonlight was more orange tonight. Tomorrow, it would return to its normal glow. Had she been gone for that long already? She tried to count the days, but everything since entering these woods had blurred together.

If she was correct in counting, today was hers and Tybalt's birthday. Twenty five years old. How she had survived her birthday, within the Wylan Woods, was beyond her. Was Tybalt alive to celebrate? What had the elves done when returning to Traifton? Ivaan was dead. Sentries were dead. Claire's ship was gone, as was she. Someone had to answer for what happened, and with Willa gone, she hated to wonder who would take the blame.

A voice came from the trees. "Willaaaaaaaa!"

Mother? Willa whipped her head around, searching.

"Willaaaaaa?" A different voice, yet one she knew all too well. Ivaan.

The deep, laughing voice of her father called to her next. "Willa!"

She let out a startled cry and, without hesitation, sprinted forward towards his voice. The tonic had helped her sore legs and arms, and there was hardly any pain as she ran past the sleeping fae commander and tore into the rows of trees.

Her father's voice called out again.

"I'm here!" she yelled.

"Willaaaaa!" A teasing, bubbly voice rang out.

Willa gasped. "Claire?"

She let out a choked laugh. It was so good to hear her voice. Willa let out another half laugh, half sob, and ran blindly past two more tree trunks. A large bush was before her, and on the other side an orange glow pushed through the thorns and brambles. A fire must have been causing the glow, her family had to be on the other side of this bush.

"Come on, Wi, hurry up!" Tybalt's voice came from the other side.

Willa grinned when Claire echoed him, "Yeah, hurry up!"

Willa shook her head at the sound of her brother and Claire giggling and whispering to one another. Lovebirds. Lovebirds she had missed so terribly.

"I'm…" She pushed through the last of the bush, grunting at the thorns grasping at her limbs and pulling on her cloak as she did. "Here!"

She nearly fell on her face as the bush gave way and let her out on the other side. Stumbling forward, she wiped her hands on her pants, a goofy smile still pulling at her lips.

A warm fireplace greeted her as she stepped into her living room. The smell of roasted meat and vegetables along with rising bread made her salivate as she took a deep inhale.

Willa smiled and spun around the room, but now no one was there. She ran down the hall to check the bedrooms, but they were all empty. Confused, she ran back towards the fire. An ethereal elf turned to her, stilling her to the core.

Merellian opened his mouth to speak, but only blood fell from between his teeth. Large streams of thick, black liquid fell to the ground and rolled towards Willa in rotting waves. With a rasping breath, she stumbled backwards only to walk into a cold, frigid body. She tripped over her own feet while turning, and crumpled to the floor. Ivaan stared down at her with glassy eyes, mouthing one word over and over again. *Wild.*

Willa heard the woman from the lake water's melodic voice and she slowly turned back to find it coming through Merellian's mouth as he stood covered in blood from head to toe.

"Three into one created by slaughter." More blood came out after each word. "Two suns forge light anew."

Willa stood and ran to the door. When she opened it, Claire was standing there. Her skin was charred and burned. She cocked her head to the side and smiled as she said in the woman's voice, "So many dead by your hand already. I wonder how many more it will take until you understand?"

"Stop with the riddles, I beg of you, speak plainly!" Willa looked at the floorboards of her home and frowned. She'd been standing on familiar wood, but it crumbled beneath her feet, turning to cold stone.

Her home was gone. The fireplace, the elf, Claire, and Ivaan were all gone.

Now in front of her was the stone dais and throne from her previous dream. Blue, twinkling lights made from the man of shadow's magic cast speckles of starlight along the cavern's floor.

"This...this was all a dream? But I was walking through the faerie camp...I saw them sleeping, I—"

"Who was sleeping?" The man covered in shadows stepped beside her from the dark space of the cave.

Willa turned to the voice and took a rushed step away from him. "Last time, you thought I was a part of your dream. Yet this time, you act as though this is normal. But it's not normal, is it? Are you a part of mine or am I a part of yours?"

The shadows rippled beside her for too long. Willa's mind was frantic from the nightmare. She looked down at her hands, noticing the fabric given to her by the faerie was gone, confirming it was all one terrible dream. "But I can't be a part of yours, or I wouldn't have seen what I had, I wouldn't even know it was happening. How do dreams even work? How does—"

A loud exhale, cut her off. "Must you speak so much? Your voice grates my ears like a squawking bird."

Willa gawked at the figure hidden beneath the dark ripples. "I'm sorry. Have I ruined your brooding again?"

An irritated groan rumbled from the dark clouds as the voice replied, "I'm not brooding, Freckles. I'm concentrating. *Quietly.* "

She huffed. "I would like to wake up now."

"So would I." The shadows ebbed and rolled, growing and shrinking with every irritated breath before the voice within it asked, "Where are you?"

"Oh, I can speak now, Your Majesty?" Willa dipped her chin down towards her feet in a mocking bow. She stood and crossed her arms. "I am beside you, unfortunately—"

"Where are you, Freckles?" The voice cut her off. "Really?"

Willa sighed and shook her head. "I actually have no idea. Maybe the fae did kill me like I asked for. This seems like a nightmare."

The voice deepened. "Why have they kept you alive?"

"Your guess is as good as mine." Willa sighed and looked into the shadows.

She asked a question that had pricked the back of her mind ever since the last time they had met in her slumber. "Are you my subconscious?"

"No."

She frowned and mumbled, "Sometimes you sound like it."

"What do you mean by that?"

"At first I thought it was shock." Willa shivered, recalling the voice that had spoken to her inside the Wylan beast's stomach. "A deep male voice whispers to me. It...helped me."

"Perhaps the Wylan's magic has made you sick with fever." But the voice spoke thickly, as if lost in thought.

"Maybe I am." Willa looked down at her palms and frowned. "I thought this happened before, when I was awake. Can you explain this?" She lifted her hands to show the shadows the eerie white glow, coming from her scars before the cavern shook violently around her.

CHAPTER 40

WILLA

A deep, rumbling voice spoke loud enough to wake Willa up. "So the past has come to greet me like a stubborn wound that refuses to close."

Willa opened her eyes to find herself within a cave, much like her dream. She looked down at her uplifted palms, the marks still glowing like they had been in her fevered nightmare. But as she peered into the dark, she saw no dais or brooding shadow figure. Instead she stood at a cavern's edge. Glancing behind her, she saw rows of the Wylan's trees. Gone was the fae and the camp she had fallen asleep in. There was enough moonlight to cast shadows into the long cave, though the back of the cavern remained cast in darkness.

"Where am I?" Willa's voice was cracked and tired. Mud and twigs were sticking to her weathered boots. The cloth she had wrapped around her palm was torn and dangling between her fingers. She thought of how her dream began and realized she must have sleep walked out of the faerie camp. How had no one caught her leaving?

The deep, grumbling voice spoke again from the back of the cave, "You reek of faerie."

A growl rumbled after the words—the sound so low in vibration it shook the very ground beneath her. She fought to hold her balance while pebbles littered from the cavern's ceiling bounced around her, choosing to say nothing to the voice, in case it was another Wylan beast, trying to entrance her with magic.

"And yet you are not one. Tell me, how were your dreams?"

Willa crossed her arms and stepped closer to the voice, despite the warning bells ringing in her mind. "You gave me those nightmares? What sort of creature are you?"

She reached for her pocket and silently cursed her faerie captor. The sight of Claire's fishing knife had made her sick with memories of Merellian, but now she wished the faerie hadn't cast it into the fire. She would give anything to attack what had held her in that tormented dream. Her family and friends had all seemed so real before the visions had turned dark and sour. She was sick of these mind games. Sick of being easily tricked and trapped by the magic in this foul forest.

"Your mind was easy to find. Easy to lure, easy to coax. I've been bored and listless in these woods. Nothing but mindless creatures who roam and rot." A deep rumble had her stumbling back as the voice said darkly, "Until you."

She contemplated running, but there was no telling how far she and her fae captors had traveled on horseback. The faerie's promise to check on her family kept her rooted in place while she tried to form a plan. A low growl reverberated around her, loud enough this time to knock her off her feet.

Willa clenched her teeth as the cave floor shifted beneath her. "You speak of creatures as if you are not one of them. Show yourself, so I may see who tricked me."

Rows of sharp, bone white teeth appeared beneath a dripping, wet snout, like that of a dog. She moved to stand but paused, noting how the snout moved with her. It sniffed furiously, black lips curling up from the teeth as they moved to speak.

"You may not be a faerie, but there is something I smell on you. As I predicted before when you stepped into my den. You are a thorn, digging into my aching wounds. Here to taunt me for what I've done." The teeth clamped shut so loudly, Willa nearly fell.

She stumbled back, but caught herself with her hands before pushing into a crouch. "I am sick of riddles and tricks. Leave me be so I can find my way back."

"Back where, girl? Back to the faeries? Or home?" The creature slowly revealed more of itself, the dim moonlight beginning to shine upon it. "If I had to guess, home is very far from you now."

It was right. Home was too far away for her. She would never survive the Wylan on her own.

Black fur sat in large, matted clumps above the giant sets of jutting teeth. Willa searched for green glowing eyes, but could only find a scarred patch of skin between the mangled fur. On the other side of its snout, a white eye stared at nothing in the dark, as if it were blind. A creature blind in one eye and missing another. She frowned. Soft whining noises whistled through the jagged teeth while the snout sniffed the air. Two long legs stepped from the shadows. Although much taller than her, its legs were scrawny despite the size of the animal's head. Its jaw and teeth took up most of its mass.

It stepped even closer, but a clanking sound echoed in the back of the cave and it stopped. Willa tried to look past the two front paws and frowned. For the size of the creature, it should have been muscular and strong, yet ribs poked out on either side of its elongated neck. How long had this beast been here? It looked starved. Deprived of all light. It might have resembled a large wolf before, but now it was frail. Forgotten in this cave. Another vibrating sound came from the wide maw, making Willa regret her thoughts of its fragility instantly.

"What are you?" she asked.

A large paw stepped towards her, but the loud clanking noise echoed again from the dark, stopping it from going any further. The teeth swung over her head and snapped to the back of the cave. She frowned at the small, sad whine.

She almost pitied the creature, until its canine teeth snapped back to her and it snarled. "I am the Harbinger of Nightmares. Death's Divine."

Willa had to hold her arms out to keep her balance as the cave shook beneath her muddied boots. In all her studies, she had never heard of such titles. Whatever names it had given itself, clearly it was no longer, if it were stuck here in this cave like she suspected.

"It's hard to believe a creature with such villainous titles is so lonely for company." A smug smile spread across her face as she continued, unable to hide the sarcasm in her words. "I am sorry it is me you found, for I am only a mortal, trying to survive your world. Or the one you are forced to watch from the shadows."

A bark came from the rows of teeth, its canines biting furiously at the air. "How dare you mock me, girl? You should fear my titles, not laugh at them."

Willa wanted to smile again, knowing this creature couldn't get to her. But pity rose within her the more she watched its snapping barks turn to frustrated whines. A sudden sadness sobered her as the creature pulled at its chains and searched for her blindly. She knew what it was like to be an outcast. To be caged within the walls of Traifton.

She looked over her shoulder, out into the woods, and frowned. Raw emotion cracked in her chest. She had no right to speak. Her situation was just as dire if not worse. She was still caged. She had run from one and stepped into another. She sighed and turned back to look at the chained beast.

Clearing her throat, she said, "I cannot fear that which I pity. Though someone clearly feared you enough to lock you here within this cave. What nightmares did you give them to receive this punishment?"

The leathered lips snarled over sharp teeth. "I could wait for you to fall asleep and show you rather than tell you. Your king did not fear us either and look what happened to him."

"You speak of something I had no part in," Willa retorted. "That was centuries ago."

"And yet you have done what he has." If the elongated mouth could smile, it tried now. "You have killed an elf."

Willa opened her mouth and closed it. The creature barked as if it were laughing, the sound shaking the cave walls around her. She gasped, the ground shifting too quickly for her to catch herself, and she stumbled. Grasping the stone wall with her nails, she blindly searched for any holes or jagged cracks to keep herself standing as the cavern continued to quake.

"I smell the fear of what you did. Your confusion."

She turned to look at the creature, pressing her back against the wall as its snout turned to her.

"Ah..." It took a deep inhale, and a long, slime coated tongue crawled out, wriggling in the air before licking the sharp teeth and snout. "You do not understand how you did it. It haunts you. You don't understand how you killed an immortal being with magic."

"How?" Willa was shackled by the truth of the creature's admission.

The beast sniffed furiously towards her before answering, "Do you bear any marks upon your skin?"

Willa let go of the cavern wall to lift her palms. Were her eyes playing tricks on her or did they still truly glow a pale white now within the cavern?

"My hands. It was a ritual," she whispered. "The Ritual of Vitality. But this happened a year ago. It's something my town has done for centuries to assure we are within balance."

The beast only barked out another laugh. Its maw was hanging directly above her now, sniffing towards the cave wall. One wrong move and those teeth would snap her in two. She could see its ribs as the two feet shuffled in front of her line of vision. She could be its first meal in gods knew how long if she didn't step or speak carefully.

The creature repeated her words slowly, as if tasting each syllable. "Ritual of Vitality. Oh, that is a rich title."

Warm saliva dropped onto Willa's forehead, and she practically gagged as the liquid rolled into her hair.

"Tell me, girl, what do they look like?"

"A sun and a star. Star of the Scales and the Dawn of Harmony."

The snout snapped towards the sound of her voice and sniffed deeply, a small rumble coming from the beast's chest, rattling the wall behind her. "I will give you answers, but not without something in return. I wish to strike a bargain."

"And why would you help me make sense of this?" Willa crept away from the snout, sliding across the wall. "And what could I possibly do for you?"

It was time for her to leave. She didn't want answers to how she'd killed the elf. She didn't want to consider what she had done at all. She had murdered someone. Another title to add to her list of names. Another nightmare to haunt her. She stepped away as quickly and quietly as she could, but the sharp rows of teeth snapped in front of her, hiding the entrance to the cave.

"To help you make sense of it could stop history from repeating itself. Though I was a deity of the dark, I abided by Forsetyr's rules of balance. Too long have the scales been broken." Willa flinched as the teeth inched closer to her. "You will listen to my bargain and go forth with secrets that have kept this realm broken. Secrets that can tear a kingdom down with the snap of your fingers."

Willa's voice trembled as she replied, "There are no kingdoms left to fall."

SOREAN

Sorean awoke with a cold slap. The faerie prince groaned and sat up, rubbing at his stinging cheek as Harland hovered over him with wide eyes.

"Gods, Sorean, I knew it was bad, but I didn't realize your essence did that while you slept." Sorean gaped at Harland's still outstretched palm as the faerie continued, "I'm sorry, I couldn't snap you out of it."

Sorean frowned, confused. The tonic he had taken, along with the fae wine, had sent him into a restless slumber. It was odd for his magic to hover over him, especially if it was unable to give him his nightly dose of terrors. Sorean clenched his jaw and rubbed his face. Memories of the sentries back at the cabin resurfaced. Harland was lucky his magic hadn't attacked him for getting so close while he slept.

"The mortal fled camp," Harland said breathlessly above him. "I fell asleep leaning on a tree. I... I don't know what happened. One minute I was wide awake, the next I was dreaming."

His gaze roamed Sorean's face with concern, but Sorean didn't take the time to decipher whether the concern was over his essence or what he had announced.

Blinking away his sleep drugged haze, Sorean surveyed the camp. It was still night, the fire reduced to a few, humble embers now by his feet. He looked to his side, but the girl was missing, as Harland had said.

Adrenaline cut through his groggy mind. Jumping to his feet, he ran towards his horse. "Where is Iara?"

"Gone," Harland replied, mounting his own horse and kicking in the stirrups.

Sorean cursed and followed him through the narrow trees. A flock of ravens flew up from the bushes in front them, spooking both of their horses, but he managed to settle the steed right as the rocks beneath them trembled and shook.

"What the fuck was that?" he asked.

But Harland was too busy controlling his own horse to answer.

Another sudden shake of the ground had his horse rearing back. Sorean dropped the reins and tumbled off with a loud grunt. He jumped up and shoved the horse's side, pressing him to run back to the camp. Harland did the same after reaching for his bow and arrows.

Sorean watched the rocks below him bounce upon the shifting dirt. Quakes like this were not natural this far from the mountains and shorelines.

His essence rolled beneath him, eager to find out what was going on, when a piercing scream belonging to the mortal girl tore through the valley below them.

"I did not argue with you when you decided to keep this girl, Sorean. But if Iara is hurt because of her, I will kill her myself." Harland nocked an arrow and pushed through the bushes.

Sorean cursed again and chased after him while the mortal girl's cries greeted them once more.

Crouching behind the malnourished wolf, Willa rubbed her aching throat as she stared at the shackles around its back two ankles. The fur around its paws had been rubbed raw from the constant pulling of the two chains embedded into the stone wall, and the heavy smell of wet iron and piss crawled into her nostrils while the soft hum of magic buzzed on each side of her, coming from the chains themselves. A mix of man-made and magical restraints to keep this so-called Harbinger of Nightmares in the dark.

"Again," the creature commanded.

Willa swallowed with a wince, but obeyed. Her vocal cords were still tender from Merellian's show of power and brute strength. Closing her eyes, she screamed as loudly as she could, the beast following her cry with a low growl. Willa grasped the chains to steady herself from the shaking cave as the two sent out another signal of despair.

"Maybe they left me to die," she croaked. "They said if I ran, they would leave me."

"Someone comes. Another fell into my sleeping trap when you entered this den. This is the same soul I smell now." His back legs shifted slightly, as if to brace himself. "Remember our bargain, girl. If you trick me, I will kill you and delight in feasting on your tender flesh."

Willa shuddered at the thought. She repeated her signal of despair, and again the wolf made the rock shake with his noise. She prepared to go again, despite her aching throat, when a sudden burst of air pushed the beast back towards Willa. Claws scraped at the stone floor and the beast slid towards her. She dropped to the ground as another gust of wind hit the beast, and it let out a startled bark and fell to its side, avoiding her entirely as it did.

This was it. Willa rolled over the loose chain and pulled the slack around her waist as she stood.

"Help!" Her voice was raspy as she called out to whoever had entered.

A sudden flame appeared in the middle of the cave and bobbed towards her. Willa had to blink and look away from the sudden brightness. It was no surprise the beast had become blind back here in the shadows. She looked back towards the light and blinked furiously, only to find her captor's companion, the female faerie, sprinting towards her with wide eyes.

The orange light bobbed, glistening on her ebony skin as she searched her. "You mortals always seem to find yourself in the worst of situations." She hissed and looked her up and down, "I should leave you here to rot."

Willa knew she wouldn't. She'd watched her argue with the male faerie, but this one always listened to him. She remembered her captor had muttered her name back at camp after his attempt at questioning her– *Iara*– she would be the one to help get her answers now. There was a clear hierarchy between these faeries, giving Willa the upper hand with who had entered their trap.

Willa dropped her head and looked at the chains she had wrapped around her waist, rasping the single word, "Help."

The wolf lay on its side beside her whining through a tightly closed jaw. Willa fought to hide her smile at the pathetic noises coming from the creature. In another life the pair could have caravanned together, like a traveling theater act, with how well they performed their plan now for the unsuspecting faerie.

Iara cursed under her breath in a rich, lilted accent before stepping cautiously around the beast's long paws. He shifted slightly, and the faerie paused to watch the creature's raspy breaths before she continued delicately towards Willa, eyeing the beast the whole time as she did.

Willa stared, transfixed, at the bobbing flame hovering beside her. The blast of air had come from this faerie. She tried and failed to repress her shiver. Did each fae control every element? But her faerie captor had shadowed terrors crawling from his palm. Those terrors had been no natural element—what sort of faerie magic could conjure such things?

Iara brought her hand out towards the chain but paused, her pink lips thinning. Tilting her head, she looked at Willa through narrowed eyes. "How did you sneak away from our camp so easily?"

Willa gulped at the silver rim encasing Iara's brown irises, frozen in fear as she assessed the chains. She could easily see they barely held her with her eyesight. Her sudden stillness reminded Willa of the elves—reminded her once again of the true predators and monsters in this realm, like the one assessing her now.

Willa stepped forward, to tighten the chain's loop around her waist. She let out a dramatic hiss and grabbed at the chains. "I was tricked out here. It called to me from my dreams."

Not a lie. She gave the fae a horrified look before cutting a darting glance to the beast. Why hadn't he done it yet?

The faerie mumbled something in her foreign language. The wolf had said he had another trapped in dreams. Iara had been sleeping before Willa took the tonic. How long had she been trapped within her own mind before wandering out of camp like Willa had?

Iara stopped her grumbling and asked cautiously, "How did it wrap you up when it is also chained?"

Shit.

Willa followed the chain towards the beast's ankles and whimpered. "I don't remember. One minute I was dreaming of my family." She paused and thought of what came after and actually trembled. When she was ready, she continued her half-truth, "I woke up here. The things I saw...I ..." She sucked in a breath and thought of Merellian bleeding out in her family home. "I want to go home. Please help me."

Willa forgot herself for a moment, so wrapped up in the story telling of half-truths. She ran a shaking hand through her curls.

"What is that?" Iara asked darkly.

Willa looked at her with wide, doe eyes and blinked. The fae ignored her ignorant look and stepped closer.

"Why do your marks glow?"

Willa winced and dropped her hand, but Iara stopped her by groping her wrist with unprecedented strength. Willa cried out as the faerie lifted her hand up towards the floating flame and studied the soft glow pulsing within her scar.

Before she could say anything, the beast groaned into the cavern floor, causing it to shake violently around them both. The shaking cave caught Iara by surprise and knocked her balance off kilter. She stumbled forward and let go of her wrist to grasp onto the chains around Willa's waist to stop from falling. As the faerie's hands latched onto them, a thrum of energy came to life around her from the metal links.

Just as the wolf had predicted, the magic binding the chains to the cavern came alive at the touch of the female's hands. Faerie magic had put this creature here and now a faerie was helping to release him, unknowingly. The chains rattled around Willa as the wolf whined and shifted beside them, the irons around the wolf's ankles beginning to shrink in size.

Iara gasped and stepped back. She tried to let go of the chains, but it seemed like she could not. She grunted and tugged hard, pulling Willa forward as she did. The faerie was so focused on freeing herself from the buzzing, rattling metal, she allowed her conjured light to disappear, casting all three of them into darkness.

A hissing sound came from the chains as they dissolved and crumbled. Willa pushed up against the cavern wall and listened to the beast slowly standing, its snout furiously sniffing in the dark.

The fae's fire light reappeared and Iara stepped towards her with a chilling calm. "What did you do?"

Pressing her forearm into her chest, Iara pinned Willa further into the wall with a snarl. She whimpered, opening her mouth to speak, but all her thoughts emptied when a shift in shadows bobbed behind the fae's head and her floating flame. The faerie's ears twitched between her thin braids, and she spun around, revealing what she had unwillingly released.

This was the Harbinger of Nightmares Willa had been warned to fear. Its eye, once milky from years trapped in darkness, was now a glowing blood-red ember. Thick layers of black fur filled out the once narrow snout, and an impish, monstrous smile displayed rows of jagged sharp teeth. A leg stepped forward, no longer emaciated and slender, but rippling in shining black fur and muscle.

A wolf of shadow. A wolf of death. *Death's Divine.*

Iara whispered an accented word in horror, "Eth'tinok."

The wolf studied the fae, sniffing furiously. "You are right to fear my name, faerie."

It leaned back on its haunches, readying itself for attack and turned the red, glowing eye to Willa. "Run, little mortal. Before I change my mind."

Iara shifted into a defensive stance, raising her hands, and Willa lept to the side as Eth'tinok lunged for them both. The faerie grunted, sliding on the wall and slumping between the wolf's paws as the cavern shook around them.

Willa scrambled over the shaking floor as quickly as she could. She didn't stop her fumbled run until a cold breeze nipped at her skin from the mouth of the cave.

Her only concern was to escape. The faerie was on her own.

Scanning her surroundings, Willa ran from the sounds of gnashing teeth behind her, latching onto the first tree she could. A mere gust of air pushed her into the bark and she hissed, looking back into the dark cavern.

Eth'tinok slid on his side towards the cave opening as Iara followed with outstretched arms. It stood and lunged, but she was much faster and lighter on her feet. Dodging its snapping muzzle, Iara dove to the side, and Willa watched, mesmerized as the faerie rolled her landing. She stood quickly and pushed her open palms out towards the wolf, another gust of wind bursting forth, but the ancient beast predicted her magic and dropped to its belly. Iara lifted her left hand and fire appeared. Different from the bobbing light, it danced around her fingers like a worn leather glove before shooting out in a steady stream towards Eth'tinok.

Flame hit its back haunches and the wolf barked before pushing up and leaping away. Ignoring the flames licking its thick fur, he dipped his long neck, letting out a deafening howl.

Willa slapped her palms over her ears as she dropped to the trembling forest floor. Dead leaves and pebbles bounced around her boots from Eth'tinok's cry. The tree she held onto moaned and swayed before the trunk snapped, and she rolled away as it crashed onto the roots and rocks before her.

Willa crawled towards the fallen tree and peeked up over the bristled bark. As she watched the two magical monstrosities fight, Willa knew, without a shadow of a doubt, if Iara survived she would kill her for this; damning the consequences of her faerie leader back at camp.

This was her chance of getting away from Iara and the ancient creature she had helped to release, but her body was rooted to the fallen tree as Death's Divine spoke once more. "Retribution is mine."

The faerie was still pushing herself up from the ground when he lunged. Sinking his teeth into her side, Iara cried out as the beast lifted her in the air. With shaking jowls, he tossed her around like a broken doll before spitting her out. She hit a large boulder, falling in a heap.

Turning from the scene, Willa ducked her head. She couldn't watch this. She couldn't be part of another death. She pushed her back into the bark, panting towards the endless rows of trees and rocks. The bargain had been freeing the wolf in exchange for answers, but she didn't give a damn about the answers now. She needed to run.

She raced through the trees, gritting her teeth at the sounds of pained moans and crunching, urging her to move faster. If Iara died, there still was no guarantee Eth'tinok would let her live. Faerie magic had kept him in that cave. He had been starved, forgotten, left to rot for years because of her people. And now he was relishing in it, tasting blood and power once more.

But Willa's gut twisted as the fae's cries filled the night. She slowed her pace and sucked in a rattled breath. She was shackled by her inner moral compass—a compass cracking with her indecisive thoughts—with the thought of this faerie's death. She was no better than the ancient beast if she ran now. Another immortal creature dead by her hands. And if Iara died, the other faeries would rather hunt her than let her die by the hands of a Wylan Creature.

She cursed at herself and her moral conscience before spinning back to the gruesome scene.

Clenching her palms, she shouted, "Our bargain is not complete, wolf. I want my answers!"

As she dared to step closer, the wolf loomed over the unconscious faerie, ignoring her approach.

Willa raised her voice. "Now!"

Eth'tinok went deathly still before turning to find her shaking stance between the trees. One red eye focused on her, blood dripping from white teeth as his shoulders heaved, a wicked, hungry smile spreading on his terrible face.

CHAPTER 43

WILLA

Distracting Eth'tinok was a terrible plan. A stupid, foolish, terrible fucking plan.

Willa spun and ran, but the wolf pounced on her quickly, his blood-covered snout flipping her over easily as if she weighed nothing. Willa's sob was pitiful as rows of canines grazed her cheek, the smell of rusted iron turning her stomach. His gruesome snarl sent stale hot air and spittle toward her face, lifting strands of hair to obscure her vision.

The wolf lifted his head and snarled. "You performed a ritual the night you killed the high elf, Merellian. The marks on your hands are more powerful than your townspeople could have ever predicted."

Willa looked down at her shaking hands. "But—"

"Rune work. Any blood you touched after you were branded has been absorbed into you."

The past year of Willa's life flashed before her eyes as she thought of the countless, careless acts she had put herself in the way of. She thought of Branlon in the temple, and how close she could have been to touching another's blood. She shuddered at the thought. She was lucky to have been an outcast, she realized, to be reproached so fervently, no one dared get close enough to her palms...Until Merellian.

Eth'tinok confirmed her thoughts with a stenched huff of a laugh. "Yet you lasted twelve full moons before absorbing any noticeable amount of blood. The ritual was sealed when your scars touched the elf's blood. You mortals have been unknowingly performing sorcery."

The wolf put a paw on either side of her head and sniffed the air around them before letting out a small grumble in its throat.

It licked the blood from its canines before continuing. "Blood magic is binding and everlasting. It was how King Ammanar killed King Erlathian and stole his essence."

The weight of Eth'tinok's words sank deep into her stomach like a rock tumbling through the Minison's black waters. King Ammanar had performed sorcery to break the Law of Balance. To kill an elf, like she had. Merellian couldn't have known this, but did Commander Enrel? Did Claire?

The wolf cocked his head to study her with its one red eye. "Heed my words, girl. Before I was cast into darkness, I witnessed the elves leave with the gods. But I saw what most did not. Three elven families stayed within our realm to hunt for answers. Now, centuries later, according to your dead friend, these elves are out of hiding to search for something." Willa's heart pounded loudly in her ears as the wolf continued. "Revenge is potent, is it not? Its festering call is more addictive than any use of magic, drug, or drink. Not just any elf would follow a mortal ship back to the place where this all began. If King Erlathian's son is still alive, he is back to avenge his father, upon ravened wings and vengeful talons."

Willa's mouth parted. *Ravened wings and vengeful talons.* It was the beast who had tried to take her from these woods.

"Commander Enrel," she whispered in horror.

"*Prince* Enrel." Eth'tinok's lips curled slightly. "Kauis Enrel Sylpetor: The Prince of Reckoning."

The wolf's given title to Prince Enrel embedded into her skin with chilling clarity. An ancient royal hunted her now, with a black winged beast, and she had killed one of his men. What had she done?

Only one question remained. "You say King Ammanar did the same thing knowingly. But he stole the elf king's essence." She sucked in a quivering breath as Eth'tinok slowly lowered his snout towards her. "I did no such thing. I have no magic."

"You lie." Teeth snapped above her, spraying more saliva and blood over her face. "I feel it within you now. It burns my nostrils like blazing fire."

Willa gasped at the truth in his words. *Fire.* A fever had itched and burned beneath her skin. Its searing warmth came when Merellian died beneath her fingers. Flames had flared within her again when the Wylan Creature had tried to swallow her whole.

"Your fear tastes sweet, girl." Its snout lowered to shove her face to the side. She whimpered as it sniffed into her curls and hissed, "You say you have none and yet you have used it before, haven't you?"

A flash of being inside the Wylan beast danced in her vision. Her stomach rolled and twisted as she remembered the way her markings had glowed as they had in the cave tonight. She closed her eyes, shying away from the truth of what had happened. The voice in her mind had helped her. She remembered what Merellian had told her about the elves' essence. What he had said his essence longed for. *Power.*

Willa opened her eyes and found herself staring into the wolf's red eye. It bore into her as if trying to find her soul to haunt and devour in death's embrace.

"I should kill you now before you learn how to truly yield it. It has not yet awakened in you."

Willa whimpered as the paw near her shoulder lifted into the air. Long claws extended from its fur, shining in the moonlight.

"You did not flinch when I spoke of revenge before. You mortals are all alike. Exactly like Ammanar. Greedy, angry, cunning. I smell your anger beneath your sickly stench of fear. It burns hotter than the magic mixing in your blood now. Even as you cower below me."

Willa shook her head and rasped, "I am not like him. I do not want this. This is a curse!"

A rattling cough tore Eth'tinok's gaze from hers, and she almost cried in relief at the sound. The faerie was still alive. The wolf's paw crashed beside her, his claws digging into the dirt.

As he turned, Willa yelled up at him, "How do you know this is what King Ammanar did?"

"I am Death's Divine. Called upon when someone wants to perform unspeakable acts. In the shadows of the woods, I spoke of the ritual to the ones who called my name. Because I did, I was chained here to rot for eternity. To hide their secrets."

"The gods chained you away?" Willa asked, horrified.

"No. The gods do not know what really happened that night. Only you and I share this knowledge now. However ..." The wolf slowly inhaled, settling above her once more. "Our bargain is fulfilled. I should have killed the mortal king when I realized what they had planned. Now I can stop the wheel before it spins again." Eth'tinok's open maw rushed towards her.

She turned her face right as an arrow hit the dirt beside her. The wolf's face snapped up as another arrow hit the dirt, narrowly missing his paw. The wolf retracted above her, snarling.

Eth'tinok spun back to the cave. Iara was struggling to stand, but she managed to lean on the fallen rock, hugging her arm with clenched teeth, blood dripping from her torn shirt. She looked out through the trees and grimaced before turning to Willa and the beast between them. The faerie let go of her bleeding arm, raised her palm, and Eth'tinok howled.

Willa lifted her hands to cover her ears but paused, staring at the brands still glowing on her skin.

"Do something," Willa hissed through clenched teeth. The wolf's howl stabbed her ears and rattled her thoughts as she stared at her hands.

Her stomach rolled, raising bile into her throat before the voice within her returned.

Why?

"I need to know if the wolf speaks the truth. I need to understand." She flinched as Eth'tinok howled again. More arrows dropped around her.

I tire of proving my worth when you have so clearly given up. You asked for death by the hand of a faerie. This deity is right, you reek of fear. It makes me sick. You do not realize what we could do together, if only you surrendered.

"I am not Ammanar," she gritted out.

She knew the horrors his temporary reign of stolen magic had done. The havoc he had caused was unthinkable, as was his body count within minutes of his use of the elven magic.

Yes, you are no king, mortal girl. A burning sensation stirred to life deep within her stomach as the voice spoke again. *But you could be.*

Warmth bubbled beneath Willa's neck and rolled down her shoulders. She gasped as the heat licked down her forearms before crawling into her hands.

Death's Divine flew at the faerie as Iara tried to throw a blast of wind at him, but the beast dodged it before crashing down with snapping teeth.

Willa's eyes nearly rolled back as the inferno grew. Her skin had to be melting away, for it was devouring her from the inside out. The heat finally found release from her palms, and bright, blinding light flew from her hands, like two beacons in the dead of night. The trees before her ignited from the intense beam, and within seconds, the cage of the woodlands she had found herself in was burning by her mortal hands.

Set ablaze by the mistakes of her past.

CHAPTER 44

SOREAN

Sorean dropped to the dirt, covering his eyes from the abrupt stream of light before them. The smell of fire overwhelmed his senses while the Wylan's trees groaned and shifted beneath the crackling embers falling like snow in the Menyamere mountains.

"Do something," Harland called as the ground trembled.

Sorean pushed his legs out to stop his body from sliding any further down the sloping rocks to the scene below, but his heels could not find traction. He was going too fast. After a few yards, his right heel finally slammed into a jutting rock. It slowed him enough to lean forward and pull himself into a run. Sorean lowered his arms to look at where he was going, only to be blinded by the bright light again.

He called to his essence, but nothing happened. Reaching for it again as he ran blindly, no whispers answered, and he dared open his eyes to look at his marks. But they did not glow blue. They did nothing at all, despite his desperate call.

The mortal girl let out an agonized cry before the blinding light dissipated. Falling embers landed on his tunic while he searched the valley and he followed the line of charred trees encasing the small cavern within a cluster of boulders, then studied the burnt forest floor. Following the blackened dirt, he found the mortal girl lying on the ground, and near the cavern's entrance was Iara, face down on the rocky forest floor. He could hear the mortal girl's raspy breaths, but Iara's were too soft. Too shallow.

Before they reached flat ground, Harland cut away from Sorean and wove through the trees, spreading out in the opposite direction. They had seen a wolf when they reached the top of the small valley and, although it was black like a Wylan beast, something about the creature had Sorean's hackles raised. Maybe it was one of the creatures Noi had warned them about, but the real question was, where was it now? Sorean scanned the trees and slowed to a steady crouch as he neared Iara and the mortal.

"More faeries to feed my aching hunger."

Sorean froze. His muscles tensed from the deep, primordial tone of the voice. He turned slowly to look at the Wylan wolf. A glowing red eye watched him through a large bush, and his skin rippled with a tingling awareness as realization dawned on him.

"It cannot be," Sorean whispered. A large snout pushed through the dead, brown leaves before rows of stained teeth curled back into a monstrous smile.

He was unable to hide the tremor in his voice when he said, "I was told you were dead."

The Deity of the Dead stepped out from the trees to show himself fully. "I cannot die." A long tongue darted out to taste the air. "Your kind did the closest thing to death and chained me to this poisoned land."

The faeries had locked this god away? His mother had only mentioned the Death Dealer once. Sorean had woken from a nightmare when he was a child. He was so inconsolable, a servant was left with no choice but to wake the queen and bring her to his chambers. As she calmed him down, she'd quietly cursed the wolf's name. When Sorean had asked who he was, she had explained the faeries cursed Eth'tinok's name when they had night terrors, blaming his dark, nightmarish gifts. He was a legend. Dead and gone, she had said.

Did she know he was alive? Did she know who kept him hidden? It seemed the longer he was in the Wylan, the more he realized his perception of his mother was one entirely made up of what he wanted to see. She kept too much hidden from him, despite being heir to the throne. There was no way the Queen of Lithelle was unaware of Eth'tinok being alive. Iara was right. He was blind to her ways.

Sorean stood tall and pushed his shoulders back. As he did, he silently called upon his essence, but it continued to ignore him. He was fast and an agile fighter, but deities fought with words and prophecies. He would not survive with brute strength alone against the wolf tracking his every move.

Sorean heard Harland move behind him, so he raised a hand. Daring one glance over his shoulder, he gave Harland a tense nod. He forced his face to mask his panic, allowing a cold calm to settle his features. His friend loosened the grip on his bow and stood straight as well, mimicking his stance. Knowing he'd understand, Sorean shifted his eyes toward Iara before turning.

Eth'tinok was tracking Harland, his red eye trained on him with a calm, killing focus. The wolf's muscles were tight, as if ready to attack, when he said, "You are offspring of Queen Morielle."

Reaching for his essence in a silent prayer, Sorean said, "I am."

"And she is still the queen?" The deity's voice held a bitter bite of hostility.

Sorean hesitated before answering. He adjusted the high collar of his shirt, feigning boredom as if he were at court, answering questions about tithe or small faerie politics. He would not endanger the kingdom by admitting anything to Death's Divine.

A trickle of sweat rolled down the back of his neck as he drawled, "She is still alive."

"Answered like a true royal." The wolf blew out a huff of warm air. "And how old are you?"

Sorean crossed his arms and sighed. "Your confinement has dulled your formalities, Eth'tinok. One never asks an immortal's age so openly. I could ask you the same, but I know you would not answer." He shifted in his stance slightly and countered, "Who was brave enough to chain you away?"

The wolf stood from its poised position and looked up at the canopy of burnt trees. It sniffed for a moment, then brought its left eye towards Sorean. "You smell like her. I have sat in that cave salivating over the memory of her scent. Fantasized what the queen of the fae would taste like."

A deep, throaty rumble vibrated out of the Death Deity's chest. Sorean widened his stance and slowly dropped his crossed arms.

The mortal girl's breath hitched loud enough for both Sorean and the deity to look her way. Sorean watched her twitch and mumble in her sleep, her brow deeply furrowed, sweat beading her pale face.

"Her brief display of power will be enough to haunt her sleep without my assistance."

Sorean thought of his own night terrors, remembering what his mother had said of Eth'tinok's powers. *Harbinger of Nightmares.*

He watched her rapid chest and quick, twitching jerks before noting the charred dirt and ash around her. What power could she have displayed? This had clearly been Iara's doing, for she could control fire elements, not a mortal girl.

Sorean listened for Iara's shallow breaths while asking, "If we locked you away, it was with our magic. How did you free yourself?"

Eth'tinok snarled. "The girl, whom you have so foolishly overlooked, bargained with me."

Something finally stirred inside of Sorean. The hairs on the back of his neck stood while his essence at last presented itself.

He turned to the wolf with a complacent stare, bringing his arms behind his back to hide the marks showing on his forearms, and shrugged. "Kill her if you want. I have no use for her. Let me take the faerie you have hurt and we will leave peacefully."

The deity laughed and gave a shake of his furred shoulders, his ears pinned to his head while he focused on Sorean. "I do not want peace, Son of Morielle."

"That's a shame, for peace is all I want, Eth'tinok." Sorean frowned and closed his eyes.

Like a key sliding into place, Sorean's essence turned from a mild restlessness to a chilling awareness of what threatened its master. Sorean knew his essence, although dark and different, was intensely loyal. Its whispers slowly floated to his mind, and the door to his essence unlocked and swung wide open. Sorean opened his eyes and Eth'tinok cocked his head to the side, sniffing curiously.

Closing its large red eye, it inhaled deeply and loosened a loud, rumbling warning. "It all makes sense now."

Sorean didn't wait to gain clarity on what it meant as his essence bubbled out of his clenched hands behind his back. Like a spilt vial of ink, Sorean's shadows crawled behind his back and pooled around his feet in midnight swirls.

As his shadows rose from the ground, Sorean rolled his shoulders with a sigh. *Cover Harland and Iara,* he said sternly in his mind.

His essence crooned softly, *What of the mortal?*

She is the reason Iara is hurt. Leave her to die or kill her. I care not. He would tell the queen what he'd seen without the girl. She had proved to him what mortals were truly like by hurting Iara.

The only answer Sorean received was a sudden wall of towering black mist shooting up between him and the wolf. Sorean sprinted with Harland towards Iara as his magic swallowed the deity in rolling waves of darkness.

The two bent on either side of Iara and carefully lifted her up. Sorean helped drape her over Harland's shoulder.

"The girl?" Harland asked quickly.

"Iara was right. We should have killed her nights ago." Sorean shook his head. "Run. It will not touch you two."

"I know what it does. I am not afraid." Harland adjusted Iara on his shoulder, loosening a soft moan from her.

A loud howl rang out through the thickness of his shadows and Sorean whispered, "You should be."

SOREAN

Sorean ran from his wall of magic as another barking whine tore from the mist. Harland was close on his heels, carrying Iara as delicately as he could while they ran.

He glanced back as his essence hummed happily within the marks on his skin, the wall of his magic climbing higher and higher towards the treetops. Giving the mortal girl one last look, he wondered what bargain she'd made to release the deity. He didn't want to know. She was as good as dead now.

Sorean waited until they breached the top of the hill before recalling his magic. He had been hidden away from this life, but he wasn't naive enough to believe he could kill a deity. He only hoped his essence would be enough to slow him down.

Staring at the wall of pulsing shadows, he listened for the wolf's cries, again reaching for his essence to cease the attack.

A wall hit him as he was thrust down the hill. Long claws and gnashing teeth scratched and fought to grab ahold of him as the wolf dragged him towards his magic and the mortal girl. He landed on his back with the wolf hovering over him.

"Your shadows cannot harm the very one who breeds nightmares."

Sorean tried rolling away, but the wolf's paw hit his chest and shoved him into the dirt like a wall of elemental air. Sorean's essence responded to his strain and dove towards him, the mist entrapping them both.

He could only see Eth'tinok's red eye as claws ripped into his shirt to scratch his skin. "I will strike a bargain with you, faerie. Take me to your mother and I will not kill you now."

"But you would kill me later, is that it?" Sorean grit out from his clenched teeth.

His essence shoved and nipped at the wolf's sides, trying desperately to claw inside Eth'tinok's mind, but the wolf only shook his head, as if Sorean's magic was merely irritating gnats buzzing near his ears.

"I will save you for last, after you've listened to your mother concede her offenses and I take her heart for what she has done." Eth'tinok brought his teeth right above Sorean's brow. "Come now, Prince. I know what you are. Don't you want to know, too?"

Sorean hissed as blood rose to the surface beneath Eth'tinok's pressed paw. He struggled to free himself from under the weight of the wolf but Eth'tinok hovered there, waiting for Sorean to agree to the terms.

He refused.

His essence barreled against the wolf like a battering ram. It was no use.

Eth'tinok raised his head and growled. "So be it. I'll find the queen on my own."

Lifting a strained hand, Sorean called for his air element as a last attempt to get the deity off him, but Eth'tinok released Sorean with a startled bark. The beast sidestepped away before falling onto his side.

Sorean's essence reared up into the air and crashed upon the wolf like a tidal wave. Eth'tinok whined and kicked towards the mass of midnight, attempting to push Sorean's shadows away, and the prince stood, holding his chest as he watched.

The shadows gave way long enough for Sorean to spot the mortal girl shoving one of their poisoned arrows into the wolf's back leg. Faerie poison wouldn't be enough to kill a god, but it would hurt him more than anything else could now. The valley had to be littered with them from their earlier attempt to attack from above.

The wolf howled and kicked at the girl, but she had already fallen away. The forest shook, the surrounding scorched trees cracking from the strain.

Sorean spotted another fallen arrow and called his air element. The arrow dislodged itself from the dirt and flew towards Eth'tinok. It stuck in between his ribs, causing the wolf to let out another, louder howl.

When Sorean turned back to Eth'tinok, he found the girl clinging to an arrow lodged within his neck, holding on as the wolf shook his head furiously. His essence was as startled as he was by the girl's sudden attack, but now it reared up behind her, preparing to pull her off, so it could have her for its own.

Shadows lined Sorean's vision as his essence grew more eager, and hungrier.

"No," Sorean gritted out.

She's ours.

The girl didn't notice his magic growing bigger and darker behind her, like a storm cloud ready to strike only her.

Eth'tinok stood and the girl fell, kicking at his chest while he snapped towards her. Sorean was too focused on the arrow she clung to, missing the one held between her clenched teeth. Dropping a hand, she swiped at Eth'tinok's turning face. She wasn't quick enough. The deity stood to his full height, his open maw larger than her upper body, and caught her with one paw, throwing her in the air, perilously close to his jagged teeth. She lifted her left hand and jabbed it into the patch of skin where his eye once was, right as he latched onto her.

Both girl and god screamed while falling away from one another. Sorean ran forward but was pushed back by the storm of his essence swooping down to grab her as she hit the ground. Eth'tinok's growl was low and guttural, and instinct forced Sorean to focus on the beast.

The wolf tried to stand but stumbled as blood ran from his eye socket. Four poisoned arrows were in him now, eating at his bloodstream.

Sorean called his essence back, but the shadows protested, *She's ours!*

He ran towards his magic as the girl cried out.

"We don't have time for this," Sorean rasped.

An unspoken code of honor had him pushing forward to find the mortal. If she could stab a deity with arrows, she easily could have tucked her tail and ran the other way. Instead, she had helped him—saved him—by attacking Death's Divine. But the wolf couldn't die. They needed to get out now while they still stood a fighting chance.

He pushed through his essence, though it clawed and fought him the whole way. He had almost reached the center when the whispering, hungry cloud around him shrieked loud enough to drop Sorean to his knees. Blood fell from his nose while he covered his ears from the panicked cry of his essence.

Realization dawned on him. His magic wasn't attacking the girl, it was protecting her. Cloaking her from the wolf, as its tendrils lashed at Eth'tinok from the rolling swarm outside of this shadowed dome.

Its panic rattled Sorean, and a shadow of his own making rolled towards him with clawed fingers, as if to attack its own master.

Sorean hid behind his outstretched palms. "I am not here to hurt her."

She's. Ours. The whispers were cold. Demanding.

The girl was standing in the eye of his shadowed storm, with both palms outstretched. Blood dripped from her side where the wolf had sunk his teeth. Outside his fighting cloud of magic, Eth'tinok let out a haunting noise, and a crack formed between Sorean's boots in the dirt from the vibrations of the wolf's call.

The girl laughed, *actually* laughed, at the Harbinger of Nightmare's pained sound. Sorean watched her, stunned, as she lifted two fingers. A shadow figure of his essence lashed at her raised arm, as if to stop her, but she ignored it, bringing her two fingers together.

Sorean's shadows recoiled instantly. Lifting away from him and the girl, they clawed their way up through the trees with frantic whispers, *It burns! It burns!*

But nothing burned for him. Whatever the girl was doing, it was directly hurting the wolf and scaring his essence.

Sorean stood, calling his essence to come back, right as Eth'tinok barreled towards him and the girl with a vicious bark. But the girl let out a throaty chuckle and snapped her two fingers together. The wolf fell to his side, letting out another agonized howl. The crack beneath Sorean's boots fissured and yawned wider. He jumped away from the stretching ground, now widening into gaping holes and crevices.

Eth'tinok whined, standing, as the ground spread his paws apart. He lowered his head towards the girl and bared his bloodied canines. But the mortal had dropped her hands, trying to balance on the shifting dirt beneath them. The wolf leapt for her, pushing the cracking rock and soil to crumble into the forming pit behind him.

Sorean ran forward, practically blind from the dark fog still encasing his vision, and called for his air magic. A gust ran through his fingertips, rolling towards the deity. But before it could touch him, his shadows returned to rain down upon Eth'tinok like a fist of fury, shoving him into the pit of his own making.

She's ours.

Sorean's eyes widened in surprise at his essence's attack and it pushed him into action.

He stumbled over the cracks to reach for the girl as she crumpled towards the yawning pit. Eth'tinok had said she'd shown power and Sorean had ignored it. But whatever act she had performed was enough to scare his magic-made horrors. She had stood against the Death Dealer twice and lived. He lifted her into his arms and winced at the shadows blinding his sight.

She is ours, Prince. Not the wolf's. Ours.

The words were so spiteful, Sorean feared his magic would find a way to kill the girl if it ever got out again.

What had happened to his essence when she lifted two, fragile fingers together? Turning, he ran from the still howling wolf within the pit. Sorean fought his essence as he jumped, avoiding the cracks racing him out of the valley.

There may come a time when you can have her, but it is not now. His essence didn't like the small bargaining tool he offered, but Sorean moved faster as his vision lightened.

He had entered the Wylan Woods to find answers and Niarath Loch was right, there was nothing more for them here. Not when his answers could be found from the bleeding girl he held firm within his grasp. He didn't look back as another howl sent tremors through the valley while he raced to their veiled camp.

CHAPTER 46
KAUIS

"How is our prince today?"

Ulrond's voice rattled Kauis out of his restless sleep. He squinted at the dim cavern ceiling and wet his lips. His body ached without his use of magic, and he sat up slowly, clenching his teeth to muffle the groan as he did. But the banished god caught it.

Ulrond chuckled and knelt beside him. "Are you ready to agree to my terms?"

A Wylan beast's cry rattled from outside of the cave. Kauis shot Ulrond a glare before bending to rub at his raw ankles. Merellian's death was haunting him. His dreams teasing and taunting him with visions of the girl his friend had chased into the Wylan, continuously stumbling into a cave, much like the one he was trapped in now.

Kauis had to swallow several times before he could speak. "What do you want from me, Ulrond?"

"Your help." Ulrond studied Kauis closely and hummed. "In all of your years, did you ever search for the Key of Sanctity?"

Kauis straightened, shifting his shackles as he did.

Ulrond slowly stood, a knowing smile spreading across his face. "I wondered if anyone would start looking for them." His voice was hungry. Eager. "That is why you came here, isn't it? To Kalandrae?"

"Is it the power you want?" Kauis asked carefully.

The key could grant certain immortality and more. Unlimited, untapped, raw power when put together. If one could get over mixing faerie magic with elven, which was an abomination in itself, they could be untouchable with magic and might. Until he saw the arrow in Greer, faeries had been as good as dead to him. For what they did to Greer, he would destroy their piece. Destroy them.

As he watched Ulrond and his glowing green eyes, a trickle of fear crawled over his body. This male was already stealing and using poisoned magic—taking what didn't belong to him. Kauis heard those beasts outside of the cave each night. This banished god was doing something more than using the magic, and Kauis was frightened to find out what it was. Scared to wonder what would happen if the God of Chaos ever found the key and tried to wield it for himself.

Ulrond hummed again and looked around, shrugging. "As I said, I am like you. Revenge is more potent than power. The conquest of gaining back what was taken from you is more addictive than any magic or bargain I have ever come across."

Kauis thought of the girl, and Merellian's death. His father's death. He would never admit it, but it was easy to understand this banished deity as he ticked off all the harm done to those he cared for.

Ulrond continued, "I want to find Queen Morielle. What she has taken from me is why I carry my own vendetta."

The queen of the faeries. Kauis had seen her in the Kingdom of Domnhall the night his father was killed. She was there, too.

Until Greer was poisoned by *her* arrows, he hadn't given a damn about a queen in a hidden realm. But now he wanted to find them, too. He wanted to avenge his companion, his friend, by drawing out her death and making her feel fear as he had. Perhaps their wants were closer than he thought.

Kauis tensed his jaw and rubbed his chin. His father and Merellian were dead. Most of his race gone with the gods, and the rest left here to die slowly while he struggled to help them. He had no one aside from Greer. And Greer was tainted now. Changed.

The God of Chaos waited for Kauis to speak. He was a patient deity; letting Kauis sit in this cave for so long rather than demanding an immediate answer. He had to be for sitting in a forest for centuries, soaking up the gods' magic and waiting for the right opportunity to come stumbling towards him. He studied Ulrond more closely and the banished brand on his neck. Greer and Kauis would not be alive if not for this unhinged deity. But they would never be like him.

If he could bargain with Ulrond, get out of this fucking cave, and see sunlight again, he would find the artifacts and get him and Greer out of this poisoned mess.

Kauis stood on trembling legs. "If you can tell me one thing, Ulrond, I will make a bargain with you." Resting on the cavern wall for support, he lifted his chin and asked, "How did King Ammanar kill my father?"

Kauis sat beneath the blue twinkling lights of the familiar cave and waited. He understood now what this was. Anger laced his veins as the girl with blood-red hair entered the cave. These were not dreams haunting and terrorizing him each night. This was real. She was still living.

This was a piece of Merellian, still alive, trapped within this mortal girl's body. He didn't know how it had happened, and it didn't matter. What did was why his friend's essence still called to him.

The God of Chaos' story had confirmed how she'd killed Merellian—the marks on her hand performing a ritual. Rune work and blood magic. It always went back to fucking sorcerers. The sailor girl had been a sorcerer and now this girl had done what King Ammanar had.

The mortals had learned nothing. They all deserved to die.

Kauis shifted on his throne, catching the girl's attention.

She turned to him and smirked. "What are we brooding about this evening?"

Kauis was in no mood for games or banter tonight. He no longer wanted to be curious about the murderous mortal in front of him.

As he thought of his father and what King Ammanar had done—what *she* had done—he said one word with a bitter bite, "Balance."

The girl straightened, dropping her smile.

Kauis didn't waste any time as he stalked towards her. He expected her to cower or flinch at the ebbing shadows covering his form, but she didn't. Instead, she lifted her chin and silently assessed him. A haunting familiarity rolled through him with her changed demeanor. Merellian's essence sat beneath the surface of her pathetic, mortal frame. The girl had connected with the stolen magic already. He saw Merellian in the way she stood now as he slowly circled her with curled lips.

He stopped before her and hissed. "I'm curious how a freckled little thing like you can walk around pretending like she is helpless. *Normal.* But you're not normal, are you, Freckles? You're not helpless either. I must admit, I underestimated you before."

The girl raised a brow. "Underestimated me before as in... When you thought you'd met me?" She scoffed, shaking her head. "I still don't see the fairness in you being able to see me, but I cannot see you."

And she would never see him if they were to keep connecting like this. He wanted the satisfaction of watching the surprise and recognition upon her face when he found her.

The girl sighed. "I want to make sense of this as much as you."

Kauis ignored her remark and snarled. "How does it feel to be a murderer and a thief? You have so many titles, Freckles."

"I don't know what you mean." Her pursed lips effortlessly pushed out the lie.

"You can't run from it forever, you know. It is a hungry force once you give into it."

The girl frowned. "I don't know what you speak of."

"I talk about what is inside of you. You mentioned a voice in your head, yes?" He reached through the shadows. Lifting her scarred palm, he continued, "You've drawn from it already. It's only a matter of time."

"What is only a matter of time?"

But she knew exactly what he spoke of.

She was too calm now. Too still and calculating. Too much like his dangerous friend already, before even giving in fully to the bond of Merellian's magic. Kauis wondered how long she would survive with it inside her. Merellian's essence had been a terrifying force when he fully gave into it, and she was a weak mortal. She wouldn't last with Merellian's malice within her.

His voice snapped through the silent cave like a biting whip. "Until I find you, Freckles."

He lunged for her, wrapping his shadowed fingers around her neck. He squeezed as she thrashed and screamed, begging for mercy. She couldn't die here, within this sleeping realm. But he would find her and the sleuthing faeries harboring her. And when he did, there would be no mercy for her—not after what she had done.

CHAPTER 48

WILLA

Willa sat up with a rattled gasp, blinking furiously in the dark, but nothing could push away what had just happened. A cold breeze nipped at her bare shoulders, and she tried to catch her breath. A white bandage was wrapped around her ribs and chest, hugging her skin tightly. With a trembling hand, she lifted the large fur blanket laying across her waist. Thankfully, she still had pants on.

A popping noise had her dropping the blanket with a startled flinch. Remnants of a fire were trying to stay alive inside a stone hearth. The glowing embers gave her enough light to inspect her pale torso between the wrappings. She wheezed while rubbing her neck absentmindedly. Was nowhere safe? Visions of the shadowed man strangling her invaded her thoughts. Every step she took, whether awake or sleeping, someone wished her harm. Her own mind was trying to kill her now, for fuck's sake.

She lifted her palms to find the marks weren't glowing, but a gnawing feeling deep within her stomach rolled and shifted. As memories bubbled to the surface, she covered her mouth to muffle her rasp of alarm. These hands...something had come from them.

She pulled her hand away from her open mouth and studied the marking of the sunburst. She wiggled her fingers warily, recalling the bright light streaming between them. The smell of burning bark still singed her nose.

A shiver of awareness pimpled her skin when she remembered the wolf she had freed—Eth'tinok. It was a wonder she was still alive. She had stabbed him with arrows and the faerie's magic had tried to kill her for it.

Tried.

Willa clamped her mouth shut to stop the bile from responding to the voice within her mind.

Memories of the Wylan's forest floor opening beneath her feet had her straightening in the bed. Her hand had been lifted, two fingers snapping together on their own accord. But she had been numb as her body moved on its own, despite the pain in her side from Eth'tinok's bite. And that voice...it had laughed and cackled within her as if pain and chaos brought it joy. It laughed like...

Willa gasped, remembering Merellian standing over the Wylan Creature with a raised fist and crazed smile.

What had she done? What had *it* done?

A dark, echoing laugh bounced inside of her, stilling her racing heart. *Do not act so surprised at the power I showed you. You know you have always wanted it. You managed to startle Death's Divine with your rage and my might...Imagine snapping your fingers to have Lord Nalore drop to his knees before you. Imagine the things we could do if you gave in to me fully.*

Willa gagged and shook her head. She had said something similar when she threatened Branlon in Traifton; saying if she were tainted by the Wylan's magic, she would snap her fingers and watch him suffer.

But now she had something much worse. Something capable of doing such things. She had stolen Merellian's magic. It was inside of her. A part of him had taken control for a brief moment while the wolf had barrelled towards her.

Another laugh bounced in her mind, too close to the sound of Merellian's unhinged cackles. She covered her ears and fell onto her shoulder. Pushing her face into the pillow with shallow whimpers, she silently pleaded, *Get out! Get out of my head!*

When the echoing laughter subsided, she uncovered her ears to wipe away fresh tears from her lashes. Rubbing at her eyes with a groan, Willa froze when the blanket around her pulled and the bed's frame shifted.

Someone else was in bed with her. Peering through the dark, she studied the pillow beside hers.

Brown curls splayed onto the dense pillow beside her in shadowed tendrils. Willa sucked in a breath as she followed the curls towards swirls of marks running over a tawny-skinned, bare back. Clusters of ferns and leaves twisted and danced around one another all the way toward two small dimples at the base of a male's spine. The markings rolled and moved as if they were living, breathing plants. A deep blue color twisted within the markings, like sparkling rivers made of starlight. Willa wanted nothing more than to touch them.

Ever so slowly, she lifted a shaking finger towards the moving design. She was about to touch it when something from above caught her attention. Willa shifted her head from her soft pillow and gasped. She tried to speak, but nothing came out as a black mass of shadow crawled out of the stone ceiling towards her.

White rows of teeth appeared in the shadow and hissed, "Mine."

Willa tried to move as the teeth chomped towards her. But she was frozen on her side. Paralyzed by what rolled towards her. She had heard that voice before. She had seen those teeth. They belonged to the wolf she had bargained with.

The shadow figure grazed its teeth over her cheek, a low growl coming from its throat as it repeated, "Mine."

Willa closed her eyes and waited for pain, but nothing happened. She opened her eyes to be met with hundreds of glowing green eyes. All blinked as one before saying the same word. Over and over again.

"Mine. Mine. Mine."

Black clouds hovered over her vision, blinding her, as the voices chanted louder and louder. This was worse than the visions Eth'tinok had given her. This was real—unlike her dreams. This was raw terror, feeding off her past and taunting her with it. It was fear in its purest state, changing and shifting above her in dancing, rippling black masses.

She couldn't breathe. Couldn't move as the eyes grew larger and larger. Flapping wings and talons fought each other as they raced from the ceiling to get to her.

Willa was pushed onto her back with a sudden brute force. Lifting her hands, she clawed blindly through the pulsing, vast mass of shadows clinging to her. She struck something hard and hit it again with a clenched fist. She went to strike once more when a strong cold force wrapped around her wrist and squeezed. Willa tried to shout, but nothing came out. Her wrist was pushed back behind her head and held over the pillow. She used her other hand to claw at whatever pinned her, but something again grabbed her wrist and shoved it above her head, next to her other one.

"Mine. Mine. Mine!" the shadows shrieked into her ears.

The layers of shadows continued to blind her. Willa thrashed and bucked, but her body was sinking further into the soft padding of the bed. She tried to get her chest to move, but her body wouldn't listen. Panic seized her. The shadows were suffocating her. Stealing every breath, the thicker they got. Black, rippling fingers crawled around her neck, precisely like Merellian's had, and squeezed her esophagus. She bit at the air and thrashed her head from side to side, but nothing worked.

Her eyes rolled back into her head as her body twitched and convulsed. She let out a silent prayer for air to return to her lungs where it belonged, but none came. She would die from the thick swarm of shadows and nightmares around her. Her chest rose from the bed as her body spasmed upwards, fighting for life, when something warm and soft crashed against her lips.

The force of the sudden touch pushed her body back onto the bed and held her there. Willa tried to pull her face away when air rushed into her lungs. She widened her mouth and gasped as another hot push of air entered her. Closing her eyes, she greedily inhaled the next rush of air. The tender force upon her lips pressed deeper, making her gasp again and again. Willa moaned as another burst of life fell into her. She would never take her breathing for granted ever again. The sudden rush of adrenaline with her newfound breaths was overwhelming.

She wanted more. *Needed more.* To assure she would never, ever run out of air again in her mortal life.

Willa lifted her head, pressing closer to the soft, plush mass touching her lips. A weight shifted over her hips as she tried to lift herself up, but something still held her wrists above her head. The grip around her wrists tightened and pressed down, forcing her head back into the bed. She fell back and gasped as the warm pillows pushing her lips closed and moved with hers. A deep moan vibrated against her lips.

When her mind caught up to what was happening, Willa opened her eyes right as the warmth on her mouth pulled away from her like a snapping whip.

Her faerie captor hovered inches above her face. The silver rims in his eyes glowed as he roamed her face with heavy-lidded hunger. His mouth hung open and he panted quick, rattled breaths as his bare arms braced either side of her, his hands gripping her wrists. Willa's body tensed as the air between them grew taut. She sucked in a breath and pulled her bottom lip between her teeth. It tingled from the pressure she put on it, practically making her spasm from the currents of tingling shocks rolling through her.

The faerie stilled above her. She stopped watching the blue rolling marks and looked back up to his eyes. He had stopped breathing and was watching her with an unnatural stillness. The only thing he seemed focused on was her lip as his hard body pressed on hers.

His glowing eyes focused only on her was like being doused with cold water. Ice rushed through her body, taking away every warm, tingling thought from before.

Willa raised her knee and slammed it towards the inside of his thigh—narrowly missing the mark she had intended, but it had been close enough. The faerie hissed, leaning towards her face in surprise. His grip loosened on her wrists enough for her to slam her forehead against his, but this time, she aimed for his nose. Having made this mistake before, she knew it would hurt, but it didn't stop the pained groan she made as she fell back onto the pillow.

The faerie recoiled with a grunt and rolled off her quickly. Grasping the bridge of his nose with both hands, he growled, stumbling off the bed.

Willa winced at the throbbing between her brows while sitting up. "Do not fucking touch me again, faerie."

She leaned forward and pulled up the heavy furred blanket to cover her bandaged chest, stinging, shameful heat flooding her cheeks as she glared at him from across the room.

The faerie still held his nose and said darkly, "I was trying to help you, mortal." He cursed under his breath. "You are here, *alive*, because of me. And yet, every time I turn my back or close my eyes, you fray the threads of my patience, nearly getting us all killed in the process!"

"How dare you—I saved you from the wolf!" But the words soured on her tongue with the thought of *what* had helped her.

"*You* put us in that mess. And it was not you who saved me. It was something else. Something you're hiding." Willa recoiled from the anger in voice. He pointed to her and hissed. "*That* is why you still live. Whatever you did and whatever you know, go to the queen now."

As if listening, a small vibrating hum echoed in the back of her mind. She pushed the thought of Merellian's essence down deep into her subconscious.

The faerie pinched his nose and shifted it side to side. It popped, and he cursed, shaking his head before turning to the door. Swinging it open, he stomped out and slammed it shut behind him.

Willa jumped as the oak door rattled on its hinges. Help her? *Help* her? His magic had tortured her, stealing her breath away. She clung to the blankets and waited for his return, but he never came.

Furious, she cursed and threw the blanket back. Why was he even in here? Sharing her bed? She slid off the soft mattress and stumbled forward in the dark.

She was about to wrap the blanket around her when her eyes caught the small pile of clothes and her boots near the fire's hearth. Shoving her feet into the familiar worn leather boots, she lifted a long, furred jacket and threw it over her hastily before rushing to the door. It went well past her knees and hands, but she didn't care. Anything was better than being practically naked in front of these rude and ruthless creatures.

Before she could open the latch to the door, it burst open from the other side. A female appeared in the brightly lit doorframe and laughed.

Brown, shoulder-length hair framed a perfectly symmetrical face. But pink lips were curled back into a snarl, taking away from the female fae's breathtaking beauty.

Willa was surprised to hear such a melodious voice come from the feral frown directed at her as the faerie said, "It pains me to say this, Harland, but you are right. The queen is going to burn us all."

The female pulled Willa out of the bedroom, dragging her through a narrow hallway covered in fur pelts and rugs of all shapes and sizes. Her cold, long fingers dug into Willa's arm as she rounded a sharp corner. They entered a large sitting room lit by sconces and candles littering various tables and shelves. A fireplace on the opposite wall roared brightly, exuding enough warmth to make her uncomfortable in the thick jacket she had found.

The faerie thrust Willa forward with a disgusted grumble. She stumbled, but caught herself with the back frame of a velvet-lined couch, wincing from the pain in her side.

"Seriously, Sorean? A mortal? *This* is what you found?"

Her fae captor, *Sorean*, turned from the wall he leaned on. His darting eyes met hers before he looked at the female fae behind her. Willa noticed red marks lining his tanned cheek and neck, and she smiled, remembering she had been hitting and scratching at something moments before he …

"We went on the word of a faerie shifter *you* asked us to meet in the tavern, *Princess*," Sorean retorted. "You know we couldn't just bring Noi's words to the queen. He's considered a deserter of the crown. So, I did what you suggested, Farren. I brought back living, breathing proof."

Willa flinched and looked at the female Sorean had called a princess. Farren wore a long, silver velvet dress, lined in brown, spotted fur. It was elegant and too fancy for what seemed to be the cabin they were all huddled in now.

She half-heartedly pointed at Willa. "And what proof is this, Sorean?"

Willa looked at her beautiful, terrifying face with silver-rimmed blue eyes before noticing another fae behind her. He was sitting at a long table, littered with half empty plates and cups of food and what smelled like wine. This one had been with them in the Wylan. He noticed Willa staring and gave her a wink before leaning back to lift an amber glass. As he drank, Willa ignored the hunger pains in her stomach. Something shuffled behind her, and she looked back at the couch to find the other faerie who had traveled with them.

Iara was lying on the couch, assessing her with narrowed eyes. Willa remembered the last time she had seen this fae and gulped. Willa could have sworn she saw her lips twitch slightly at the nervous movement.

She spoke from her reclined position, silencing both Sorean and Farren, who seemed to be arguing now in another language. "You saved me. Why?"

All noise subsided, except for the popping and crackling of the fire.

Willa looked away from her cold, unblinking gaze to the arm that was bound in a tight sling across her chest. Her upper right thigh was also bandaged, much like Willa's chest.

Willa shifted her stance and gripped the couch tightly. "I did nothing heroic. I left you at first. Tucked my tail and ran." It didn't take magic or immortality to feel the sudden tension falling over the room from her unfiltered words. She had no choice but to continue. "I have been a part of too many deaths as of late. You all keep saying 'mortal' as if I am nothing and yet I feel things exactly as you do. Or maybe you have no emotion to understand what empathy and common decency means."

The air thickened, and Sorean shifted in her line of sight. Willa took a breath, her chest aching as she thought of Merellian, Claire, and Ivaan.

Her nails dug into the couch, her shoulders beginning to shake, but she straightened her spine and continued. "I won't say it was kindness towards you that brought me back. Guilt is what did it. I have a conscience and am trying to clear it. And I couldn't do that by leaving you to die at the hands of the deity."

Iara cocked her head for a moment and studied her face. No one moved, including Willa, while she waited for her to say something. Surprise flooded her when the hardness in the faerie's face cracked. Small wrinkles creased around her dark honey eyes, a slow smile forming before she let out a loud cackle.

"Well, at least you're honest, girl." She laughed, but then hissed, shifting on the couch. "And honesty is hard to come by when you're constantly surrounded by scheming court faeries."

The tension in the room subsided, a heavy weight lifting from her throat and chest when Iara gave her a tentative smile.

"Willa. I have a name, and it is Willa."

"Willa." Farren's feminine voice repeated her name with disgust. And when she turned to face her, the faerie rolled her eyes. "Thanks for the introduction. I'll have them put it on your grave."

Farren shouldered past Sorean as she swung the cabin's front door open. A cold gust of wind and snow blowing in from outside was cut short by the faerie slamming it behind her.

"It was clever, what you did to get Eth'tinok out of his binding magic," Iara said, pulling her attention to her.

"Eth'tinok," Willa repeated the word slowly, frowning at how clumsy it sounded from her lips. "I heard you say it in the cavern, and he gave himself many titles, but what does it mean in your language?"

"Sleeping carnage," the fae at the table said. "Bloodshed of the mind. Night's unholy bringer of bargains and bloodied balance."

Willa's gaze flitted to the dark marks rolling over Sorean's neck and tried to imagine anything but the shadows attacking her in bed, as descriptions of the wolf she had freed filled the room.

"Forsetyr's counterpart," Iara explained, shifting on the couch. She appeared as uncomfortable in her bandages as Willa was. "He was the horned bear's shadow, to keep the gods' balance in check. Really, he was there to do what they could not."

"Which was?" Willa asked.

"Killings. Slaughter." The fae at the table's eyes darkened as he answered. After a long drink from a refreshed glass, he added, "The wolf was aware of everyone's wrong doings. Worse than death and torture, he dabbled in selling secrets and knowledge."

The wolf's words and shared secrets washed over her with the answers she'd gained from freeing him. "Eth'tinok said you locked him away, is it because of what he is?"

"The Deity of the Dark is a predator before anything else," Sorean answered, his lips twitching as his gaze wandered over Willa's scowl. "Even the fae have reason to fear him. Eat or be eaten. Kill or be killed. It was for protection."

"Precaution," Willa countered.

The fae behind her mumbled something, and Iara again shifted uncomfortably. Sorean darkened his gaze upon her, and Willa lifted her chin.

"You said he dabbled in knowledge and secrets. Bargains," Willa said. "Were you scared of what he knew or what he did?"

"I did not chain him, girl," Sorean bit back.

She stepped forward with shaking shoulders. "Then who did?"

"It doesn't matter now that he is out again."

"And hunting us," the faerie behind her grumbled. Willa looked back to him, catching his smile as he took another pull from his cup. He was either enjoying this or extremely drunk.

"He lives?" she asked breathlessly. His howls still rattled her mind.

None of them answered her.

Willa rubbed at her chest and ribs, remembering its teeth tearing into her side. She had stabbed a deity. By listening to the voice within her again, she'd done *something*. Enough to knock it down and startle it, if only for a moment. And her captor had witnessed it.

His queen would want answers, but how could Willa explain that her town had been unknowingly performing sorcery? And because of their mistakes, she now harbored an elf's essence within her. They would kill her instantly with these damning confessions based on her late king's actions.

The only noise to follow her question was the popping of the fire until Iara pushed herself up into a fully seated position. She turned to look at all three of them with a pained face before speaking, "I don't know what your bargain was—"

"Iara, we don't have time," Sorean said darkly.

Iara looked at Sorean with a glare before giving Willa a small smile. "If we live to see tomorrow, I want to know your story and how you ended up here. I want to know how you bargained with Death's Divine and came out alive, for most do not."

Willa's stomach clenched. She assumed it to be her hunger until it stirred again, making her flush with a sudden heat the fire hadn't caused. Had Iara heard Willa and Eth'tinok's conversation? Sorean had admitted to witnessing part of what she had done, but had Iara seen what came from her palms?

Willa fought to keep herself from checking her hands in front of them all. To fight the sudden temptation, she brought her hands back to the couch and gripped the velvet. Willa unclenched her jaw and nervously rolled her neck to shake away the sudden flush within her.

"Do you have a last name?" Iara asked.

Willa shifted nervously on her feet, glancing between her and Sorean. "Thesalor."

She hadn't heard or said her last name in ages. Her chest was torn in two as she ached for home. She was so caught up in her own emotions to notice Iara standing from the couch with slow and painful movements.

It was the faerie's words pulling her from the emotion she swam in when she said, "Willa Thesalor. Allow me to formally introduce myself. I am Commander Iara Holavaris of Lithelle's aerial division." Her tongue rolled with the r in the last name. "I am the right hand to the queen's heir to the throne. The voice of reason in council and—"

"The voice of reason?" The faerie on the table behind them coughed loudly. He wiped liquid from his dark beard as he clutched his belly, letting out a howl of a laugh.

"Yes, the voice of reason, Harland," Iara countered with irritation.

This was a terrible time for Willa to smile. She ducked her head from Harland back to Iara, fighting her amusement of the drunk faerie. She glanced at Sorean, who was still scowling deeply at her. It was then, she realized, the heir to the throne Iara and Harland argued over was him: her faerie captor. She wasn't just going to his queen, but his mother. Willa shifted uncomfortably in her stance. If the queen was anything like him, she truly was destined for death.

"Do you think *you* are? You are in a wine induced haze most days, Harland," Iara hissed. "Forgive me, but it is I who takes the title easily."

Harland continued to laugh loudly and Willa discovered a sudden interest in the fur rugs to keep from joining in with his infectious laughter.

Iara pressed on, "I am giving you my title before I make you an oath. I, Iara Holavaris, swear a life debt to you, Willa Thesalor."

CHAPTER 50
WILLA

Harland's laughter stopped abruptly, and a cup fell as he stared at Iara with a slackened jaw. Confused, she looked away from the bearded fae and froze when she saw the way Sorean now glared at Iara.

The prince spoke slowly, as if to rein in the rage so clearly plastered on his face, "Do you understand the consequences of what you've said, Iara?"

Harland grunted behind them. "You just said we do not know what bargain she made to trick you into helping Eth'tinok escape. Voice of reason, my ass."

Sorean nodded, hissing through clenched teeth, "She is a mortal and you are a faerie. Life debts are everlasting. Do you want to die when she does? Their lifespan is but a blink of an eye for us, and if she dies because of her constant, careless actions, you die with her."

Iara countered with shrugging shoulders. "Why does it matter? Farren is right; the queen will kill us all for this. I am well within my honor to offer this to her. She did the same for me unknowingly, against all odds, knowing she would probably die to save me. And you brought her back despite what had happened. It is you who should do the same, for we are living and safe from Death's Divine because of this mortal." Iara pointed a finger at Sorean's chest and continued. "And it is *not* everlasting, prince. If we survive the night, I can sever the bond whenever I choose."

Harland grunted, as he stood. "With rune magic—sorcery." Willa's eyes widened, a cold sweat rolling through her as he continued, "Sorcery is forbidden and you know it, Iara. That will guarantee your death from Queen Morielle. And *if* you kill the bond and she dies, you will wash away all we have done to get her here. You are stuck with this oath now, you damn fool."

Invisible roots crawled over Willa's feet, holding her in her stance as the faeries argued over how or when she would die. Anger rippled from Sorean's tense shoulders and ticking jaw in thick waves. He looked like was ready to say more but he rolled his neck and adjusted his jacket. Willa, Harland, and Iara watched him tensely, but he ignored them all to turn and leave through the front door of the cabin.

When the door slammed shut, Willa loosened a deep, trembling breath. Iara cursed and grabbed a bundle of bags near the door before walking out to trail after him.

"Eat. Drink. The night's ride will be cold."

Willa jumped at the sound of Harland's voice. He had been so quiet when coming to stand beside her. Even for a drunk, as Iara had called him, his steps were more graceful than she could ever hope to be.

She grabbed the bread and cup from Harland's warm hands and nodded to him in thanks. "Why feed me when everyone anticipates my death before dawn?"

Harland's eyes twinkled, but he didn't smile. He watched her take a bite of the bread before stepping away. Savory meat and cheese were nestled inside of the roll, making her hum with satisfaction as she chewed.

"In another life, we would have been friends, Willa Thesalor. I bet you can hold your drink, too."

He hadn't denied the fact she might die tonight, and Willa had to force down her bite of food to keep from vomiting from his kind yet lancing words. She chased it with the drink, coughing and hissing at the stinging bite that followed. It tasted sweet, like wine, but much more potent. At once, the dull throbbing behind her bandages settled from the instant buzz of the drink.

Harland only laughed and opened the door. He held it open and raised his brows. Willa realized he was waiting for her. She quickly finished the roll and drink before following him out of the entryway and into the dark.

As the two walked down a tight, snow-packed trail, Willa heard nothing aside from the crunching of snow beneath her boots. Harland's steps were silent despite the moving snow they packed down. She looked up at the falling snowflakes and tried to recall Traifton ever having this much snow as she tightened her oversized coat. It happened seasonally but never stuck for more than a day. Usually, it only fell in sheets of wet ice before melting into more stinking mud puddles around the dreary town. The Wylan Woods had been humid and putrid, and this was vastly different. No green menacing mist, only crisp fresh air, and as she turned, her steps faltered. They had just stepped out of what she'd assumed was a cabin, but all she could see for miles in every distance was snow covered rocks and thick pine trees at the base of a mountain.

"We are out of the Wylan?" she asked.

The path narrowed, and Harland stepped in front of her, quickening his pace. He replied with a simple, "Yes."

She thought of her bandaged ribs and frowned. How long had it taken them to leave the Wylan Woods? How long had she been asleep?

As if to read her mind, Harland spoke again. "All we had was sleeping tonic and wine, and with the blood you lost, we weren't sure you would live. You're more stubborn than I thought and surprised us all by making it here." He chuckled and continued, "We managed to stitch you up with what we had in the cabins but a healer will need to further assess your wounds."

If the queen didn't kill her right away.

Willa looked over her shoulder and frowned. "You say cabins, yet I see only rocks and trees behind us now."

"They are invisible to anyone without faerie essence." Harland said smugly.

So this was how the fae had managed to remain hidden for centuries. Willa struggled to keep up with Harland's effortlessly lengthy strides. She pressed further while walking in his footprints, two times the size of hers. "If this is veiled to someone like me, is this Lithelle?"

"No."

Fine. Willa glared towards his towering frame and studied the terrain around them instead.

The trees were different, as if bred for constant snow and cold. Fog lay high above them, covering the rocks and mounds crawling up beside her. Clearly, they were in the mountains. The air was tight in her chest as she looked around through puffs of her breath hovering in front of her. Aside from the cliffs and hills around Traifton, the only mountains on Kalandrae were the Menyamere Mountains, but they were clear across the maps.

"Harland?" The faerie grunted in front of her but kept walking. "How long were we in the Wylan?"

Harland was quiet for a moment before answering in the same, clipped tone. "Six days. I don't know how long you were there before us, though, mortal."

Willa almost tripped on her feet. She thought of the lake she had fallen into and the elf's beast pulling her from it. Its wingspan had been large enough to carry her for miles with a few simple pumps in the air, there was no telling where she had been dropped. She would be dead if the winged beast hadn't been attacked.

Her eyebrows raised. "Did you shoot at a winged creature above the Wylan's trees?"

Harland grunted. He continued walking without her while she stood frozen from the realization. If Sorean found her after the bat-like beasts, they were unaware they had saved her, not knowing who the beast belonged to. Although, 'save' was a funny word. Really, her death was continuously being prolonged— escape dangled in front of her like a slice of tempting apple pie.

Her stomach rumbled at the thought of her favorite treat. If she had been in the Wylan for over a week, Traifton's festival was long since over. Had it even continued with the elves being there?

Harland pulled her from her spiraling worries. "Hurry up, girl."

The sounds and smells of horses greeted her as they passed a tree, but she couldn't locate the large beasts. Despite Harland's grunting and quickened steps, she halted as he disappeared before her eyes.

He was no longer speaking to her, or at least she hoped not, as he cooed softly. She took one hesitant step when she heard a neighing response. Her brows furrowed. Where had he gone?

The crunching of snow behind her caused her heart to lodge in her throat.

She spun to find a furred cloak blocking her vision. She followed the black fur up to Sorean, who was glaring down at her from the bridge of his nose. Before she could say or do anything, he threw a dark material over her head, ropes quickly knotting over her wrists.

Willa kicked at the faerie as he hoisted her up over his shoulders and led her towards the sounds of whinnying horses and stomping hooves. Like a sack of flour, she was thrown onto a horse. She tried to roll herself off the saddle, but he was too quick and she was lifted into a seated position, with both legs hanging over one side. She groaned from the stinging pain beneath her bandages.

Gloved hands pulled her wrists forward as the rope binding them was shoved around the leather knob to keep her seated. Those gloved hands moved from her tied wrists to hold her hips and shimmy her back towards a warm, firm body. Willa snarled through the thick material covering her vision. At least she could breathe and talk in this one.

Sorean said harshly near her ear, "Not a word."

She wondered why she couldn't have ridden with Harland or Iara. At least those two tolerated her. Iara had sworn a debt to her, even. A debt Willa didn't understand, but she knew it had made the prince behind her very upset. If she made this less than enjoyable, maybe he'd force her to sit with Iara instead.

She waited a moment beneath the dark material covering her face. He leaned away from her, the horse shifting forward in response, and Willa bucked her head back to hit him in the face. Sorean predicted her movement easily and dodged her.

Clenching a fistful of the material and her hair, he yanked her head back with a swift jerk of his arm, causing her to yelp. The cold air nipped at her exposed neck, sending a shiver down her spine.

Blind from the material, she jumped as the faerie's cold, sharp teeth grazed her neck. A sudden, stinging pinch had her letting out a cry. The pinch grew harder, right above her collarbone as his teeth bit into her skin. Before he could draw blood, however, the faerie pulled back, sending another wave of shivers down her body from the lack of sudden warmth. Sorean tugged her head back again, making her whimper in fear and dreadful anticipation.

"We are in the fae lands now, girl. We play differently here." Sorean's breath was hot on her stinging neck as he growled. "The rules are simple. The gods do not exist, leaving only the faeries and elves to hold power. Mortals are once again beneath us, and we will let that be known. So, listen when spoken to and do as you are told."

"And if I don't?" Willa asked quietly.

She stared into the material with watery eyes as she envisioned a realm worse than the nightmares the fae had procured in bed. A realm worse than the Wylan if all faeries acted like the one behind her.

Sorean huffed coldly before kicking his horse into a run. "You die."

CHAPTER 51

SOREAN

Sorean clenched his jaw as his horse led the party closer to his veiled home. He took in deep, lingering breaths as they rode, as if to pocket the freshness of the cold air before entering the magically procured land he had grown up in.

His body itched uncomfortably behind the tense and quiet mortal as they traveled in taut silence. The color of his marks was the only thing to keep his nerves settled. They were glowing white, not dark blue. A quick glance back to the cabins they left behind had him clenching his jaw even tighter.

Sorean had been fighting to keep his essence in check ever since their precarious escape from Eth'tinok. He had veiled their travels as they rushed out of the Wylan and to the mountains. For a while, Sorean had dared to believe the wolf was stuck within the crevices he had created in the forest. But when they'd pushed through the cursed veil of the woods to enter the mountain trails, he had heard Death Divine's howl. They didn't dare stop until they reached their veiled land within the snow-capped rocks. Only then did his essence settle into a complacent slumber beneath his skin. He should have known why when they'd drawn closer to the cabins. He should have realized why his essence was suddenly satisfied and quiet, but it was only when he got off his horse, he realized what had happened. The queen's sentries were dead.

Harland had offered to help him gather the bodies, but Sorean had refused. He'd dealt with his own destruction. Weeping as he burned the bodies, he'd screamed and pleaded with the gods to take his essence away. He'd even tried to pull his essence out so he could punish himself for what he had done, but it had ignored him. In fact, it had seemed to nestle further within him, wrapping around his soul, forever marking him as a monster.

Sorean hadn't looked at his friends when he'd entered the cabin. All he could do was mindlessly take care of the mortal girl's wounds with the small reserve of medicines and tonics they stored in each cabin, while Harland tended to Iara. Sorean had left a piece of himself there when he'd cleaned his mistake from the ground and walls. The essence had helped him several times in the Wylan, but it would be the last time he would allow it. It was evil incarnate.

He had fought sleep for as long as he could until the darkness embraced him like an old friend. The night terrors had been worse, keeping him trapped within a web of hauntings until his essence had awakened. He'd woken to find the room clouded in his magic. Sorean had stayed with the girl to ensure she didn't wake up and try to run, but had forgotten what his own essence had wanted the most—*her*. She would have died if he hadn't broken the connection between her and his terrors.

The girl shifted on the horse in front of him, snapping Sorean out of his recollections. His jaw ticked as she adjusted her position with a shift of her hips and his grip tightened on the reins. The sooner he was off this horse, the better. Digging his heels further into the stirrups, he urged his steed to go faster. The horse obliged, which had the girl sliding back further between his thighs, flooding him with a sudden rush of heat. Sorean suppressed his groan as the smell of his scent on her overwhelmed him.

The two had camped beside one another and ridden together all through the Wylan. His scent on her was nothing new. But when she leaned into him, Sorean's essence shifted within him. It wanted her. To kill her or study her, Sorean no longer knew. It had teased and terrorized her before trying to suffocate her with its wrath. It was, above all else, curious about its promised mortal. And its curiosity was festering within Sorean with a raw and primitive ache. He had never loathed something so small and fragile so fervently as he shoved his essence deep down within him.

When they neared Lithelle's veil, Sorean readied himself for the sentries. Slowing his horse, he donned the mask of the arrogant, dark, and brooding royal they all knew him to be. When Iara announced their party and led them into Lithelle, he did not look at them. He couldn't, knowing he would see their dead comrades in their faces. He would tell his mother he was responsible for what had happened at the cabin. Let her punish him for what his magic had done. For what he could not control. Perhaps then she would understand he was not meant to rule.

A dry heat greeted him immediately as they entered the realm. The mortal girl's body responded to it too, flushing warmer against his. They all could use a bath and a week's worth of rest, but the queen would be aware of their return now. Lifting his hood to cover his face, he followed Iara's horse through the narrow alleys of the southern quarters.

Surprisingly, the girl didn't fight him when he pulled her off the horse behind Lady Talarin's tavern. He was glad she was heeding his warning. He had enough to deal with now without a brat questioning or fighting his every move.

Sorean checked her neck before hoisting her over his shoulder and veiling them both. Thankfully, he hadn't bitten her hard enough to make a mark. He shouldn't have bitten her at all. His body had reacted instinctually before his mind could stop him. Biting was something only lovers did when two faeries wanted to claim each other, letting the rest of the fae know they were spoken for. But Sorean's instincts had been on high alert ever since his kiss of life turned into something more heightened between the two of them. It was natural to need and want...Unless it was with someone you hated with every fiber of your being. His essence purred as if to agree with his thoughts, reminding Sorean it was his magic making him feeling this way and nothing else.

He needed to calm his body down and find release. He needed this tension gone before he arrived at court. It would be bad enough bringing a mortal girl into a viper pit of feral beings, but even worse if his body wanted nothing more than to protect and claim her if anyone so much as looked in her direction.

The girl didn't dare move as he walked them into the back of the tavern. He didn't lift their veil until he found an empty room to throw the girl into. Pushing her onto the bed, he ripped the rope away from her wrists with a few rough pulls, and lifted the cloth from her face, slowly, preparing for her to fight. Not willing to take any chances, he immediately put a finger over her mouth, signaling her to stay quiet. Her round, green eyes sharpened on him as he did, and Sorean startled, ripping his finger from her when her sharp teeth bit into his skin.

Feral little thing. The girl's laugh grated on him, and he shook his hand in the air as he glared at her.

With an arrogant smirk, she spoke up to the velvet tapestries and said, "Now we're even."

Even, His essence repeated the word in a harmonized awe. *Yes, we're even.*

Sorean tensed, rolling his shoulders. He didn't know why his essence was agreeing, and he didn't want to know. He didn't want to give it any attention, for fear of it unleashing on her now.

And his body wanted nothing more than to shove her further into the mattress and wipe the smirk from her mouth. An odd and terrible tension thickened between them as she sat up to assess him with narrowed eyes and flared nostrils. Blood rushed to his ears as he tracked her racing pulse.

He could admit her green eyes and freckled nose charmed him. She would be devastating had she been born a faerie or an elf, especially with her less-than-charming personality. Immortals would have puddled behind her tempered steps, like lovesick puppies. They were lucky she was a mortal—*he* was lucky.

He turned and rubbed both hands on his face with a low groan. She was a curious mortal, nothing more, despite her rising allure.

The smugness in her voice was gone when she asked in a panicked rush, "Wait! Where are you going?"

Sorean reached for the door handle. "A healer will be in to assess your wounds. We patched you together with what we had, but she'll want to check you herself. She'll bring a change of clothes as well."

"What's wrong with what I'm wearing?"

Insufferable mortal.

Sorean fought the desire to slam his head on the door to rid him of this irritation and desire wrapped into one. He, of course, did no such thing, and instead turned to her, leaning on the door frame with a tense smile.

"It's my jacket, for one. For two, you smell terrible and there are twigs and mud caked so far into your hair I've nearly forgotten it's red and not black. This is not appropriate for the faerie court."

The girl's smile fell away as she snarled at him, much like a faerie would. She looked down at the oversized jacket in disgust. Grabbing its hem, she started to lift it off, as if it burned to touch her skin.

Sorean cocked his head, his smile widening as she pulled it up over her pants, exposing a freckled patch of skin above her navel before revealing the bandages he had poorly put on her.

"Oh, by all means, just wear the wrappings and pants like before. That will make *quite* the impression."

The girl dropped the jacket and stood. "You didn't seem to have a problem with it when you kissed me this morning."

Sorean was constantly surprised by the anger beneath her brash, unfiltered words. She must have been a dragon in another life; he was sure of it as he took in her flaming hair to match her temper. Her anger and his surprise only seemed to excite his roaring pulse more. No one spoke to him like this, aside from Iara and Harland. No one looked at him like she did now; like she was planning to murder him while he slept or push him up against this door and—no.

Mine, His essence hummed beneath his sweat slicked neck.

No. She was a fucking mortal and nothing more. He needed to leave.

He shook the curls from his forehead and turned to open the door. "Trust me, mortal. I will never willingly touch you in such a way again. I did it to keep you alive for my queen, nothing more."

"You are an arrogant, pompous, wretch of a monster!"

Sorean barked a laugh, surprising himself with the rasping sound, but the girl apparently wasn't finished. "I may hate you more than anyone I've ever met."

"The feeling is mutual, *Ohirlyn*." He opened the door and stepped into the candlelit hall. "I'll be back in an hour to take you to the queen."

Sorean wandered the halls, nodding to those he recognized as he went. He let out a sigh of relief when he saw a familiar blonde faerie leaning on the bar. She was flirting with a handsome male with thin black hair. The two were sharing a drink, unaware of who walked towards them as they exchanged niceties.

Sorean said nothing as he strolled past, grazing a hand on her lower back as he went. He smiled to himself when he heard her excusing herself from the bar.

Within minutes, Sorean had Dasyra pushed up against the doorframe of a private room, her legs wrapped around his waist, while he nipped and kissed the small of her neck. Her hands clenched the curls of his hair while he thrust into her with a fast and fevered tempo. The two faeries found release together quickly, and he moaned into her shoulder as she loosened around him, sliding down the door. Sorean followed and sat beside her with a hazy smile.

The pair laughed and she bobbed her head onto his shoulder with a sigh. "It's good to see you again, Prince."

Grabbing his chin, she brought his face to hers and gave him a slow kiss, before pulling back and searching his eyes. The look she gave him filled him with regret. He shouldn't have done this with her. He had used her.

"Relax, Prince. I know what this was. I needed it, too."

He nodded but avoided her gaze, looking instead at the freckles dusting her flushed cheeks. His pleasant mood dampened further as he was reminded of another female with freckles. One who would most likely die today by the hands of his mother.

WILLA

Aromatic scents of lavender and orange wafted around Willa as she floated in a large tub of warm water. She had found the bathing room easily enough after Sorean had left her alone. The water was already steaming when she had found the entry behind a large red tapestry. She didn't want to understand how the water filled the tub on its own accord. She didn't want to ponder faerie magic, or any magic at all, while she soaked in silence. Willa certainly didn't want to envision the prince of the realm who so easily poked at her nerves with one arrogant dimple.

As the minutes passed, anxiety ate away at her insides.

She should have been preparing to meet the queen of a race she didn't believe existed a week ago. She should have been practicing how she would speak of the elves without mentioning Claire, or how she had killed an elf and stolen his magic with an unknown ritual.

But all she could focus on was what Eth'tinok had said. Over and over, his words repeated in the back of her mind. She had killed Merellian by stealing his essence. Essence that was inside of her now.

She could no longer deny the changes within her after having used it on the wolf. It had been brief but too much as the bright, burning light had fallen from her. It had touched the deity as it overwhelmed her senses, allowing her to *feel* the wolf's surprise and even fear. But how was it possible? It didn't make any sense. Maybe it had been her own emotions heightened by fear and adrenaline before she passed out. She needed days to dissect everything, but there was no time.

Willa sat up in the water and studied her brands. There was no glow to them now. They looked as ordinary as any scar would be upon one's skin. It needed to stay this way.

The faeries hated mortals; Sorean had made that clear, time and time again. They hated her for what King Ammanar had done—for what she had accidentally done five centuries later. If Iara or Sorean prodded her more on what had happened in the Wylan Woods, she would admit to sharing their confusion. Simply because it was true: just because she knew how she killed an immortal, it still didn't help her understand what was happening to her now. She could only hope Iara had heard nothing of what Eth'tinok said to her.

It took her fifteen minutes to comb through her hair. As she pulled through the knots, she sat on the edge of the bed and studied the ornate tapestries covering the entire room. A portrait of a beautiful faerie lay in the middle of a green tapestry. She had fine jewelry and wild blue eyes. A large crown sat nestled on her head with flowers and twigs entwined in the gold headpiece.

Willa took in the vibrant colors of the painting and thought of the hair clip Claire had given her. It was better off at the bottom of the lake. A secret that would die with Willa, like it had with her friend. A secret she still didn't understand. She didn't know why it had been so important or why the elves had chased Claire to

Kalandrae for it. An answer she didn't need to know now. She could only hope the elves would never find it within the Wylan Woods.

Someone cleared their throat behind her. Another breathtaking faerie was inspecting her curiously from the doorway. Long golden hair cascaded in waves on either side of her face, stopping at her shoulders. She looked a few years older than Willa, as did all the faeries she had met so far. Her eyes appearing wise, with small crinkles along the edges, silently assessed her. Her tailored silk pants and a button up tunic were both a deep royal blue, the cuffs and hems embroidered with swirls of ferns and vines, reminding Willa of the markings on Sorean.

The faerie looked at Willa with a tight smile and lifted a leather bag. This must be the healer Sorean had sent. Willa gave a nod and the faerie quietly set the bag onto the bed, opening it to reveal rows of vials and sharp instruments. Willa smiled softly. Her mother had a bag exactly like this. Even the small vials were the same as they used in Traifton. She wiped at her eyes quickly to hide the tears.

The healer looked up and nodded to the silk robe Willa had found in the bathroom. Willa dropped the comb to shift out of the robe. She winced at the movement and straightened when revealing her bare torso.

"You look at my instruments with nostalgia. Are you accustomed to healers and their work?"

Despite the emotionless observation, the faerie's accent was rich and hearty. Willa nodded while the fae walked towards her with a handful of items.

"My mother is a healer in our town," Willa said quietly.

The faerie hummed before tilting her head to assess her ribs. The faerie's golden hair shifted as she moved, uncovering more of her celestial features. Willa's brows rose when she saw a bright red scar traveling across the healer's cheek, down her neck, and into her high collared tunic. Willa knew she shouldn't stare so openly, so she looked away, tensing as the healer poked at her wound.

"The prince made quick work of this, though he could use some practice in stitching."

Willa looked at her side with pursed lips. The uneven stitches, holding her skin together in tiny knots, covered her ribcage, showcasing the large bite mark. Black and blue bruises spread from the mended wound all the way towards her hip.

The healer asked quietly, "Does it hurt?"

She shifted to assess her torso further. Willa shook her head. "Not constantly. I know it should be worse; I shouldn't even be upright. Why am I?"

"You were given tonics by Prince Sorean to help speed your natural healing process." The healer reached for a tub of ointment and dabbed it on her skin. "I am surprised how quickly your body reacted to it. Or that it did at all. But I will give you more tonight and tomorrow to assure the wounds don't fester." She sighed through her nose and continued, "Though I've never met a mortal, so I cannot say what would normally happen. Aside from the tonic, I'd say you are lucky. Lucky to breathe and lucky the prince tended to your wounds so carefully."

Willa cringed but gave the healer a polite nod, wondering if it was Merellian's essence within her that was helping more than the faerie tonic. The thought of Sorean tending to her had her frowning. His hatred was so contradictory. She almost laughed aloud when realizing he assured she survived for his queen and his own personal wants. Nothing more. She was only a means to an end for him.

"You'll take this for the fever." Willa focused on the healer, who held up a small brown vial. She lifted another clear vial and said, "This is for sleep."

"Fever?" Willa asked with a dry throat. She cleared it and straightened her back as the healer wrapped her up with a new, clean cloth.

"You're covered in sweat, and you look like you are about to pass out. If the wound is hurting you more than you say, speak now. It'll be your own fault if it worsens when I leave." The matter-of-fact tone had her straightening, as if her own mother was about to scold her.

"I'm a mortal who took a hot bath, and I need to eat." Willa regretted the needled pitch she used and winced, but the healer only laughed.

"It is okay to be in pain. The prince said you have been through quite an ordeal, Willa." She pulled back and nodded to the wrappings before smiling at her.

Her eyes narrowed. "How do you know my name and yet I don't know yours?"

The healer let out a warm chuckle as she walked back to her bag. As she packed up her items, Willa again caught herself staring at the scar across her face.

"I can see why they like you, though you'll do well to not ask so many questions in front of the queen." The healer raised her gaze from her task only to give Willa a stern look, much like her mother would have with any of her patients.

Willa hid her trembling chin, checking her hands. She unclenched them, staring at the marks, her chest aching for home.

"My name is Elliana. You may call me El." The healer's words were soft now. Kind.

Willa looked up from her hands and allowed a small smile. "Thank you, El. For helping me."

Elliana was focused on her open palms with a frown, but she nodded, letting Willa know she'd heard her. She supposed a healer branded with her own scar would find hers interesting, too.

A knock sounded at the door before Iara walked in, changed and bathed, looking more otherworldly and intimidating than she had before. Holding a bundle of clothes in her hands, her long, thin rows of braids were pulled into a low ponytail, a few with bright blue beads framing her face. She wore a button up tunic, much like the healer's, embroidered in the same woodland design on the cuffs of her sleeves. They were bunched up slightly above her wrists to show white leather cuffs on each of her forearms.

"What happened to your injuries?" Willa asked in awe while inspecting her. Iara's tunic was a creamy beige, practically glowing atop her dark skin tones. It was unbuttoned at the top to show layers of silver necklaces, and she noted matching earrings dangling from her pointed ears. She was breathtaking and terrifying all wrapped into one.

Iara and Elliana exchanged a knowing look, making Willa ache with loneliness. She knew nothing of their world or magic. She was all alone, with nothing but questions.

"El is one of the best healers in Lithelle," Iara answered. But Willa caught her wince as she deposited the clothing on the bed.

The female commander lifted a simple silk gown and dangled it before her with an impish grin.

Willa groaned. "Dressing me up for my death? How kind."

She ripped the dress from Iara's hand and turned quickly to step into it.

"If you keep speaking so openly, then yes, you will die in this finely made gown," Iara scolded.

Willa tensed before putting her hands through the short sleeves. Although the design was simple, the fabric was still elegant and finely crafted, rippling down in one layer, covering her bare feet like a puddle of melted iron. There was no need for wrappings or ties as it clung to her skin, hugging the curves of her body with little effort, yet it was thin enough for her to breathe comfortably in. The top of the dress swooped right below her collarbones, showing off her pale neck and freckles. She twitched with a shiver as she remembered a faerie who had bitten her there only hours before. A faerie *prince*. If royalty acted so feral, she could only imagine what the queen was like.

Dread hit her, making her shift nervously and fidget with the deep gray color of the thin satin. Willa turned to find both fae women watching her with amused looks.

She braided her hair in a single plait, swinging it over her shoulder. "So, I keep quiet and answer questions. This is an interrogation, correct?"

Iara pursed her lips but nodded before waving Willa towards her. She gently pushed her to sit on the corner of the padded bed before handing her two matching silk slippers.

"I cannot ask the queen any questions of my own?" Willa asked as she donned the shoes. "For I have several."

Amusement flashed in her eyes, but her growing frown deepened. "It would be wise to not ask any. If we make it out of her throne room tonight, I will answer any questions you have tomorrow."

"Because of your debt to me?"

Iara tensed as Elliana gasped.

"The debt I gave has nothing to do with this. I told you before, I want to know more about you. I apologize for how I first acted, but I have never met a mortal."

Willa bent forward, ignoring the tense looks the two faeries exchanged in silence. "I'm afraid there is not much to tell. I will behave, but I am like you, Iara. I know nothing of your customs or even what separates you from the elves. I am lost here in a world of those who can kill me without even touching me. In a world I never imagined because we were told the fae were gone."

Elliana spoke first in her kind, matter-of-fact tone, "Speak only when spoken to, and stay by Iara's side if you can. Eat and drink as much as you like and observe our customs."

"I am not seeing the queen by herself?" Willa asked hesitantly.

Iara placed two blue silk gloves with green fern and vine embellishments sewn into the sleeves in her hands.

"We have brought you here at an untimely moment for the realm of Lithelle," Iara answered. "This is the week of Prince Sorean's coronation. A week of games and celebration within the castle."

Willa lifted the gloves and blew out a nervous breath. "Does she know I am here?"

"She knows we are back," Iara replied. "I am not certain she knows what we entered the realm with."

What they entered the realm with. Not who. As if she were a Wylan Creature, dragged in for observation. Willa said nothing as her nerves grew thicker than the mist in that cursed forest. She could feel Iara's hardened gaze as she put the gloves on, and she looked up to find the faerie's attention fixed on the brands on her hands. Her face was pinched, almost as if she pitied Willa.

Willa covered her right palm quickly and snapped, "Do not pity me for these. This was a punishment."

Iara answered simply with a shrug of her shoulder. "I do not pity you."

"Pity is not something you'll get here," Elliana added. She tilted her head to reveal more of her scar. "Sometimes scars show power. They can show what you've survived and how you now laugh at those who have never had to bear their hardships on their skin like a painting out on display, rather than hidden deep within the soul. Everyone has them. What matters is how you wear them."

Iara sighed, pulling Willa away from the healer's heavy gaze. "But you will have enough stares tonight, and there is no need for the queen to view your past so openly."

Willa quickly put on the other glove and cleared her throat. She thought she was done until Iara slid two white cuffs over the silk gloves. Willa flinched as she clasped them over her wrists, allowing them to fall like bangles. She looked at Iara's wrists and the same white straps around her.

"What do these mean?"

"The castle will be filled with many royal faeries and their family members. Those who serve the families or specific royals wear their colors with these bands."

Willa scoffed, making Iara straighten. She looked up at her and crossed her arms to hide the straps. "But I do not serve any of you."

Iara pulled her arms away from her chest and gripped her wrists tightly. Willa froze at the quick movement.

Knowing she had scared Willa, she smiled and tugged her closer. "Listen to me, girl." Her kind, yet testy tone from earlier was gone. This was the faerie she had met in the cavern with Eth'tinok. Her voice was low and intimidating while she said, "These are to protect you. With these around your wrists, no one will dare touch you or speak to you."

Willa stared at the silver rims in her eyes and asked carefully, "How can I be protected by cuffs belonging to the queen's house when she is the one who may kill me?"

Prince Sorean answered before Iara could, "It is not the queen's color. It is mine."

Sorean was leaning on the doorframe with his usual, pompous smirk. He nodded to Elliana, who quickly packed her things and left.

Before she passed Sorean in the doorway, she looked back to Willa and mouthed, "Good luck."

Willa gave her a small smile, but it died when she looked back to Sorean, who was giving her his usual icy scowl. She wanted to rip the leather cuffs off, but she seemed to lose herself as she took in his new royal attire. Standing there in his moss green jacket and shiny black leather shoes, this was not the faerie captor who had taken her from the Wylan Woods. This was a royal, immortal being. A prince of a hidden realm. The Prince of Lithelle.

His usual mess of curls was combed back and tucked behind his pointed ears. Although there was one stubborn curl managing to pop out and hang near his left brow, which was the only telling resemblance of the unkempt, prickled faerie she had come to loathe. She couldn't help but notice the high collared jacket hid the marks on his neck. And the sleeves of his jacket were tightly pressed, showcasing his strong arms all the way down to his hands, covering the rest of his strange markings. He, too, wore gloves. Black thick ones made of leather, matching his shoes.

Aside from the stark white buttons lining his jacket, she saw no white leather cuffs on him to indicate she wore his color. But when she took his full outfit in again, she realized he had no need for them. He was painfully unforgettable in looks and status.

Sorean cleared his throat, and Willa pulled her gaze away from the details of his jacket to sneer at him.

"Do not take those cuffs off, tonight or any other night when in the queen's castle. Do you understand?"

She crossed her arms. "Don't pretend to care for me now, *Prince.*"

In the corner of her eye, she saw Iara pinch the bridge of her nose and turn with a shake of her head.

Willa gave him a defiant smile and continued, "You would not care if anyone touched me. This is all for show. I am a trophy of what you found in the Wylan, nothing more. The prince found a mortal, lost and afraid," she said in a mocking tone. "The poor girl would have died without the immortal prince. The elves chased her into the woods, and he saved her. Now he brings her to his perfect realm to show how magnanimous he is. The prince could have killed the mortal easily, but ever the dashing knight, he spared her pathetic life and brought her into his."

Sorean's face deepened into a rush of crimson. Had she struck a nerve? She snorted with a shake of her head. Good.

He lowered his brow, deepening his icy stare, and said, "I do not owe you any explanation. We made a deal, remember?"

He pushed from the doorframe and met her halfway. She tried to step away from him as he reached for her, but he was too fast. Pulling one of her crossed arms away from her chest, he lifted her wrist and the white cuff around it.

"Do you forget what I promised you in exchange for answers so easily, *mortal*?" His dark, condescending tone made her flush with anger.

Through clenched teeth she answered, "No. I did not forget."

She needed to know if her family was alive. She needed to know what had happened to Traifton after she'd left. Had the elves or council hurt the ones she loved? Or had the elves covered up what happened and continued to pretend they cared for mortals?

His green eyes glittered while he drank her in with a cold smirk. "Good. Behave and I will get you what you want." He looked at the white cuff and said, "And you are right about one thing. I have brought you into this realm. Which means you are mine and no one else's. If anyone touches you without permission, they will answer to me."

Sorean stepped into the hall and crossed his arms, waiting for her to follow. He cut Iara a stern look before taking in Willa's full form. He looked away before she could read his features, but she caught the muscle ticking in his clenched jaw. He kept his chin low, and scuffed his toe along the floorboards, as if lost in thought.

Iara handed her a black velvet cloak before passing Sorean in the hall. Willa thumbed the material wistfully, remembering her cloak from Traifton, now discarded and torn within the Wylan's veil. She threw it on, swallowing her somber thoughts of home.

She struggled to keep pace with Iara's quick footsteps through the candlelit hallway. Paranoia had her pulling the cloak's hood over her face. Her ears and eyes were a dead giveaway of what she was not. And, although she walked between two powerful faeries, it seemed they did not want to make any unnecessary risks or stops.

She remembered what the healer, Elliana, had said. She had never seen or met a mortal before. This realm had been hidden and secluded for five centuries. Willa knew they were immortal, but were any of the faeries here older than the curse? Would they be just as shocked to see a mortal?

As they walked, Willa looked at the doors on either side of them with curiosity. The prince appeared to have hidden her in some sort of brothel. Loud moans, groans, and pants could be heard easily by her plain, mortal ears. Her cheeks flushed at the thought of what Iara and Sorean could pick up with their faerie hearing as they made their way through the corridor.

Music and laughter greeted her as they rounded a sharp corner, and Iara lifted the hood of her cloak. A look behind showed her Sorean had done the same. All she could see were two silver bands glowing around his eyes.

Willa steadied herself and turned back to the bustling room filled with tables and booths. A long bar was built into one side, with stools lined up against a counter coming from the wall. Long, swaying beams hung above the crowd with hundreds of lit candles, the wax dripping down on the customers, but no one seemed to care or notice.

The crowd captivated Willa as Iara pushed them between the tables. Thin, strappy silk gowns littered the room in a wide variety of vibrant colors. The faerie women were all strikingly gorgeous. Some were tall and slender, standing out from the crowd as they walked and talked to those they passed, and others showed off curved hips and thicker thighs beneath their dresses. Despite being surrounded by such mystical beauty, Willa didn't feel like she stuck out so terribly in her tight silk gown with her own curves and short, mortal frame. Different skin colors and textures of hair blended in a mix of neutral swirls as they laughed and clapped along to the music.

The faerie males were, of course, unnaturally handsome as well. They, too, varied in shape and size. Some wore cloaks like Willa and her party, hiding their faces, where others were dressed simply in plain cotton tunics tucked into cloth pants. A few were dressed the same, with colorful silk ties to match the dresses that surrounded her. It was then Willa realized, all of the matching faerie men and women worked here.

Willa noticed how closely Sorean walked behind her as she fought to keep up with Iara's bobbing hood. They stepped behind the groups of faerie men and women and stuck close to the bar as they made their way through the tavern.

They were nearly past the bar when someone reached for her arm, stopping her mid-stride. Willa jumped at the sudden contact and a warm presence pushed up behind her.

"Relax, Prince," a woman's voice crooned.

An older woman was leaning over the bar with a roguish smile.

"Impossible," Willa whispered.

CHAPTER 54

WILLA

Bright, bulbous blue eyes framed long white hair as the woman behind the bar smiled at her. It was wide across the woman's aged and wrinkled face, and a shiver ran down Willa's spine.

She had met this face before, in the lake within the Wylan Woods.

The woman regarded Willa with knowing, twinkling eyes before speaking to Sorean. "I take it you found everything you needed?"

Willa shuddered at the sound of her voice. It had to be her, but it didn't make sense. Willa had thought the woman in the water to be a mirage, or magic from the cursed land. But here she was in front of her, cleaning the counter with a wet dishrag and speaking to Sorean with a toothy, crooked smile.

Sorean's voice was closer to Willa than she'd expected, making her shift uncomfortably when he said, "Yes, Lady Talarin. Thank you."

The woman winked at him and asked, "Will you need a room tonight?"

"No need."

Sorean's voice was clipped and cold, but either the woman didn't notice, or she didn't care. Her smile only widened, and she gave a quick nod of her head, the white hair around her face bobbing eagerly as she did. "I'm sure I won't be seeing you for quite some time with the week at hand."

She wiped the counter in quick, circular motions, and Sorean pushed Willa forward, but she couldn't stop gawking. How was she here?

The woman looked up from her rag. "It's raining outside, do be careful when you leave." She sighed and lifted the rag to throw it over her shoulder. She gave another bob to Sorean with a dip of her chin before settling her gaze on Willa. "But clear skies always come after the rain, don't they, girl?' She gave them both another toothy smile and turned without saying goodbye.

Hands gently pushed at her side, urging her to move out of her shocked stupor. Numb from the woman's words, she followed Iara out of the tavern and into the cool evening.

Iara looked up at the stars twinkling in the clear night sky and grumbled, "She's always been odd, that one. Says it's raining when it's not."

But Willa understood. The woman had said those words before. And those had been the last words exchanged between her and Claire. This Lady Talarin had been the woman from the Wylan waters. But how could she be in two places at once? She wanted to run back into the brothel and demand answers—ask for help—or at least beg for a crumb of clarity. But Sorean grabbed onto Willa's arm and pulled her past Iara, stopping her from doing anything.

Willa followed him silently through a narrow alleyway until the sound of horses drew her gaze up from her feet. Harland was atop a horse and dressed as well as Sorean. A black tailored jacket hung open to reveal a black, silk shirt cut in a deep vee to show the faerie's taut chest. His beard was trimmed to frame his strong jawline and his black hair was slicked back into a small bun. He winked at Willa as she was steered toward the horse she recognized as Sorean's.

Without saying a word, Sorean lifted her up with two sturdy hands around her waist. Willa reached for the leather saddle and pulled herself up the rest of the way, the slits in her thin satin dress allowing her to straddle the horse easily. Sorean was up and behind her seconds after. As she adjusted herself in the seat, his gloved hand fixed her hood, before wrapping around her middle and urging the horse to take off into a steady walk.

Nerves bubbled and frothed inside her stomach and throat as the horse led them through the cobblestoned alleyway. When they exited the dark alley, Sorean led his horse onto a wide road made of flat stone. Elegant buildings towered over them on either side of the path, the sandstone walls rich in deep orange and sanded colors and the rooftops made of red clay in small, square tiles. Vines and creeper flowers crawled over the roofs, dangling from the sides of the homes. Market stalls with brightly colored flags and blazing torches sat in front of the grand buildings. Piles of exotic looking fruits, hanging meats, and bread filled the stalls as they trotted by them quickly. Though it was late in the evening, many fae were bustling around the stalls, speaking in clipped tones to one another. It didn't take long for them to notice the horses go by, and they all stopped what they were doing to stare at her.

Willa tensed in her seat, but remembered she was hidden beneath the cloak. It wasn't her they stared at, but the one who held her. She turned her head from the onlookers to focus on where Sorean led them. The wide path seemed to go on for miles at a steady incline between the rows and rows of the sandstone buildings. The further they went, the more crowded the road became with stalls and booths filled with clothing, jewelry, food, and even weapons.

Sorean turned his horse to cut between two stalls, relaxing Willa's stiff shoulders. They went through a short alley before stepping into another wide path. Cheers and screams greeted them, making her sit forward once more in alarm.

The sound of brass instruments called out ahead of them as the crowd thickened on either side of the road. Willa didn't know where to look as faeries clapped on either side of Sorean's horse, cheering and chanting in words Willa could not understand.

Sorean kicked his horse to move faster, but the further they got, the thicker the crowd became. Willa heard Iara and Harland's horse before they came up on either side of her and the prince. Harland was waving and winking at the crowd, while Iara assessed each faerie with narrowed eyes.

Sorean's hand tightened around her waist when Harland said loudly, "Look up, Willa."

Curious, Willa obliged. Looking ahead, above the endless crowd of pointed ears and moving flags and torchlights, the road gave way to large stone stairs crawling up between taller, sandstone buildings. Higher and higher they went before she saw the twinkling lights above her. Tilting her chin further back, she noticed tall bridges high above them, with wide arches leading to one central place.

A large stone castle sat nestled high up in the sky within a hill, crested with large waterfalls. Willa's eyes widened as she followed the rushing water back down towards the winding roads and buildings before her. She tried to count the buildings as they made their way to the long winding staircase, but there were too many; the sight of it all astonishing her.

This was not a simple, hidden realm. This was a whole, grand kingdom, kept secret for centuries. Yet somehow wiped out from all maps and realms completely.

She heard Harland's voice again, beaming with pride as he said, "Welcome to Lithelle."

"And it won't bond to me?" Kauis gave Ulrond a tense look. "You're certain of this."

Ulrond smiled coyly while answering, "Not unless you want it to, Prince. It sits here, floating around, grasping a hold of whatever it wants. If one is strong enough, I'm certain they could will it away after pulling from it. Although, I wouldn't know." His eyes darkened to shift into the glowing green color. "I wanted it. All of it."

"We are not the same," Kauis said quietly. Saying those words out loud was an oath to himself: no matter what happened, he would never be like the God of Chaos.

Ulrond's laugh bubbled up again, so hard he doubled over to grab his sides. Kauis turned away from him in disgust and bent down to rest upon the forest floor of the Wylan. He sat on his knees and leaned forward, pushing his palms into the wet dirt.

Ulrond came to kneel beside him. The banished god slapped Kauis on the back with an open palm and let out another crazed laugh. "We will see, Kauis, we will see."

Something shifted behind them, and Greer pushed through the trees. His companion stared only at him as he crept closer to what was happening.

Sucking in a tense, readying breath, Kauis looked at the forest floor and then towards the rolling green and black mist within the trees. It called to him right away, much like when stepping into Kalandrae; a soft, undeniable whisper of powered promises. The gods' magic was thick and buzzing all around him.

He closed his eyes and stilled his breathing, listening to the calm of the forest, soaking in the smell of rotting leaves and moss. His essence stirred within him in anticipation.

Much like soul shifting, Kauis let his body relax into the earth he touched. As he grounded himself, he let his thoughts float mindlessly away. His soul reached out to Greer first through their bond, but it bounced back in quick rejection. Refusing to acknowledge the sting, it floated away from Greer, and like a puff of smoke, rolled slowly above Kauis and his elven body.

Kauis heard his body thrash and twitch below while his soul touched the tainted magic in the trees. His soul was hesitant when the two rubbed against one another, until he heard it. Like rain dropping over stone from miles away. A soft pattering at first, but as it came closer, it escalated into a dull roar. It wasn't the roar of pelting rain drops. It was the roar of a god.

His soul swam through the mist, chasing the sound until it latched onto it eagerly. Kauis was suddenly looking through the eyes of a large, winged beast, flying high above the clouds. It let out a shattering roar, and fire ate up the clouds before him with hungry heat.

Then, he was falling, and his soul broke away from the connection. And as it did, Kauis watched the dragon deity, Velithor, fly past him in the sky, unaware of what had just happened.

Kauis had attached to a memory, a piece of Velithor's own soul, sitting within this cursed magic. His soul bubbled with ecstasy as he realized he could touch and feel the gods themselves within this hovering mist. It was as close to being a god as he would ever get.

Kauis clutched his chest and fell to the ground, his soul crash landing in a buzzing, rattling heap of energy within him.

Ulrond's voice was distant while Kauis tried to settle back within himself, "How do you feel, Prince?"

Kauis took heavy, gasping breaths as he grasped the leaves and dirt, groaning as a wave of euphoria rolled through him. The further he dug his hands into the ground, the more his magic strengthened to newfound heights of possibility.

He let out a startled laugh and opened his eyes. Sitting back onto his knees, he stretched his arms out wide and looked up at the rolling mist of magic. His voice was deeper, distorted, as he stated, "I feel like a god."

It took well over an hour to reach the castle nestled high over the faerie realm. They had left the cheering crowd halfway up the winding staircase, warm air whipping around them, threatening to pull off Willa's hood as they faced the grand arched entryway. Together they stood silently, shrouded in thick, nervous tension. Even Harland's bright mood was gone as he shifted from side to side with clasped hands.

Two glass doors yawned open beneath the large arching stone, sending a nervous shiver down Willa's spine. Shining metal poured through the doorway as sentries holding torchlights marched out in rows of two. Between them strode a familiar faerie wrapped in an elegant, draping silk dress.

Farren smiled at them as she neared, her navy gown trailing after her in sparkling waves of small, encrusted gems. The gown was cut low between her breasts, showcasing a long, jeweled necklace, and her glittering tiara sparkled in the torch lights, enhancing her ethereal beauty. Black liner rimmed her eyelids, making her blue eyes pop and shine.

Sorean had called her a princess in the cabin like it was an insult, but Willa wondered if she truly was one now as she took in her finery. Adjusting the black silk gloves around her arms as she walked towards them, she exuded royalty as every woman had in the fairytale books Willa read growing up.

She stopped before Willa and turned back towards the door to lead them inside. Over her shoulder she said, "She's in a rare mood tonight."

Sorean handed a sentry his cloak. "Does she know what we bring?"

Willa fought to hide her scowl upon hearing another faerie say 'what' again, as if she weren't a living being trembling in her bones beside them.

Farren's brown curls swayed side to side behind her pale shoulders. "It doesn't matter now, does it? It was clever to come this way. She won't do anything with an audience."

The prince's dimple appeared as he said smugly, "Of course not. Her parties mean more to her than anything else. Bloodshed tends to dampen the mood."

Willa flinched at the word 'bloodshed', nearly stumbling over her long skirt. The prince seemed to catch the movement, deepening his dimple and arrogant smirk.

They walked swiftly between the large glass doors, reaching another set of grand marble stairs. A long blue carpet covered the middle, winding up towards another large arched entry. As they walked up to the steps, Willa surveyed the room. The walls and ceiling were made of glass, the bright yellow moon providing light through the glass dome above them. The night was clear, and stars sparkled clearly from the step she had paused on, seeming to calm her growing anxiety.

She practically wept at the sight of the beautiful moon. The two had been parted for too long, the past week nothing but a suffocating ceiling of trees and green mist. Willa smiled as the moon's white light trickled over her body behind the glass, as if to say hello. Here, everything was open and grand, so safe compared to where she had been.

Walking closer to the glass dome, Willa inspected a large waterfall rushing beside them. She followed the patches of lush, green moss, sticking out from the roaring water, as far down as she could. A bird flew beside them, bright blue and green feathers glistening from the sprinkling water before it flew towards the cloudless sky. It was all so lush and untainted.

Iara spoke beside her, "Most of what you see is a mirage. A mix of elemental magic from all of us."

"It must be hard to maintain," Willa mused bitterly.

Music filtered towards her in echoes of drums and light strings. How grand it must be for this kingdom to hide and celebrate while the rest of those on the map suffered.

"It is. But there are thousands of faeries below us. And a few hundred within the throne room we near. There are enough of us to gift our essence to the realm without feeling the loss." Iara grabbed her arm and pulled her along before continuing in a hushed tone, "The queen would never admit it, but the realm has dimmed over the years. Some parts have grown to be quite plain and sickly. Our illusions are harder to upkeep in certain quarters of the city."

Hundreds of twinkling lights blinked below them, illuminating the rocks holding the castle. Willa thought of all the faeries they had passed below and scowled. Thousands of magical beings, hidden and untouched by the curse. Only dealing with their beautiful illusion not sparkling as nicely as they wanted it too. *Good.* She wished for the beautiful waterfalls to fall away, wanting nothing more than to see this place for what it really was. She thought of Traifton with every step she took, bubbling with rage the more she compared the two places. Did they not realize how well they had it?

When they reached the top of the steps, Willa had to wipe away the sweat beading her brow. She thought of the fever the healer, El, had spoken of. But was it her temper or the fever making her feel like this? No—it was because of where she was and how such grandeur made her sick, knowing her town suffered.

The music was louder now, beyond the long navy tapestries they neared. Farren waited below the arched entry, watching Willa carefully. The faerie looked her up and down slowly before stopping on the leather cuffs around her wrists. Farren didn't wear cuffs. The prince didn't either, confirming she was a princess or a royal of some sort. Farren cocked her head to the side, staring at the white leather on Willa, and for a brief moment, Iara's arm tensed around hers. But then the fae smiled, although it was cold and hard. She brought her stone smile up towards Sorean who was stepping forward now with shoulders pushed back.

Farren extended her hand to him, and he held it delicately with his black, leather glove. The two gave each other an odd look, one that spoke volumes without any words, even if Willa didn't understand the meaning behind it. They stepped forward in unison and the tapestries pulled back. Her pulse kicked up as blasts of brass instruments halted the merry music. The two faeries stepped under the archway and waved their hands towards the sea of faeries below. Claps and cheers rang out to the two of them.

"The two are to be married after Sorean is crowned," Iara whispered as she dragged her towards the archway.

Willa gaped at her, recalling how Farren had spoken to him in the cabins. "Is it normal for a couple to be so cold a week before their marriage?"

She caught Iara's smile, but the faerie commander merely said, "Do not leave my side."

Willa didn't plan on it. She gave the faerie a nod and stepped closer while looking out at the grand room and scene below.

Salted meat and rich seasonings tickled her nostrils as they stepped under the pulled curtains, and she stared at the lustrous braziers attached to each of the twelve limestone columns lighting up the lower levels of the throne hall. The flames from the metal cast the colossal room in dancing shadows and a warm radiance. Willa followed the wide columns up to a high ceiling. Instead of glass, this ceiling was made of white, glittering marble, an illustration of the gods dancing along it. A massive, black dragon took up most of the space. Velithor. Below him was a brown bear with antlers. Forsetyr ran through a forest, flanked by rows of horse riders who looked like the faerie sentries she had seen outside of the castle.

Iara pulled her away from her gawking, leading them both down the winding staircase. They stepped onto a long golden carpet separating the ballroom. As they moved through the bustling crowd and columns, Willa noted tapestries embellished in gold, vine trimmings with white flowers decorating the walls. A band stood beside tables filled with food, playing a fast tempo tune to match Willa's thundering heart.

No one looked their way, despite her being the only one wearing a hood, as they moved deeper into the cavernous hall. Clusters of faeries dressed in ball gowns spoke with one another in loud, boisterous voices, holding goblets. The stench of sweet faerie wine tickled her nose and she remembered how much stronger it had tasted compared to human wine in Traifton.

As they walked, Willa surveyed the leather cuffs accessorizing the royally dressed faeries. Leather in colors of deep red, blue, green, and gold. She saw a few white ones throughout the moving crowd, matching hers and Iara's, but they were walking too swiftly for her to remember the detail in their perfectly chiseled, otherworldly faces.

Iara slowed beside her, and Willa followed her gaze towards a short line of faeries standing on the gold carpet. Willa cocked her head to the side, following the line to its destination. The line veered before stopping at the base of a wooden stage, holding a formidable redwood throne. Nerves settled in her stomach like a pit of vipers, slithering and hissing within her.

Looking anywhere but the empty throne, Willa found her gaze drifting toward the painted ceiling once more. Her eyes roamed towards the right side of the ceiling where land turned to water. Black waves covered the arched marble and through the largest wave was a sea serpent. Nathayus.

She studied the illustration until she found more intricate details within the trees and waters. Ships littered the waves. In the trees, she saw normal forest creatures. She looked up to the mighty dragon and craned her neck back towards the door, searching for what Velithor was attacking. She stifled a gasp as she spotted them: rows and rows of elves stared at her, also wearing armor much like what she had seen in Traifton. It didn't escape Willa that there were no mortals in the painting above her.

The music stopped abruptly, as did all chatter, making the nervous snakes in her stomach grow restless. Sorean and Farren stepped up onto the stage where a row of royal fae now stood. Two faerie males and one female looked at the crowd, all sharing Sorean's striking features with brown curls and tense smiles. Willa wondered if Prince Sorean's siblings were as insufferable as he was. The prince and princess parted hands to stand on either side of the throne, as a booming, male voice announced, "Queen Morielle Valkian of Lithelle."

Claps danced around her and the band picked right back up where it had paused, overwhelming Willa's senses. The line was moving now, and Willa did everything in her power not to turn and run the other way.

"Keep your wits about you," she whispered to herself and raised her chin, remembering her father's saying and her mother's words before her whole life had been ripped away from her.

Iara tilted her head with pursed lips, but said nothing of Willa's quiet peptalk. Alarms rang in her head, but she managed to stand tall, as Iara ushered her towards the throne, showcasing the queen of Lithelle.

A faerie nearly identical to Prince Sorean and his siblings shifted on the plush velvet cushion lining the seat of the throne. Long, dark brown hair fell in rolling waves on either side of the queen's face, stopping above her navel. White flowers were woven into small braids throughout silky strands, enhancing her golden-brown skin. Much like the rest, she had sharp cheekbones and a profound feminine jawline with striking full red lips. Although she was otherworldly in her beauty, her green eyes held a hardness focused only on the prince beside her.

Willa looked at the silver rims in her eyes before noting the small wrinkles around them. Although appearing young and immortal, her unblemished skin showed small signs of a long, tiring life. A golden crown embellished with white petals and vines amidst deep blue sapphires sat low above her brows. It cast shadows onto her glistening cheeks, making her all the more intimidating.

Queen Morielle smiled and waved to each fae who bowed before her, quickly thinning the line in front of Willa. She steadied herself as best as she could when it was time for them to step forward.

If the faeries hadn't noticed a mortal walking in their midst, they were sure to now.

The only sound she heard was her own footsteps and thundering pulse as she inched closer to the queen. Sorean stepped off of the stage and walked towards her and Iara with strong, graceful steps. The music faded, bringing all attention and focus towards the three of them.

Sorean nodded to Iara, jaw clenched tight, before brushing up beside Willa. She jumped as his hand grazed the small of her back, gently helping her forward. All eyes seemed to be focused on her now as she walked between the prince and his second in command.

When they reached the foot of the stage, Iara and Sorean bowed on either side of her, and Willa quickly mimicked them.

The three stayed low until a frigid, accented voice spoke. "Rise."

They stood slowly together. Sorean took a step forward, partially covering Willa's view of the queen. The queen gave him a cold stare before leaning to the side to peek at Willa. Her hard gaze cracked slowly as a small, creeping smile bloomed upon her face.

"Just what have you been up to, Prince?"

"I have brought you a gift," Sorean announced.

Willa straightened. A gift? She took a half step back, but Iara tightened her grip on her arm to stop her.

The queen's smile widened. The royals standing behind the throne murmured but ceased as her voice seemed to grow colder when she looked at Sorean. "A gift from the mountains? Tell me, what did you find while preparing for your crowning day?" She leaned forward and clasped her hands together.

Willa stared at the jewels covering the queen's slender fingers and swallowed thickly.

"A piece of our history was found roaming the hills. Starved and nearly dead, she unknowingly entered our veil. She has quite the story to tell." His commanding voice filled the room as he addressed the crowd, before turning back to the queen. He matched her icy tone as he said, "And I know how you love stories."

Iara pulled her towards Sorean, who crouched low enough to look at Willa beneath her hood. There was no kindness in his eyes as he pulled it back.

Gasps tore out from the room. The crowd shuffled around her, whispering to one another in harsh accents. But soft footsteps stopped the growing whispers. Sorean stepped behind her to unclasp the cloak from her neck, and she shivered as it fell away and all eyes took her in fully.

The queen stood before walking rigidly towards her. She studied Willa, from her dress, and hair, roaming over her bare skin. Her cold eyes finally trailed up to her face. Although her smile never faltered, her green eyes were dark and deadly.

"A mortal girl with a story to tell? You even dressed her like one of us." The queen laughed as she circled Willa, and the sound was like a rusted blade against her ear. But all the faeries in the hall soon joined to laugh with her, raising Willa's hackles as the queen stood inches from her and crooned, "A nice attempt, but nothing can hide those plain features."

As Queen Morielle clucked her tongue, she leaned closer to Willa as if she were closing in on her prey. Sorean had stepped aside, as had Iara.

"You say it is a gift, and yet she wears your colors?" Willa's skin pimpled as cold fingers lifted one of her gloved wrists, and the queen inspected the white leather band.

"A gift I thought we might share until I am crowned." Sorean's voice was emotionless as he said, "The mortals were once our servants. It would be a waste to kill her when we could see what they have bred after all these years. She is stubborn and a bit wild, but it won't take long to break her in."

Willa clenched her jaw. *Wild.* The word sent her right back to Traifton, before Forsetyr and the council. Sweat tickled her neck as a rush of shame and anger washed over her. He wanted to break her in? She would love to see him try. Willa pushed her anger towards the prince who was focused on the queen with calculating, narrowed eyes. She watched his jaw tick as they all waited for her reply.

The queen hummed softly behind her. A sudden clapping sound had Willa flinching. Music played instantly.

"Come, sit with me." The queen walked past her, back up to the throne.

A few simple wooden chairs had been pulled beside it, but all royals had left to mingle amongst the assembly except for Farren, who held a drink in her hand as she took at seat at the end. The princess eyed Willa warily as she drank before looking out and smiling at the crowd. Willa searched for Iara, but she was walking towards Harland, who stood near the tables of food and wine.

She paused, unsure of how to proceed until she saw the prince sitting near the throne, leaving a seat between him and the queen. Willa walked slowly towards them both. Some of the faeries had begun to talk and mingle, but those closest to her tracked her every step.

Willa sat between them and fixed her skirts nervously. The queen smiled at her before waving a hand towards her subjects. The music grew louder, and the faeries came together over the gold carpet to dance and drink.

"Do you know how long it has been since I saw a mortal?" Queen Morielle drawled. "Five centuries. In fact, the last mortal I saw was King Ammanar."

Willa tensed in her seat.

Queen Morielle noticed right away and let out a dry laugh. "Oh yes. I was there when he broke the scales of our laws. I saw him kill the elf king." She shifted on the throne enough to fully look at Sorean before saying, "King Ammanar is a reminder that mortals, no matter how frail they may seem, are dangerous. Nasty creatures. You should have killed her for entering our veils, Sorean. You and I have no use for her."

"Why did you hide?" Willa asked before realizing she'd spoken. She mentally cursed herself, but managed to keep her chin raised, waiting for the queen's reply.

Instead of drinking from her goblet, half raised towards her red lips, the queen chose to drink in every bit of Willa's features with hardened eyes. She took in her simply plaited hair, her nose, lips and paused when reaching her neck. Willa's pulsed kicked up from the too calm stare and the queen's lips curled into a soul shattering sneer.

Willa continued, wincing from the tremble in her lips as they moved. "The elves dissipated and scattered, but you managed to hide an entire kingdom. Your realm, Your Majesty, is more beautiful than anything I have ever seen." Willa shifted nervously as the queen listened, unblinking. "Ammanar may have killed an elf, but we mortals did *nothing* to you. It has been centuries, and yet we still suffer for his mistakes. The Wylan Woods are growing worse every year because of the gods' wrath. We have repented time and time again for Ammanar's treason. I have seen what your magic can do to those creatures."

She shouldn't have spoken. She would surely die for this, but she had to try. "Help us. Please."

The queen studied her for a moment longer before her snarl curled into a feral smile. Her eyes flicked to Sorean before she said, "You are the reason we are hidden, girl. Do not forget this."

Sorean took a breath, "Your M—"

"I have had enough of your lies, Sorean. So ungrateful. After all, this party is for you." The queen turned to Willa and leaned forward with a snarl. "You mortals are all the same. Greedy and self-righteous. I do not answer to you or any of your pathetic kind."

Willa could have sworn the room brightened with her words, the fire around the throne snapping and popping louder. "But I will admit, you are a curious little bird." She snapped back from Willa's face and fell into the throne with a dramatic sigh. "Get her out of my sight before I burn her here and now."

Kauis stared at the pit with a passive scowl, a hot, rolling breeze shoving tendrils of his white and black hair in front of his vision. He could feel everything around him. Every shift in the ground to small leaves falling from the trees. He anticipated the breeze moving towards him before it even touched his skin. With every movement, his body tasted energy in rippling waves of adrenaline. The emotions and thoughts of every tangible thing walking or crawling below him tickled his nostrils. He rolled his shoulders back and stretched his neck from side to side.

The Kingdom of Domnhall was gone. In its place was a pit, breeding nightmares made of the gods' magic. He looked into the dark hole and listened to the guttural calls of the creatures taking shape.

A gust of wind coming from behind Kauis had him turning to watch as Greer came from the mist and landed before him. The two looked at one another as Ulrond dropped from his back.

"What do I have to do?" Kauis asked. His voice did not sound like his own. It was empty. Hollow.

Ulrond adjusted his black cloak as he walked past him, and Kauis followed the God of Chaos back to the edge of the pit.

Putting his hands in his black pants pockets, Ulrond smiled at the large crater he had created. "You know what you have to do, Prince."

Kauis nodded, emotionless, and turned back to Greer.

He closed his eyes and absorbed the magic all around him, letting it trickle further into his body. He took as much as he could until a soft pull snapped tight within him. This was why he had agreed to this madness. The companion bond between him and Greer tightened in his belly like a crackling bolt of lightning. The humming familiarity almost made Kauis weep with sudden relief. But his mind and body were too numb from the cursed magic. It was so strong. A raw force, dragging Kauis further and further below unkempt waters of wasted potential.

When he opened his eyes, he was seeing through the griffin—through Greer. Having this connection again was like returning home after a long, weathered trip. Despite the gods' magic now running through them both, he was back in his sanctuary, beside his oldest friend. Kauis looked down at his own elven body with a slow, assessing tilt of his head. His body stood still before the griffin, his mouth open slightly in a silent cry for help. But his eyes were not the usual, shifting black color. They were a bright glowing green.

A sound of snapping leather pulled their attention away from Kauis' elven frame. Together, they looked past Ulrond and into the pit. A deep, guttural sound of thunder came from the hole. Green lightning scattered above the sky as rain crashed around them. Greer's ears twitched above them, and he stepped back and let his wings fan out nervously. His tail swished over the rocks and dirt behind them as another, loud call came from the massive hole.

Ulrond called out over the rolling, thunderous sound, "Queen Morielle and I had a deal the day Ammanar killed your father, Prince!'

Another sound of wings pumped up towards them from the chasm, making Greer step back in anticipation.

Ulrond yelled as more creatures started to screech and moan around them. "She should have known better than to run from a bargain made by the God of Chaos himself!"

He let out a bark of a wild, crazed laugh of a mad man and stretched his arms wide towards the pit. "If we find your mortal thief, we will find Morielle and what she has kept from me. What is *mine*."

Ulrond looked at Greer with wide, pulsing green eyes. Stepping backwards towards the edge of the pit, he smiled and repeated their bargain. "Together, we will find the Key of Sanctity. Together, we will take what we are owed. Then you are free to rid yourself of this magic. *If* you both so choose."

And then he jumped.

Kauis shifted back into his body and ran forward. Greer dipped to the ground quickly, allowing him to climb up in two, swift movements. As Kauis settled above him, the griffin pushed up from the ground with a screeching yowl. And the pit answered.

A loud roar came forth as Greer flew them over the crumbled kingdom's crater. A sudden black mass of shadow and leather pushed up out of the pit with another loud rumble and Greer careened away from it before they slammed into its massive size.

Kauis stared up at the body of the beast pushing higher and higher into the sky. Its eager emotion rippled over his skin with a new layer of energy. All of the creatures in the pit touched his mind and body with waves of restless vibrations. Hungry and primed for dominance.

Greer flew them up higher into the air, following the shadowed beast, and Kauis reached out to the creature with his essence, mixed with the gods' magic. Raw adrenaline greeted him, coming out in a loud thundering roar.

The beast dipped towards Kauis and Greer, revealing Ulrond nestled atop its shoulders. Long leathered wings made of shadow and mist pumped beside Greer's rain slicked feathers. This was a dragon, birthed from the gods' curse. A creature mocking the dragon deity, Velithor, the God of Justice.

But this shadowed creation was not justice. The beast pumping its wings beside Kauis had been put together by the banished god for one purpose: Vengeance.

This was a beast of retribution.

Greer's bond tugged at him as he flew them up higher and Kauis answered his companion with a satisfied snarl, "We go to Traifton."

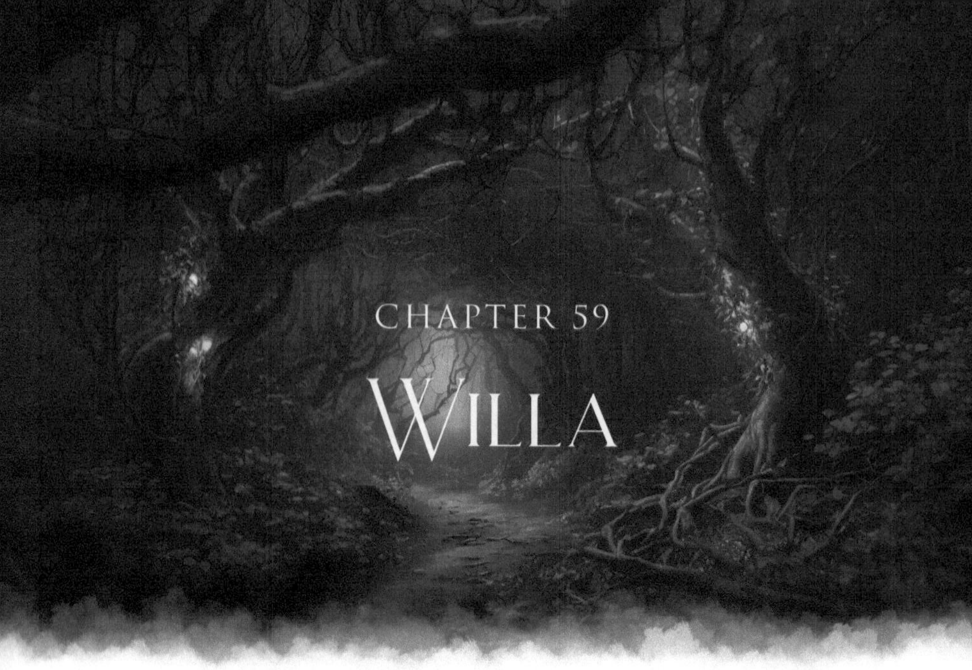

CHAPTER 59

WILLA

The door shut softly behind Willa and a lock clicked into place. She ran to the tapestry concealing the bathing chamber, and rushed to a large wooden pot, bending forward to vomit. She crouched there for a few moments, emptying what little food Iara had given her on their way out of the throne room. The queen's words echoed in her mind, along with what she had foolishly said.

A cloth dangled in front of her, and Willa grabbed it eagerly to wipe her mouth.

"That went better than expected."

Willa glared at Iara as she sat back on the cold floor to wipe away the sweat on her brow. "What did you expect the outcome to be, Iara?"

Iara did not reply. Instead, she turned and walked out of the room. Willa looked at the dress clinging to her cold and clammy skin, making her feel claustrophobic. She was ready to get out of the faerie clothes Queen Morielle had publicly mocked. She was ready to have a moment alone before Iara came back in, holding two vials. Willa recognized them from Elliana's bag and reached for them eagerly. Sleep would be better than anything now, as long as her dreams didn't haunt or try to harm her.

Iara crouched in front of her and spoke quietly, "Sorean handled that well. Offering you as a gift to the queen made you look favored and desirable to the court. His story of your survival, stumbling into our veil, showcased your resilience."

Willa grimaced. Almost every faerie she met had called her lucky, stubborn, or resilient for having survived what most would not in only a week's time. Her mother had called her resilient after being branded. She was sick of it. She hadn't chosen any of this; the fates had placed her on this path, pulling her on invisible strings for their own entertainment. She was tired of tenaciousness. Fatigued with resolve. Her whole life, and nature, was built on survival from growing up in Traifton. Even within her own frame of mind, she was constantly running on adrenaline from the quakes of her own actions. She wanted to live without fear. Live and celebrate like these magical immortals, who had openly mocked and studied her with their queen.

Willa downed the vial and shivered at the thick minty taste. Looking up from the glass, she said sourly, "I am only looked at with resilience because I am a weak mortal who has somehow managed to stay alive. I am a spectacle and nothing more. And your queen made it very clear she does not care for what I am. I did not look favored or desirable."

And she didn't want to look desirable. She didn't want any part of this place. Sorean's promise to her was the only thing keeping her from running now—-for the sake of having a moment of ease over resolve within her mortal blink of existence.

Iara hummed before musing, "But you and I know there is more to you than being a mortal, isn't there?"

Willa almost dropped the amber glass as she looked up at the faerie. She thought of the shadowed man's words in her dreams from before. He had said the same thing before choking her. Iara's knowing smile enhanced her deep, glittering eyes and she pushed to her feet to pace in front of Willa.

"I was in and out of consciousness after Eth'tinok attacked me. The only thing keeping me from dying was my essence. Essence is what gives us immortality. It is how we faeries hone the elements for our own purpose. Do you know what mine felt as it kept me breathing despite the blood that fell from me?"

Willa set the vial down beside her quietly, but Iara didn't wait for an answer.

"It stirred and itched uncomfortably, as if it were trying to hide from something. I managed to open my eyes, assuming it was Eth'tinok's doing, when suddenly I was blinded by a bright, unnatural light. There was fire, not like mine; not even like the queen's famous white flame. I know Harland and Sorean's magic. It was not theirs. But it couldn't be you, could it?"

Willa gave Iara a pained look as the faerie studied her with unnatural stillness.

"Afterall, you are only a *simple*, mortal girl." Iara's lips curled back into a snarl as she watched Willa's racing pulse and quickened breaths. "And then, Sorean said you managed to drop the beast with a snap of your fingers, despite a wound that should have killed a mortal instantly."

Sweat dripped from Willa's brow, as the tension rose between the two of them in thick, sweltering waves.

"Why did you hide my marks, Iara?" Willa whispered. Iara had seen their glow in the cavern and she had brought her these gloves to wear. "Why keep me alive at all, knowing what I have?"

"We don't know what you have. That is why you live."

Willa rested her forehead in her gloved hands and squeezed her eyes shut. "If I tell you, you will kill me."

"I cannot kill you."

Willa opened a single eye to find Iara still watching her too calmly and closely. "The life debt?"

The faerie nodded. "A magical bargain. I cannot kill you and you cannot kill me. If one of us dies, the other will shortly after. Usually meaning the two with the bond will protect each other to the bitter end. But I will admit I did not do it for this reason. This was to assure my safety."

Willa dropped her hands, shaking her head. "Your safety? From what?"

"From you."

Willa flinched as if she had been slapped.

Iara crouched, staring into her eyes. " I do not know how you survived Death's Divine, but one thing is for certain, my essence is never scared. And yet it was paralyzed by your fire. Petrified of you."

How could it be scared of her? Willa didn't even understand what had happened or what she had done. What Merellian's essence had done.

"You don't want to know more about me or my life, do you?" Willa said bitterly with a quivering chin.

Iara said nothing, giving Willa the only answer she needed. Her body suddenly ached with years of fatigue. Willa closed her eyes to hide her tears. No one cared for her here and no one would. She thought she had been despised in Traifton, but it paled in comparison to Lithelle. She was still an outcast, just in a different land and outfit.

Lifting the other vial, Willa drank from it. Sleep was all she wanted now. No nightmare could be worse than this.

"Sorean wants to change this realm," Iara said. "In a few days' time, he will be able to. I haven't told him what I know, and I am not going to. He saw part of what you did, the rest is up to him to put together."

Willa let out a bitter laugh. "So you are testing him now before he is even crowned. And you are testing me... Waiting for me to turn into a monster. And what do you think he will do when he finds out? Even I know the answer."

He would kill her or take her to his queen and have her burn Willa like she had so effortlessly threatened in the throne room.

"Change can come in many forms, Willa. Sometimes it is petrifying, but only because every single being in this realm, magical or not, fears the unknown. We all fear what cannot be controlled."

Iara's voice grew distant, as the sleeping tonic caressed Willa's pounding head. She couldn't be the change the faerie spoke of. The shadowed figure in her dreams was right; she was nothing but a thief and murderer.

Iara's voice rolled towards her on the waves of coming slumber. "Prince Sorean yearns for change. Yet he runs from things unknown in the same breath. He makes monsters out of nothing." She sighed. "But he cannot run from monsters. He must embrace them or be devoured by their wrath."

Willa tried to make sense of Iara's words. She thought of the prince's brief yet terrifying displays of magic. She thought of his mother, and wondered what scared the prince before mulling over what scared her. Nausea bubbled up. Merellian was inside her, waiting to come out again. And Iara had sensed it, had sensed Merellian in those woods. It didn't matter when or if the prince found out what she had. She knew Sorean would kill her regardless. It was part of their bargain.

"I will be watching you, Willa. Tread lightly with the queen next time so we both don't die."

Sleep took her quickly. Willa dreamed of rows and rows of trees. She wound through them quietly until she saw the woman from the lake leaning on a tree trunk. She turned and smiled at Willa before her body morphed into a large, black snake. It grew taller than the trees around her, lashing out with large white fangs. Willa screamed and dodged the attack.

When she stood, she saw the snake's eyes were bulbous and green. A screech tore out above her. Black talons were reaching for her and she fell to the forest floor, covering her face. The last she saw was the hair clip Claire had given her to protect. It glistened amongst the muddied leaves in front of her, glittering beneath the green mist.

CHAPTER 60

WILLA

Someone was shaking Willa's shoulders, attempting to pull her out of her night terror. She tried to push them off as she was being lifted but failed. She was so warm. The bones in her body were melting away. Had the queen finally burned her like she'd threatened?

Cold water encased her body and she gasped, rising with sputtering coughs. Wiping away her curls, she blinked to find herself in a shallow pool. She coughed out more water, looking up to find the night sky and beautiful moon. Glass surrounded her in a private, fogged dome. Humid air filled the vine covered glass and large palm trees surrounded the body of water she shivered in. The faerie dress clung too tightly to her body in the cold water, and she covered her chest, coughing with rasping, shakes.

"How long have you had a fever?"

Willa followed the voice to find Sorean crouched near the edge of the pool. His jacket was hanging from a small stool behind him, and although he was still in his tailored pants and leather boots, the sleeves of his white under shirt were rolled up his forearms, the fabric disheveled. He reached out a hand and dangled his fingers in the pool. Slowly, he swirled the water around, creating little ripples.

Willa could hear her own teeth chattering as she said, "According to Elliana, a few days."

She covered her eyes and yelped as water splashed towards her. Sorean stood and shook his head, throwing water at her once more before running both hands through his long curls.

Willa turned to swim away from him, but the water sloshed as the prince slid into the pool, his hands gripping her, pulling her back against his hard body. She tried to shout, but he covered her mouth with his hand, and when she tried to bite his hand again, he chuckled behind her, spinning her around to face him.

His shirt was soaked, clinging to his chest and showing every ripple and hard line of his primordial strength. His strange markings were glowing white beneath, rolling down his arms and chest.

Willa covered her chest and scowled. "What is the meaning of this, Prince? Am I here so you can *break me in*?"

Sorean rolled his eyes. "The queen put you near my chambers. I could hear your screams from my bed."

"You took me from my own bed and threw me into a pool? All because I woke you up?" Willa scoffed. "Forgive me, Your Highness. I will try to avoid my night terrors the next time sleep takes me, so as not to wake you." She tried to step away, but his hand moved to the small of her back, pulling her closer.

"Your fever wasn't letting you wake up," he said through a clenched jaw. "I did what I had to do. The water clearly helped."

Willa pinched her lips to stifle her irritated huff. She had her own washing basin in her room. He had done this to be an ass, nothing more. She gave the prince the most hateful look she could manage between her chattering teeth.

"Elliana cannot watch you all through the night. She has more important things to do." Willa deepened her scowl, but he ignored it and drawled with his arrogant, dimpled smirk, "You'll stay in my chambers."

Willa's jaw dropped. "And you don't have more important things to do, *Prince?*"

His smirk widened into a feral smile. Willa froze. Sorean had gifted her to his mother as though she were an animal. He'd said he would break her in and use her. Her teeth chattered as she refused to look at anything but him.

Sorean sighed and let go of her. Willa stepped back immediately and rubbed at her arms.

"I don't trust anyone else in this castle more than myself. And as I said, you're mine and no one else's."

"Right. To break me in. Tame me. Use me as a slave."

The prince's smile dropped, and he tensed. "I needed to say those things to Queen Morielle. I am not like that."

"But some are," Willa hissed. "Your *mother*, the queen, is like that."

She let go of her chest to run her shaking hands through her hair, realizing she still wore the silk gloves and cuffs. She cursed and ripped the leather bands off before removing the soaking gloves as well.

Letting them sink below the water one at a time she asked, "What makes you so sure she will listen to anything I say? She made it very clear she does not care about what happens outside of her precious, pretty realm. And why do you care? Why did you go into the Wylan, *Prince?* Why go through all this trouble to keep me alive after witnessing ..."

She paused and looked at her reflection on the rippling water to control her tempered words.

Sorean's searing gaze bore into her shaking frame as he answered, "Despite our differences, we want the same thing. You made it clear tonight with your unfiltered words towards the queen."

"We are not the same, *faerie*. Your immortal wants and desires are self-centered. Selfishness and hatred are the only emotions you have."

"I have lived through thousands of emotions, *mortal*." Willa blanched at his venomous retort. "Emotions your ordinary mind cannot even fathom. You feel grief, loneliness, love, and joy for seconds compared to the endless years and countless hours I have to sit within the swarm of feelings. I would say I pity you for what you will never experience, but I meant what I said in the woods. You mortals do not deserve pity."

"You say you have spent years with emotion, ones my mortal brain could never comprehend, and yet you are a still a fucking fool!" Willa shook her head and hissed, "I at least know I will die by the end of this. Whether it will be by your hand as promised or your mother's. What makes you think you are immune to her wrath? You are wasting your own time, she does not want to help those who suffer."

"I will be king," Sorean retorted. "For too long, we have sat back and done nothing while the curse grows and worsens. It is only a matter of time until it comes knocking on our door."

"Kings die, Sorean. A crown on your head will not save you. I spoke to your queen for less than a minute and can see she cares little for what you plan to do or how you want to rule."

Queen Morielle's malice had dripped from her tongue in only a few shattering sentences. She was worse than any creature or beast she had encountered so far. Willa shook her head and looked away from him, thinking of the woman's words to her in the lake. She'd spoken of serpents eating their own tails until it was too late. Perhaps Lady Talarin had been warning her of this realm and the queen who ruled it. She was the snake in the lake's story. Willa looked back to her reflection and shivered. It was what Queen Morielle was doing after all, sitting back while her realm slowly dulled and the life outside of her magic burned and crumbled. She was blind to her own power, intoxicated by it—wanting nothing else but to celebrate it in her safe little cove.

A rush of heated anger flared through her. Willa lifted a hand from the water and wiped away the sweat lining her brows. The cold water only helped lessen the fever, not take it away entirely. But she knew what this really was. It was Merellian's essence latching onto her anger. He had told her what his essence liked when he'd healed her back. Power and control. It loved emotions—fed on them.

Sorean cut through her fevered, angry thoughts, the water sloshing as he crept closer.

"I am *not* a fucking fool. I know my mother hides things. I know she has her own selfish reasons for why we have been kept away." His steps had water lapping at her sides as he repeated their bargain. "I need you to help me find out why. Tell her about your life, give her your story. Tell her about the elves."

Heat rolled up and down her body with such a force, Willa wondered if the cold water lapping upon her would turn to steam as soon as it touched her burning skin.

"She won't care about the elves. I think you know this." Willa looked up slowly, he was an arm's length away, watching her with a predatory focus.

"For once, I agree with you." His dimple popped with a tight lipped grin. "I need to know if she fears hearing of their return and, if she does, why. Are they the reason we hide? Or is it something else."

She sighed. "There are more of you than the elves. I don't know what they want or why they returned, but if you could make sense of it, you could easily stop them."

"You fear them?"

Another rolling wave of heat moved through her body, as if Merellian's own essence answered Sorean's question. "I do."

More than he could ever know.

Iara's admonishing words played between Willa's knitted brows. "You saved me from Eth'tinok, despite Iara's injuries. Despite me freeing him."

"I did." He sighed and continued, "You attacked the wolf with the arrows, freeing his release from me. I may not swear a debt to you like Iara foolishly did, but I kept you alive for an unspoken code of honor. You helped me and I helped you."

Her eyes narrowed. He had witnessed more and she knew it. "But why?"

"As I said, we want the same thing." Water sloshed as Sorean narrowed the gap between the two of them further. "I have witnessed your brash, flaming words to match your ember hair. But behind your stubborn facade, I see what you are searching for."

She rolled her eyes. What could he possibly know about her within a week's time?

"I see it in your gaze and trembling chin. You said it to my mother tonight. You want peace. A storm free day with clear skies and with it a clean, balanced slate. No inner turmoil, no fear, no fights, no running." His voice was calm and quiet when he continued, "I do not understand what you did to Death's Divine and the more I watch and listen to you, I realize you also question how you are still alive."

Willa scoffed, "Do not pretend to know—"

Sorean's voice raised as he cut her off, "Because I search for the same thing. Answers and with it peace. I see your fear and how it drives you." He pushed back the wet curls from his forehead with agitated movements and continued, "And I know what it's like to fear the unknown. The endless search for answers is desolate and all consuming. A small piece of me had given up on finding clarity centuries ago. Until fate pushed me into the Wylan Woods, to meet a girl who has the same raw and stubborn spark in her eyes that I once had."

Her body trembled beneath the weight of what he said. But it didn't mean she could trust him. She couldn't trust anyone in Lithelle.

"Sorean, if you tell the queen what you suspect, whatever it is, I will die before you get the chance to gain your clarity with our bargain. Iara will die with me." And yet she had asked for death. She had asked him to kill her after their bargain. Why would he care now?

Willa had to lift her chin to keep their taut eye contact. Her chin quivered slightly as she searched his impassive gaze. If she told him what she had done, he would kill her here and now despite his curiosity about her.

Sorean's thumb reached out to cup her chin. "I know this, *Ohirlyn.*"

Willa flinched from the unknown word, moving to pull away but he held her firm.

His hold tightened as he warned, "And I know I could ask you here and now for the truth. You've seen what I can do."

Willa's pulse kicked up, nearly drowning out his words.

"You know I could rip it out of you with my shadowed fingers."

Her fear of what his shadows had previously done to her was dampened by a gut wrenching twist of heat within her. A dark, forewarning hum of Merellian's essence crawled inside her veins and another pulse of heat had her trembling beneath Sorean's firm grip on her face. His nostrils flared and his eyes darted over her features, somehow sensing her inner turmoil.

"And yet, I know you'd lie, even beneath the grip of my essence. You would evade the truth, to the bitter end, wouldn't you?"

Willa hissed as he pulled her closer to his chest.

He was right. She wouldn't tell him what was inside her—she couldn't.

"You would rather die than tell me anything, aside from our bargained promise. In fact, you asked for death by my hand when this is through. Your hatred for me is powerful, but the way you fear yourself is much stronger." His eyes darted from her eyes to his grip on her jaw while continuing, "I can practically smell it on you now, see it in your darting eyes. It has built strong, stubborn walls around you. But know this, *mortal.* I relish in the hunt. I will stop at nothing to find out how you survived Eth'tinok before our time together has ended. The queen will not know what I do not understand and you will fulfill our bargain. *If* you don't get yourself killed first by simply opening your feral little mouth in temper alone."

Willa's racing pulse and scattered thoughts clashed into one another, stealing her words as Sorean's thumb brushed over her bottom lip. She hated this faerie, with every fiber of her being. He said he saved her for honor when admitting he loved the chase for answers. The hunt. He was a predator through and through. Though she would never admit it, his words had done something to her. He had seen some small part of her, despite his hatred and equal wariness with her. Despite her walls, practically coated in poison, he saw through them enough to understand how scared and alone she was. To see the spark, as he'd called it, showing how desperate she was for home and her family, and with it peace. He understood she was just as alone and confused in her world as he was in his.

Sorean's face was tense. His eyes continued to dart from her wide eyes, to his hand on her face, and then to her lips. He scowled as he brushed his thumb along her lip again. Heat flared in her, nearly buckling her knees. Her vision blurred as

Merellian's essence grew more restless with the quick pumps of her racing heart, from the faerie's feather light touch.

Another rolling heat wave had her seeing spots, the room and water spinning around her as she puddled in Sorean's hand. Sorean let go in time to grab her shoulders, steadying her stance.

"I thought the water would help the fever," he murmured darkly. "I will get Elliana."

Willa nodded with clenched teeth, squeezing her eyes shut to stop the spinning.

It is not the fever. Giving in will be easier than this pain, mortal.

Willa gasped. Her eyes flew open, focusing on Sorean's arms holding her upright. Her stomach knotted, another heat wave tearing at her insides.

The prince's white marks seemed to sparkle beneath the moonlight, she narrowed her eyes on them right as they shifted from white to blue. "Why do your marks change before me now, Prince?"

CHAPTER 61

SOREAN

Sorean set the mortal on his bed with gentleness that surprised him. Shadows blurred his vision as he commanded, "Do not leave this room."

She nodded, though it was strained. Sweat beaded her skin as she clenched her stomach and hissed in pain.

Let us out so we can play with it.

Sorean paused while turning from the bed. *You said 'it', not her.*

She's ours, was the only response he received before the darkness dimmed his sight further with a rolling intensity.

He needed to leave before his essence took over. It had never been this bad before. He needed to find Elliana.

Sorean swiftly pulled his wet shoes off before throwing them near the fire he walked past. He peeled off his tunic and pants next with irritated jerks. Rubbing his hands over his face and hair, he desperately tried to blink away his shadowed haze. He grabbed the first set of clothes he saw within his unkempt drawers and barreled his way out of his rooms.

His essence hummed and whined for him to go back to the mortal girl, but Sorean grit his teeth, ignoring the plea, and stumbled through the hallway. It had been frantic the whole time the two were in the pool, but Sorean had sensed something right when his essence did. She had a fever, that much was clear, but whatever mortal trick she had used to momentarily stop Eth'tinok was rearing its head now and his essence loved whatever she had hidden.

Faerie essence and magic could sense other fae's magic and their gifts naturally. It was like meeting an old friend, the two essences of each fae warming up to one another and feeling out what each could do. But she was a mortal. She had no magic. The closest mortals could get to magic was sorcery. A simple curse or spell could have thwarted the wolf's attack. And if it was sorcery like he suspected, the price of performing it always came with a cost, which could explain the fever. Sorean couldn't wait to figure out what tricks she had used. He had been telling her the truth when he said the hunt excited him. It thrilled him, giving him a brief distraction to what other answers he searched for; from the queen and himself. He only hoped she wouldn't die by his mother's hand before he could figure out her freckled, feral puzzle.

It took him twice the time it normally would to reach the other side of the large stone castle with his essence blinding and berating him.

He had almost made it to the healer's quarters when a servant cut through his shadowed haze. "Prince Sorean, Queen Morielle requests your audience."

Sorean clenched his jaw and straightened. "Please bring Elliana to my chambers.".

He had managed to settle his essence enough for him to see clearly by the time he had entered the queen's chambers. He cleared his throat and tucked in his ruffled tunic before rounding the corner to his mother's grand and overly decorated sitting room.

Queen Morielle faced a large arched window, showcasing hundreds of glittering lights from Lithelle's lower quarters. "Some told me not to crown you."

Straightening his shoulders, Sorean clasped his hands behind his back and walked slowly towards her.

"They said your magic was dangerous and therefore *you* were dangerous. But I didn't listen." Queen Morielle clicked her tongue against her teeth. Turning her head, she narrowed her eyes on him before moving on to study his dark markings. "Perhaps I should have. I did not listen as a ruler. I listened as a mother who only wanted what was best for her son."

Sorean halted, grinding his teeth together while she continued. "And yet I have five sentries dead because of you. And a curious little bird who does not belong in my kingdom."

The sentries she had insisted he bring to the cabin. The sentries he had killed. Guilt rolled through him, but his essence ate it away eagerly. Its whispers purred beneath him, proud of what it had done to her guards.

She took a step away from the window and breezed by him. Endless layers of her skirt's fabric trailed after her as she rounded the couch to stand before a formidable stone hearth lit up by a large white fire. Fire conjured by her own precarious magic.

"Tell me why you thought it so important to break my rules before I kill her. I would hate to waste all the effort you went through to display her like you did tonight."

The cold, emotionless hatred in his mother's voice did not surprise him. She had always been this way. She spoke of being a mother when all he really knew was a queen almost too cold to wield her famous, white flame.

"Did you know the elves were back?"

The queen stared into the fire. She watched the flames with more love than Sorean had ever seen in her gaze.

He continued, "This girl has witnessed the elves firsthand." He thought of the mirage in the lake, Niarath Loch, and said, "They are searching for something, Mother. They're searching for the Key of Sanctity."

She sighed and quietly spoke into the flames. "It was only a matter of time. But it doesn't matter, it's been gone for years."

"How do you know?"

His mother turned from the flames. "Before Nathayus could bury the key with Ammanar, I took our piece from those deep waters and hid it myself. It was one of the first things I did after hiding Lithelle. It is gone, on a forgotten part of the map and safe because of where it dwells."

Sorean frowned. "But there is enough magic in our piece to keep Lithelle strong for centuries to come. Why not keep it with us?"

"It is because of what you brought here that I did no such thing!" She seethed. "I knew, despite my efforts, someone would find this realm eventually. The key holds our life force, Sorean. If our kingdom is revealed, we can fight and defend ourselves. But to have our piece of the key stolen would end all of us and what we have accomplished."

Sorean's frown deepened in response. "If you had found both pieces, what would you have done? Would you have destroyed the elves' piece?"

To destroy theirs would have killed off the elves instantly. And she would never mix the two pieces for strength—it was an abhorrent abomination.

"I would have destroyed theirs, yes." She caught Sorean's wince and scoffed. "Do not look at me like that. You have not witnessed their true nature like I have. The elves are worse than the mortals. Lying and evil in their ways. You don't understand what I have sacrificed to keep us safe. And yet you lie like them. You left Lithelle and entered the Wylan Woods."

Sorean stepped forward. "Moth—"

"The girl said she saw what our magic could do against those cursed beasts." She stepped towards him, her voice teetering above a yell. "You found her there, in those woods. You left the Menyamere mountains, as an heir to *my* throne, *my* kingdom, and entered the Wylan Woods!" Her shoulders heaved as she stared at him with wide, accusing eyes. "And then, you have the nerve to bring her back here?"

Sorean crossed his arms and said carefully, "Her town has met the elves. I don't know what has happened to her, but I believe she has witnessed what they can still do firsthand."

"She could be a spy."

Sorean shook his head. "No. She saved Commander Holavaris' life in those woods. If the elves are as bad as you say, a spy would do no such thing."

"Saved her from what?"

Sorean cocked his head, assessing every inch of her face as he said, "Eth'tinok."

His mother didn't blink. Didn't breathe. It looked like she had seen the dead as she turned her head to look into her flames within the hearth.

"You told me he was dead. Who chained him there? The bindings were of faerie magic."

"It doesn't matter who put him there," she replied coldly, "What matters is how he got out."

He groaned and turned away from her, looking instead to his rolling marks. "You are more worried over a deity who cannot find us than what has happened while we've been kept away." His essence flared beneath him, responding to his quick temper. "There are creatures in those woods being created entirely on their own from the gods' cursed magic. There are monsters crawling from Domnhall's ruins."

He turned back to face her with clenched fists. His essence was ready to explode from his chest, racing his breaths as it beat at his ribcage. He could do it now, with how angry he was. Unleash his own hidden monsters upon her. They would tell him what he needed to hear from her. They would help him understand.

Queen Morielle lifted her chin and sighed. "It doesn't matter what happens out there. What matters is we are safe and alive. There are thousands of us, Sorean. You will have no time to worry for anyone else but them when you are crowned."

"I do not want to be the king of a realm that turns its back on everyone else. You have been in your own safe web of lies, unaware of the spiders drawing closer to us each day." He stepped closer to her. Shadows crawled along his vision while he spat, "What if the elves find our piece? If a mortal girl can find the chained Death Deity, the elves can easily find your hiding spot. And if they are what you say, we will die, unaware and unprepared. They will do what you had considered."

The queen recoiled as if he'd physically slapped her, but he looked out of the window and shook his head. "And if the gods' magic worsens, those monsters will find our veil eventually." It didn't matter how long it took, what mattered was they existed in the same world as Sorean. "I refuse to sit on a throne and throw parties night after night, waiting for it to happen."

The window grew dark as the shadows blinded him.

"How long has this been happening?"

Sorean couldn't see her through the shadows covering his vision. He took a few long deep breaths, ignoring the whispers growing louder inside of him. He hadn't heard her footsteps as she neared him. Her warm fingertips gently touched his arm, making him flinch. When she repeated her question, it was with a hint of actual concern.

Shadows poured from his hands and his mother screamed.

"Do not pretend to care for me." He hated the sudden, cracking emotion in his shout. He hated her, he realized. "I have only ever been a tool for you. Another way to help this realm stay hidden."

Sorean could finally see. The Queen of Lithelle was pinned up on the wall, shadows holding her wrists and legs as she stared at Sorean, horror etched on her face.

Sorean stepped forward slowly. "It has always been like this; you have just chosen to ignore it. Ignore me. All the while working hard to get me crowned and loved by our people, despite what you think of me and this." He looked at his hands while more and more shadows crawled out. "This is not natural. Fae control the elements, but this is not one of them, and you know it."

"Sorean." His mother's lips trembled.

He wanted to laugh at her. She was never scared. But when he focused on her, he saw it. True terror was etched into her features.

"You have kept me in the dark for centuries while I searched high and low for answers." He took another step forward and smiled as his shadows tightened around her wrists and legs. "If you had the answers all along, I need you to tell me right now."

The queen looked at the shadows and hissed, closing her eyes when one got too close. Sorean studied her panicked movements and waited.

Finally, she spoke. "I will tell you everything the moment you are crowned."

Sorean's jaw ticked. Three days. He had searched for hundreds of years, he could wait three more days.

"Fine." He tilted his head and watched her wiggle within his wrath. "I will not be a ruler like you or Father. A new age is approaching, and I will not let us die beneath its footprints like cowards."

He called his essence back in. Eager to have been let out, it crooned and obliged with no hesitation, and he rolled his shoulders as it crawled back into him. But despite its quick response, his marks remained blue.

Sorean shoved the whispers away as his mother slid to the ground with a rattled wheeze. To her credit, she was quick to stand and straighten out her dress as if nothing had happened. When she was composed, Sorean headed towards her doors. This conversation was over. He needed to get sleeping tonic from Elliana and see what she had done for the mortal.

"You will listen to the girl's story tomorrow with me. I want you to hear what is happening outside of Lithelle. I know you will not act on it, but know that I will."

He reached for her doors as the queen said coyly behind him, "As you wish, Heir Apparent. Bring her to the dance tomorrow night."

Sorean growled. "Absolutely not."

She's ours.

Sorean nodded in agreement. His brows shot into his curls, shocked by his own movement, but he masked his alarm.

"I saw those cuffs on her wrists, no one will touch her." Queen Morielle laughed, although it was slightly shaken. "Though I don't know why you care."

Sorean bit out through clenched teeth, looking over his shoulder. "I don't."

"So bring her." His mother gave him a sweet, cold smile. "I command it."

WILLA

Elliana closely examined Willa's side with a tense frown. After setting fresh wrappings around her ribs, the healer sighed and shook her head. She straightened and pointed to three new vials on Sorean's nightstand as well as water and a steaming plate of food.

"I've tweaked the tonic's ingredients. The vial you had before may not have been strong enough." She frowned and continued. "I wasn't sure what your mortal body could handle, but now I'm hoping this will stop the fever."

Willa's stomach turned as if to argue with Elliana, but she managed a pained smile. Elliana eyed her warily before nodding. Reaching into her bag, she pulled out a notebook, scribbling something hastily.

As if feeling Willa's puzzled stare, she spoke, still writing. "I don't know when I'll ever see a mortal again, Willa. Forgive me, but I am noting everything on your health and progress to better understand. Eat, drink, and rest tonight." She closed the notebook with snapping finality and smiled. "And may the gods reward you with a restful slumber."

Willa winced slightly from the mention of the gods but she politely replied, "Thank you, El."

The healer gave another curt nod and packed up her items. She gave a pointed look to the furthest vial from Willa as she did. "The prince's tonic for sleep. Yours is the closest to you. Drink his, and your heart will likely stop in minutes."

Willa drank the middle vial for her fever, scrunching her nose at the peppermint taste and what Elliana had said.

She looked at his vial. "Gods, it's that strong?"

Elliana only hummed in a distracted reply. Willa's mind was brought back to the prince's deep colored marks before he had carried her out of the small pool. She thought of his threat to torture her for information with his shadows. And the way he spoke of her fear, as if he truly understood. What haunted a prince enough to have need of something so strong? To understand fear as she had?

When El had finished packing up, she gave Willa a quick look over before turning towards the door.

"What does *Ohirlyn* mean?" Willa wet her lips, reaching for the plate of food as Elliana paused to look back at her.

The healer's brows were raised and her eyes held a sparkle of amusement. Elliana surveyed Sorean's room, humming again, before she stopped to inspect the other side of the prince's chambers. Willa took a bite of steaming potatoes, watching her curiously. The healer tilted her head, assessing Sorean's bookshelves littered with open books and half stacked papers.

"Where did you hear this word, Willa?" El's voice was light and airy, like it was on the verge of a giggle.

Willa rested her plate on the blankets and sighed with content. "The prince has called me it twice now."

Elliana's cheeks flushed as she dipped her head to stifle a laugh. Willa raised a confused brow. The healer continued to giggle while she walked towards Sorean's bookshelves. Feeling the spines with her pointer finger, she tapped it twice on a large, leather bound spine, before pulling it off the dusty shelf.

Her smile widened as she gracefully walked back to the bed, handing Willa the large book. "Remember, I am only the messenger."

Willa gave her a confused scowl which only had her chuckling. The healer winked and spun on her heels, leaving before Willa could open the book.

Willa lifted the heavy hardback and was surprised to find she recognized the title. It was a history book. More specifically the history of the gods, other deities, and famous creature descriptions. It read more as a children's story book than a textbook and Willa remembered having read brief chapters of it in Traifton's small school as a child. It was easy to forget how close Lithelle and Traifton were, all things considered. They shared the same air once—the same gods, even the same books.

She opened the cover and lazily flipped through it, squinting at the black and white drawings, taking up some of the weathered pages from top to bottom. She stopped on a drawing she recognized with pursed lips. The dragon God of Justice flew across two pages and below him were branches sprawling across the paper like scattered lightning. Scribbled names popped out on either side of the lines, showing the dragon's family lineage. She halfheartedly read the names and frowned when she recognized one: *Ohirlyn*. A small page number was beside the word and Willa flipped to it, scowling.

"*Ohirlyn*. 'Before the dawn'. The female dragon was known for her temper above all else. Legend states, her eyes glowed red when angered, hence the name, in relation to the burning red of morning. Smaller than her siblings in wing size and maw, she made up for it with tenacity. However, Ohirlyn was rare in her abilities. Unlike other dragons, she could not wield flame like Velithor or the rest of his bloodline. It seemed her bite was the only notable distinction for her. But because of her differences, she was outcast from her siblings. Studies say Ohirlyn lived an isolated life before the dragons parted from the realm."

Infuriated, Willa re-read the summary of the female dragon.

Temper. Outcast. But without flame to back her bite.

"I will kill that bastard." Willa hissed.

She angrily flipped past the definition to settle her temper. She stopped when recognizing another drawing. The Kingdom of Domnhall and its grandeur sat before her. Willa touched the edges of the castle with a single finger before flipping the page over, smiling softly, happy to be distracted from the prince's nickname for her.

Her smile faltered and a soft gasp fell from her parted lips.

On the page was Claire's broken hair clip. But it wasn't a broken clip at all, it was part of a key. Her and her mother's theory was correct: the star on the hair clip was for the Star of the Scales. She traced the star with her finger before studying its counterpart, The Dawn of Harmony. She looked to the half sun and back to her left palm in awe. In the drawing, the two were side by side and behind it, holding them together, was a small dagger dangling on a chain. She moved on from the drawing with darting eyes to read the description. Her jaw went slack before she shoved the book off of her lap in panic.

Another wave of heat raked her insides, making Willa groan. She ran a trembling hand through her hair and cursed.

She lowered her shaking hand to look at the star on her palm, matching the hair clip she had kept for Claire. Not a hair clip, but a piece of a dormant artifact. One with either elven or faerie essence embedded in it. And now it was at the bottom of a lake. Her friend was dead because of it—because the elves had been searching for it. The book said the pieces held the races' lifeforce within them. Held by the mortal kings to establish balance between the three creations. But what could one piece do without the other? And where was the sunburst?

She focused on the book thrown across the bed with racing breaths. Tears coated her vision as another question repeated over and over in her head: Who had her best friend become all those months at sea, and how did she wind up with a forgotten piece of history?

Willa cursed. Commander–no– *Prince* Enrel and his winged beast had been searching for her. *He* was searching for her. If he had been the one to enter the lake, not his beast, would he have found the clip? Most importantly, what would the elves do with it?

A cold chill settled her racing thoughts. If the elves were in the Wylan, they were too close to where she had unknowingly hidden an ancient artifact. Willa hoped the elves thought her dead and gone by now; assumed she had been eaten by a Wylan Creature. She traced her brands, forming a plan as another ripple of heat barreled through her.

If she survived the queen and this realm, she would go back to the lake within the Wylan. She would take back the artifact and find a place on the maps so far from this poisoned continent, the elves would never be able to find her or it.

Yes, keep it for us.

Willa's heart seized.

With the Key of Sanctity, we would be unstoppable.

"But what would it do?" Willa whispered, horrified.

You would be wielding an entire race's lifeforce.

Her face flushed as it hummed.

Untapped power. I told you before, you could be king, but why stop there? This sort of power would rival the gods.

Her eyes widened, realizing the essence knew this because Merellian knew what they searched for in secret. Prince Enrel had been partially truthful in Traifton. They wanted to bring back the old construct of laws, but not for the sake of balance. For the sake of power. A new era of immortals in a lawless land with no gods to stop them.

CHAPTER 63

SOREAN

Sorean wanted nothing more than the warm embrace of his silk sheets and pillows as he opened the door to his chamber. He stepped inside, frowning to find his bed empty.

His essence nipped and whined beneath him, mirroring his concern. *Where is our friend?*

Sorean pinched the bridge of his nose and cursed at his essence. He stepped further into his room, dropping his hand as he did, and was greeted with a jarring slap across his face.

He grunted, stumbling back as a large, leather book fell to the ground. "What the fuck!"

He rubbed his face and shifted. The mortal was balancing on a chair, by the tips of her toes, seething at him.

He had been so focused on his essence and Mother's words, he hadn't noticed her waiting there. Waiting to hit him over the face with a fucking book.

"*Ohirlyn?*" The girl's shaken voice was an octave below a yell as she stared daggers into his shocked features.

Sorean rubbed his face and bit the inside of his cheek to keep from laughing. She had proved the very nickname by lashing out at him. The dragon had been known for her temper and bite, but nothing else.

The two regarded one another tensely before Sorean lunged for her. She yelped as he wrapped an arm around her hips and hoisted her over his shoulder. Small hands beat at his back as he stomped towards the bed. He smiled, despite the sting on his face, before throwing her onto the bed like a sack of flour.

The girl let out a wheeze and clutched her side. Sorean froze. Elliana had given her a silk nightgown but wrappings were still visible along the low cut sides. Sorean's gaze flit to the nightstand, showcasing an array of vials. When he looked back at the girl, she was rolled over and lying on her side with her back to him.

His essence stirred eagerly beneath him as he watched her heavy breaths, moving her shoulders up and down atop his blankets. Sorean rubbed his stinging face and groaned before grabbing his vial of sleeping tonic.

He settled onto his side of the bed with irritated huffs. Kicking one leg over the other, he gave her a pointed glare and finally spoke. "Does this make us even?"

Even. Yes we're even.

Sorean winced at the sudden whispers, again confused as to what it meant.

The girl's scowl cracked slightly with a small twitch of her lips. "Yes."

She took in his face and her smile widened. Sorean imagined it was as red as her hair from how hard she had managed to throw the book.

He narrowed his eyes on the bandages he could see and followed it up to her flushed face, still lined with sweat. "Are you okay?"

"Don't act like you care."

He flared his nostrils to hide his breathy huff of a laugh. The thought of irritating the girl delighted him, but what had transpired with his mother had left him fatigued. Tomorrow would be a test for both him and the mortal. He needed sleep.

"I am confused on the difference of faerie and elven magic."

"I have books for it," he drawled, popping open the cork to his sleeping tonic. "Clearly you know where they are."

"I'd rather you tell me," she said quietly.

Sorean sighed, remembering her question about his marks in the pool before he had left her.

The girl spoke again. "The elves call their magic 'essence'. But I do not understand what their magic does. In fact, I can hardly tell the difference between you both aside from the rims of your eyes."

"It's one way to tell us apart." He glanced at his arms and dark markings. "The other is our ears. Ours are a bit shorter in length. The faeries were born from the land. We merely borrow the elements from the land we came from and wield it when we desire."

He shifted on his side, mirroring her by resting his head on his pillow to study her freckles. He had always liked freckles. If she were a faerie he would be envisioning other things to do in this bed beside reciting history. He closed his eyes, attempting to wipe away the thought, but when he looked back at her green eyes and puzzled brow, his essence rippled through him with a sudden tension.

On second thought, reciting this would be good for him. In fact, he now wanted *nothing* more than to do this and only this. Sorean cleared his throat, pushing away the odd rush of desire, and continued, "The elves, however, were not born from land. The gods made them first. They took pieces of their own essence to create the elves. Because of this, the elves' gifts have a wider range than ours. And from what I've read, they work more closely with controlling others, rather than the elements like us."

The girl nestled further into her pillow, taking in all he said with quiet curiosity.

He continued, "And essence is the correct term. It is a separate living soul within us. Without it, the elves and fae would live a mortal life. Despite the favored gifts we are born with, each essence has its own personality. For the fae, you can tell who favors fire based on their personalities. Same with water, and air, and the ground workers and earth shifters."

"And what of the elves?" She winced while sitting up and grabbed her vial of sleeping tonic. Pulling the blanket back, she nestled back into his bed.

Sorean's lips twitched. No one slept in this bed besides him. And yet here was his common enemy, a *mortal*, getting comfortable under his blankets.

"From what we know, the elves' essence rules emotions and the mind. Some can control others' emotions or manipulate them. Others can step into minds, walk around within another while they are unsuspecting. Elves were amazing healers because of their ability to work with others' bodies. But they had darker gifts as well. Mind tricks and foul play happened often with elven magic."

"Don't act like you faeries are so innocent. I've seen what your magic can do."

His essence hummed beneath him, making him tense. As if she were one to talk, hiding tricks up her sleeves. He should be asking her about sorcery, but tomorrow he would investigate. His mother's fury had zapped his energy tonight like a bloodthirsty Wylan beast.

Carefully, she asked, "Does every faerie control each element?"

"No and yes. Each fae is born with one predominant element. It is usually passed through our blood lines. We can wield all elements to some degree, but none are stronger than the one passed down from our predecessors."

He knew what was coming before she asked it.

"And what are yours?"

"My mother's line is fire. White fire. Rare in its heat and everlasting when it burns. My father's was air. It is how I veil objects."

"And your other element?"

"I was born with it." He brought a hand behind his head and shifted to lie on his back and stare up at the bed's framed canopy. "This thing. It lives and breathes within me, like any essence. But it has its own wants and desires. It's constantly aching and starving for things I do not want, or things I cannot have."

He refused to look over at her, waiting for his essence to speak. It stirred but no whispers came. He flinched as cold fingers grazed his other outstretched arm. Sorean looked, wide eyed, at the girl who now traced two fingers over his deep colored marks. He scowled but didn't pull away, waiting for his essence to say something.

It was attracted to her because of her secrets and its morbid curiosity. This wasn't him—it couldn't be. Yes, he found her attitude alluring. And the features he'd once found plain were becoming harder to pull away from. He wanted to count and study every freckle on her fragile body, like a map of constellations. His scowl deepened at the thought. But the more he watched her trace his marks the more apprehensive he became. She didn't retract from the marks as they squirmed beneath her touch. In fact, he caught a small smile forming as she trailed her fingers back towards his clenched hand.

It was in this moment, Sorean realized this mortal girl would be the fucking death of him.

"Do not look at them like that," Sorean snapped.

The girl's gentle tracing stopped. She blinked and withdrew her hands with wide eyes, as if she hadn't realized what she was doing or whom she was touching.

She cleared her throat and whispered hoarsely, "Even I can admit they are beautiful."

"They are not." He growled. "I am no better than the creatures we saw in the Wylan Woods. I am worse. I am a monster."

The girl bit her lip, watching the marks with knitted brows. She followed the markings up to his sleeves before finding the ones on his neck.

She spoke quietly, making Sorean's ears twitch to listen. "Have you heard from your scouts?"

"No. Tomorrow you will speak with the queen. After, I will check in with the shifters. Answers for answers."

She gave a small dip of her chin before looking past his shoulder, to the window behind him. Her eyes glassed over like they had in their camp within the Wylan Woods. "I'd like to change my bargain. I will tell your queen what I know, and you will tell me of my home as promised. But after, you will not kill me like I asked."

Sorean tensed but she looked at him with a new, determined gaze and continued. "You will take me back home if there is one."

She opened her cork before Sorean could argue, and downed the sleeping tonic. Sorean's eyes were already closing on their own accord, but he took his tonic as well for fear of his essence attacking her.

"I will do it on one condition," he mumbled.

The girl hummed, her eyes already closing when Sorean looked at her own marks and said, "If I take you to your home—if you survive tomorrow—I kill whoever put those marks upon your palms."

It was as if his own essence had said the words for him. Her eyes shot open with a surprise, mirroring his own inner shock. But he didn't take it back. If it was his essence, it was right. The girl had been branded for fucks sake, as some form of punishment. No one deserved that, not even his enemy. And yet she still begged the queen for help, for her town and vile race, despite whatever horrors she had grown up with.

Sorean stared into her eyes, searching for fear of the monstrous thing he had vowed, but fear wasn't there. Back was the spark he had caught time and time again. It was hope and anger mixed into one. Perhaps she wasn't *Ohirlyn*, for he swore he saw a flicker of actual fire within her green eyes before a peaceful sleep embraced him.

CHAPTER 64
WILLA

"I cannot wear this."

This was a dress for royals, not mortals. A gown made of silk rippled over her body in layers of sage and forest green. The back was tied tightly like a corset, clinging to her fresh wrappings around her ribs like a warm embrace. The top of the gown was open and sleeveless. It would have shown some of her cleavage and bare arms if not for the sheer blue arm and neck piece Elliana was clasping around her throat. Gold embellishments wrapped around her neck like a choker before melting into the thin fabric, swooping above her chest and hugging her arms. More of the iridescent fabric bubbled out from the elbows of the stretchy material, hanging from her forearms like thin wisps of air.

Willa lifted her arms to wave the fringed fabric around her arms in awe and confusion.

Elliana sighed behind her in the mirror. "It is as I said, Willa. The queen likes to have shiny new things to present at court, especially this evening. She requested you look every bit a faerie as we could make you."

Willa scowled in response, shivering as Elliana tied her hair into a simple braid. Her red hair came alive above the earth tones, but she didn't look faerie. It somehow only made her look more human, beneath such finery. Elliana plucked a few curls from the front to frame her face before adding white flowers into the braid. Willa thought of the queen's hair from the night before. Her lips had also been painted a deep red, much like the queen's had been. This was certainly bold for someone who would already be scrutinized so closely.

"All done," Elliana said, stepping back to admire her work.

Willa only frowned at the healer before turning to face her fully.

"Why are you helping me prepare, El? I am grateful for the company, for you are kinder than the rest, but why not servants?" Even Iara would suffice. It was bad enough Elliana had tended to her late in the night previous and now this.

Elliana handed her a vial. Willa nodded and hurriedly drank from the bottle. She shivered as the cooling liquid soothed her stomach. She had been burning up all morning, but had thankfully managed to hold down food and water.

The healer handed her another cup and said, "For the nerves," Willa scrunched her nose at the cup as Elliana continued. "And Sorean doesn't trust many. He asked for me to specifically care for you today and help with whatever you needed."

Willa studied the dark, strong scented wine and took a long sip. Thankfully, unlike human wine, she buzzed with a stinging force of liquid courage at once. She silently chewed on El's words, remembering what her and Sorean had discussed late into the night.

Despite their differences, something had shifted between her and the prince's shaken relationship last night. It was nothing close to camaraderie, for the faerie irritated her more than anyone she had ever met in her twenty-five years of life. But the two understood one another on some level now. When he didn't look at her like she was scum beneath a ship, Willa found it easy to envision a friendship with him. It made her ache with loneliness, knowing the two could never have that. Friendship was built on trust, not hatred. And she still couldn't trust him. Not with his mother as the ruler of Lithelle. The queen of this realm could never know what she had or what she had done. She could never know what Willa had unknowingly hidden within the tainted woodlands.

Sorean had helped her understand Merellian's magic more last night as well by informing her of the differences between both races. He may have found the questions innocent, but she needed to better understand what she had found in the book. She needed to understand what the elves, or even his mother, could do if they were to find both artifacts and wield the Key of Sanctity. Prince Enrel was bloodthirsty, but Queen Morielle was a wolf among sheep. A wolf worse than Eth'tinok. It had only confirmed her poorly panicked plan of getting back to the lake within the Wylan Woods. To find the hair clip within those waters and hide, like her and Claire planned originally. She would lose the prince one way or another if she had to, despite what he had said after changing the terms of their bargain.

The venom in Sorean's words when he'd sworn to kill Lord Nalore for her brandings had shifted something within her. She didn't want to be avenged and she didn't need to be. She had brought the punishment onto herself, despite the vile ritual and betrayal from Ivaan. Her foolish actions had been the catalyst of all of this, yet something deep within her chest had cracked from his vow. A small stone had crumbled from the walls carefully sealed around her heart.

She frowned at the cup, swallowing the rest of the wine to wash away the thought. He was attractive—yes—perhaps even the most gorgeous male she had ever, or would ever, meet in her mortal life. This small itching change within the back of her mind didn't matter. She knew he only wanted answers from her, and still was trying to figure out what she had done to save them from Death's Divine. He couldn't know or he *would* kill her. It was the only thing she was still certain about while the rest of her thoughts continued to shift and tremble.

The door opened and Iara stepped in with a low whistle. Her eyes crinkled with amusement as she took in Willa's cleaned up state and faerie gown.

"You threw a book at Sorean, and yet you stand? If I didn't know better, I'd say the Prince of Lithelle liked you."

Willa almost dropped the cup in her hands from Iara's teasing words. But Iara caught it, smile widening, and a rush of heat flared to Willa's cheeks. She cleared her throat and looked at Elliana whose jaw hung slack.

"*Ohirlyn?*" Willa crossed her arms and raised a defiant brow to the healer.

Elliana blinked slowly, shaking her head in surprise. Grabbing onto her waist, the healer clutched her stomach and crumpled in a deep, bellow of a laugh.

The fae's laugh was infectious, making Willa giggle as well. Gods, it was good to laugh. She couldn't stop now and it became funnier remembering the shocked look from Sorean when the book thumped to the floor from his face made of stone.

"Is there something I'm missing?" Iara asked, eyes darting between the both of them.

Elliana and Willa only looked at one another again, laughing harder.

Iara let out an irritated sigh, but Willa saw the tug of her lips as she fought to hide her smile, while Elliana and Willa composed themselves.

The faerie commander wore a more eccentric outfit than the night before. A strapless red shirt sat tightly on her chest and torso, revealing the taut muscles on her abdomen. Tight black pants made of silk hung right below her hips. Long gold chains hung around her navel and waist. The chains rattled and shimmered as she walked to Willa with a tight-lipped smile.

Iara brought her arms forward and revealed a pair of short green gloves, matching her dress and sheer sleeves. Willa reached for them silently and put them on, sobering with the memory of her and Iara's last conversation. She sighed when she saw the white cuffs Iara held up but added them regardless.

Willa gave herself one last lookover in the mirror before asking, "This week is in celebration for the prince's coronation?" The two faeries nodded behind her in the reflection. "So why can't I help feeling like I'm dressed as Queen Morielle?"

Iara said, "Tonight we honor the past and present. Most will dress like the queen to honor her rule. Others will dress like the gods or lesser deities. It is a wild night—one of fevered dancing and drinking."

She nodded while nerves frothed within her stomach. She had crossed a line last night when speaking to the queen. She needed to be on her best behavior. Speak when spoken to, answer the queen's questions, and get Sorean his answers in exchange for hers.

Elliana stayed behind to clean up while Iara escorted her to the throne room. The two were silent as they walked. Iara seemed to be lost in thought while Willa was too nervous to talk.

Iara broke the silence before entering the throne room. "Behave."

Willa only sucked in a rattled breath and nodded. She wouldn't argue with her, she had been telling herself the same thing over and over throughout their clipped walk.

Beautiful harps were playing a slow ballad from the other side of the grand parlor. As Willa followed Iara down the stairs, she noticed an organized dancefloor where the golden carpet had been, and faeries slow dancing in a matching rhythm to the music.

The stage once holding the queen's throne now bore a long banquet table. A humbler throne sat beside it, though the same design of flames etched into the back of the chair didn't lessen the formidable intimidation. White fire, Sorean had called her magic. She shuddered, hoping to never witness it.

This time upon entering, everyone noticed her. The mood shifted instantly as the crowd gathered at the bottom of the stairs, parting as Willa reached the last step. Now, the faeries openly stared at her and whispered. It chilled her to the bone to be watched so carefully in a room full of those with magic and strength. But Willa lifted her chin. She was used to stares and whispers. Sneers and jests. She could handle this. For once, she would do as told and not speak unless spoken too. She just needed to make it out alive.

Iara didn't blanch at the sudden shift in mood, instead Willa watched her back straighten as she pushed through the onlookers.

Like a plague settling over a land, the further they walked, the quieter and more dismal the hall became. She noted some of the faeries barely wore clothing, A few males had only low-slung breeches with an open jacket, exposing their bare chests and jewels laying atop of it. Many of the females had silk shawls, or dresses like Willa's, only with layers of necklaces and bracelets. But almost all the women had elaborate head ornaments, like different sized tiaras. A few had larger head pieces shaped like giant antlers or animal ears, making them look even more animalistic and predatorial than they already were.

Hard glares and tentative gazes met hers for anyone she dared to look at. The music stopped, but the whispering faeries had made their own, haunting harmony in place of the harps and strings.

Willa took a slow turn around the room to take in all the faeries watching her curiously. Bright white flames appeared around her. Willa covered her eyes, but everyone erupted into cheers as the brass instruments played again to introduce the royals. Willa lowered her hands as a male's voice called the queen's name.

Queen Morielle strolled down the stairs, flanked by two gorgeous, shirtless fae males. She looked as regal and intimidating as the evening before. Her dress was stark white and followed her down the stairs in a long train. She looked like the flowers Willa wore in her hair. Golden beads hung from the puffy bell sleeves of her dress. The beads twisted and rolled over her back like golden, shimmering vines. Her crown was woven into her hair, braided around the golden headpiece. Willa took the moment to relax as all focus shifted to Queen Morielle. But she found herself tensing again when she saw who entered next.

Prince Sorean looked positively sinful as he stepped into the throne room. Dressed in all black, he exuded every bit of the monster he had claimed to be. His black tunic was unbuttoned all the way down to where it tucked into his pants. Even his marks were glowing dark blue, the same way they had been before the two fell asleep. Willa had never seen him wear a crown until tonight, and it too was black. Sitting high on his forehead, it held back his slicked curls, although that one curl still managed to escape to fall above his eyebrow. He gave a tight nod to the cheering fae as he was announced.

Princess Farren wasn't beside him. Willa looked around to search for her, but Iara pulled her away from the royals.

"Tonight, you will sit beside Queen Morielle. You are her guest of honor."

Willa bit her lip to hide her reply. So many fae stared at her still, she knew they would be listening to everything she had to say.

She followed Iara up to the banquet table and sat beside her, waiting for the approaching queen. Faeries crowded around her, excited chatter following Queen Morielle's parade. She took the time to speak and smile with each of them as she neared the table, and Willa fought to hide her sneer. It was amazing to find the queen was so esteemed and cherished by her people, considering how terrible she truly was. Again, Willa looked for Farren in the crowd nearing them, but didn't find her.

She caught the prince walking a distance behind the queen with a scowl. It seemed his outfit also matched his mood tonight. Like the queen, many were gathered around him, but he hardly paid them attention. He didn't stop scowling until Harland appeared beside him. The two exchanged quick words before the prince threw his head back and laughed. The smile on his face transformed him from an intimidating force to a beautiful man. No. Willa looked away from his unrecognizable smile. He was not a man. He was a faerie with terrifying magic. Magic even he didn't understand.

"You look wonderful, little bird."

Willa rigidly followed the sound of the queen's voice. Queen Morielle watched her from the dance floor with a wide smile. Willa forced a smile of her own and gave a small dip of her chin. The queen's eyes sparkled while she took in Willa's dress and makeup.

She clapped and spun back to those who circled her. "Begin!"

The music at once changed to a rolling tempo of drums. Willa anxiously shifted in her seat as the fire around them dimmed. She watched as Harland and Prince Sorean passed the table below her. Harland whispered something to the prince before clapping him on the shoulder. The two laughed as Harland stepped out into the crowd.

Prince Sorean turned with him but didn't follow. Instead, he watched as the faeries, and even Queen Morielle, stepped aside to open the large dance floor. The drums beating grew louder, and fiercer. Willa sat forward in her seat to better see Sorean. He was bouncing up and down on the balls of his feet, as if he too was anxiously waiting for something to happen. The drums were going so fast now, Willa almost wanted to cover her ears from the rushing thunderous noise. As swiftly as the beating grew, it stopped. A hush rolled over the crowd, the fire dying to mere embers around them.

Willa jumped at the sudden dark. Iara chuckled beside her right as a sudden burst of bright orange light appeared from the middle of the dancefloor.

Within the flame was Princess Farren. Her gown was a deep, rusted orange, matching the flames dancing all around her without touching her. Her hair was twisted around her head, wrapped in a black crown, nearly identical to Sorean's. She walked slowly towards the table, with a playful smirk on her face. It was not the table she walked towards, Willa realized, but the prince.

Sorean stepped out to meet her halfway and the drums picked back up. He reached out a hand as if the two were about to engage in a dance, but she jumped away from him. Confused, Willa watched her smirk widen as again Sorean reached for her. A few in the crowd clapped at Farren's teasing display. The prince however, did not seem amused.

Sorean stopped and rolled his shoulders. Farren tilted her head before letting out a dramatic yawn. The crowd clapped and laughed as she did. She looked around to them with a dazzling smile, waving her hand and winking at those who called her name.

Farren stumbled back as a blast of air snuffed out the flames surrounding her. Willa saw the prince had a hand raised towards her, and the crowd switched their direction of chanting toward Sorean instead. He raised his other hand and cheered with them.

Spinning, he turned towards the table with a victorious smile. But it dropped when he caught Willa's gaze.

His eyes widened as he took in her outfit before he lowered his brow to give her a deep scowl. Willa rested her elbow on the table and then her chin on her gloved hand, tilting her head to meet his scowl with a dazzling smile of her own. Willa could have sworn the large fern markings on his neck and chest deepened with his glare. He stepped towards her, his lips curled into a snarl, but was quickly thrown back.

All the vines dangling from the tapestries and ceilings were now crawling down towards him. They wrapped around his wrists and ankles, lifting him higher from the ground, and the faeries clapped and cheered as Farren rounded on him. Holding him above her, she smiled as he thrashed and kicked. When he knew he was stuck, he tilted his head back and laughed. His smile was so wide Willa saw, not one, but two dimples as he looked down at Farren. She loosened the vines, erupting more cheers from the watching fae.

Willa wondered whether Sorean would show his unkempt magic, but when he landed on the ground he pulled Farren in towards him. She yelped and fell against his chest with a loud giggle. The crowd cheered wildly as Sorean lifted her chin and pulled her into a deep kiss. The kiss was long and full of passion. Long enough for Willa to grow uncomfortable. His hand snaked around her waist and pulled her closer, veins popping in his forearms as he squeezed her sides.

A warm shiver ran through Willa as she watched. Whatever she had thought about Sorean and Farren's cold betrothal quickly died away as she watched him bring his hands onto her thighs to hoist her up. The princess wrapped her legs around his waist, letting her slitted orange dress trail behind her.

The crowd grew frantic and wilder as Prince Sorean walked her backwards to the middle of the dancefloor. Willa thought of the way the prince had touched her before. Never with kindness and never like this. But she couldn't shake the way he had looked at her in the cabin after he'd saved her from his magic. She sucked in her bottom lip, remembering the way his mouth had crashed into hers. He'd looked like he wanted to devour her.

The two faeries grabbed each other in a frenzied heat, and a sudden, twisted longing burned Willa's stomach as she watched the prince spin Farren round while he kissed her chin and neck wildly. The drums were quickening along with Willa's racing pulse, and she had to turn away from the scene to catch her breath.

Iara's jaw was tense as she stared at the dancefloor, her hands tight over the seat of her chair as she practically sent daggers towards the prince and princess.

"Is this normal?" Willa asked.

Iara swallowed. "This is the start of the Fever dance. In a moment, the two will be veiled beneath Sorean's magic. Whoever can find them first within the throne room gets to dance with either the prince or princess. For the rest of the night you will see more dancing and displays like this. Each one more heated and driven than the last."

Farren's giggle rolled towards the table and Iara's scowl deepened. The commander pushed her chair back quickly.

"I'll bring us food and drinks. Do not leave this table, Willa."

She followed Iara's clipped steps off the dais before slowly looking back towards the dance floor. Sorean still held Farren against him, the princess' back to Willa with her arms wrapped around Sorean's neck as he held her. One shoulder was bare, the bell-sleeve of her dress dangling from her elbow. The prince's face emerged from hers to kiss down her neck, towards her bare shoulder.

Willa adjusted her dress as another flush ran through her. This was something private, something she shouldn't be watching.

Prince Sorean lifted his lips to graze his teeth over Farren's shoulder, and a chill ran through her as she watched him lightly nip at her bare skin. She absentmindedly brought her fingers beneath her sheer covering and traced her collarbone, remembering he had bitten her once, too.

The drums pulsed through her, and the hall's energy seemed to buzz with intense fever. Willa closed her eyes and listened to the beat of the drums, entranced by a tingling awareness of the restless energy in the room. The hair on her bare arms rose like she was being watched and she opened her eyes to find Prince Sorean's powerful gaze focused on her.

Sorean smiled above Farren's shoulder. Willa was unable to look away as the prince's dark, hooded eyes watched her intensely.

She shifted in her chair, her cheeks flushing to a dark red, which only grew when Sorean's brow rose beneath his crown, telling her he'd noticed what this was doing to her. He closed his eyes, giving Willa a moment of reprieve, but then his green eyes boldly raked over her as he bit into Farren's shoulder.

Farren threw her chin back and let out a loud moan. Sorean smiled against her skin, all the while staring into Willa's very soul. A dark and wretched soul if the faerie she loathed was disturbing her pulse in such a way, without him even touching her. Her skin tingled, and Willa wanted nothing more than to crawl out of it, to cool her overwhelmed senses.

Sorean let go of Farren and pulled away from her shoulder, but she continued to hold onto him with her arms around his neck. Sorean looked away from Willa and wrapped his arms around Farren's waist once more. He leaned forward and kissed the top of her head as the drums quickened, the crowd continuing to holler and sing, and then the prince and princess vanished. Sorean had veiled them, just as Iara had said.

Willa searched the dance floor, knowing she wouldn't find them with the prince's magic.

The fae in the room went wild. Suddenly they were rushing past one another, chanting loudly. Female and male faeries shoved at one another while running around the hall, reaching out to the air in front of them and around them. All to search for their prince and princess.

Queen Morielle stood in the middle of the chaos with wide sparkling eyes, laughing as the fae sprinted around her as if they were on fire.

Willa jumped as a plate of food plopped down loudly in front of her. Iara fell back into her chair and handed her a glass of faerie wine. Flushed, Willa grabbed the cup and took a small sip. The food in front of her smelled divine. Roasted vegetables and steaming potatoes as well as some sort of salted dark meat. She dug in quickly, eating while the fae around her danced and ran around the large hall. No one had found the prince and princess yet. Based on how Farren and Sorean were acting minutes before, Willa wouldn't have been surprised if they'd left to go somewhere more private.

She sighed happily after filling herself with the savory food and leaned back into her chair. Licking her lips, she took another sip of wine. It buzzed through her quickly, making her more flushed than she'd been before. Willa nearly moaned from the heat and satisfaction of a good meal. She went to set the cup on the table, but her plate was in the way. Standing slightly, she leaned forward and set the cup in front of her plate.

She glanced at Iara who had foregone food for drink. She was already finishing her glass as Willa went to sit back down. Before she could ask about the commander's sour mood, Iara was up and gone again.

Willa practically fell back onto her seat, the strong wine coating her limbs. But, as she sat back, she frowned at the odd sensation. Her seat didn't feel wooden at all now.

Gods, how drunk was she? She leaned her shoulders back only to be met with an invisible warmth. Confused, Willa shifted. It was only a chair, but something was off. She could see the gap between her and the chair now.

A warm caress rolled over her stomach and Willa tensed. Wafts of rich, citrus spices and leather overwhelmed her senses while a deep, rolling chuckle stroked the chills running down her spine.

The heavy weight around her pulled her back and Prince Sorean whispered, "Did the mortal enjoy our show?"

Willa's eyes widened. An unwelcome surge of excitement bubbled within her as he shifted further into the chair, pulling her along with him. Warm breath tickled her shoulder.

"Your pulse gives away what you do not say. Your cheeks are still flushed." His invisible hand tightened on her waist again, pushing her backside into him more.

"It's only the faerie wine," Willa's voice cracked in her whisper. "Shouldn't you be with your betrothed or letting another beautiful faerie find you?"

She looked around the room as the fae ran frantically around, unaware of who she sat on.

Another chuckle rolled behind her, jolting Willa's pulse. "Jealous?"

"You could kiss the gods on the mouth and I wouldn't be jealous," she managed to say. "In fact, I'd pity them. Besides, why should I care who you marry or flirt with?"

Her thighs cradled one of his as he slid her as close to him as she could get. She leaned into him as if he was the anchor keeping her steady from beating waves of reckless abandon. But he was not the anchor; he was the rebellion within the rolling tides, threatening her resolve with every movement of his chest behind her. Willa cleared her throat and wiggled slightly. Her shift upon his lap pulled a low, warning sound from him.

"Oh? But I saw the way you bit your lip." His voice was deep beside her, its tone vibrating her very core as he spoke over her shoulder. "What were you thinking about, I wonder, if it wasn't jealousy?"

Willa hissed. "I was picturing all the ways to kill you."

Sorean chuckled, and the sound shook her against him. But they both tensed as his warm fingers caressed her knee before slow invisible tingles followed his circled motions towards her thigh. She swallowed thickly, and watched the frenzied crowd, the drumming beat in time with her rising pulse.

When his hand left her thigh, she relaxed into him, cold air lingering in the wake of his sudden absence. She squirmed from anticipation of where his hand had disappeared to when suddenly warm fingers grabbed her chin.

Willa gulped as her face was tilted back towards the seat of the chair. She searched the empty air, imagining his face and scowled, drawing out another heated laugh from the invisible prince.

Warm breath tickled her ear as he whispered, "Were you thinking of me when I did this to my betrothed?"

Her sheer shawl lifted, her bare shoulder pimpling from the movement, before a stinging pain came from above her collarbone, followed by a rush of warm heat as he softly kissed the bite. A pulsing tremor ran through her, making Willa shiver. Her hips rolled over his hip and thigh of their own accord, shocking her senses.

Another low, warning noise came from the lips now exploring her shoulder.

"Careful now, Willa."

Willa. She blinked through the flushed haze, realizing this was the first time he had said her name out loud. Not *girl* or *mortal.* Not the vile, nickname *Ohirlyn.* Just Willa.

She gasped as his tongue rolled up her neck before another stinging bite came right below her jaw.

Someone in the crowd cheered wildly. Willa sat up, Sorean's hand tensing around her waist as her thighs tightened around him.

Princess Farren suddenly appeared in the middle of the dance floor. She let out a laughing yelp as the male fae who had found her lifted her up and hoisted her over his shoulders.

Queen Morielle clapped and laughed before looking around with a frown, "But where is our prince? No one has found him yet?"

Sorean whispered in Willa's ear, "I am surprised."

Willa licked her lips. "At what?"

She tried to focus on Farren and the male laughing and spinning on the dancefloor. But all she could hear was the frantic beating of her pulse in her throat as Sorean's warm fingers caressed her neck like the embellished choker she wore.

His teeth grazed her ear lobe as he said, "That your pulse would beat so strongly for someone you loathe, with every fiber of your mortal being. For someone you called a monster."

CHAPTER 66

WILLA

Willa's eyes widened in horror, and she jumped off him. Sorean's arrogant chuckle trailing after her. The faeries nearest to her gasped, all of them gawking at her with frozen, startled looks. No, not at her, but behind her to where Prince Sorean leaned smugly back in the chair with his chin resting on his fist.

He smiled out at Queen Morielle and said, "Your little bird is quite the hunter."

Her cheeks flushed again as Queen Morielle narrowed her eyes on the both of them with obvious disdain. Farren and the male were dancing behind her, not paying attention, and the others, despite who they'd seen sitting on Sorean's lap were joining in, too. It seemed the fevered energy in the room outweighed the shock of what had just transpired.

Willa yelped as she was lifted into the air. Sorean hoisted her over his shoulders and walked her to the dancefloor.

The queen bared her teeth at Willa as she was dropped to stand right beside her.

Sorean stepped between them and said, "What? You wanted her to attend and here she is."

The queen gave him a cold look before smiling at Willa, though the smile was frigid and forced. "We will talk after, girl, so I may get to know you better."

She raised her chin and walked away from the crowd drawing in to dance around their prince and princess.

"You berate me for acting foolish, saying I will be the one to get myself in trouble and yet this is what you do?" Willa whispered harshly, her eyes darting around the faeries moving beside one another.

Sorean answered by lifting her wrist to show her leather cuff. "No one touches you, remember? Even if they hate mortals, they would hate my wrath more." The prince's voice rang with command, stilling her nerves.

He smirked, pulling her towards him. His arrogance had her scowling as the drums quickened, but Sorean ignored her glare to move with the beat. He lifted one of her gloved hands and pulled it towards his neck. He was so much taller, her palm could only rest on his chest. When he went to grab her other hand she swatted it away.

Sorean tilted his head back and laughed loudly. Willa's brows rose from the freeing sound falling from his mouth.

She let out a sputtered gasp when she was lifted above his shoulders. He spun them around in quick circles and she cursed, kicking at him, but he only laughed harder. The room mixed in a frantic swirl of colors. Making her dizzy. Finally, he relented, and dropped her with his usual, arrogant smirk.

Willa stepped back, fighting her dizziness with furious blinks. The wine had been too much. Dots were lining her vision. Groaning, she rubbed her eyes. Her forehead was sweaty when she touched her face, but Sorean grabbed her waist and brought her into him so they were flush.

He swayed her more gently side to side, rolling his hips towards hers as he did. Willa didn't want to dance with him, not when she could feel these faeries staring, but it was better than sitting with the queen. She soon found her rhythm and rolled her hips when he did. For a brief moment, she allowed herself to wonder what it would be like if the two didn't truly hate one another, despite their implied understandings from the previous night. If they weren't natural enemies because of a history they had nothing to do with.

She looked up at Sorean and tried to fight her smile, but found she could not. Not wanting him to catch her change in attitude, she tilted her chin further up to better study the mural on the ceiling. The painting began to swirl and move. Was this part of the Fever dance? The name fit, for suddenly her flush grew within her. Sweat coated her skin as they continued to roll against one another. Willa moved her gaze from the ceiling to look over at the tapestries. They also seemed to bob and move to the rhythm of the music.

Willa giggled and closed her eyes to feel the music. The sounds caressed her skin so wonderfully. But everything was so hot. So tight. This dress was too much for her, she needed more air.

Shoving Sorean, she backed away and frowned at her dress. "I'm too hot."

She reached up to unclasp the jeweled shawl from her neck but Sorean's hand was there in an instant. "Willa, what are you doing?" A tinge of concern laced his deep voice.

Willa rolled her eyes and swatted him away. "I want to feel the music."

"Feel the music?" She tried to paw at the back of the clasp on her neck, but his fingers tightened around her wrist, "What are you talking about?"

Willa ignored him. She needed his hand off her so she could free herself from this wretched material, so she leaned over to bite Sorean's wrist.

He hissed and let go of her with a step back. He gave her a confused look, making Willa laugh. She giggled and stepped away from him. But when looking down to her own wrists she huffed with irritation. Everything was too tight.

These white cuffs were squeezing her skin like thousands of needles. She hastily ripped them off of her, faltering only for a moment when a warning growl said, "Willa—"

She ignored the intolerable prince and threw them both to the dance floor. She sighed with relief and started to do the same with her gloves, backing away from the seething faerie in front of her. But her dress was too long, and she tripped over the skirts, falling back into another warm and hard faerie body.

Willa turned towards a handsome faerie with ebony skin. She brought her hand up to his cheek and said, "You are beautiful!"

The faerie, stunned for a moment, stared at her with an open mouth. But as Willa swayed in front of him, his arm slid around her waist.

She smiled, but then frowned at how hot she was. She glared at her dress as the faerie moved them side to side, she reached to pull at the strings knotted at her waist, but her fingers slipped over it. Willa seethed, looking at the gloves. The faerie had pulled her closer again, but Willa pushed away.

She was abruptly met with cold air. Willa fell back onto the ground and saw a swirl of movement in front of her. Everything was so blurry. So hot. She rubbed her eyes and beneath the swirls of colors she saw Sorean on top of the faerie she had been dancing with.

Willa groaned and sat up. Too hot. She remembered what she had been doing and grabbed at her gloves. She pulled one off and then the other as gasps rang out around her. She heard crashing sounds followed by a grunt of pain. But Willa ignored them. She was too focused on her body blazing in an invisible inferno.

Someone called Sorean's name. Willa smiled and stood, recognizing the voice, she called, "Harland come dance!"

He would be more fun to dance with anyway. She waited for him to join her in a dance while everything swirled around her. Willa brought her palms up above her and spun them in circles, giggling at the brightness coming from her pale and clammy skin.

Why dance with the faeries when you could join me instead?

Willa gasped, her eyes shifted past her lifted palms to the swirling and spinning painting on the ceiling high above her. The horned bear, Forsetyr swirled within the moving colors with a silent roar. The God of Balance was the last thing she saw before her eyes rolled back into her head and darkness wrapped her up within its warm embrace.

Sorean carried Willa from the throne room with quick, angry steps. He should have known his mother would have planned something like this. He should have seen it coming when she'd been so adamant on Willa attending, when the evening before she'd wanted nothing to do with her. This was punishment for what he had done to her in his chambers. For what his essence had done.

Ignoring the servants and mingling guests, he carried Willa down a narrow corridor. She should have been awake by now. He checked her pulse. Something wasn't right, and he clenched his teeth in anger, his essence purring at the feeling.

His essence had been awake and aware ever since he had entered the throne room and laid eyes on the girl. She was intoxicating in the faerie gown, tracking his every move from the stage like an enchanting royal while he danced with Farren below. It had taken everything in him to ignore her for most of the night. He shouldn't have danced with her. He shouldn't have teased and touched her, or attacked the fucking faerie who'd danced with her. But the moment she had ripped those cuffs off, Sorean knew what would happen. She was a rare delicacy dressed for display amongst fevered faeries who had so openly been captivated with her just as he had.

He needed to get his thoughts under control. He didn't want her—his essence did. And she didn't want him, it was the wine and the dance.

Sorean pushed through a door with his shoulder and stepped down the curling staircase quickly in the dark. He didn't stop until he saw the fogged, glass doors to the aerial garden.

This had always been his favorite getaway. The garden itself was self-sufficient, gaining moisture from the waterfall splashing through the top of the dome. It was high enough in the sky to get sunlight all year round for the exotic plants to flourish, and aside from the beautiful walkways, it was quiet and private.

He walked to a tucked away bench between a wall of palms and water reeds and set the girl down. Watching her carefully, he checked her pulse again before settling his own temper.

Sorean pushed a curl away from the girl's face.

Let us out, Prince. She's ours.

Its never-ending persistence was wearing his resolve with every whisper.

"What happened?" Elliana stepped out from behind a row of tall plants, dropping her basket to rush over to Sorean.

He stood to give the healer room, watching as she leaned over Willa to swiftly assess the mortal's pulse and body with skilled thoroughness.

"Queen Morielle gave her a tonic." Sorean's words were too rushed. Too angry. He rubbed his hands over his face and bit out, "I didn't know who else to bring her to."

The healer stiffened while hovering over the girl, but caught herself. But it was enough for Sorean to catch it. A pit fell in his stomach.

Sorean rolled his shoulders and walked towards the healer's basket. The queen was cruel and loved to play tricks, but she never dirtied her hands to get what she wanted. He crouched beside it and looked through the contents.

"I'll admit it was clever of my mother to hide it in Willa's food. But I caught her surprise when the girl reacted to it so quickly." His gaze rolled over each tonic bottle and vial carefully as he said, "She had also been given fae wine. I can smell it on her breath. I can smell it in her pores. We know it is powerful to those who have never drank it. But to a mortal, it could be deadly if mixed with other medicines."

He pulled out the small amber glass he had been searching for and stood. Hiding it behind his back, he paced behind the bench and watched Elliana continue to fuss over Willa's state.

"How is her fever?"

She shook her head in frustration before pushing into a stand. "It seems like it has a mind of its own. It comes and goes when it pleases, despite what I've tried to give her. I've tried different mixes to no avail." Wiping her hands over her legs she said formally, "She will sleep this off. I can help you take her to her chambers and give you something for her to take when she awakens."

She had been looking at Willa while speaking, and when Sorean didn't answer right away, she looked up and startled at the vial he held in front of him.

"And this is what you've been giving her for the fever, yes?"

Sorean threw the vial up in the air and caught it. He did the motion over and over until it slipped from his hands. The glass fell onto the stone pathway and shattered. A plume of purple and green smoke came rolling out from the glass immediately. Waves of peppermint stung his nostrils, making him snarl as he stepped away.

"Forgive me, El. I am not a healer. But we have been peers, and even friends, for centuries, so I was hoping you could answer my questions candidly."

The healer stared at the broken vial with wide, unblinking eyes. Her light skin seemed to pale more between the vibrant garden around them.

She seemed to remember herself and said with a quick nod, "Of course, Prince."

"It has been years since I've studied herbalism, so please correct me if I'm wrong. I didn't know edderway helped with body aches and temperature. I thought it was the herb given in training to help awaken our essence. They stopped, of course, when the herb blew up in a student's face." He slowly followed her scar up and down her neck. Elliana averted her eyes and swallowed thickly as he continued. "But I have been wrong before, so please correct me, friend. Because why would a mortal be given this? She has no magic. If anything, it would make her worse over time."

Unless she had in fact used sorcery and 'the cost' was fighting the faerie herbs and tonic.

"I forget how smart you are, Sorean." They smiled at one another, though both were forced and tense. "Edderway, when mixed in a tonic, can be used for many things. Powerful and finicky to make, I know better than anyone. I should have known you would pick up on it eventually, I had only hoped to get results before you did."

"Results?" Sorean raised a brow and Elliana laughed.

"You are smart, but you choose to ignore many things. Ignorance is bliss. Your mother would know better than anyone." She shook her head and gave him an impish grin before saying, "Iara told me you were fascinated with the marks on Willa's hand when you first found her."

Sorean nodded. He looked back to Willa with a frown. Elliana brushed by him to walk towards the girl.

She asked over her shoulder, "And now?"

"She has mentioned hardships from her home. She was going to tell the queen her story tonight."

And he would kill the bastard who had scarred her.

Yes we'll kill them. Kill them all for hurting what's ours.

Elliana scoffed and looked out to the garden with narrow eyes. "You wanted to shame your mother in public. You wanted to wait and have this poor girl tell her sad story so everyone could see what you saw in the queen. So everyone could understand what she ignores. Admit it, you have been using this poor girl."

Sorean blanched at the harsh truth of the words. He stepped forward to argue, but the healer was quick to continue. "And yet you ignored something far greater. How did she survive Eth'tinok?"

"She bargained with Eth'tinok. But I suspect she knows sorcery. It's the only thing to explain what I saw." He frowned at the healer. "She is not immortal so anything else would be impossible."

His essence crawled uncomfortably beneath him, as he remembered what Eth'tinok had said to him. Looking down at Willa, who shifted slightly on the bench, he found sweat dripping from her cheek and onto the stones below. It was like she had been dunked in water.

Elliana bent over Willa and Sorean rushed forward to stop whatever she was doing, but he froze as she lifted the mortal's hand. The brand on her palm was glowing. It was a soft white color, almost matching the white of the scar and the paleness of her palm. But when he stepped closer, he could see the pulse and throb of the glowing color. As if it had its own heartbeat.

His essence clawed hungrily within him.

Elliana looked up at him and asked, "You believe she has no magic. Even with this?"

Even. Yes we're even. Let us out so we can touch it.

Sorean shook away his curls as if to shake away the panicked whispers screaming in his mind. Again his essence said *it* when pleading over the girl.

The healer was watching him intently with pursed lips, and Sorean blew out a frustrated breath, taking three large steps back from the both of them. Vines met his shoulders as he backed into a wall of greenery.

The healer touched the glowing scar gently, her finger tracing the edges of the sunburst before she set Willa's palm back on her chest. "The edderway mix wasn't working fast enough. What I slipped into her food tonight was rash, but I didn't know what else to do. I didn't think it would respond so rapidly."

"What do you mean? What is happening to her?"

But a familiar voice replied behind him, "She is a thief."

Sorean turned and looked through the swaying vines as Iara stepped casually around the greenery.

He narrowed his eyes and commanded, "Explain."

Iara held up a rolled parchment and waved it before her face with a sneer. "I suspected something when she came back for me. I was in and out too much to hear what Eth'tinok said to her." She walked towards Elliana with casual, bored steps, as if she weren't shattering his perception of a seemingly innocent, albeit aggravating, mortal girl. "The words I did hear didn't make sense. Not until I saw the queen's face after the girl ripped her gloves off on the dance floor."

She handed the paper to the healer. Elliana unrolled it briskly and skimmed the writing. Her eyes widened the further she read. She looked up to give Iara a questioning look before glancing at Sorean with concern.

Iara turned to look at Sorean. "You saw the fire in the valley, Sorean. You saw her attack Eth'tinok."

"I thought the fire was yours." He paused and cursed. "It's sorcery. It has to be."

Iara barked a laugh. "You're more like your mother than you realize. I hoped you would have figured it out by now. I hoped she would, too. I didn't want to tell you for fear of what you would do to her. But tonight proved you have a soft spot towards the mortal."

Sorean snarled, but Iara snapped, "Don't deny it. You carried her from the hall after lashing out at my cousin for dancing with her."

His essence growled to Iara in his mind, *Touched what is ours. We don't share. Mine. Mine. Mine to play with.*

"I sensed your presence when she went to sit in her chair. I see the way your marks change color when you look at her. You may not know what it means, but I can smell it on you. You're at least attracted to one another."

"Speak plainly—both of you!" Sorean yelled.

His essence was growing more and more uncomfortable by the second, begging and whining within him. Saying the same word over and over: *Even. Even. Even.*

Sorean stiffened as his essence continued to chant. Every ounce of his being emptied to be filled with the one, simple word instead. Iara had called her a thief but it couldn't be. She couldn't have magic like the faeries.

His essence hissed, *Magic like ours. She's ours.*

A cracking realization struck his insides. And the tower within him, holding his beliefs and understandings, crumbled. Shattering everything he thought he knew about the girl. And himself.

Elliana said nothing as she crossed over to him and handed him the paper.

"The report from the shifter you sent to Traifton," Iara said quietly.

WILLA

Willa awoke to the sounds of an argument. Groaning, she pushed herself up with her elbows and looked around. She was back in Lady Talarin's tavern. Strange. She had been in the queen's court only a moment ago. What had happened? She winced, thinking of faerie wine. Perhaps she had indulged too much in an effort to settle her nerves.

Yawning, she looked around the room to inspect the tapestries and candles. It seemed to be a much bigger room than where she had been before. A small hallway showcased shadows of a crackling fire from the foot of her bed. Angry, clipped whispers echoed down the hall of what she imagined to be a sitting room. Willa shifted further to sit up, wincing as a flush of heat ran from the bottoms of her toes all the way up to her head. She quickly pushed the blankets from her body as the heat rolled violently through her.

Willa reached for the glass of water at her bedside with a shaking hand, gulping it down as quickly as she could. Water spilled over her chin and neck, temporarily cooling her skin, but it did nothing to help douse the fire inside her. She wiped at her neck and mouth, to find someone had put her in a nightgown. She thought of the elegant dress she had worn to the dance and frowned. Why couldn't she remember what happened? She scowled at the nightgown in confusion, the blue sweat-soaked satin clinging to her chest and thighs. The fever was getting worse. Much worse.

Willa thought of Sorean's pool. She needed to get to the bathing chamber. Pushing up from the bed, she stood, but stumbled forward as the ground tilted beneath her. She reached for the nightstand and when she fumbled to grab ahold of it, the glass of water fell to the floor and smashed. A deep, male voice came from the hallway, silencing the others she had heard before. Willa panted and clung to the nightstand as everything continued to spin.

She focused on a candle, trying desperately to get everything else to stop spinning, when a voice whispered, *Finally, you're awake.*

Ignoring the voice with an irritated groan, she pushed away from the nightstand and stumbled towards the wall beside the hall and bathing chamber. She clung to a tapestry and pressed her cheek to it. Everything was still spinning. She needed to hold onto this while she caught her balance, before calling for help.

A voice spoke loudly beyond the hall. "She couldn't have done it purposefully. The girl is brash and temperamental, but she is not like him."

Sorean. Willa sighed against the tapestry. He would know what to do. The arrogant prick always knew what to do.

Another voice snapped back harshly, "And yet she did it. Just like Ammanar. It doesn't matter if she was unaware. What matters now is what she has."

Iara. Willa frowned and opened her eyes. The room was done spinning, but her mind was not. They were talking about her. But the words they were saying didn't make sense. Willa sucked in a breath and tiptoed closer to the open arch of the hall.

The healer's voice piped up, "You know they will come looking for her, Prince."

Who? Who would?

Iara spoke again, "Burning Traifton was a clear message. We knew taking in a mortal was a risk but now, by the queen's law, we harbor something much worse."

Willa's eyes widened. Her ears started to ring. Traifton— burned? No, she hadn't heard correctly. She couldn't have. She pressed further into the stone, wincing at the sound of the wood creaking beneath her feet as she moved.

"Enough!" Willa flinched from the anger in Sorean's words. "I know what it means. Let me go in there, let me speak to her. She's awake, I can hear her moving. You all can."

"No!" Iara yelled.

Willa flinched as loud footsteps echoed over the cobblestones.

Iara spoke again, "I can see your eyes right now. Your marks are practically black. I cannot let you go in there."

"I won't hurt her," Sorean growled.

Elliana spoke softly, "But your essence might. You said it yourself; it is curious about her."

Iara quickly followed the healer's words, "I agree with her, Sorean. We can't risk you killing her. She has become something far bigger than you and I could have predicted."

Willa lifted her head from the tapestry she clung to. Sorean's voice sent a chill down her spine, mixing and fissuring with the heat rolling through her. She shivered violently, waiting for the other two faeries to answer.

"We wanted to know what the elves were doing," Iara continued. "We have some answers, but we now have what they want. We have an advantage. When you are crowned—"

"She is not a tool!" Sorean barked.

"By law and nature of what she has, she is an elf now," Elliana chided. "We are harboring an elf within our faerie realm. She cannot stay here with the risk of your mother finding out, or them finding us."

"And where would she go?" Sorean hissed. "Her town is gone. Traifton has been reduced to ash and rubble. Everyone she knows is *dead*. We'd be taking her from one poisonous pit to the next."

Willa's clammy grasp on the tapestry gave way, leaving her to stumble backwards with ringing ears. Sorean knew about the stolen essence. They all did now. She was considered an elf to him and the faeries beyond that hall because of her mistakes. But Traifton was *gone*. Her family was *gone*.

Willa fell back onto the bed with panicked gasps. Her eyes blurred from tears as her body flushed with another wave of heat. Grabbing her stomach, she leaned forward to vomit. Another heat wave ran through her and she grimaced, slipping off the bed, and landing on her knees amidst the broken glass.

Dead. All dead. Mother. Tybalt. Burned to the ground. She dry-heaved and let out a pained gasp. The council was gone. Claire. Ivaan. Merellian.

She dropped forward and put her head in her hands. Her heart and body were breaking at the same time. Bursts of anger and pain rolled through her in one giant wave of stinging sensations. She had to get air. She had to get out. She needed to get back home and see for herself. She needed to see what she had done.

Willa looked up from the floor and the room tilted. Grinding her teeth, she pushed into a stand with a low moan.

"Perhaps I can be of some assistance."

Willa wiped the tears from her eyes and looked behind her. The woman from the lake, Lady Talarin, was leaning on the wall between the bathroom and hallway. She gave Willa a sad smile and glanced toward the hall where Willa could still hear the three faeries arguing in hushed tones, before pulling back a tapestry to reveal a hidden door.

Willa stumbled through the dark tunnels, following the white flowing hair in front of her. Sweat dripped from her nose and chin, mixing with her constant stream of tears. Her body ached from the biting waves of heat, but her mind was numb. She could think of little else besides her family and Traifton as she followed the mysterious woman.

Traifton was gone. All of her family was gone.

A hollow thought had her steps persisting despite her need to crumble: Her mother and twin were reunited with her father. Father would be overjoyed with how much Ty looked like him and he would be so proud of the man he had become. Her mother would smile again. And Claire...Claire and Ty would have uninterrupted time together in death's realm.

She stopped when the woman did. A creaking sound came from the dark before a dim light appeared before them. Willa wiped at her eyes and face to focus on the sleepy buildings of Lithelle.

Lady Talarin leaned on the stone door she had opened and sighed, looking out at the town with a soft smile before rolling her head lazily towards Willa. "Remember what I asked you?"

"So it *was* you. You were in the water with me." Willa shivered and shook her head. Grabbing her chest, she let out a rattled sob. "I feel like I am breaking from the inside. I have known grief, but this is too much."

The woman's blue eyes glittered and crinkled, but her smile was somber. "Sometimes grief will ask too much of us. But in its dark embrace it will hold us gently while we come undone. It will hold our hand in the dark and help us grow into something else entirely. And when you are ready to face the light again, you will find yourself remade."

Willa rubbed at her chest and continued to cry. She swore she heard her own heart shatter beneath her palm, but Lady Talarin pushed from the door and hummed thoughtfully, bringing Willa's focus back to her.

Stepping out into the town, she looked at the sky and stared into the night. Willa clenched her teeth and shuffled forward. Standing beside her, she followed her gaze. The moon was shining above them, clouds hovering around it as if a storm was coming, but the air was humid and warm, and no breeze touched her skin.

In Traifton, clouds like this would have brought a bitter chill. You would have been able to smell the rain before it came. Perhaps it was the veil over the kingdom, protecting them from the forces of nature.

"The storm is here. Dawn is approaching." The woman watched the clouds above them and turned to Willa with glittering eyes. "I'll ask you again. Will you be the fire or the rain before it?"

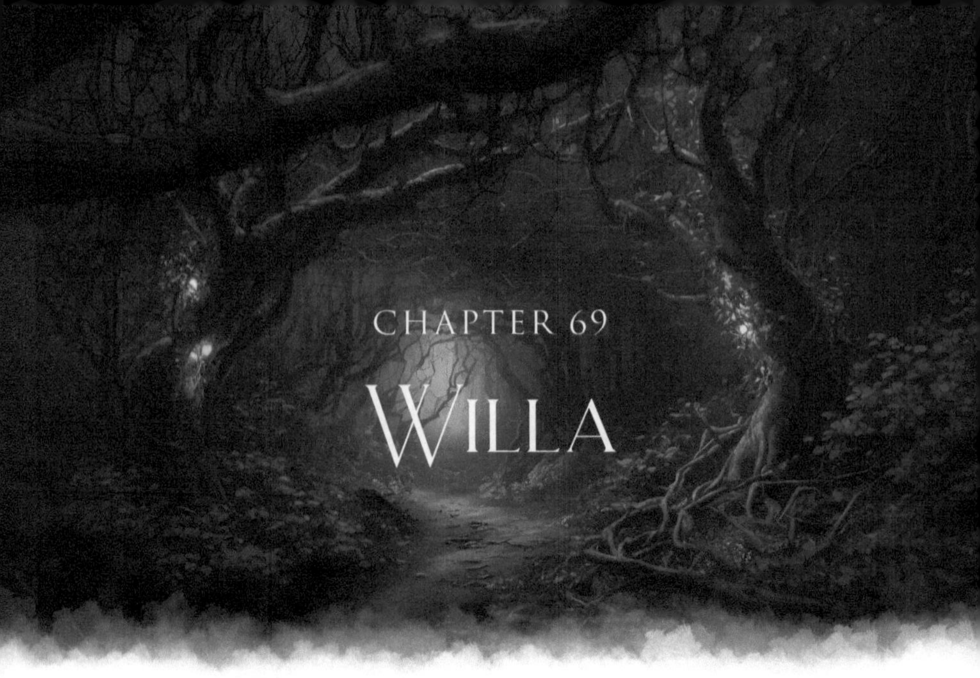

CHAPTER 69
WILLA

Willa ran through a dark alley, blinded by her sea of tears. Her caving chest threatened to stop her run, but she continued as fast as her body would allow.

Damn the bargain with the prince. Damn the faerie queen. As she ran through the sleeping kingdom, she recalled every embarrassing thing from the dance. It didn't matter. None of it mattered. She would find the lake on her own. She needed to get back home and see for herself what had happened.

Pushing past a stack of crates, Willa looked out from the alley at the street. Empty market stalls littered the large stone path, flags shuffling in the warm, calm breeze. When something flashed above her, she looked up at the sky to find the clouds had darkened. Another flash confirmed there was lightning outside of the veil. It was so calm here compared to what was happening above.

"Keep your wits about you," Willa choked out the words, trying to push herself to keep moving.

She hobbled out into the street, grabbing her stomach with both hands as she did. She looked around wildly, trying to find any sign of a gate or way out of the kingdom, but warm hands suddenly gripped her shoulders.

Willa opened her mouth to scream as she was spun towards a tall, hard body, but a hand covered her mouth to silence her.

"Where do you think you could go that I would not find you?" Sorean asked darkly, his chest rumbling against hers as he spoke. "You stomp so loudly with your *mortal* body, I'm surprised the whole kingdom isn't awake."

Willa's eyes widened as he focused on her face. He knew everything. He knew what she had done. What she had. She tried to pull away from him, but he pulled her closer. His hand moved from her mouth to grip her curls and Willa hissed as he pulled her head back. As his fingers exposed her sweat slicked neck to him, she remembered Iara's words. She'd said she was worried he would kill her for what she was. Worried his essence would kill her.

Watching the storm beat into Lithelle's invisible fortress, she asked, "Are you going to kill me now, knowing what I have?"

Her voice was hoarse and cracked, and she licked her lips, swallowing slowly. The prince watched her throat bob with dark intensity before bringing his face down to her neck and grazing his nose on her skin. She winced as he inhaled deeply, a push of his warm air tickling her shoulder. Willa closed her eyes and waited for death to come.

"I know why my essence wants you so badly. I thought it was temperamental at first. It doesn't like being told no." His nose ran over her collarbone. Willa twitched to pull away from him, but he tugged her hair to stop her. "But I had never met an elf before. My essence knew you were different. It knows what you are."

Teeth grazed over her shoulder. Willa was helpless and frozen as he nipped her skin lightly before snapping away from her and licking his lips. She stared up at him, horrified at how he might kill her. He was drawing this out as if he were enjoying it. He truly was a monster. His eyes seemed to darken, brightening the silver rims as he looked down at her.

"I think it's scared of what you carry. Intimidated." He broke eye contact to gaze at her with a killing, predatory calm.

"And are you?" Willa croaked, wiping at the tears streaking her face.

Sorean's eyes snapped back to hers. "Am I what, Willa?"

"Are you scared of what I carry?"

His lip curled into a snarl. "No."

Releasing her hair, he stepped back. Willa stumbled, but caught herself before she fell, rubbing the back of her head with a soft hiss. Sorean was hardly breathing as he stared at her. His chest didn't move, and he didn't blink as he watched her shift from side to side nervously.

Her palms were glowing. She grimaced at them. "I need to leave."

"And go where?" Sorean's biting tone had her looking back up at him instantly. "You knew you had this and you kept it from me. You're just like my mother. Keeping secrets. Hiding things."

"Did you know about Traifton?" Willa snapped back. "Did you know my family was dead while I tried to do what you asked? While I was *poisoned* and left to be made a mockery of?"

Anger rolled with another heat rush, and she could have sworn she heard a deep satisfied purr within her as she let her temper come to the surface.

"No. I got the report tonight." His hardened eyes looked into her very soul. Stepping forward, he lifted a hand towards her.

"I'm sorry, Willa, I swear I didn't know before. I came in to tell you, but you were gone."

"Let me leave, Prince. I cannot help you with your mother." She groaned as another rush of heat had her stomach twisting, and she stumbled forward in pain. "I never could. I couldn't tell her I killed an elf. What do you think she would have done?"

Willa looked up at him, but doubled over as her stomach clenched tighter. Sorean was holding her up in an instant. She groaned and leaned over his arms, panting at the ground while spots danced in her vision.

"Help me understand, Willa. What happened between you and the elves?" He lifted her up so she could face him, his dark eyes searching her face wildly. "I am begging you to give me a reason. Any reason for me to not kill you for what you've done."

"Why?" She tried to laugh, but it came out in a gasp. "You hate me, remember?"

She tried to focus on him as everything spun and tilted like it had in the brothel.

"You told me in the forest you were trying to clear your guilty conscience. I am trying to do the same. I am a monster for what I've done. And I don't want to be." His words were strained. As if it pained him to speak. "You are aggravating, brash, and wild."

Willa focused on him as her temper flared back up from the word, 'wild', but Sorean pulled a curl back from her cheek and smiled enough for his dimple to pop out.

"But you are also intoxicating to me in the most infuriating way. You are the past coming back into a new world. A world I want to change. If you were like Ammanar, we would all be dead already. But you are not. You have tried to help me. Your first words to the queen were asking for help for your people and the rest of the realm." He shifted to help her stand, but it only made her fall into him. "That is what I want. Let me help you."

Willa closed her eyes and let the tears fall, leaning into his hold. Could she trust him? She was alone now. No family. No friends. No one, but the faerie holding her up.

"They're searching for an artifact." Willa pulled away from him with as much strength as she could muster.

She thought of Claire and sucked in a tight breath. "An artifact I had. Merellian chased me into the Wylan. He didn't know I had it. Even I didn't realize what I carried. But he knew something was going on. He chased me down before I hid in the woods."

"And then you killed him," a cold, bone chilling voice crooned.

CHAPTER 70

SOREAN

Sorean pushed Willa up and shoved her behind him, straightening as his mother stepped out into the road.

She walked slowly towards them, with her hands clasped behind her back, glancing around the quiet buildings and empty stalls with a tight frown before looking at him. "I knew there was something curious about the little bird behind you."

She took another slow, calculated step towards Sorean. It took everything not to unleash his essence as anger roared in his ears.

He had searched for answers for centuries about his magic and differences, and she let him wonder and question for years, alone. All the while knowing what he was. He never thought a mortal thief, more stubborn than him, would help him gain clarity. And his essence had been trying to tell him for days, while he shoved it further and further away, ashamed of its whispers.

Willa slumped against his back, the heat from her body rolling over him, so hot, like he was backing into a fire as she leaned on him for support. He reached a hand back to hold onto her side so she wouldn't collapse.

His mother watched him intently before speaking. "I wasn't sure what it was about her to make you so intent on keeping her here." She sighed and shook her head, a long brown curl tumbling over her shoulder as she did. Her eyes narrowed on Sorean's before she let her gaze roam down towards the marks on his neck and chest. "But then I saw her hands. I saw those marks while she was busy embarrassing herself in front of the whole kingdom."

She looked back up to meet his gaze and sneered. "I warned you about mortals. I told her the night you brought her to me, in front of everyone. I told you she was exactly like Ammanar, even when I had no idea she was!"

A cold laugh bubbled out of her, and Sorean flinched at the loud, crass noise.

Sorean shook his head. "How did the marks on her hands make you realize what she had done? We know Ammanar killed King Erlathian. But we didn't know how he did it. We don't know how she did it."

"Do not say his name in my kingdom!" His mother's words cracked like a whip.

She rushed towards him with both hands raised and Sorean blanched. Her face was pulled into a feral, terrifying scowl, her eyes bright with anger as she bridged the gap between them. He tightened his grip on Willa, who whimpered behind him.

"You are just like him! Playing with things you should not. Wanting things you should not have. Lying. Sneaking around."

"Like who?" All anger washed away within him and a silent buzzing filled his mind while he waited for her to admit what she had done.

Willa gasped behind him, and Sorean was unable to catch her as she slumped onto the road.

The queen tried to step around him to get to her, but Sorean's essence flared up beneath him. Shadows covered his vision immediately as he cut her off. His mother looked at his raised hand and shook her head with a feral snarl.

A flash of white fire danced in front of her, shying away the shadows in his eyesight enough to showcase her renowned flames dancing up both of her hands.

Sorean ignored her magic, and asked again, "Who am I like, Mother?"

She looked at the flames in her hands and snarled. "Your father!"

Sorean dropped his palm, ignoring the call to release his shadows. "King Illithor?" He clucked his teeth together, lips twisting into a pained smile. "No, I don't think that's right, is it?"

He shook his head. King Illithor had been dead for over a hundred years now. Sorean had been there beside him when he died. Like Queen Morielle, he cared little for the world outside of their hidden realm. Cared little for Sorean. The faerie king had always been distant with him, different from how he had been with his siblings. And his mother; he knew there was no love in her gaze.

His body trembled as five hundred years of loneliness and searching gave him a biting embrace. It squeezed him so tightly he thought he would die from the snapping of truth, whipping his heart with venomous lashes.

His mother spat out a dry laugh and said coldly, "So you figured it out. His name does not hold merit to you now, Sorean Valkian. It doesn't matter. You are about to be a king, *that* is what matters."

Queen Morielle paced in front of him like a beast about to pounce. The white flames danced in her eyes as she spat. "I did everything to fix my mistakes. I did everything to cover my tracks. And yet the past is here to haunt me within my very own kingdom!" She said the last two words so loudly they echoed down the road behind him.

Dread pitted in Sorean's stomach as he took in the flames licking up her shoulders, giving the queen a terrifying halo of hatred.

"My husband thought you were his until your magic shifted. Until those marks deepened on your skin when you met your elven essence for the first time. After it awakened within you."

"How could you be with an elf?"

The queen's voice was brittle and distant in her reply. "A deity brought us together, whispering honeyed words of our secret pairing, and how wonderfully we would match. And for a time, the deity was right, for I was in love. But he played me for a fool. It was forbidden to be together, but we met in secret as often as we could. Both engaged to another, about to be crowned."

Sorean chilled. What deity would bring two races together with the intent of them falling in love? No deity would defy the gods' law. Even Eth'tinok had made his disdain towards the queen clear, but he would not make deals with love involved; only death.

"I went to him one night, in the Kingdom of Domnhall and found him with another lover." She clutched her belly and blinked away her teary haze to truly focus on him, "He was with another woman. An elf. Not a faerie like me. He didn't care for me, he never did. I was merely a hidden conquest."

She let out another dry laugh. "It doesn't matter. He is dead."

Sorean's brows shot up and his lips parted. Dead. His real father was dead.

His essence—his elven essence—flared with rage, nearly blinding him with the shadows begging to be released.

Willa let out a groan behind him, and he stilled. He had nearly forgotten she was there with his mother's slap of reality, stinging his battered soul.

"So my true father is dead," Sorean spoke too calmly for the rage tearing him apart. "How?"

"King Ammanar was jealous of any with magic." The queen spat onto the ground. "He wanted magic for his own. He held so much power within the Key of Sanctity. But none for his own. He was easy to persuade. And I was hungry for vengeance. Ammanar was eager to kill him. He relished it, like the terrible mortal he was."

"King Erlathian." His true father. "You fell in love with a *royal* elf and had him killed for it."

She was colder and more calculating than Sorean ever realized. He had been so blind to it all.

Thick and terrible tension hovered between them as Sorean tried to make sense of it all before his essence could take over. It raked his shallow breaths, screeching and howling within him as he took in his mother's flames still dancing on her hands.

This was why they were hidden. She was hiding from what she had done. She had helped King Ammanar shatter the Law of Balance by murdering his true father, the king of the elves. And then she'd run from her scheme because of what she had in her belly. Him.

Sorean trembled with shock as he finally found out the truth about who he was. Of who his mother truly was. Mixing magic was forbidden by law. He'd often wondered what mixed immortals would be like, even imagining them as demi-gods. But he was no such thing.

Queen Morielle stepped forward and gave Sorean a hard stare. "Give me the girl."

Willa was curled into a ball and shaking, sweat pooling out beneath her, but she was awake and staring at him with wide, terrified eyes. Something above caught his attention. A storm was pounding upon their veil. Black clouds hovered over them, covering the bright moon, rain and lightning hammering against their magic, trying to find a way in.

Mine. Not hers.

Sorean for once agreed with his whispers. His *elven* essence.

He looked back at the girl and frowned. His essence had said *'even'* more times than he could count, trying to get him to see her for who she really was. Trying to tell him they were more alike than he could have ever imagined. It was why he was so protective. And it was why he wanted her despite his denial.

He looked back to his mother and growled. "No."

Queen Morielle stepped closer, reaching for his arm. "Do not make the same mistake as me. We need to kill her before her magic awakens."

Shadows appeared in his vision. Mistake. He was the mistake she spoke of.

An abomination in the eyes of the gods. A monster.

Prince Sorean was an elf. And a faerie. Two powerful pieces of magic rolled into one. He was a mixed creation, hidden within this kingdom for nearly five hundred years.

Queen Morielle had fled with Sorean in her belly, and hidden him from the world, after setting King Ammanar up to dole out her revenge.

Willa's own anger, terror, and pain rolled through her body, and she was helpless to the waves of misery tumbling through her insides. This was worse than when she'd killed Merellian. This was worse than any pain ever inflicted upon her.

She looked up, squinting at Sorean's shaken stance. The way he spoke to his mother was devoid of any emotion, but she saw it now in the way he was failing to hold himself together. She knew his heart was fracturing, like hers had from the news of Traifton. Her family was gone and his mother had kept him in the dark, with nothing but his terrifying essence to keep him company.

"Give me the girl," Queen Morielle said more fiercely.

Sorean's voice was dark and distant as he said, "I, Sorean Valkian, swear a life debt to Willa Thesalor."

What was he doing?

The queen asked the same thing. "What are you doing, Sorean?"

It was the first time Willa had heard emotion other than anger in her words.

"I do not want to believe the words you say. But I cannot deny them. I cannot deny this." He laughed, cold and bitter, as shadows slowly crawled out of his clenched fists. "You say the elf king broke your heart, but I don't believe you."

Haunting harmonies of whispers followed, ones she knew all too well from the cabin in the mountains. Sorean's essence. The road had become dark, and so cold, the ice clashing with the fire roaring within her still. Something tickled her leg, and a black tendril of a shadow cascaded over her feet. She kicked it away with a whimper as Sorean continued above her.

"You are not capable of love. Only anger, paranoia, and fear. Yet, you went through lengths to hide our kingdom. To hide *me*." If Willa's heart could shatter again, it would have been from the pain in the prince's words. "You ran and hid us all to save yourself from the gods. To save yourself from their wrath. Of course, you kept us hidden from their curse because it was *you* who made it possible!"

Willa ducked her head further into her chest to hide from the black mist covering everything around her now.

"You have never loved me. I knew this. I fought for your love. You kept me dangling on a thread and now I know why." His voice deepened as he said, "Or maybe you did love the elf. Maybe it's why you kept me. Raised me. Trained me to give me the crown. Because I carry a piece of him. I don't want to know the reason. But I trust whatever it is, you would not go this far to keep your secret hidden if you didn't want me alive."

There was a lengthy pause before Sorean hissed, "You cannot hurt the girl. If you kill her, I die with her."

Hundreds of shadows in different shapes and sizes were watching her. She waited for them to attack her, to tease and shift into her nightmares, but they did not. They only hovered around her, as if waiting for something to happen, like she was.

One pushed through the rest to walk towards Willa. It was in the shape of a large, black dragon, and Willa watched, frozen on the ground, as it stretched its wings out wide and stood to full height, reminding her of the God of Justice, Velithor.

The shadowed dragon looked at Willa and said calmly, *"Mine."*

These were pieces of Sorean's essence. Pieces of him. Little nightmares eager and ready to turn to monsters. Ready to attack at his command. Eager for justice, much like the shadowed replica of Velithor.

The queen's voice was almost darker than Sorean's when she said, "I will *not* let history repeat itself."

The realization of the queen's words had her attempting to sit up with wide eyes and an open mouth. The shadow of the dragon roared up into the sky and flew above her, but a sudden gust of white fire shot over Willa, lighting up the dark mist and night around them.

Something crashed behind her and Willa rolled away to find Sorean on the ground.

"No!" Willa screamed, crawling towards him.

His eyes were open, but his skin and clothes were charred. She grabbed his chest and shook him while flames danced around the ground, circling them both.

Something was happening to her. Her pulse was slowing, her eyes were getting heavy.

"No! No!" she rasped as the queen, who stood behind her flames, watched them with fire dancing in her cold and spiteful eyes.

Deep sobs racked Willa's insides while she shook Sorean as hard as she could, but nothing happened.

He was too still. His eyes were glassy. Lifeless.

He was dead.

"If you kill her, I will die with her." The life debt would kill them both.

The queen had killed Sorean to end Willa for what she was. For what the queen had hidden: her own son and heir to the throne. She tried to shake him again, but her arms weren't working. She fell on top of his chest with an airy wheeze. The shadows of his essence were gone, his monsters were gone.

Willa searched for his shadows, hoping to find a piece of him, still alive. Something, even a small whisper of a shadow remaining, so she could tell the prince he wasn't a monster. So she could fight with the realm of death and bring him back with a tendril of his essence. But all she saw was the white roaring flames around them as she took her last breath.

CHAPTER 72

WILLA

The crackling of fire was all Willa could hear aside from distant shouts.

The woman of the water asked if you would be the fire or the rain before the dawn. A familiar, deep voice echoed around her, a dark, rolling chuckle shaking her insides before it spoke again. *It seems you are the fire. You are stronger than I thought. Together we will do what Merellian and I could not. Awaken, little mortal.*

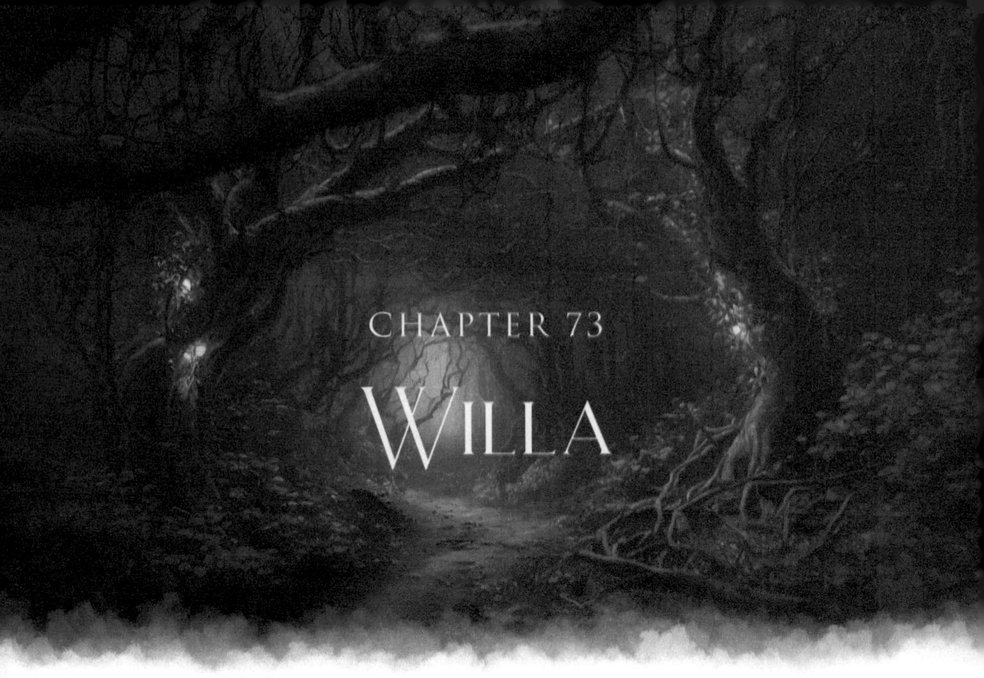

CHAPTER 73

WILLA

Rain pelted softly on Willa's face, waking her from a deep slumber. Thundering storm clouds pulsated towards her in rumbling waves. The rain soaked her skin as she watched it fall from the dark sky, but the only thing she could smell was smoke and burning wood.

She groaned, pushing herself up from the road. White fire roared all around her, the buildings burning and crumbling from its hungry force.

Thunder cracked loudly in the sky, and Willa looked up, blinking through the rain. It was when she saw it: Lithelle's veil. It was thin, almost iridescent in color, like delicate glass or a sheet of ice. A lightning bolt struck it and it rippled from the blow, shimmering enough for Willa to catch its surging movement. She squinted through the rain as a small fissure of flaming orange tendrils crawled and licked its way over the invisible dome, trying to eat through the magical fortress.

Willa watched as the thin strip of energy tore away from the black clouds. She followed the shimmering air all the way towards the castle high above her. It rippled before a loud crack rattled the sky and the ground shook and groaned beneath her.

The veil hiding Lithelle was crumbling.

Everything seemed to be moving so slowly. The flames around her bobbed and danced as if they were gently moving blades of grass. She took a deep inhale and scrunched her nose at the burning smell. She wasn't hot. Her fever was gone. She reached out towards the closest flame and gave it a puzzled look. Her fingers danced within the flame without burning. In fact, nothing hurt. She was numb.

Taking a step away from the flames, Willa lifted her arms and frowned, realizing she couldn't feel them. Turning her hands over, her mouth fell open at the sight of her palms.

The brands were glowing a bright white color. She lifted a hand slowly and turned it in front of her, the color seeming to pulse brighter than it ever had before.

An eerie call sounded above. The black clouds from the stormy sky were swallowing up the buildings and another crack of thunder rang out. The lighting to follow was green in color. Strange.

The ground trembled beneath her again. Cracks were webbing out from the soles of her bare feet. But her footing didn't falter, making her head tilt with curiosity. The ground parted slightly between her toes, as if she were the one making it break by simply standing.

Despite the surrounding flames, the warmth only came from her palms. It tingled and nipped her skin eagerly. Her hands no longer glowed white, instead, they were glowing a deep red. Much like the color of blood.

An arrow whizzed past her, scraping her cheek as it flew by. Willa followed it and snarled. She turned towards the faerie who had shot at her and lifted her hand. A flood of light tumbled from her palm.

It was red and white, mixing together to look like the fire of a dragon as it came from her. She watched as it hit the faerie square in the chest, feeling his fear lance through her as her light knocked him to the ground. The faerie's emotion rolled through her in a thick, intoxicating wave.

She wanted *more.* She had control. For the first time in her life, she was powerful. Nothing could touch her. Nothing could hurt her ever again.

Another faerie ran towards her, palms outstretched. A gust of air shoved her back, but her heels hit something, holding her upright. She only laughed before raising two fingers and snapping them together. The sentry clutched his head, crying out in pain before crumpling to the ground. Her face twisted into a wide smile as she swallowed his pain and fear with eager inhales. It was divine.

Willa searched for what had stopped her fall and frowned. A body lay on the cobblestones, face first. She knelt on the road beside the body with pursed lips and gently rolled it over.

Prince Sorean stared lifelessly up at her.

He couldn't be dead. He was immortal.

Willa lifted her hand towards his neck, frantically searching his face and chest for movement. Her glowing red palms illuminated his skin and the marks upon it. The marks weren't a deep blue. They were white, but they lacked their usual glow. They looked like pale scars now, dead upon his skin. They were lifeless; he was lifeless.

Falling back, Willa let out a horrified wail. When she hit the ground, all feeling crashed back into her. Time sped up and slowed all at once, overwhelming her startled senses. Everything was so loud. So quick. So chaotic. Screams were coming from all directions. Willa coughed from the smoke, singing her eyes and throat.

"Willa!"

She lifted a hand to better see through the flames surrounding her and Sorean, squinting until she found the voices calling to her. Harland and Iara were on horseback, narrowly avoiding a crumbling rooftop as they neared her and the prince.

"Help!" she wheezed. The sound was barely audible from her aching throat. She swallowed again and winced. "Sorean!"

Iara slid from her horse and ran forward with wide eyes.

"How are we alive?" She neared the flames and rubbed her chest, her words falling between panicked rasps. "I *died*. I felt you die from the bond."

Had they died? Willa rubbed her throat and lifted her glowing hand.

Iara spotted Sorean's body and took a haunted, stumble back. Her face snapped to Willa's. "What did you do?"

Willa crawled back to the prince, as if to shelter him from Iara's wrath. "I don't know! I don't remember anything."

Harland was nearing the flames now, too. He lifted his hand and water shot out, hissing over the flames to create an opening. They ran forward, but a stream of white fire threw them both back onto the crumbling road.

"Do not touch him!"

Willa's heart stopped at the sound of Queen Morielle's voice. As she raced towards them with outstretched arms and a line of faerie sentries behind her, she remembered everything.

The prince of Lithelle was dead. Queen Morielle had killed him. His own mother killed him...because of her.

Arrows landed beside her, bouncing off the cobblestones. But Willa didn't care. Her pulse was so loud within her ears, she heard nothing else as she grabbed Sorean's cold hand.

She had died. She'd *felt* it. She'd seen him die, too.

So how was she here without him?

A hot tear rolled down her cheek, falling onto their entwined fingers.

"Wake up," she pleaded. Another arrow narrowly avoided her cheek. "Wake up, you insufferable faerie."

She would give anything to see Sorean's arrogant dimple form on his cheek. She would take the nickname *Ohirlyn* ten thousand times, just so see him stir.

Her palms itched beneath her as Queen Morielle's voice cut through her raging grief. Willa raised Sorean's fingers to her trembling lips before turning towards the one who had murdered him.

In another life, Sorean and her would be friends. Maybe even more. They'd find days with no rain and clear skies. A life without fear, loneliness, or questions. A life where he could meet her family and she could hear his irritating laugh, and listen to five hundred year's worth of stories.

A life of peace. Together.

If a god had kept her alive, despite Sorean's life debt, Willa wondered if it was the God of Justice. Perhaps he had helped her escape death's brief embrace, to fight fire with fire, as she stood to face Queen Morielle.

Buildings continued to crash into the rising flames around her and the road beneath her bare feet quaked in rippled cracks and moans.

How had this happened? How was Lithelle burning?

We did this, the voice in her head said softly.

Willa looked to her hands as another tremor rolled beneath her.

A sudden piercing flame of rage overwhelmed her. Willa's nostrils flared and she clutched her chest. The queen was pacing behind the ring of fire, haloing both Willa and the prince. More emotions rolled through Willa: surprise, fear, and grief. She assumed it to be her own until a wave of guilt hit her, followed by paranoia.

She snarled, rubbing at her chest. The faerie's fear had enveloped her while attacking them before. These were Queen Morielle's emotions now, rippling into her soul with fevered intensity.

Willa didn't want to taste her emotions. She didn't want the queen to feel anything ever again. She raised both palms and the queen did the same.

The essence beneath her squirmed, twisting her stomach as it easily crawled up towards her palms. But something screeched right above her head and, before she could attack the queen with her stolen magic, she was being lifted from the ground.

A small Wylan Creature, much like the bats she had encountered in the woodlands, was lifting her up by the straps of her nightgown. Willa kicked her legs and lifted her palm to the beast's legs with a feral yell. Warmth cascaded from her fingers and the beast howled as the fire singed its legs, instantly dropping her to fly away.

She landed on her back, the air ripping out of her as she rolled to her side with sputtering coughs. Thunder cracked above her head, and Willa peered over her shoulder to find green mist mixed with the dark clouds enveloping the sky, the creature's screeching echo within the rumbling thunder.

The Wylan's curse. The gods' curse was crawling through the crumbling veil.

Something kicked her in the side, and Willa rolled before landing on her back, groaning as the queen stood above her with a snarl. Her hands covered in white flame, she pressed her pointed shoe into Willa's chest and leaned forward, pushing her into the ground.

"I should have killed you the moment you stepped into my throne room," Queen Morrielle hissed.

Green lightning illuminated the clouds for a few seconds behind the queen's frame. Long enough for Willa to make out what raced the falling rain. Hundreds of flapping leathered wings brushed beside one another. Thousands of bulbous green eyes focused on Willa, Lithelle, and the ruler of the kingdom standing over her.

Unaware of what sped towards them from above, the queen pressed her foot further into Willa's chest, and she gasped, shifting beneath her, but Queen Morielle lunged for her wrist, burning her arm.

Willa cried out as the fire latched onto her skin, her nostrils flaring at the familiar smell of burning flesh. The queen pulled back and kicked her ribs again. When Willa opened her eyes, she was inches from her face.

"You destroyed my kingdom. They will find me now and it is your fault."

Lady Talarin's words from the lake rang in her ears with crystal clarity, *"There are many kingdoms, Willa. Ones not yet made, and ones not yet broken."*

Queen Morielle wrapped her flame covered fingers around her throat, her eyes wide and hungry. Willa thrashed and kicked, trying to release herself as the white fire burned her hair and singed her neck. She let out a rattling wheeze, her terrified face visible within the dilated reflection of the queen's eyes. But she also saw something else.

The queen tightened her grip around her throat and laughed, but Willa could only stare at the small red dot of light growing larger and larger within the queen's manic pupils.

The ground trembled beneath her, and Willa's eyes rolled back as the queen tightened her grip. The smell of burning hair and flesh enveloped her. But then, a growl rippled through the burning kingdom, so low and guttural, it was as if it came from Death's very realm.

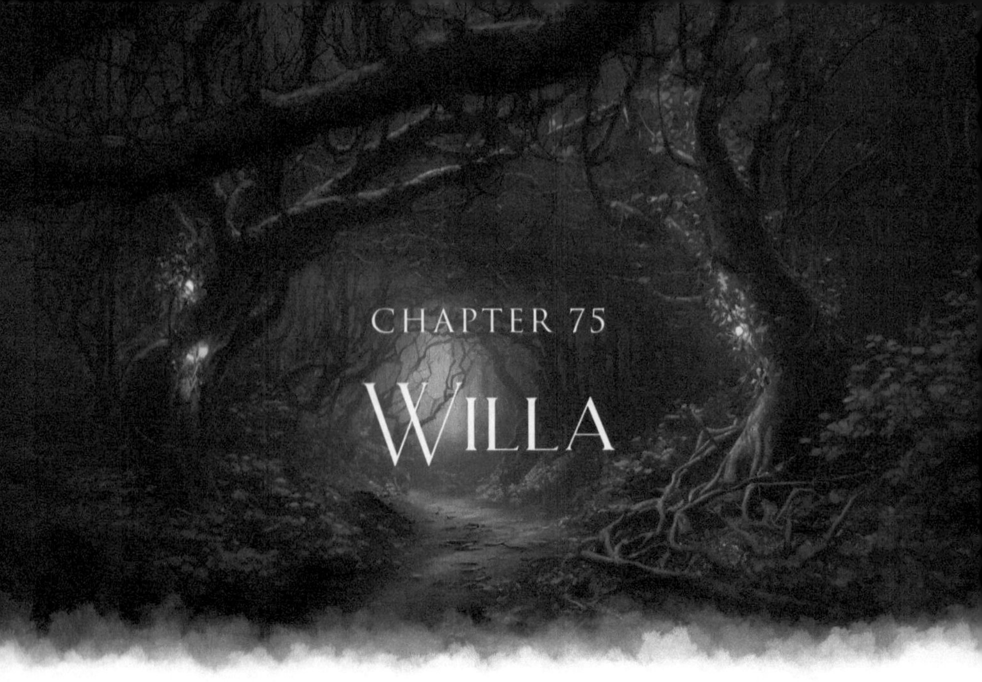

CHAPTER 75

WILLA

Queen Morielle screamed as she was ripped away. Willa sat up with a rattled gasp, holding her throat as Death's Divine leapt over the fire with the queen of Lithelle between his teeth.

Eth'tinok landed and turned to Willa slowly. Fire bubbled from his maw as Queen Morielle cast her flame upon him, but the wolf only growled and whipped his head from side to side, in a death rattling shake. He loosened another earth shattering noise and unclenched his teeth. Queen Morielle fell limply to the ground.

"Death was a kindness for you, Morielle. For locking me up for centuries, I will haunt you in the afterlife for the rest of my days. You will never find peace in the dark nights of death."

Eth'tinok lunged at the queen's still body, and Willa covered her face to hide from the horrific scene as the wolf tore into Morielle's flesh.

"Willa!"

She dropped her hands to find Harland on horseback, with an outstretched hand. Iara passed him on her own horse with Sorean's body between her and the horn of the saddle. Willa stood, stumbling to Harland's outstretched palm, but a gust of wind shot her back.

She wheezed, sitting up to see Iara galloping away, sending a cold warning to Willa over her shoulder with narrowed eyes and bared teeth.

Harland's horse spun between Iara's path and Willa's, his brows furrowed as if unsure what to do. Willa stood again, racing for him, and he turned his horse to better grab her. When he reached for her hand, she pushed it away, instead slapping the haunches of his steed. The horse reared up and Harland grasped the reins with a shocked face.

"Go!" Willa yelled, "I created this mess, do not die because of me."

Harland cursed, turning his horse to face her. Willa grit her teeth and focused on the horse, this time calling on her essence.

Heat rose to the surface and, scared to lose control, she didn't touch the horse again, but got close enough to frighten it with her bright red hands. Its nostrils flared and it kicked off into a run. Harland didn't look back as more buildings fell on either side of his path.

Black and green mist covered the streets now. The castle above the kingdom was set ablaze by green and orange flames. More warbled cries of Wylan Creatures cut through the fog and alleys around her and she wheezed, feeling her singed throat and hair. Half of her braid was gone, the frayed and charred ends of her hair now stopping at her collarbone.

A black mass of shadow caught her eye, right as a brute force barreled into her. Death's Divine rolled her onto her back, blood dripping from his teeth.

"I should have killed you in the Wylan Woods, girl." Willa was paralyzed with fear as his canines snapped above her. "I smell it now within you. You have bonded to the stolen magic. You said you were not like King Ammanar, but you are worse than him. An entire kingdom has fallen because of your wrath."

Willa trembled and looked up at the deity, bracing herself for what came next.

The wolf was right. She had done this. Willa had brought an entire kingdom to ruin. A queen was dead because of her. Prince Sorean was dead because of her.

His lips curled into an impish grin before he growled, "For the desecration you have caused, your death will be divine. Your afterlife will not."

"She is no longer yours to kill," a haunting, familiar voice called out above the cries of a kingdom collapsing.

The wolf's red eye narrowed on her before stepping back.

A loud ear-piercing call, cut through the rest of the monstrous noises raining down around her.

Realization struck her like the green bolts of lighting pelting the kingdom.

A large black beast with raven wings and vengeful talons glistening from the rain was clutching to the remains of a crumbling building. Willa stumbled to her feet, moving back with a gasp, but froze as she heard Eth'tinok's snapping teeth behind her.

The beast's formidable black wings stretched wide above her before tucking in at its massive, furred sides. Half of its body hung over the side of the crumbling building, showing its swaying, cat-like tail. But something was different about the beast now. It cocked its head towards her, showcasing its bright green eyes. Green eyes like a Wylan Creature.

"No," Willa whispered in horror.

The beast dipped its head to reveal the elf sitting atop it. Prince Enrel.

The Prince of Reckoning.

Half of his hair looked like it had been dipped in black ink, while the top of his head was as white as snow. His eyes were blown out and completely black as he leaned forward and smiled, blinking slowly.

When he opened his eyes, they too were now glowing a bright green. "Hello, Freckles."

EPILOGUE

Prince Sorean's body was pushed out into the middle of Niarath Loch. Iara knelt beside the water with her companions, and together they watched as he slowly sank beneath the surface.

For hours, they knelt beside the waters in silence, and Iara stared unblinking, unfeeling, at the misty waterfall until someone gently squeezed her wrist.

She looked down at the hand holding hers and choked back a sob. Farren pulled her against her shoulder and held her while she wept silently. They stayed embraced through the night, holding one another while they cried.

When the morning light finally trickled over her head, Iara sat up and looked around. Harland lay on his side beside her, his eyes red rimmed as he stared at the water in front of them. Elliana was sleeping near Farren's waist, her soft snores the only sound to be heard above the waterfall.

A rustling of grass had Iara turning towards a red fox pushing through the grass. It seemed the faerie shifter, Noi, had survived the falling of Lithelle. The shifter circled twice before cuddling up to Elliana's back with a soft whine.

Iara wiped at her swollen eyes and cleared her throat. "We've been here for too long."

She stood slowly and wiped the mud from her knees before turning away from the lake and looking through the Wylan's trees. A myth had brought them here. It was said the lake could bring souls back from the dead, as well as answer for those who passed. Iara didn't dare hope Sorean would rise back out of the water, but at the very least she had hoped for clarity.

But the lake also took from those who entered. If Iara had anything to give she would have dove in alongside the prince's body. She would have offered anything to bring him back. But she had nothing now. She was nothing without him. Her titles meant nothing. She was only a faerie without a home.

She had *died*. She'd felt it, knowing Willa had died too.

But she was here, alive, because of the mortal girl. She didn't know how Willa had come back from the depths of the afterlife, bringing Iara with her. And she didn't want to know.

None of it mattered now. The faerie realm was gone. Lithelle was destroyed. A queen was dead, and a prince killed, days before he was to become king. All because a mortal girl stole elven magic.

History had repeated itself, bending the broken scales even more.

They needed to find shelter and food. They needed to get moving. Iara was halfway to the horses, wiping fresh tears from her cheeks when Harland yelled her name. Startled by the emotion in his voice, Iara turned back to the lake and gasped.

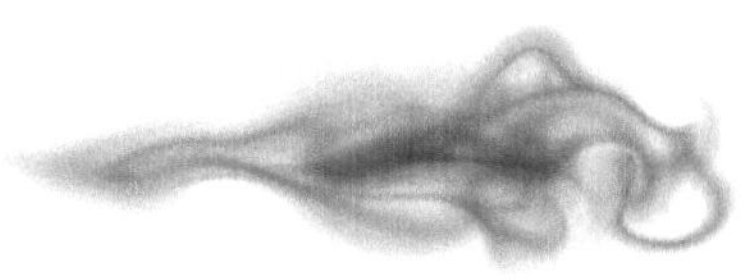

The waves had barreled into the ship relentlessly through the night. It would be weeks to make it back to Nudrith Helm, and provisions were depleting fast.

Claire ran up the stairs towards the top deck to check the damage. Her crew was already working on cleaning up as she greeted the morning sun and salty air, and she sprinted past them up the stairs to get to the quarter deck.

She had felt it in the cabin below where she stood now. But she was tired. Overworked. The days had been long, and the nights longer. It was only a matter of time before the elves came looking for her again.

The diversion she had created in Traifton had worked. The ship the elf had attacked blew up easily with her rune marks attached to it. His magic and hers combined had made quite the spectacle while she and Willa's family escaped from the other side of Fang Gulf.

She had promised her friend to keep her family safe, and safe is what they were here upon her ship. And if Willa was alive still, a piece of the Key of Sanctity was safe too. She would know if the elves had found the hair clip. The whole realm would know. Willa was smart and stubborn. Wildfire could not die easily. Willa was alive—she had to be.

The ship groaned, jolting suddenly, sending Claire sliding across the deck. She slammed into the wooden railing, the main sail above her creaking and shifting from the hit.

"What in the gods' name was that, Claire?"

She straightened, looking down the stairs at Tybalt Thesalor. She had no idea. They were in the middle of the Minison now, with nothing around for miles and miles. Nothing except the large and unforgiving waves. But she knew she had felt something earlier. It had rattled her table and candles as she looked over the maps, sending chills down her spine.

Pushing off the railing, she went to answer him when a crew member shouted. She looked past Tybalt at where the crew member was waving wildly towards the black waves.

Another jarring hit pushed into the ship's hull and Claire gasped, rolling forward. Helplessly, she slid over the deck as the ship dipped completely on its side. The black water splashed up towards her in rolling tendrils of midnight as she slid towards the Minison's endless depths.

But the lapping waters she neared suddenly crested and shifted. A large open mouth, full of jagged teeth and elongated fangs pushed out from the Minison's waters. The ship careened upwards, and Claire slid back the other way, while a pale sea serpent rose higher and higher from the waters to crash down upon them.

"Nathayus," she whispered, staring up at the mighty creature.

The God of Chance? No. It was impossible.

$\mathcal{A}$UTHORS NOTE

If you've made it this far, I know you probably hate me...and I am so fucking sorry for what I did to our fae bae, Sorean. When Kingdoms Fall has been a wild ride for me, too, trust me. This story has changed so many times throughout the years. It started so innocent and wholesome: Poor Sorean never died, and Willa hadn't faced such hardships. In the first baby draft, Willa found a speaking fox, Noi, and a handsome elf prince, Kauis, while foraging for magic mushrooms. She didn't kill an elf in self-defense, sucking up his creepy essence in the process, and Kauis wasn't so close to the edge of villainhood. But he was always a cynical, snow-capped sourpuss; at least that never changed.

Four years ago, I started this journey as a hollow shell of a person. But the voyage of writing quickly taught me that vulnerability is a weapon to wield, not one to hide from. This story made me face my own monsters, much like Willa, Kauis, and Sorean had. It taught me that fear is an immortal beast, as is anger, grief, and resentment. It embraced me when the crumbling tower of my life fell to rubble, and lifted me from the remnants of my fallen kingdom, showing me that I, a mere mortal, can survive anything.

The more I acknowledged my own story and faced new hardships when writing about these characters, the more their stories shifted and changed. I would say I was lonely while working on this story tirelessly for years, but Willa, Kauis, and Sorean were with me all along. Together, we found our voice and will continue to heal and grow with precious little sparks that will never again be reduced to embers.

Thank you, from the bottom of my heart, for reading my debut novel. I cannot wait to meet you in the Wylan Woods again for the next part of this story. ***While I won't promise happy endings for anyone, I will assure you that you may forgive me for what comes next.***

$\mathcal{A}$CKNOWLEDGMENTS

To be perfectly candid, I never prepared myself to write this next part. Simply because, for a while there, I never imagined When Kingdoms Fall would make it to the finish line. But as I sit and process the years that went into this, I am being slapped with a giant dose of humbling reality. Of course, we made it. And it is only because of *you* that we did.

As a reader, you took a chance on me and my story. As a friend, you lent me your ear, support, and patience. As a mentor, fellow author, and guide, you never let me give up. So many of you have helped immortalize my dream. A simple thank you is not enough for what you've done for me, but I will do my best to convey my appreciation below...

Thank you to my inspiring, hilarious, and brilliant editors: *Claire and Darby.* I was terrified to have my work critiqued, but you both were so kind and patient. You believed in these characters, pushing them and me to their fullest potential. The time and love you put into this show, and I'll forever appreciate what you have done for me and When Kingdoms Fall. With that, I have two promises: I swear never to make you read 'scream' so many times ever again. And I vow never to repeat the isolation process of hiding in a writing hole with no contact for months, only to come out on the other side with a completely new draft at the last minute. Yeah…as I said, you two are the most patient editors in the realm. Thank you again for everything.

Thank you, *Beck*, who transformed this manuscript into the beautiful book you hold in your hands now. I'm so honored to have you be a part of my debut novel since I have looked up to you for years. You are a true inspiration and a wonderful mentor and friend. Thank you, *Alice*, for creating an incredible cover of our dearest Wildfire and for your patience with all my ideas.

Thank you to my *friends* who consistently asked, "Have you finished the book yet?" enough times to assure me I could never back out of what I had started. Thank you to those who sat with me for hours and helped pull me out of the plot holes I had dug myself into. Thank you to those who refused to let me isolate myself. You ensured I had gotten fresh air, ate, showered, slept, laughed, and enjoyed the process: You helped keep my head above water when all I wanted to do was sink beneath deadlines, divorce dread, and busy season with work. You refused to let me drown; you probably would have come with me if I had. Thank you to those who cheered me on from the sidelines, even if you have no idea what a faerie or elf is or could care less about dragons. Most importantly, thank you for letting me be me and giving me a safe space to create, grow, and let my freak flag fly. I don't need to name all of you because I know you all laughed or smiled when reading your piece in this paragraph. We fucking did it. Holy shit, we did it.

Thank you, *Mom*, who always encouraged me to write stories, and *Dad*, who always told the best stories. Together, you nurtured and sharpened my imagination and passion since I was a little girl. I'll never forget telling you that I finally started writing a book and how pleasantly unsurprised you both were by the announcement of it. You have always been like that; supportive and kind with any idea, job, or project I decide to try. You both have helped me become unapologetically me, the most significant gift a child could ever hope to get from their parents. As promised, *Trace*, I made you into a character. No, you're not a Vokreat, but Tybalt, Willa's twin brother. (You're welcome for being nice. Consider it guilt for how cruel of an older sister I was at times when we were younger.) *Chris*, I thought of you as well when writing Tybalt. I'm lucky to have two kindhearted brothers like you and tator-tot. I'm lucky to be a Dahl.

Thank you, *Angela*, who never let me doubt myself or this story for a second. You helped me realize that this story was not Willa's but mine. You helped me find myself again and taught me that vulnerability and emotions are nothing to fear, despite how gross they may feel in the moment. Not only are you a wonderful mentor, but you are someone I look up to and will never, ever forget.

Thank you to the *bookish- Instagram fam*. I am so grateful to have met so many wonderfully talented artists, authors, and friends from afar. Thank you for cheering me on: This story is as much for you as it is for me. We did it, fam!

Thank you, *Karley*, my witchy sister and the first friend I ever made on bookstagram. I genuinely don't know what my life was like before you. You have helped me countless times with any questions I have. (I literally learn something new every time I talk to you.) Your blind support and encouragement have kept me going. I'm so proud of you and your debut novel, *Dark Fate*. I'm so proud of us. Your future is so bright, and I am honored to be a part of it.

Thank you, *Jade*, who has supported, checked in with me, and cheered me on since the beginning. You were the first person to read this story, even if it is vastly different now. You always answered my questions and helped bounce ideas back and forth with me for years. (Also, I'm so sorry for always letting the voice memos expire because of my ADHD chaos.) I'm so proud of you and your work, and I am honored to have been a part of most of your beautiful stories and your self-publishing adventures. Forever cheering you on, pal.

Thank you, *Marcella:* a talented artist and friend. You also read this story when it was just a cute and innocent baby draft. You were the first person to bring Kauis and Willa to life, inspiring me to keep going every time I looked at your sketch. You read through the trenches of countless drafts, seeing how it has changed and shifted over the years, yet helped me without fail through every dumpster fire. Thank you for loving Sorean, Willa, Greer, and especially Kauis.

Thank you, *Jocelyn.* I will forever enjoy our rants and chats. I am grateful for your support and friendship. And I am so glad you love Greer and Kauis as much as I do. (Ps. I'm sorry for the emotional damage of this story.)

Thank you, *Kristin,* another soul sister of mine. You are so inspiring, and I'll never forget our buddy reads and endless check-ins over the years. I'm blessed to know you and wish you and your family the best.

Thank you: *Megan, Eliana, Katie, Sam, Brenna, Tia,* and the list continues. You are all such remarkable humans and cheerleaders. I would like to mention many more of you, but just know that every connection made will forever be cherished.

Thank you to my *Street team: The Wylan Weirdos.* You're the fucking best. Thanks for pushing my book baby out into the wild with relentless love and creativity. Thank you to my *Beta & Alpha* readers who helped mold this story with gentle hands and hilarious commentary. Thank you to the *ARC team* for reading and reviewing When Kingdoms Fall and, in doing so, supporting indie authors like me.

Last but certainly not least, I dedicate When Kingdoms Fall to two deities that have assured I get this book out into this realm, come hell or high water: *Loki and The Morrigan.* You two repeatedly held me in the flames of creative chaos and ice-cold water of emotions. I am forever indebted to your guidance and grace. It's out in the wild now, like you wanted, so take care of it for me, will ya? (You know Kauis read this part, eyes rolling, whispering, "fucking sorcerers.")

Pronunciation Guide

NAMES:

Forsetyr [God of Balance] : For-set- EE- y-ur

Nathayus [God of Chance] : Na-thigh- Us

Velithor [God of Justice] : V- eh-l- i-tho-re

King Ammanar [The last mortal King]: A-mm-ahn-ar

Ulrond [God of Chaos] : OOL -rahn-d

Kauis: Kh- YE (or) I- us

Merellian: M-ur-ILL-EE-yahn

Greer: G-rear

Willa: Will- UH

Tybalt : T-YE (or) I-bolt

Talarin: T-ahl-ah-r-IN

Sorean: Sore-ahn

Iara: I- awr-uh

Morielle: More- EE- ll

Farren: Far-hen

Harland: H-AHr-land

Noi: N-OY

ON THE MAPS:

Kalandrae: Kh-ah-l-un-dr-ay

Traifton: Tr-hey-f-ton

Lithelle: L-EE-th-hell

Nudrith Helm: Nude-wray-th

Menyamere Mountains: Men-yaa-mere

Domnhall: D-ahm-n-all

Niarath Loch: N-hi-uh-wray-th Lock

Magic Systems

Magical essence is a separate soul within an elf or faerie, granting these two races their immortality and magic. Like you, dear reader, magical essence has unique wants, needs, desires, and personality traits. A faerie or elf host often nurtures their essence's aspirations, creating an unyielding bond with a versatile blend of power and personality.

Faeries wield natural elements: Air, water, fire, and earth. ***Elves*** also wield elemental magic, but beyond that, they have a much more comprehensive range of abilities. Two examples are telepathy and soul shifting.

Mortals have no magic. Yet some have found ways to conjure deals with shadows to become ***sorcerers***, mimicking what the elves and fae have.

About The Author

CALLIE DAHL is the American author of the enthralling new adult fantasy series, *When Kingdoms Fall.* She is so excited to have you fall in love with her chaotic, creepy monsters and deities within the Wylan Woods.

Callie is a neurodivergent, overly caffeinated, photographer who resides in Montana with her two small rescue dogs. She is actively searching for magic within the mundane, whether in the mountains with her camera or within her writing hobbit hole.